MORE THAN A FEELING

ERIKA KELLY

parents is particularly well-done -- but it is Mimi's strength that will linger long after the finish." —Sarah MacLean, Washington Post

MORE THAN A FEELING

"This was all just so AMAZING, and I feel blown away!!! Honestly, I can't say enough good things. Emotion, tension, drama, and off-the-charts chemistry and heat. I felt like my emotions were going to spill over while I was reading and by the end, my heart was bursting. **If you have not read Erika Kelly before, I highly recommend her.** This series is phenomenal! **5 I'm-feeling-so-much-stars!**" – About that Story

"*More Than A Feeling* by Erika Kelly is a powerful and epic romance novel that is sure to make readers hearts swell. This was written so well that I felt like it all was happening to me instead of the heroine, Daisy. This, my friends, is amazing on the authors part, and it has been quite a while since I felt a connection as powerful as this one. It is everything I wanted it to be and then so much more." – Pretty Little Book Reviews

Titles by Erika Kelly

Rock Star Romance series

YOU REALLY GOT ME

I WANT YOU TO WANT ME

TAKE ME HOME TONIGHT

MORE THAN A FEELING

The Calamity Falls series

KEEP ON LOVING YOU

WE BELONG TOGETHER

THE VERY THOUGHT OF YOU

JUST THE WAY YOU ARE

IT WAS ALWAYS YOU

CAN'T HELP FALLING IN LOVE

COME AWAY WITH ME

WHOLE LOTTA LOVE

YOU'RE STILL THE ONE

Wild Love series

MINE FOR NOW

MINE FOR THE WEEK

Sign up for my newsletter to find out when YOU'RE STILL THE ONE is released in June 2021 AND to read the EXCLUSIVE novella for my readers only! You'll get two chapters a month of this super sexy, fun romance! #oppositesattract #onenightstand #surprisebaby. Come hang out with me on Facebook, Twitter, Instagram, Goodreads, and Pinterest or in my private reader group.

MORE THAN A FEELING
by
Erika Kelly

ISBN-13: 978-0-9859904-7-3

Cover design and formatting by Serendipity Formatting

Proofreading by Jamie McHugh

This book is dedicated to Kristy deBoer,
for never giving up until we get it just right.

Acknowledgments

To Superman: you're always there for me, and I can't live without you.

To Sharon: your friendship means the world to me. It's your calm that gets me through.

To Olivia: thank you for the book talk and plot talk, and for being such a joy in my life.

To Kevan: thank you for your support and for never giving up.

To Kristy deBoer: you say you're pushy, but I say you're a woman who gets things done. And you've done so much for me. Thank you for making the cover pop, critiquing the book, and sticking with me until we get it right.

None of this would be possible without the generous support of the romance writing community: readers like Kathy Page and Andrea Szul; bloggers and reviewers like Guilty Pleasures Book Reviews, Obsessed with Romance, Krista's Dust Jacket, and Reading in Pajamas (just to name a few); and the support from my friends in RWA chapters like CTRWA, WRW, and CoLoNY.

Chapter One

HEAD TIPPED BACK, THE LEAD SINGER HELD THE impossibly high note, his eyes squeezed shut, features wrenched in emotion.

From out of nowhere a slice of bread came winging through the air and struck his chest in an explosion of red jelly.

Oh, shit. Cooper Hood quickly scanned the backstage crowd for a roadie. He waved one over. "Get security down there."

With a sharp nod, the guy disappeared.

The singer stared in shock as the bread slowly peeled off his white T-shirt and dropped onto his boot. Slowly, he lifted his gaze to the audience, chest lurching with erratic breaths.

The song, "This is How It's Gonna Go," a crowd favorite about a misogynistic man's expectations for his fiancée, had started causing problems for the opening act when a fan in Ohio got the idea to throw bread on the stage during the line *Hey, girl, fix me a sandwich.* Since then, as the tour had taken them west across the country, slices had been flying.

But adding jelly to the joke? *Funny, but not cool.*

At the edge of the stage, the singer pointed to a group of older teens in the crowd. "Did you do this?" They just laughed at his slurred words. "You shitbirds think this is funny?" He swiped the glop off his chest and, with a flick of his wrist, sent it flying into the audience. "Well, fuck you. I don't have to put up with this shit." He cupped the mic to his mouth. "I want these assholes out of here right now. Get 'em out."

Completely unfazed, one of the kids reached into his flannel shirt and whipped out another sandwich. He split the slices apart and hurled them, one after the other. One struck the singer's chin, spraying jelly across his neck and arms.

The singer yanked off his T-shirt, balled it up, and pitched it at the kids. "You redneck hillbillies *suck*."

The Texas audience booed, and a third jelly-covered slice of bread arced through the air and hit the singer's bare stomach. His body went rigid, hands curled into tight fists, and he looked like he was about to dive into the audience.

The roadie next to him smacked his arm. "Is he on something?"

"Yep." The opening act's partying had gotten steadily worse over the past three months, but it was the singer's drug use that had caused real concern.

Blue Fire didn't put up with that crap.

The lead guitarist and bassist raced toward the singer, boxing him in, but it did nothing to contain his frenetic rage. Punching and kicking, spittle flying from his mouth, the man fought like a wildcat.

The audience went nuts. Cell phones lit up as fans captured the display of bat-shit crazy.

Enough. Cooper pushed his way through the crowd to the stage manager. "Kill it. Right now. Cut the lights."

When he turned back, he saw the singer heaving his Stratocaster over his head and slamming it on the floor, bits of wood splintering and flying out like buckshot. A beefy security guard grabbed the guy around the waist and hauled him away.

The moment the stage went dark, the roadies charged out to clean up.

Needing to get with his bandmates, Cooper made his way through the frenzied backstage crowd. *Well, this sucks.* Blue Fire was halfway through its national tour and had a two-week break scheduled. They'd booked a red-eye to New York after tonight's performance so they could spend much-needed time with their families.

But now it looked like they'd need to find a new opening act.

He spotted the guys huddled together, away from the fracas. Emmie, their manager, was on the phone. The moment they saw him, the circle opened to include him.

"Called it," Ben said.

They'd warned the record label about the singer's substance abuse, but the band's manager kept promising he had everything under control. "Yeah, well, no more of this shit."

"No more," Derek said. "Emmie's talking to Irwin right now. These guys are out."

"This better not make us miss our flight." Ben's girlfriend hadn't been able to visit him on tour, so they'd gone three months without seeing each other.

"Let's see what she says." Slater watched his wife, as Emmie spoke animatedly.

"It shouldn't affect us," Ben said. "It's not our problem."

"It's *Emmie's*," Slater said. "That makes it ours."

And he was right. Not because she was Slater's wife and Derek's sister, but because she was one of them. They were a family.

A sizzle of unease burned in his chest. With the guys all coupled up now, he wasn't sure where he fit anymore.

"No matter what, we're going home," Derek said. "The label will find us a new opening act."

"The label gave us this one," Calix said. "But I agree. We're going home. I haven't seen my girl in a month."

Emmie turned back to them. "Okay, it's done. They're fired."

"So now what?" Derek asked.

"Now I deal with the West Coast booking agents who're blowing up my phone."

"Does the label have another opening act for us?" Derek asked.

Emmie started to speak, and then pressed her lips together, looking pained. After a moment, she said, "Kallous."

"Are you serious?" Ben said. "They want *Kallous* to open for us? How's that better than these assholes?"

Not a chance. "Did they forget that the lead singer walked off the stage in the middle of a song because he was so wasted he forgot the lyrics? We're not touring with a band like that."

Emmie's shoulders lifted in frustration. "I know, but they're not giving me a choice in the matter." She checked her phone. "Dammit. I have to take this."

"Hang on." Slater put his big hand over hers. "Let's figure out what *we* need to do, and then we'll get back to everyone else."

"Okay." Emmie drew in a breath. "Well, first, I have to let the booking agents know this band's out. No one wants a hot mess on their stage. But, then, if we're going to reject Kallous, we'd better have our own replacement act." She lifted her worried gaze to her husband.

"It's not gonna be Kallous." Slater looked to the other guys for confirmation, and they all nodded in agreement.

"Then we have to hurry and find someone else," Emmie said. "Whoever it is has to be ready to hit the ground running in *two weeks*."

Cooper looked at his bandmates—his brothers—and knew how badly they needed to spend time with their wives and girlfriends.

But he didn't. He was free and clear. He could make himself useful. "I'll do it."

Everyone shot him a look, and heat climbed up his neck. For all his talk about wanting to take on a leadership role in the band, he'd never actually done anything.

"You don't have to do that," Emmie said. "This is my job. Maybe we should book a hotel, stay the night. Get a handle on things before we head home."

Cooper held up a hand to stop her. "Go home, Em. Take a break. I got this." The guys just gawked at him. "What? You think I want in on your couples' staycation?" He gave them a teasing smile, but it didn't cover the twist of fear that went through him at the thought of separating himself. For nearly ten years, they'd lived together, worked together, and played together. They'd always been a team.

But things were changing. His friends had settled down, and that wasn't something he'd ever do. He'd waited a long time for this kind of success—and he planned on enjoying every minute of it.

"That's bullshit," Derek said. "We're all going home. We can take care of everything in New York."

Cooper thought about the guests he'd invited to tonight's show. One of them owned an indie record label, two were popular DJs, and one did Promotions for a record company. "I've got a bunch of people in town who can hook me up with some of the best indie bands on the scene. I'll hang around here for a few days and check out some gigs."

He saw the concern in his bandmates' eyes. Considering he'd only ever been the kid in the backseat while Derek drove and Slater called shotgun, he didn't blame them for doubting him. But not only did he have the right connections, he actually thought it might be fun. "Look, someone gave us a shot, right?" He knew they'd all be down for paying it forward. "How cool would it be to find a band in Austin and have them break-out on our tour?"

"Very cool," Slater said.

"I like that," Derek said.

Emmie gave Cooper an approving nod—and was that a hint of pride in her smile?

The stage manager approached them. "Hey, I hate to ask, but can you guys go on early? The audience is pretty stirred up, and it'd be great if we could get you guys out there."

"Yeah, sure," Cooper said.

The manager looked relieved. "Thanks. You guys are the best." He walked backward away from them. "We're setting up right now. Should be good to go in fifteen."

"Okay." Derek turned to the band. "Let's do this."

"Let's make Austin forget all about fuckin' strawberry jelly," Slater said.

Everyone gathered around, hands piling on top of each other.

"We got this, man," Derek said. "Let's block it all out and get our heads where they belong. The music."

They turned their arms over, revealing the Hand of Eris tattoo on the insides of their wrists, a reminder not to get sucked into the chaos of the music industry.

"I want to start with 'This is Us,'" Slater said.

Derek nodded. "That'll grab 'em right away."

Slater had written that song when he'd found out his wife was pregnant. It had become an instant hit. Even won a Grammy.

"And then we can launch into "'Get it, Boy.'"

"Excellent," Derek said. "Okay. Cooper, you're an asshole. Slater, you're a prick. Ben, go fuck yourself. And, Calix, suck my dick. I love you guys. Now let's rock this shit."

Just as the guys leaned in, Cooper's phone rang. Everyone's attention snapped over to him.

"Turn it off." Ben shook his head.

"Yeah, yeah." Cooper pulled the phone out of his pocket to silence it, but when he checked the screen and saw the area code, his heart gave a painful lurch.

Mom.

"What's up?" Ben asked.

Ah, hell. There could only be one reason someone from Snowberry would call him. "I gotta take this."

"Right now?" Derek glanced to the stage.

"Yeah." Putting the phone to his ear, he held up a finger. *One minute.*

As he started to walk away, Emmie touched his back. "Is everything okay?"

"No idea." Dammit, he'd lost the call. Calling the number back, Cooper moved a few paces down the hall, away from the noise. Cold fear squeezed his nerves as the phone rang. He had two ties to his hometown, his mom and a building contractor. This number was neither's.

Someone had to be calling *about* his mom. *Fuck*. She'd been doing so well.

Coming to a stop under the illuminated exit sign, he waited as it rang a second and then a third time.

"Cooper Hood?" He didn't recognize the woman's voice, but she sounded ballsy. Not panicked. Definitely not sad.

So his mom was okay? "Yes."

"This is Sherry Allen."

Never heard of her. Fuck, what was going on? "Okay."

"Your mom's sponsor."

Dammit. An image of his mom as he'd last seen her popped up in his mind. Eyes narrowed in concentration, trembling as she'd held a flame under a spoon.

She'd been clean for four years. When he'd lived with her she hadn't gone four *days* without using. He'd been so damn hopeful. "Is she okay?" He turned away from his bandmates.

"She's fine. She's doing great. Well, you know. Every day's a struggle, but she's doing it, you know?"

So she hadn't relapsed? *Thank Christ*. "So what's up?"

She exhaled into the receiver. "Look, I know it's not my place to call you, but you need to know your mom canceled the appointment you set up for her this weekend."

Why did his mom make everything so difficult? He

wanted to give her a *home*, for Christ's sake. "I don't know what to tell you. I tried to buy her a house, but she wanted to build one instead. Now she's blowing off the contractor?" He let out a frustrated breath. "There's not much more I can do. If she decides to go through with it, tell her to give me a call." He glanced over and found his bandmates gathered at the side of the stage. "I have to go."

"No, wait. Listen. She's not taking you up on your offer because she has something to tell you."

His mother drove him nuts. "So have her call me." And then it struck him. Her *sponsor*. "Look, if this is about making amends, you can tell her we're good. I forgive her."

All that crap of his childhood? He'd left it behind long ago. Made a great life for himself.

"It's not about forgiveness," Sherry said.

No, with his mom, he wouldn't think so. She'd never given a single shit about him. "Sherry, I'm on tour right now, and I'm about to get on stage. You need to get to the point."

"Come home, Cooper. I wouldn't bother you if I didn't think it was important for *both* of you. She needs that house as much as you need to hear what she has to say."

He headed toward his band—Slater had pressed Emmie up against a wall, and Calix had Ben in a head-lock. He'd committed himself to finding an opening act. Not a chance would he blow his first attempt at taking a leadership role. "Tour's over just before Thanksgiving. I'll plan a trip then."

The *band* was his family. Not Ronnie Hood.

Ben spun out of the hold and gave him an urgent wave. Cooper picked up his pace, that familiar rush flooding him, as his body and mind geared up for the performance.

"One night," the sponsor said. "Catch a flight out in the morning. You can have dinner with her tomorrow night and be on your way first thing Saturday."

"Can't do it. Gotta go." Just as he reached his band-mates, his finger hovering over the End Call button, he heard her voice.

"Dammit, Cooper. It's about your father."

Energy ripped through him, and he brought the phone back to his ear. "I don't have a father."

"Yeah, you do. And she needs to come clean about him."

It happened every time.

The moment Daisy Charbonneau rounded the bend and saw the sign for Snowberry, her pulse quickened. The beauty of her mountains always made her heart sing.

On one side of the road, fly fishermen, hip-deep in the Gallatin River, whipped their lines in graceful arcs. On the other side, horses flicked their tails, their sorrel coats gleaming in the sunlight. She couldn't wait to get home.

With the festival two weeks away, she'd taken a risk leaving, but a personal visit with an investor had turned interest into commitment, so it'd been well worth it.

Oh, boy, had it been worth it.

Now she just needed the mayor's signature, and every-thing would be set.

As she neared the intersection, Daisy's mind raced with all she had to do. Given the crowds they anticipated, adding a few more standby generators and Port-a-Potties made sense, and the cost would be minimal. Also, she wouldn't mind going over the lighting one more time. She hated the idea of kids wandering off. It got dark in the mountains at night.

She hit the turn signal and slowed. Dense thickets of snowberry with their bell-shaped pink flowers bracketed the side of the road leading to her valley. A line of bikers gathered at the stop sign, three of her godfathers among them.

Happiness rushed her so hard she felt the sting in her eyes. She'd been so worried about letting them down, but now, because of this trip, she'd gone from hopeful to confident.

So damn glad I flew out there.

With the top down on her convertible, she waved. "Hey, guys."

Affection warmed their weather-beaten faces until one of them pointed in confusion to her car.

"It's a rental." *Don't get me started.*

Whale dropped his kickstand and hustled over, his gray T-shirt pulled tight over his big belly. "Welcome home, girl."

Daisy punched the seatbelt and lifted to receive his hug. "Thanks. Glad to be home."

He pulled away. "What happened to your car?"

"I found out my battery died when I was heading for the airport, so I had to rent this one."

"Should've told me," Whale said. "I'd have replaced it while you were away."

"It's okay. My dad took care of it."

Whale glanced to the others, but she didn't need to see their doubt. Obviously, she knew not to rely on her dad.

Mostly, she didn't. But she'd had a plane to catch, so she'd taken him up on his offer.

"All he had to do was make a simple phone call." She shrugged as if her dad couldn't possibly have failed such a simple task. But everyone knew better. He could easily have forgotten all about his promise the moment he'd disconnected the call. "But look at me in this fancy convertible. It was *all* the rental company had." She smiled. "*Such* a hardship."

Whale pressed his lips together, likely holding back comments about her dad. But she had to get moving. She needed to get that contract signed. "Seriously, it's no big deal."

"Ah, sugar." He looked like he wanted to say something. Instead, he leaned down and gave her another hug.

She breathed in his familiar scent of leather and pipe tobacco. With her dad gone for long stretches of time, his biker club brothers had stepped right in. Her godfathers had been to every recital, performance, and graduation she'd ever had—even when her dad had been in town.

They meant the world to her.

He pulled away. "You find out your battery's still dead, you let me know. I'll take care of it."

"Thank you." But why trouble him when she could just call roadside assistance?

Whale hustled back to his bike. "See you tonight."

"Hey, have you guys seen the mayor?" she asked. "He's not answering, and I need to talk to him."

One of the guys aimed a gloved thumb over his shoulder. "Saw him heading to your mom's."

"Great. Oh, and guys, don't leave me hanging up there tonight, okay? Promise me if no one bids, you'll step up."

They shook their heads as if they couldn't believe she'd

even suggest it. One of them said, "Hon, they're gonna be fightin' over it."

Her auction package—a day on the ranch with the choice of fishing, rafting, hiking, or rappelling—was what people in Montana did for fun anyway. It made more sense to bid on Helene's year of free haircuts. Or a children's party from Barry's Bouncy House.

"We got your back, Daisy."

She absolutely knew that. As she buckled up, she watched them roar down the highway. Pulling out her phone, she skimmed her messages, stopping when she saw one from Stuart. *Oh, good.* Not hearing back from him had made her anxious.

She opened his text.

Stuart: Slight change of plans.

A clammy sensation crept across her skin. What did that mean? Her fingers tapped out a quick response.

Daisy: What change? The sun beat down on top of her head as she waited for his response. At this point, she couldn't afford any changes.

She shot him one more text before getting back on the road.

Daisy: Just turning onto Main Street. Need to meet you right away—great news!

Okay, don't invent trouble. He'd said *slight* change. It wasn't like he'd do anything major without talking to her. She made the turn, fingers gripping the steering wheel. Besides, no matter what he'd done, he'd get back with the program the moment she told him her good news. She'd flown across the country to convince one potential investor to come out for the Huckleberry Festival, and she'd wound up nabbing a powerful media mogul at the same time.

They'd always had local and state press at the annual festival, but national? That would be a game-changer, and not just for the ranch but the whole town. Which meant her mom, her godfathers, and their small group of friends who'd pooled their savings to invest in the resort wouldn't lose their money. *Thank God.*

But first, she needed Stuart's signature on that contract —proof for Mickelson Media that he was delivering the Shout! reunion.

As she rounded the bend into the historic town, she got that little kick in her chest when she took in the blue and white striped awnings of the businesses, the antique wrought-iron streetlamps, and the window planters bursting with purple, pink, and blue pansies.

Turning into a spot in front of the Sugar Bowl café, Daisy pulled the contract out of her travel folder. *What have you done, Stuart?*

Please don't mess this up for me.

Her mom and godfathers had offered to become share-holders at the beginning of summer, but she'd held off, not willing to risk their savings if she wound up with a short-fall of investors. But as soon as Stuart had offered a Shout! reunion, Daisy had known they'd reach their goal.

Cutting the ignition, she grabbed her phone and a pen and headed inside. She scanned the large café, its low ceilings and wood beams making it feel like a cozy tavern. The place was packed. Every seat was taken, including the stools facing the bay window that looked onto the green.

She didn't see him anywhere. About her height, the mayor—also known as the former lead singer of the nineties rock band Shout!—had a deep tan and shoulder-length frizzy hair. With his Hollywood-flair, he definitely stood out in a town full of people who lived in hiking boots and nylon cargo shorts.

Three firefighters stood at the register, arms loaded with white paper bags, handing cash to her mom's summer help. Joe, the fire chief, saw her and broke into a warm smile. "Daze, honey, you're back."

"I am." She took in the smudges on his cheek and damp hairline. "Everything okay?"

"Small fire up the mountain. Came close to Mr. Cudder's place, but we got it out, no problem." He nodded toward the display case. "Stopped by here on our way back to the station."

She gave him a gentle smile. They both knew exactly why he'd visited her mom's café. "Any chance you've seen Stuart? I heard he was headed here."

"He wanted turnovers, but they weren't ready yet. Your mom told him to come back in twenty minutes."

"Rats. I must've just missed him." She pulled out her phone and called him, but it went to voicemail. "Stuart, it's Daisy. I've got big news and need to talk to you. I'm at the Sugar Bowl. Call me or come over right away, okay?"

Just then, the door to the kitchen swung open, and her mom backed out with a tray of apple turnovers. When her gaze landed on Daisy, her tired expression lightened. "Sweetheart, you're back." She handed the tray off to one of the college kids and came around the counter to embrace her daughter. Daisy wrapped her arms around her mom, breathing in her cinnamon and warm-butter scent.

"So glad your trip went well." When her mom pulled away, she cupped her chin. "You okay?"

Her mom could read her so well. "Yeah, of course. I just need to talk to Stuart."

"Hannah." Joe looked at her mom like he wanted to

bury his face in her neck, close his eyes, and breathe in all her wholesome goodness.

Her mom gave the chief a smile. "You guys all set?"

"Yep. Gotta head back."

Daisy figured she knew another way to get Stuart's attention.

Daisy: Guess what my mom just pulled from the oven?

"Well, hang on," her mom said. "Let me grab some turnovers to take with you."

"You don't have to do that." Joe cupped a hand over the side of his mouth. "Please do that."

Her mom laughed and took off behind the counter, Joe watching her every move. "She works too damn hard."

Well, sure. Daisy's parents hadn't married, so her mom had to support herself through retirement. And a town that made most of its money during the summer tourist season didn't make it easy on its residents.

If they didn't build the resort, and her mom lost her investment, retirement wouldn't even be an option. But Daisy was getting ahead of herself again. A slight change of plans could mean any number of things.

"The trip to New York went well?" he asked.

"So well. I've been working on this guy for months, and I just couldn't get him to commit. He thought it sounded great out here with all the outdoor adventures, but I guess he was looking for razzle-dazzle because as soon as I mentioned the Shout! Reunion, he got all excited and said if we can book big-name acts like that, he's in. And then he got on the phone and told his friend to come out with him. And his *friend* just happens to be Dan Mickelson."

His eyes widened in surprise. "Mickelson Media?"

"Yep. So, yeah, it went great."

"This is really going to happen, isn't it?"

"It is." She could see the relief behind his smile. He didn't have a lot of extra cash for investments. "I'm not going to let you down, Joe."

"Good to hear, honey. And not just for me." His gaze tracked her mom. She loved the look in his eyes as he watched her mom chat with a customer. "I sure would like your mom to slow down."

Anxiety banded around her chest. She had to find out what Stuart had done. "I'll see you later, Joe. Bye, Mom." Just as her hand hit the door, her phone vibrated with a text from the mayor.

Stuart: Stay put. On my way.

Finally. As she headed outside into the bright sunshine, she saw Stuart dashing across the street and waved him over.

"Daisy." As Stuart stepped onto the sidewalk, his gaze traveled down her peach linen dress to her wedge sandals. "Didn't you just get off a plane? You look like you're going to a garden party."

"Yep, came straight from the airport. Okay, tell me about this change you mentioned." She motioned him away from the doorway.

"Nothin' big. Give me your news first."

"Oh, I just had the most amazing meeting in New York. That investor I told you about is coming out for the Huckleberry Festival. And you know what sealed the deal?"

His eyes glittered with joy. "Knowing he'll get to hang out with me?"

"Pretty much." She laughed. "When I told him about the Shout! reunion, he was in. Just like that."

"That's great."

"It is. It couldn't be better. Well, actually, it *is* better. He invited his friend, who just happens to be Dan Mickelson."

The mayor's eyebrows shot up. "No kidding?"

"And he's offering the full force of his media empire if you just sign a contract confirming you're going to produce a Shout! reunion here in Snowberry."

"Awesome."

What was that? Did his smile just falter? "He needs it today, though, so his media outlets can get going on the event." She smiled as she held the contract out to him. "How fast can you sign?"

He didn't immediately reach for it. Instead, he cupped his mouth with his thumb and forefinger.

"What is it, Stuart?" *Just tell me already.*

"Had to shift things around a little."

Everything in her tightened. "I need you to be specific."

"Well, you know the guys like Blue Sky."

She held her breath, waiting for him to go on.

"It's more upscale."

"So, are you saying they're going to stay in Blue Sky? Because that's fine. I don't care where they stay." It would also open up six cabins at the ranch, which was booked solid.

He eyed her warily. "They're gonna play there."

A stinging sensation ripped through her. "No, they're playing here. The Huckleberry Festival is *here*. In Snowberry."

He raised his hands, palms up. "It's all set, Daze. We're playing the Blue Sky Amphitheatre. Same date, same playlist, just…different venue."

"No, Stuart. They're playing here. We've already built the stage for this show. We've advertised it. People planned their vacations around it."

And my family and friends invested what little money they have in the resort because they trusted me to deliver.

"I know that. And I'm givin' you the reunion concert, just like I promised. This is a big deal, man. You have no idea how hard it was to get all the guys to agree to it. But I did. They're in. So, believe me when I tell you we're gonna put on a show you'll never forget."

"Here, Stuart. You'll put it on here. *That's* what you promised us." God, how did she get through to him? "You're the mayor of *this* town, not Blue Sky. You ran on a platform to revive *this* economy. Turning the Blackstock Ranch into a resort is the only hope of doing that. It's going to bring in jobs, tourists, and year-round business to the entire community. But it won't happen if we don't get the investors. And this is it, Stuart. Our last shareholder weekend of the summer." She shook the contract at him. "I need the concert at the ranch, and I need you to sign this contract."

"The investors don't give a damn where it's held. Long as they get the show they're coming out here for, who cares if they have to drive fifteen minutes down the road?" He pulled the contract out of her hand. "Mickelson sure as hell won't care. He's in it for the reunion. Give me a pen."

"No, Stuart. He's in it because our town draws this level of entertainment. Which is why he's having you sign a contract stating that you're playing in *Snowberry*."

"It's fine. I'll just write in Blue Sky."

"No, you won't." She saw a way to get what she wanted. "If you want *Entertainment Update* covering your show, you have to hold it in Snowberry."

All his energy faded, and he just looked tired. "Daze, come on. If I had any damn control over this thing, you know I'd have it here. But I don't. It's out of my hands."

"Then so is the contract." She snatched it back. *How do I salvage this?* "Give me your manager's number."

"You can't call my manager." When she stared him down, he let out a frustrated breath. "He hardly returns my calls. He's sure as hell not gonna return yours."

"When he hears about *Entertainment Update* covering your show, he will."

"Trust me, Daze. He won't."

This isn't happening. "Dammit, Stuart. I had The Desperados, remember? I was all set. You're the one who told me you could pull together a Shout! reunion. I *trusted* you."

Failure for the professional investors wouldn't change their personal lives, but it would do serious damage to Joe, her godfathers. *Mom.*

She watched him for a moment, looking for the slightest indication he could be swayed.

"I *am* pulling off a reunion. You have any idea how hard it was? The guys barely talk to each other anymore. They've turned down every offer we've gotten for a tour or an album. I made this happen for *you*. For this town. So, work with me, okay? We'll get some limos, some champagne. Set up a VIP suite for them. It'll be a hell of a lot cooler for your investors than having it on some raised platform on a *ranch*."

She closed her eyes and took in a slow breath. "It won't be better, Stuart, because we're selling the investors on our location. We need to show them that Snowberry is a destination resort. It's not a destination resort if we hold our concerts in Blue Sky."

Ethan. She needed to talk to Ethan. Get the Blackstock brothers together to brainstorm a Plan B. She'd call The Desperados' manager, but she suspected it was too late to rebook them at this point.

Reaching into her tote, she pulled out her phone and pointed it at Stuart. "Confirm with me right now that there's no way to have the concert at the ranch."

One terse nod gave her the answer. She strode to her car and hit Ethan's number.

He answered on the second ring. "Daisy. You just land?" In the background she heard persistent hammering and a buzz saw, letting her know he was overseeing the festival grounds' set-up.

"We've got a problem."

"Talk to me." He sounded terse, alert.

Getting into her rental car, she shoved the key in the ignition. "I'm on my way to the ranch. Can you get everyone to meet in my office in ten minutes?"

"You got it." He disconnected.

Stuart stood beside her, a hand on her window. "Don't be like this, Daisy. The guys and I'll take care of the investors. We'll spend a day with 'em at the ranch. It'll be fine."

"I'm not looking for fine, Stuart. I'm knocking it out of the damn park."

Chapter Two

You've got to be kidding me.

Dead. Completely dead. Not even a ticking sound when Daisy turned the ignition.

Okay, calm down. In the scheme of things, a dead battery was an inconvenience and not a problem. She'd call roadside assistance, simple enough. But when she reached for her phone, and it flew out of her hands like a live trout, she had to acknowledge that she was upset.

No, let's be honest. She was *angry*. Crazy angry. Wild energy raced through her, making her body tingle with anxiety.

She would never have asked her family and friends to touch their savings. She'd only accepted their money because she was so sure the Shout! reunion would push them over the finish line. *Slam dunk.*

And now Stuart had blown it up—two weeks before show time. How was she supposed to find another big-name act *now*? She would, though. Of course, she would. She didn't have a choice.

And her dad, God, he couldn't have made one phone

call? If she'd talked to Whale instead of him, she'd have a working car right now.

Mostly, though, she was angry at herself for trusting them. Because she'd *had* an act lined up, and she'd known not to trust her dad.

Oh, hell, no. This is not my fault.

She lunged toward the passenger side to grab her phone off the floor. Flipping the visor down, she punched in the number for assistance—the same one she'd given her dad four days ago. It took her a total of five minutes to give her location and arrange for them to replace her battery. They'd be here within the hour.

That's all he'd had to do.

The moment she got off the phone, she punched in her dad's number.

He answered on the second ring. "Daisy, love of my life, how's it going?"

In the background, she heard loud conversation, music, and shrieks of laughter. "I thought you were going to get my battery replaced."

A moment of silence, and then, "Oh, dammit. Hang on a sec, sweet pea, let me get clear of all this chaos."

As she waited for him to find a quiet place, she wondered why she'd bothered to confront him. Hadn't twenty-eight years of disappointment taught her anything?

Because of *hope*. She'd yet to extinguish that tiny flame flickering deep inside that one day he'd come through for her. Become dependable.

"Hey, yeah, listen," he said. "You won't believe what happened. Right after we got off the phone, this moron driver backed his bulldozer over a pipeline creating the damnedest mess you've ever seen. There was oil every-where. It was like Lake Michigan over here. I could've finally gotten some use out of that damn boat I bought for us when you were a kid."

"Dad." Listening to his excuses only hurt worse.

"Flowed for an hour before they got it shut off. Now we've got Feds, state, local…damn government employees crawling all over this place. I—"

"*Dad.*"

He stopped talking.

"I have to go. The auction's about to start, and I have to get changed. I just…I'm disappointed. I really wish you'd have come through for me."

"Yeah, sweet girl, me, too. How 'bout this? I'll fly out for your birthday—"

"No." Her abrupt tone silenced him. "Last-minute tickets are too expensive. I'll just talk to you later."

"Sure thing, doll. I'll get on the horn and get your car taken care of."

"It's already done. Bye, Dad."

"I'll call you on your birthday, sweetheart."

That promise and five bucks would get her a latté.

Hunching a shoulder to hold the phone tight to his ear, Cooper let himself into the cabin.

"Wait, she blew you off?" Emmie sounded surprised.

She didn't know his mom. "Yeah. She works house-keeping. If they offer a catering event she's got to take it." He obviously understood that, but what the hell? He'd interrupted his plans to come out here.

The shriek of laughter in the background told him his bandmates and their families were hanging out at the beach. He ignored the sharp tug in his chest and reminded himself how much more fun he'd have with his Austin buddies, who were single and down to party.

"But she asked you to fly out there. I mean, we're talking about your father."

His *father*. Jesus. Cooper's heart pounded. Of course, it could turn out to be nothing. It could just mean Slider, the man his mom had had an off-and-on relationship with throughout Cooper's childhood, had gotten sober and finally decided to acknowledge him.

Man, as a kid, Cooper had done everything he could to win that man over. Being quiet so he didn't wake him up, fetching him beer, an ashtray, a bag of chips—whatever. He'd even stolen a handful of lighters when Slider had tossed the house looking for one. But nothing had earned the man's attention.

Christ. He didn't want to dig back into those memories. "I'll see her in the morning."

"Well, don't worry about anything, okay? Just take care of your family stuff."

Cooper dumped his duffel bag on a leather club chair. "What're you saying?"

"Just, you know, don't stress over finding us a new act."

"Em, those guys I hung out with last night? They're all over this. They're putting together a whole list of bands for me to see." He wouldn't bother unpacking. Just head into town. "There's no stress here."

"That's good." She hesitated. "It's just that I'm getting a lot of pressure from the label. They're pushing hard for Kallous. It's their next break-out band, and if we don't come up with an alternative pretty fast, they're going to go ahead and book them."

"I'll have an alternative."

"Yeah, but you're in Montana right now. You know?"

"Doesn't matter where I am. I'll listen to a bunch of bands, and by the end of the weekend, I'll have the field narrowed down to two or three. Then, I'll be back in Austin and can meet with them and their managers. Okay?"

"Yeah, sure." She didn't sound convinced.

"And don't count Snowberry out. It's a hotbed of talent."

She laughed. "Why? Because you're from there?"

"Hell, yeah. But actually, you'd be surprised at the scene here. In fact, I'm heading out right now to hear some live music."

"Doesn't Pearl Jam's bassist live in Montana? Maybe we can get them to open for us." He heard the smile in her tone. "I think John Mayer lives there, too."

"See? Hotbed. I'm even renting a cabin owned by Hunter Blackstock, a famous rockabilly and jazz musician." *Well, around here anyway.*

"Really?"

"Yeah, he's the local land baron. And, other than a few B&Bs, his ranch is the only lodging in town."

"Well, I don't want you to worry about it. Family comes first. So, if you get caught up in things, let me know. I have to give the label an answer by Monday morning, so they have time to pull a tour together."

"Tell them now. No way's Kallous touring with us."

"Jeez, Coop. I don't think I've ever heard you so serious. How about this? I don't have to tell them anything this weekend, so I'll hold off a couple of days, see what you come up with. If nothing lights your fire—"

"I'll find us a band." It struck him that her concerns had less to do with him and more to do with balancing the conflicting demands of the label and the band. She was in a tough spot. "Em," he said softly. "I got this."

"I know you do." She let out a breath. "So, are you going to see any old friends when you're in town?" He was about to respond, when she said, "Any old *girl*friends? Bet you were a heartbreaker."

And just like that, the memory of Daisy Charbonneau slammed him. He'd thought about her a lot over the years. When he'd first moved away, he'd felt the relentless ache of regret. All those years of crushing on her, and he'd never once acted on his feelings.

But, of course, he could never have asked her out.

She'd been the light to his dark, the pure to his filth. He'd wanted her with a fierceness he'd only tamed because he knew she deserved so much better than the son of the town's addict. What was he supposed to do? Entertain her in the rotting hunting cabin? Take her on a date to Tandy's Grocer so they could share a stolen bag of beef jerky?

"I won't have time to hang out with anyone." To this day, when he closed his eyes, he could still see Daisy's smile—and it packed the same punch. She was the only woman he'd ever truly wanted.

He doubted he'd run into her, though. He was only in town two nights.

Patting his pocket, he made sure he had his key, and then looked around the room. A classic A-frame, the cabin had soaring ceilings, a high-end galley kitchen, leather couches and chairs, and a separate bedroom and bathroom. "All right, Em, I'm going to head out. If I like what I see tonight, I'll send you a clip."

"Thanks, Coop. Have fun."

"Talk to you later." He yanked his ball cap from the side pocket of his bag and headed out. Pulling the door shut, he took a moment to get his bearings. From what he'd seen on the drive in, this cabin was off the beaten path. Closer to the base of the mountain and more isolated. If he recalled correctly, the walkway led to the back of the main building.

Cooper struck off, breathing in the pine-scented air. For the last ten years, he'd divided his time between Austin and New York, so it felt strange to be back in Snowberry. The majestic mountains and vast expanse of purple-tinged sky hurtled him back in time.

It left him feeling a little disoriented. He might not be poor, angry, and unwanted anymore, but all those feelings rose to the surface as the world of his childhood enveloped him.

Time hadn't washed them away after all.

The river roared, and a golf cart whirred by. The driver, dressed in a black Polo shirt with the ranch logo, waved to him. Automatically, Cooper lowered the bill of his cap. Not that it mattered, but he'd rather get through this weekend without anyone from his childhood recognizing him. Giving the guy a nod, he pulled out his phone to see if his mom had texted back about meeting him for breakfast.

Mom: Working in the AM. I'm off at 3.

What the hell? No fucking way.

Cooper: You asked me to come out here. I'm in the middle of a damn tour. Just pick me up tonight after work. Don't care how late.

He waited several long moments, knowing full well she might not respond. No one forced his mom to do anything.

So, he was almost surprised when his phone chimed.

Mom: Can't.

That was it? *That's all she has to say?* Why did every interaction with his mom have to be so damn frustrating? Part of him wanted to grab his duffle and head right back to the airport. But dammit, he needed answers.

He kept replaying the sponsor's words. *And she needs to come clean about him.*

Did that mean Slider wasn't his dad? If so, who *was* his father?

Jesus, why wouldn't she just tell him?

Drawing in a deep breath, he looked down at his black boots. He reminded himself that his mom hadn't called. Her sponsor had. Plus, he'd only changed his plans that morning, so it wasn't like she could've arranged her schedule to see him.

Okay, so, if she'd only see him tomorrow at three, he might as well use the time to meet with the contractor and get the house project started. In the meantime, he'd stay in touch with his Austin friends, check out the demos and videos they sent.

He texted her back.

Cooper: Pick me up after your shift.

Too bad he hadn't rented a car at the airport. But he'd been thrown by his mom's text telling him she couldn't pick him up. Since the ranch had offered car service, he'd taken it.

Approaching the main building, he heard a strange rumbling, groaning sound. When he came upon the dumpsters behind the restaurant, he caught sight of dark, beady eyes watching him. Sleek fur and long-ass claws.

The shock of it seared through him, practically frying his skin. A huge black bear balanced on the corner of the dumpster, a garbage bag in its paws.

"Holy shit." But then he laughed, automatically

rubbing the scar on his forearm. Growing up in deep woods, he'd encountered bears all the damn time. He wasn't scared of this guy.

"Go on inside, okay?" A hand pressed reassuringly on his shoulder, and he breathed in a faint vanilla scent. "I got this." A woman wearing waders and a fishing hat stepped in front of him, clapping her hands at the bear. "Hey. Go on now. *Go*."

Cooper had to smile at the way this slight woman was protecting him.

The bear dropped the garbage bag, turned so his ass faced them, and climbed off the dumpster.

"It's okay." The woman spoke gently but confidently while keeping her eye on the bear. "Don't worry about a thing. He's far more interested in the six-tier cake one of our waiters dropped than you. You just head inside the building."

Like he'd let her alone with a hungry black bear.

But before he could say anything, the bear started lumbering toward them.

"Oh, crap." The woman dashed into a door at the back of the restaurant. Reaching up, she brought down a shotgun, racked it, and shot it into the air.

The bear took off into the woods.

She turned to him. "Are you okay?" And then her eyes went wide, and a smile burst across her features. "Cooper? Oh, my God." Her hand clapped over her mouth, and she pulled off her hat. "What in the world are you doing here?"

Daisy Charbonneau.

Oh, fuck. She was gorgeous.

"Hey." His mind went blank. The circuitry shorted out. "Daisy." He heard his voice. Knew how dull it sounded. And he saw the way her joy dimmed. But his heart thundered painfully. Daisy Charbonneau in high school was so beautiful he could barely look her in the eye, but the woman she'd turned into was a stunner. Long, dark hair, blue eyes, the lushest mouth he'd ever seen, and that body. Jesus Christ, she had a body that made men stupid.

Even in stockingfoot waders.

Cheeks blazing a furious red, she gazed down at herself. "I can't *believe* I'm wearing this when I finally see you again."

"You look beautiful."

She gaped at him. *Awesome. Way to make her uncomfortable*. He scrambled for something intelligent to say. "You've become a real mountain woman."

What the hell—why had *those* words come out of his mouth?

"Oh." She laughed, holding up the shotgun. "Right. Let me put this back. Hang on." She leaned into the doorway and set the gun on the rack. "That's the summer help. They leave the dumpster open so they can bring out more garbage bags but then get distracted by something else."

His body heat clashed with the cool evening air, leaving him clammy and robbing him of speech.

"God, I just…I can't believe you're here." She'd always looked at him like that—as if he'd reached into the sky and pushed the clouds apart so the sunshine would spill down onto her. "Have you been back even once since you left for college?"

"Nah, been busy."

"Busy?" She stuttered out a laugh. "No kidding. *Blue Fire?*"

He smiled. "Guess it worked out all right."

"Uh, yeah, I'd say so. Hey, you have to see Mr. Walker while you're in town. You're his one and only success story."

That would've been nice. He owed the man every-thing. "Wish I had time."

"I just...I'm sorry for being such an idiot. I'm just so surprised to see you." She shook her head. "So, what brings you home?"

Home. Associating that word with Snowberry felt all kinds of wrong. "I've got some business to take care of with my mom."

Warmth suffused her features, and she reached out to touch his arm. "My first job out of college was at the Blue Sky Club, so I'd see her from time to time. She looked like she was doing great. You must be proud of her."

"Sure." He tried to get command of himself, but she was just so fucking beautiful. Her vibrant personality, her warmth...she was just *so much woman*.

But he didn't want her to think he was still the same messed-up kid. He wanted her to see the man he'd become. "I'm glad her...well, you know, her quality of life's a lot better."

Oh, Christ. Kill me now.

"I'll say. So, how long are you in town?"

"Just the weekend. Getting started on a project for her tomorrow."

"Aren't you guys in the middle of a tour?"

"Yeah. We're on a two-week break." *Jesus, Cooper, talk to her.* "You still sing?"

"I do, sure. But, you know, just for fun. I work here now."

"At the ranch?"

She laughed. "Well, we like to call it a *resort*." She leaned into him. "We can charge the tourists more that way."

"It looks great." Not only had they replaced the run-down rental cabins, but they'd put in roads, landscaping, and a fancy lodge-like restaurant. Plus, golf carts.

People used to give Hunter Blackstock a lot of shit for paying more attention to his music than his kids and the rental cabins—his family's only livelihood. But it looked like the guy had done all right for himself.

Music in the distance grew louder, as a stretch limo approached the portico of the restaurant. Hard rock blasted out of the sunroof. The door opened, and a short man in a blue velvet tuxedo stepped out.

Wait a minute. Was that Stuart Neil Goff? In *Snowberry*?

You've got to be kidding me. Talk about timing. The former lead singer of Shout! would have exactly the kind of connections Cooper needed. He wanted to snap a picture and send it to Emmie. *Look what just fell into my lap.*

Stuart headed toward Daisy, holding his palms up like a supplicant. "Hey, Daze. We okay?"

The look she gave him should've flash-frozen the man's balls.

"Aw, come on. You know I'm not gonna let you down." His tone sounded almost patronizing.

"You already have. But this isn't the time." She nodded toward the restaurant. "You'd better get in there."

"Daze, whatever plans you make here, you know the concert's still happening at Blue Sky, right?" He gentled his voice. "Your investors are gonna be my VIPs at the show."

Four older men wearing western clothing and cowboy boots slid out of the limo. Stuart gestured to them. "Daisy, these are some friends of mine who flew in from Aspen for the weekend."

Cooper didn't like the way the tallest one—the one with the black Stetson—looked at Daisy. Like he'd just swiped right on her Tinder picture. "Evening." The man reached for her hand.

Daisy grasped his firmly. "So nice to meet you. I don't know what your plans are while you're in town but let me know if you're interested in exploring the ranch. I can set you up with Remi Blackstock. He's the best guide in the state. Fly fishing, white water rafting, you name it, he'll give you an experience you'll never forget."

"Sounds great," Stetson said. "Weekend's wide open."

"Are you a guide, too?" One of the other men turned a confused expression on the mayor. "I thought you said she was in the show tonight."

The mayor laughed in his gravelly, rough voice. "This isn't a show, man. It's an auction. I told you we're raisin' money for the high school music program. Besides, Daisy's beautiful no matter what she's wearing." Stuart reached for her as if he might draw her in for a side hug.

The moment Daisy flinched, Cooper stepped between them. "Cooper Hood." He thrust out his hand.

"Cooper, this is Stuart Neil Goff," Daisy said. "He's the mayor."

As they shook hands, Stuart flashed him a big grin. "You got a pen? I can sign somethin' for ya."

"You gentlemen better get in there." Daisy gestured to the entryway of the main building that held reception, a restaurant, and a fitness center. "The auction's already started."

"Nice to meet you." Stetson led the group toward the entrance.

Stuart held his arm out for her. "Come on. I'll walk you in." He leaned in close. "Wanna make sure we're okay."

The look she shot him said, *We're not.* "You go on. I'm catching up with an old friend."

"This your date?"

She stepped closer to Cooper. "We went to high school together. We were voted most likely to form a band...and then join the 27 Club."

Tension snapped across Stuart's features, but Daisy just laughed. "Those of us in the music program didn't have much street cred."

"Yeah, but we're twenty-eight now," Cooper said. "So, they obviously did get us at all."

She beamed a smile up at him, and he loved sharing a joke with her.

"You played, huh?" Stuart asked with a self-satisfied smile. "Give Daisy your email address, and I'll have my publicist send you somethin'. You got a phone? You can take a picture if you want."

"He's the lead guitarist for Blue Fire." She sounded proud.

Stuart's eyes widened. It took him a moment to process the information, and Cooper thought he saw the mayor go from surprised to calculating. "Well, hell, man, we gotta jam. How long you in town for?"

"Just through the weekend." Cooper took his shot. "I'm actually looking for an opening act. Ours blew up halfway through the tour."

"Ah, that sucks. We should talk. You got any free time?"

"I do. How about we get a drink after the auction?"

"You got it."

"You should hurry up," Daisy said to Stuart. "You're missing out on some amazing packages."

"Not gonna miss a thing." Stuart gave her a strange smile. "I'm just here to show my support for the music program." The mayor cocked his thumb and forefinger like a gun. "I'll see you in there." He gave Cooper a hearty handshake. "Catch you after the auction." He followed the group inside.

Cooper shook his head. "I can't believe I ran into Stuart Neil Goff in Snowberry. And the *mayor*? What's up with that?"

"I know. It's crazy, right? He's been going to the Blue Sky Club for years. Somehow, he found his way here—though, frankly, I think it was the smell of my mom's cinnamon buns." She gave him one of her dazzling smiles. "He wound up running for mayor a couple of years ago. You should definitely meet with him about an opening act, but if you're looking for something a little different, talk to Hunter. He plays with some amazing bands. Tonight's not a good night—we've got a little crisis on our hands—but if you have time tomorrow, the three of us can talk about the local music scene."

"Sounds good."

She looked to the restaurant. "Okay, I have to get in there. Where were you headed before I turned all Annie Oakley on you?"

"I was going to grab some dinner and then head into town. My driver told me about a club with live music."

She grinned. "He's talking about the Sugar Bowl."

"Your mom's bakery?"

"It's now a bakery-slash-café-slash-super-cool-coffee-house-with-live-music. Hard to make a living in Snowberry." Her features fell. "Unfortunately, there's no music tonight because of the auction. But let me get the chef to put together some dinner for you." She tipped her head, looking thoughtful. "Actually, you should join us. Like Stuart said, we're raising money for the music program. It's always the first thing to go when they're looking at budget cuts. But you know Hunter. Music's everything to him. No way the program's going down on his watch." With that brilliant smile and the sparkle in her eyes, his blood went fizzy, just like in high school. "Feel like bidding on a day with a mountain woman?"

A day with Daisy. What he would've given to spend that kind of time with her as a teenager. Actually, though, he hadn't thought of dating her so much as folding his whole self into her. In his fantasies, they'd been inseparable.

But he wasn't that pathetic kid anymore, and he had different fantasies these days. "I'll definitely donate, but I have to pass on the auction. Like I said, I leave on Sunday, so I won't be around."

"Okay, then, let me at least get some dinner for you."

Instead of walking through the door he'd opened for her, she stopped and gazed up at him, studying his features. In the light of the foyer, he could see the dimple at the side of her mouth, the rim of black around her deep blue iris, and the creamy complexion of her skin.

He held his breath, afraid he smelled from the long day of travel. Worried she thought he was a total dick for his awkward comments. But, after a moment, she smiled softly. "It's really good to see you." And walked into the building.

He finally took a breath, inhaling the trail of her sweet scent. Jesus, he'd follow that woman anywhere.

Heading straight for the arched doorway into the crowded, loud restaurant, she called over her shoulder, "See you in a bit."

Actually, he ought to get Stuart's cell number, in case they lost each other in the chaos after the auction. He didn't want to risk losing the opportunity.

He made his way to the hostess's podium and took in the cavernous room. Well, damn. The Blackstocks had done well for themselves. A picture window comprised the length of the restaurant, with a massive stone hearth at one end and a long brass and polished wood bar at the other.

Everyone had their chairs turned to the stage, where a woman dressed in an aviator jumpsuit held up a red and white gingham-lined picnic basket.

The microphone screeched with feedback until the MC pulled his mouth away. "Sorry about that. Okay, ladies and gentlemen, let's introduce our next package. Gallatin Valley Charters is offering a helicopter tour hosted by Elena Broadhurst. This family-owned business has been around for sixty years, offering airborne surveys of the Greater Yellowstone region as well as all over the Gallatin Valley. And if you're nervous about getting up in the air, you should know your pilot graduated from Embry Riddle Aeronautical University, and her specialty is Search and Rescue." The MC smiled, his gaze fixed on someone in the audience. "As Harold can attest."

An older man lifted out of his seat, waving his casted arm. "Trust me, the only one you want rescuing you is Elena. She's got a cooler of beer on her chopper."

Laughter rippled across the room.

"I'm sure he meant iced tea." The MC wore a teasing expression. "Okay, moving on. Gallatin Valley Charters is offering a half-day tour of Yellowstone with a stop in the valley for a picnic lunch. You'll see seven mountain ranges and a whole world of wildlife that people in cars never have a chance to see. Plus, you'll have all of lovely Elena's tales of adventure from her family's sixty years in the business. Let's start the bidding at one hundred dollars. Do I hear—"

"Two hundred," Harold stood up.

"Thank you, Harold," Elena said.

A young woman dressed in a simple black cocktail dress and black cowboy boots approached Cooper. "Hey, there. Daisy wanted me to let you know your dinner should be ready in a few minutes."

"Sounds good."

"Why don't you grab a drink, and I'll be back as soon as it's ready?" With a smile, she headed over to the hostess stand.

He'd pass on the drink. He needed to find Stuart. Scanning the crowded room, he recognized way too many people from his childhood. His gaze snagged on Ed Tandy, and the hot shame of stealing from the man's grocery store burned through him. He tugged his hat lower.

When bawdy laughter erupted at a table near the back of the room, Cooper turned to see Stuart and his buddies flirting with the waitress who poured their wine. *Bingo.* He headed over.

"And now for our next package." A shriek of feedback from the microphone cut through the buzz of conversation in the room and jerked Cooper's attention to the stage. "I'll get the hang of this just about the time we close the auction. Okay, next up."

The MC smiled as Daisy climbed the stairs in her wading boots, a fishing pole in one hand and tackle box in the other.

Clapping and boot-stomping thundered in the room. She gave a wry smile and shook her head like she thought they were messing with her. But Cooper knew they weren't. Everyone was a little in love with Daisy Charbonneau.

When she hit the stage, she set the box down and pretended to cast a line.

"Forget the bait, Daze," some guy called. "I'm already caught."

She laughed, and Cooper felt a pull in his gut. Her innate happiness had always affected him.

"Damn, Stuart," a low voice said. "No wonder you want a slice of that pie."

A shock of energy tore through him, and Cooper looked to see which guy had said it.

"Told you." The mayor chuckled quietly. "Been here a couple years now, and I still can't get her to go out with me." He fixed a hungry gaze on Daisy. "I'll get her now."

What the hell did that mean?

The MC read from a notecard. "Most of you know all about the Blackstock Ranch, but for the out-of-towners, I'll let you know it's one of the oldest homesteads in Snowberry, founded when Galen Blackstock planted his Scottish flag on the soil in 1862."

"Galen was too cheap to buy a flag," someone in the audience called.

The MC waited for the titter of laughter to die down before continuing. "That was a metaphor, Carl. As an English teacher, I'd expect you to know that." Another burst of laughter. The speaker looked up from the card.

"But, hey, doesn't legend have it that the old spendthrift buried his box of gold coins somewhere on the property? Maybe the Blackstocks would get better bids if they hosted a treasure hunt instead of an adventure tour."

When the audience members started shouting out comments, Ethan Blackstock stood, raising a hand. "It's just legend, folks. There's no money buried on our property."

And then Nash, his younger brother, said, "Trust me, we've looked."

Cocky bastards. Of anyone he wanted to avoid while in town, it was Hunter's three dickhead sons.

"Okay, since the Blackstocks *aren't* offering a treasure hunt, let's find out what we're bidding on. For more than a century, adventure seekers have come to the ranch to take advantage of all it has to offer. From Blue Ribbon fishing and level four white water rapids in the Gallatin River to rappelling off Rocky Top Ridge, the Blackstock Ranch has everything an outdoorsman could want. Your host for the day of fun on the ranch is our own Ms. Charbonneau, a Snowberry native."

Stetson, in his black blazer and turquoise bolo tie, lifted a hand. "Five hundred."

The MC found him in the crowd. "Hang onto that thought. We're not quite there yet. The package includes a full day on the ranch with the winner's choice of two activities, a picnic on the Hell Roaring Creek trail, and dinner in the Blackstock Ranch restaurant. And *now* we'll open for bidding—"

"Seven-fifty," Stetson called in his booming voice.

"Hey, man," the mayor said. "What're you doing?"

"Just having a little fun." Stetson kept his attention on Daisy. "That's what you brought me out here for, right?"

Cooper didn't know what these guys were up to, but he didn't like it.

A huge man stood up—probably one of Daisy's godfathers. He looked intimidating as hell in a black button-down shirt, black leather vest, and black jeans. "Eight hundred." The others at his table—all wearing similar black vests—turned hard eyes to the mayor's table.

"Eight-fifty," an older woman called.

Cooper felt better once he saw others were bidding. He had no idea what the mayor and his horndog friends thought they'd get by winning a day on the ranch, but Daisy shouldn't have to find out.

"A grand," Stetson said.

"Hey," the mayor said in his rough voice.

"What?" Stetson grinned. "It's for a good cause, right? Besides, she all but invited me to spend the day with her."

A woman in the middle of the room raised her hand. "Eleven hundred."

The MC pointed the gavel at her. "The bid for a day on the ranch with our own Daisy Charbonneau stands at eleven hundred dollars, do I hear—"

Stetson lifted a hand. "Twelve hundred."

"Shit, man," the mayor said. "You're costin' me money here."

"Thirteen hundred," one of the bikers said.

"Fourteen," Stetson called.

While everyone paid attention to the volleying of the bidders, Cooper watched Daisy's beautiful smile fade. With a look of concern, she shook her head at her godfathers, but the large one folded his arms across his ample belly and gave her an implacable look. "Fifteen hundred."

Stetson remained calm. "Sixteen hundred."

Cooper hadn't had any friends in Snowberry. Well,

he'd had Daisy, but he couldn't claim her as a *friend*. They'd only hung out together because of the music program. But he'd spent more time with Daisy than anyone else. She'd never treated him like the others had, like the drug addict's son. She'd seen him as the one kid in the program who could play well enough to make performing fun. She'd always chosen him to accompany her.

So, he knew her expressions, knew her gestures. And he'd watched her enough to know what made her uncomfortable. He didn't know the whole story, but he could see she didn't want her godfathers getting into a bidding war.

And he sure as hell didn't like how the mayor's buddies viewed the auction. These assholes thought they could buy *her*.

Not gonna happen.

"Keep it up, folks," the MC said. "We're well on our way to funding the music program. We've got sixteen hundred dollars for a day on the Blackstock Ranch. Can I get seventeen hundred?"

"Seventeen," a biker called.

Daisy strode to the podium and gestured to the microphone. The MC handed it over. Facing the room with all her easy confidence, she said, "This is great, you guys. Your generosity tonight is overwhelming. I think most of you know how much this program means to me and so many other kids who benefited from it, so keep the bids coming. And just to sweeten the pot, I'm going to point out that all three Blackstock brothers are available as guides, so there's no limit to the number of people who can participate in this package. You can bid on it for your whole office, family, or team. You bring the adventure-seekers, and we've got the guides."

She handed the mic back, and the MC gave a broad smile. "Well, how about that? A day on the ranch with Daisy *and* the Blackstocks—no limit to the number of participants—is going for seventeen hundred. Do I hear—"

Stetson raised a hand. "Two grand." He leaned into the table and in a low voice, said, "Feisty thing."

Dazzling, more like it. Daisy Charbonneau was a force to be reckoned with.

"Hey, there." The hostess handed him two paper bags. "This one's hot. It's got your main meal. And this one's got your salad, rolls, and dessert."

"Great. Thank you." He reached into his back pocket and pulled out his wallet.

She held up a hand. "Daisy says it's on the house because the restaurant's closed for this event."

"Okay. Thank you." He swiped a twenty out of the billfold and handed her the tip. Then, he looked back to the stage.

"And at two thousand dollars, going once, going twice…" The gavel went up. "A day on the ranch with Daisy and the Blackstock brothers goes for—"

The mayor stood up. "Four grand." He lifted his glass of bourbon to Daisy with a victorious smile. Then, he faced the room. "Music program's not goin' down on my watch."

"Going once for four thousand dollars, twice…"

Just as someone from the biker table lifted his hand, the mayor shot out of his seat. "Five grand. Okay?" His expression said, *We done yet?*

"Thank you, Mayor," the MC said, "but you're already ahead at four."

The audience laughed.

"Leave it at five." The mayor nodded to the bikers. "It's my gift to the program."

"A day on the Blackstock Ranch for five thousand dollars, going once, going twice…"

Stuart turned back to his table with a smug smile, bumping fists with Stetson. "Got her."

But the moment the MC raised the gavel, Cooper stepped forward. "Ten grand."

The gavel cracked on the podium, the MC pointing it at Cooper. "A day on the ranch sold for ten thousand dollars to the man at the back of the room."

Chapter Three

Ball cap tugged low, Cooper made his way out of the restaurant.

Good job pissing off the guy who could land you an opening act. But seriously, man, using the auction to try and score a date with a beautiful younger woman? *Dirty old bastard.*

Whatever. At least Daisy wouldn't have to waste a day with the entitled lech, and Cooper had donated to the program that had saved his ass.

Time to get back to his cabin and check out the links his Austin buddies had sent.

Nearing a bend in the pathway, he heard voices. Three big, brawny men surrounded Daisy. The Blackstock brothers. The oldest glanced over, narrowed his eyes, and then the twins turned as one, giving Cooper that all-too-familiar look. *Keep your filthy hands off her.*

Yeah, well, he'd let them mess with his head when he was sixteen. He was done with that shit. "Daisy." His voice carried in the still of the night, maybe a little too loudly. A little too defiant.

As she leaned into the circle of men, he thought he heard her say, "I'll talk to him." And then she headed his way. "Hey, there."

"Hey." Something flickered at the back of his mind—something he'd wanted to say to her—but with her attention focused on him like that—like there was no one else in the world she wanted to see more than him—it slipped from his grasp.

"I'm glad I ran into you." Her leggings and simple T-shirt accentuated her feminine curves, and her shiny hair tumbled over her shoulders. As she gathered it into a ponytail, twisting it and somehow getting it to stay in a bun, she noticed his take-away bags. "You still haven't eaten?"

"Got distracted by the bidding war."

She smiled. "That was crazy, right? Come on, I'll walk you to your cabin." They headed down the dimly lit path. "The last thing I expected was a fight over a day on the ranch."

He didn't bother pointing out that the bidders weren't fighting over the package. They all just wanted time with her. "Yeah, I got the feeling you didn't want your godfathers involved."

"Oh, God, no. And it's my fault because I *asked* them to bid. Just in case it was like crickets, you know? I mean, come on. It's Montana. People can fish and hike on their own. And it's not like Stuart can't come to the ranch whenever he wants."

"Pretty sure it's not the ranch he's interested in."

"What?" She gazed up at him, worry crinkling the skin between her eyes. "No, it's not like that. I've known him for years. He's never shown any interest—well, I mean, he flirts with everyone."

Cooper didn't want to stir things up, but Daisy needed to know the truth about the mayor. "I don't know about that, Daze. I heard him say he hasn't been able to get you to go out with him since he got here. He basically used the auction to be with you."

"Are you serious?" Confusion clashed with hurt on her beautiful features. "Is that what he thinks of me? We'd fish, eat a sandwich, and then I'd hike up my skirt? I'm not…" She let out an exasperated breath.

Oh, holy hell. That image. Every muscle in his body clenched at the visual of Daisy bent over a picnic table, skirt hiked over her sweet, round ass. *Jesus.* He shut that shit right down. "Daisy, he's a washed-up old man, and you're…" There was nothing he could say that wouldn't embarrass them both. She was stunning. And way too good for a scumbag like Stuart Neil Goff.

"He's the *mayor.* We have a professional relationship."

"Don't worry about it. He didn't win."

"That's right." She leaned into him, her shoulder brushing his arm. "Because you charged in at the last minute." She flashed a mischievous grin. "So, you *do* want to spend a day with me."

Right. *That* was what he'd wanted to talk to her about. "I can't. Like I said, I'm not going to be in town long enough. Just consider my bid a donation to the music program." Her silence went on a little too long, and he wondered if she thought he was rejecting her. "Hey, it's a win-win. The program gets the money, and you don't have to waste a day with some chump who'd rather play in a Nickleback tribute band than spend a day fishing." Yeah, he hated fishing that much.

"What if I want to go through with it?" she asked softly.

The moment she gazed up at him, they hit a break in the towering pines. A shaft of moonlight spilled across her pretty face, giving her complexion a silvery glow. He nearly lost his stride. "I've got too much going on."

"Cooper. You can't turn me down again." Whatever had held her hair back stopped working because it sprang out, bouncing over her shoulders like something right out of a shampoo commercial.

Her tone was teasing, but at the same time...he sensed something more. "Again?"

"Yes, *again*." She tipped her head back, shaking her head as if imploring the stars to make him see reason. "How do you not remember my greatest humiliation?"

"I remember everything." He looked at that beautiful mouth, the gentle bounce of her breasts in the tight T-shirt, and desire hummed in his dick. *Stop it.* "And I'd sure as hell remember if you'd asked me out."

"You really didn't get it, did you?"

He had no idea what she was talking about. "I guess not. Did I hurt you?"

"Uh, you only destroyed my seventeen-year-old heart." She was serious.

And her sadness made him ache. "What am I missing here?"

"It was the prom. I'd crushed on you for years." She eyed him tentatively. "But you knew that, right?"

"No." What was she talking about? He'd gotten hit on a lot in high school. Once he'd stopped wearing dirty clothes and grown into his big feet, girls started flirting with him and handing him notes. Carrie Levitt, his first, used to wait for him outside his last period class. She'd grab his hand and lead him into the textbook storage room for a quick romp.

She must've told her friends because he'd found plenty of entertainment the rest of his time at Snowberry High.

"I don't know how you couldn't tell," she said. "I mean, we were together all the time."

"Yeah, because of the music program." *Because just occupying the same room as you made me happier than ten minutes in a closet with anyone else.*

He couldn't wrap his head around the idea of someone as pure and wholesome and flat-out talented as Daisy being interested in him. If he'd known…nah. He wouldn't have done anything. She'd deserved way better than what he'd had to offer.

"Oh, come on." She nudged him. "It was more than music for me. You had to have noticed. I wasn't exactly subtle about it."

"You were nice to me when nobody else was. That's what I noticed." *Way to sound like a sad sack.*

"I asked you to prom."

"We did go." Understanding rushed him hard. "You meant as your *date?* I thought—"

She patted his arm. "Yeah, I know what you thought. And I took it. *That's* how much I wanted to be with you."

He would never have thought she'd been asking him on a date. When Mr. Walker announced the school had hired a DJ to play, Daisy had leaned over and said something about the prom. He'd assumed she'd wanted their band to play live instead. "I had no idea. Jesus, I'm sorry." What an asshole. She'd asked him to the prom, and he'd turned it into a performance *at* the prom. *Fuck me.*

"Would you have gone with me, if you'd understood what I was asking?"

He didn't have to give it much thought. "I don't think

so." Again, her features tensed. "Daze, I wasn't the right guy for you."

They walked along in silence for a bit. "I thought you were."

Fuck. She'd wanted him. *Me.* How was this happening? "I was a pissed-off kid who wanted to get the hell out of here."

"Well, of course, you did. People treated you terribly. They were awful." She reached for his arm, stopping him. "But look how you handled it. Given your home life, you could've been a high school drop-out. You could've been a drug addict. But you graduated with honors and got a full ride to the University of Texas's School of Music." The pride shone in her eyes. "Cooper, you were amazing. And I was crazy about you."

Blood roared in his ears. His vision tunneled to her face, those searching eyes, and that mouth he'd wanted to kiss for too many empty, lonely years.

All that yearning...*fuck.* She'd been right there. Right fucking there.

He wanted to cup those creamy cheeks, press his mouth to hers—just to have one sweet taste of the girl who'd brought him more—no, the *only*—happiness he'd known in this town.

"It's okay that you didn't see me the same way." She sounded resigned. "You were a huge part of my childhood, and I'm glad I finally got it out there."

Noise filled his head, and a current of energy pulsed through him. He couldn't leave her thinking he hadn't felt the same way. And, in typical Daisy fashion, she'd held nothing back. He'd be a pussy if he didn't do the same. "I did."

"Sorry?"

"I did see you the same way. I thought about you all the time. I…" He sounded agitated, and his skin went all hot and prickly. He needed to calm down. They were talking about feelings from ten years ago. *This is closure for her, nothing more.*

But the way she gazed up at him, eyes full of disbelief and longing, just undid him. "I wish I'd known that," she said.

No, no, no. Do not *look at me like that.* "Nothing could've happened. I wouldn't have brought you into my shit."

"That's not what it would've been about at all."

Did she think he could've somehow separated his home life from his time with her?

Not possible.

Drawing in a breath, she looked down at her black leather flats. When she tilted her chin, she'd pasted on a smile. "Well, that does it. I'm not letting you out of it. Even if we only have coffee or lunch together, I'll get the date I never got in high school."

As hard as she tried to look unaffected, he could see the vulnerability underneath. This mattered to her. And so, he'd give it to her. "Yeah, sure. I've got some business to deal with in the morning, but we can have lunch."

"Business with your mom?"

"I'm building a house for her." They resumed walking.

"Seriously? Cooper, that's…" She let out a breath. "See? You are amazing."

"Well, I'm trying to, anyways. She's not making it easy."

"I think that's probably just her way."

He let the simplicity of her comment sink in. He'd spent a lot of years trying to figure out why his mom made such bad choices, and in one sentence, Daisy had nailed it. *That's what she does. She makes everything difficult.*

"So, have you bought the lot yet? What's the plan?"

He hadn't discussed it with anybody yet. Not even his bandmates. "She wants to renovate the hunting cabin."

Her brows shot up. "But it's so remote."

He smiled. "That's just her way."

She glanced up at him, their gazes locking. That connection they'd always had flared hot and bright, and it stirred the long-buried yearning he'd lived with for so much of his childhood.

But he quickly doused it. He'd moved way the hell past all that.

She gave a faint smile. "Do you have a contractor?"

"I've been talking to one over the phone. My mom was supposed to meet with him this weekend, but she blew him off. I'll head out to the property myself tomorrow. I haven't seen it in ten years. For all I know the cabin's nothing but an outhouse for bears now." His grandfather had won the oddly-shaped parcel of mostly unusable land in a poker game. He'd built a hunting cabin. It had never been meant for a family.

"That's incredibly nice of you. She rarely comes to town, obviously. But I see her sometimes in Blue Sky."

"What do you mean, 'obviously?'" Did people treat his mom badly?

"Oh. She's not...people in small towns have long memories."

That didn't sit right with him. "Well, that explains why she didn't want me to buy her a house." She didn't want to live next door to people who saw her as the addict that had neglected her son. "I showed her listings from Bozeman, though. West Yellowstone. She insists on living here." On that barely accessible plot of land. He really didn't understand his mom.

"She grew up here. It's her home."

"Wherever she buys a house would become her home."

"Maybe. But don't you think one great act of courage at a time is enough?"

He liked the sound of that. "Yeah, Daze. I do." Still… "We don't have a lot of good memories on that land."

"No, I imagine you don't. But if her dad only knew her as a hot mess, maybe on some level she wants to live on his land as the kind of woman he'd have been proud of."

Damn. He'd never thought about it like that. Determination dug in. "Then I'll give it to her."

"I might be able to help you." Those lips curled into a delectable smile.

"How's that?"

"Contractors, vendors, all that stuff? That's what I've spent the last few years doing. All the changes the Blackstocks have made so far? These are all just developmental phases as we turn the ranch into a world-class resort. In September, we break ground on a luxury lodge." She cringed—true worry in her eyes. "Well, that's the plan anyway. But I know every contractor and vendor in the area. *And* I can get you the best prices."

"So, you want to give me some names and numbers? That'd be great."

"Nope. I want to help you with the project."

The sparkle in her eyes let him know she had something up her sleeve. "That's…nice of you."

"Not really." She gave him a mischievous grin. "Cooper Hood, I have a proposition for you."

Closing her eyes, Daisy bit into the crunchy drizzle, her teeth sinking through the buttery-rich goodness of the bread. *Oh, dear God.* Her mom made the world's best cinnamon rolls. With a sigh, she looked up to find someone heading toward her on the path.

Of course, her childhood crush would show up the moment she'd stuffed her mouth full of pastry. Leaning against the hood of her car, Daisy chewed quickly—which sucked because, basically, time should stand still while savoring her mom's desserts.

But Cooper wasn't looking at her. Scowling at his phone, he stopped on the path, fingers furiously typing. Was he dealing with his mom?

Or maybe a girlfriend. Instantly her skin tightened, and her heart thudded. If Cooper had a girlfriend…after she'd gone on and on last night about how much he'd meant to her?

She looked away, mortification crashing through her system.

First, she'd bumped into him wearing waders and a fishing hat, and then she'd forced him to go out with her. *Awesome.*

He couldn't have been clearer that he didn't want to hang out with her, but she'd gone and made an offer he couldn't turn down. Not if he wanted to get his mom's house built and get himself back on tour.

Feeling a little sick to her stomach, she licked the sticky drizzle off her fingers and shoved the treat back into the bag.

As he paused on the path, thumbs working over the phone's keypad, she took in his powerful physique. A white T-shirt strained across his broad shoulders, hugging his thickly rounded biceps, and worn blue jeans cupped his hard, muscular thighs.

The colorful ink covering his body made him look like a total badass. She'd noticed a strange symbol on his inner wrist and a cartoon image on his forearm of a pin-up girl holding a barbell, a sexy slash of red for her lips.

The man he'd grown into made her soul wake up, and *God*, she couldn't even remember the last time she'd felt this kind of fluttery attraction for a guy.

As if he felt someone watching him, he looked up sharply and found her. The worry lines eased. But he didn't smile. "Hey."

She pushed off her car. "You ready?" Forced or not, her plan was good for both of them. She was sticking to it.

"Sure." His posture, the way he held himself back, screamed apprehension. "But I want to make it clear I'm not asking the guys to come out here and play the festival." His expression said, *You still want to do this?*

"They might like it out here, you know. They could bring their families out. We'd show them a good time."

"August is a busy month for Violet and Mimi's businesses, and Emmie's managing the tour *and* an eighteen-month-old kid." He shook his head. "I'm not blowing up their one-and-only break."

It was hard to hide her disappointment. Blue Fire replacing Shout! would've been unbelievable. "Okay, but I've set aside the time today, and I already have the relationships you need, so I'm still going to help you."

Once he saw what was involved in a building project, he'd figure out pretty quickly his mom couldn't handle it. He'd need someone to oversee it. At which point, she'd make her offer again. Blue Fire headlining the concert in return for her acting as the project manager seemed an obvious solution to both their problems. But if he still refused, she'd ask *him* to do it.

It might not have the same impact, but Blue Fire was a Grammy-winning band. Their lead guitarist would definitely attract interest. And he'd only need to come back to town for a night or two before his tour resumed. It was a good deal for both of them.

She swung around to the driver's side door. "Let's head out to the property first. See what we've got."

Approaching the metallic blue car, he gawked. "This is your ride?"

"Yep." When her godfathers had tried to get her into a Volvo sedan, citing safety issues on the Gallatin Road, she'd gone right out and bought herself a Camaro ZL1.

He got in the car and reached for the seat belt. "It's got some serious horsepower."

"Don't bother asking." She stuck the key in the ignition and fired her up. "No one drives my baby."

Wait—did the side of his mouth just curl? Her heart nearly stopped in her chest. Cooper Hood had a devastatingly sexy smile.

The sweet and buttery scent of her pastry overwhelmed the usual smell of her leather seats. "I don't know if you've eaten yet, but I got you one of my mom's cinnamon rolls." She handed him the paper bag.

"Thanks."

"Maybe it'll make up for the bad news you just got."

His features hardened. "Yeah. Maybe." Pulling the roll out of the bag, his nostrils flared as he breathed in the scent. "Looks good."

She was about to point out that he'd grown up eating those rolls, but it struck her he might never have had one.

"So, what do you think? Should we get your mom to meet us at the site? She'll need to make some decisions."

"She's working today." He gazed out the window, looking pissed. "And, apparently, later this afternoon, too. Whatever. If I have to camp out on her doorstep tonight, I'll get what I came here for. It's not going to be a wasted trip."

"You're sitting in my badass Camaro eating the best pastry on the planet...there's nothing wasted about this trip."

He turned to her, his gaze taking a leisurely tour from her hair to her eyes down to her mouth. He gave a slow nod.

His intense expression set her nerves on fire, and so she focused on backing out of the parking spot in front of her cabin. She nodded toward the roll. "Go on, bite into it. This will be a changing moment in your life." People came from all over to eat at the Sugar Bowl. It was listed in Montana travel guides.

Setting the bag between his legs, he leaned over it as he took a bite. The drizzle cracked, and little bits clattered into the bag. She liked that he'd gone out of his way not to mess up her car. Eyes closed, he tipped his head back and moaned. "Damn, that's good."

She had a flash of him making that sound for a different reason—one incited by her touch—and a jolt of lightning hit her chest. "So, how involved is your mom going to be? I mean, if you plan on making decisions today, how do we do that without her input?"

"Honestly, Daisy, I don't care. She's not cooperating, and I don't have time to screw around. I'll get things in motion. Maybe set up accounts, so the vendors get paid. And when she's ready to build, she'll be good to go."

Daisy wasn't so sure about that. She'd run into Ronnie Hood occasionally over the years, and the woman seemed in no way equipped to handle building a house. "I can help her, you know." At that moment, she realized she'd help him even if he didn't want to come back for the festival. He was doing a really nice thing for a woman who hadn't known much kindness in her life.

"No, you've got enough on your plate." He must've realized how harsh he'd sounded because he looked away and let out a slow breath. "Sorry." His tone softened. "You're a good person, Daisy, and I appreciate your offer. But she's going to have to handle this one on her own."

After a three-point turn, she was on the road leading off the property. "Does she actually want you to do this?"

"She does." He chewed, watching out the window.

A family picnicked at a table by the river, and a couple of hikers sprawled on the grass, faces tilted to take in the early morning sun. As she passed under the wrought iron Blackstock Ranch sign that arched over the road, her tires rumbled over the wooden bridge.

Cooper swallowed. "I got a call from her sponsor. Apparently, my mom can't move forward with the house until she talks to me about something." He shrugged. "I'm here. But she doesn't seem to have time to see me."

Daisy nudged his shoulder. "Come on."

He swung his gaze to her. "What?"

"You have to know what's going on."

"I don't have a clue."

"When was the last time you saw her?" she asked.

"I haven't seen her since I left town after graduation."

"Right, so not since she got clean."

He dropped the rest of the roll into the bag. She hated that talking about his mom upset him so much, but he seemed interested in hearing her perspective, so she continued. "It's got to be hard for her, you seeing her sober for the first time. You're a grown man—a famous man."

"I'm doing something *nice* for her."

"Exactly. And that must sting a little since she's supposed to be doing nice things for *you*. You know? She knows she wasn't a good mother. So, you doing something so incredible for her..." She shrugged. "She probably doesn't think she deserves it."

His shoulders relaxed, and she was happy to see him reach into the bag and pull out the cinnamon bun. He eyed it from different angles. "Yeah." He cleared his throat. "I can see that."

It was probably not the best time to notice the flex of his powerful biceps as he brought the pastry to his mouth. Or the way his big hand rested on the thigh of his well-worn jeans. Or, worst of all, the incredible blue of his eyes. She'd never seen eyes that color. A startling pale blue, like a marble.

He was *so* handsome.

She definitely shouldn't be looking at him like that. "Just to let you know, I've asked an architect I know to meet us there."

He looked at her a moment too long. And then gave a short nod. "Thank you."

She couldn't tell if she was too pushy or if he was just uncomfortable with the situation. "Is that okay? I don't want to take over your project. I just figured you didn't have much time, so we should try to get in as much as we can."

"No, it's good."

"Okay. He can help us decide which direction to take. I don't know the condition of the cabin or how extensive the renovation might be. I'm also wondering if the easiest solution might be to buy a log home package."

"What's that?"

"You just pick out the model you want, and they come in and build it. It's the simplest, most efficient way to do it. Anyway, we'll look at all the possibilities. Then, if we have time—"

"I'll make time, Daisy." Again, his intense expression made her wonder what he was thinking.

He had this way of looking at her that shut out the world and sealed the two of them in a strangely intimate bubble. It made her think of tight spaces and bodies pressed together in dark, quiet rooms. Clothes rustling, hot breath on her skin. She shifted in her seat, too aware of his hand on his thigh.

She wanted to put *her* hand there, wanted to feel the heat of him through his jeans, the power of his muscles. It made her restless. "Okay, then. After that, we'll head into Bozeman and open up accounts with vendors. You can set price ranges for the lighting, cabinetry, and plumbing fixtures. All that stuff. Sound good?"

"It does." A moment later, he said, "Thank you. I appreciate you doing this for me."

"Hey, you paid for my time. And instead of wearing waders, I get to wear cute sandals." She hated that his mom was avoiding him. He deserved so much better. She reached for his arm and gave it a gentle caress. "This'll be fun."

When they turned off 191 onto the dirt road of his childhood, they crossed a rusted metal bridge that led deeper into the forest. Cooper tensed. She wondered what it felt like to be back after escaping ten years ago.

His fingers curled on his thigh and, when the dilapidated cabin came into view, he went perfectly still.

Daisy eased to a stop, her hand on the gearshift. Sunlight glinted off the fender of the architect's car. He leaned back against it, one arm across his chest, the other holding a cell phone to his ear. When he saw her, he held up a finger. She nodded, understanding his request to finish his call.

Cooper wasn't getting out of the car yet, anyway. He stared at the house, mindlessly rubbing the ink that took up most of his forearm. A geometric series of bear claws covered the scar he'd gotten on this very property.

He'd said he didn't have a lot of good memories of this place—was he thinking of the bear attack just then?

"It's got to come down." He made it sound more like a question.

The roof had collapsed on the back end, the porch sagged, and the wood had rotted. "Most likely. But I'm sure they can salvage parts of it. If it means something to you—"

"It doesn't." He stared at it. "Raze it."

She couldn't even imagine what life had been like for him inside that cabin. With the architect still on the phone, she thought she'd try to shift his perspective a little. "Tell me one good memory."

With a vague shake of his head, he lifted his eyebrows. "I don't have any."

"Even as a little boy? Like your mom reading to you or a bedtime routine." There had to have been something good. "A cup of cocoa on a bad day. A hug?"

With a thoughtful expression, he gazed out the window. "I can't think of a single time she touched me. Not even to put on a Band-Aid." He shifted his long legs.

"I think I was eight or nine when I figured out something was wrong. It was fourth grade because I remember Mrs. Patterson's expression when she sent me to the nurse's office. I'd cut myself that morning opening a can." He shrugged. "I didn't think anything of it, just wrapped a piece of paper around it and walked to the end of the road to catch the bus."

He stared unseeing out the windshield. "I could tell Mrs. Patterson was trying to keep her cool, but she looked at me like I was walking around with a bloody cleaver in my hand. And I'll never forget the nurse asking if my 'mommy' was home and how come she hadn't given me a Band-Aid."

He looked at her so abruptly she lurched in surprise. "I got it, you know? That my mom was different. That she wasn't doing the things she was supposed to do. And I didn't want anyone to ever look at me like that again, so from that moment on, I was very, very careful. I didn't show them anything."

"What about your grandfather?" *Please tell me someone showed you love.*

"Nah, he died when I was young. I don't remember much, but I got the impression my mom changed after my grandmother died. I think my mom was pretty young— maybe early teens—and she didn't handle it well."

A car door slammed, and they both looked over to see the architect approaching.

Cooper reached for the handle. "Let's get this done."

Chapter Four

TEN YEARS AGO, THE SUGAR BOWL HAD BEEN A bakery that served breakfast and lunch. So, to see it now at eight o'clock on a Saturday night, the tables packed, musicians setting up on the stage, and people lined up to get in, impressed the hell out of Cooper. Snowberry had changed.

Daisy's fingers trailed across his shoulders as she breezed past him, her warm vanilla and honey scent swirling in her wake. Once again, he felt like that boy who'd lived in a state of hyperawareness around her. The boy who'd noticed the way her dark hair pooled onto the desk as she'd hunch forward to write, her fingers curled around a pencil. The way the tendons in her neck strained when she'd hit and held a high note. Her burst of laughter in the music room had made him stop whatever he'd been doing just to witness her joy.

He'd hoarded all those images, those sacred moments, to pull out and comfort him as he lay alone in the dark woods, waiting for his home to be safe enough to go back inside.

She would never know it, but she'd been his saving grace.

Taking her seat across from him, she set two little pots on the table. Her vivid blue eyes sparkled in the candlelight. "This day couldn't have gone better."

"We got a lot done." Everything was set for his mom's house. All she had to do was pull the trigger to get the contractor and vendors in motion. "Thank you."

His phone vibrated in his pocket, and his stomach pitched. Was his mom blowing him off again? Each time she did it, she upped his anxiety. *How bad could it be?* She wouldn't be this freaked out to tell him Slider wasn't his dad.

So, what then? What dirty little secret did Ronnie have? Of course, it might not be anything. She might be putting him off because she couldn't be bothered to make time for him.

But when he checked the screen, he saw a message from one of his Austin friends.

"Everything okay?" Daisy asked.

"Yeah. I've got another band to check out."

"Well, there you go. House project ready to go. Opening act almost in the bag. Life's good." She reached for a spoon. "I can't wait to share the plans with your mom. I really think you made the right choice going with the log cabin."

One look at his childhood home, and everyone had agreed it needed to be razed. And since he wanted to get his mom into a house before winter hit, the package made the most sense. After he'd chosen a layout and put down a deposit, they'd spent the rest of the day in Bozeman checking out vendors. If his mom cooperated, she could be in her own home before Thanksgiving.

Daisy leaned toward him. "Okay, I don't want to pry —well, I mean, I obviously *want* to…okay, I'm going to pry. What does your mom want to talk to you about?"

He hesitated, not wanting to share the sordid details of his life. But it was Daisy. He trusted her. "My dad."

"Slider?"

A kick of anxiety had him drawing his legs under the chair. "That's what I'm here to find out."

"You don't know?"

Cooper reached for a sugar packet and tapped the edge on the table. "Nope."

"So, that's why you're here? She's going to tell you?"

He gave a deep nod, unwilling to say more.

Just then, the waitress brought their espressos and a slice of strawberry cream cake. Daisy's features lit up. "Oh, yum. Thank you, Jen."

As Daisy and the waitress chatted, Cooper checked his phone yet again. Still nothing from his mom. Were they meeting after her shift at eleven or not?

He didn't know why he was so worked up over this. If some random guy had knocked up his mom, it wouldn't make a damn bit of difference. It wasn't like he needed a dad at this point in his life.

No, it wouldn't matter if it were some random guy. But if Slider had sobered up, if he and his mom were together, he'd have…well, he'd be part of a family. Something rustled in his chest, then popped, spreading warmth along his limbs. *Family.* His mom sober—happily married. Cooper could see coming to visit, staying with them in the log cabin. Waking up to the smell of coffee and bacon. The three of them sitting around—

"Try this." Daisy's voice broke through his ridiculous fantasy. She held a spoon out to him.

Letting her feed him was just too damn intimate, so he took it from her and fed himself. Creamy dark chocolate filled his senses. "Mousse?" Although it was denser, richer, the chocolate velvety. "It's good."

"It's a Pot de Crème." She scooped another mound for herself. Turning the spoon upside down, she brought it to her mouth, closing her eyes when she tasted it. She moaned, and her tongue swept across her bottom lip.

Desire surged through him, and he couldn't help wondering if she'd look like that in bed. If she'd go all slack and dreamy-eyed when he sucked a nipple into his mouth.

Fuck. His blood rose at the image of Daisy naked beneath him, back arching, her hands digging into his hair, holding him to her as if she never wanted him to go away.

She opened her eyes and *licked the fucking spoon.* "I had my mom make it just for you." The silky fabric of her shirt draped over her breasts, accentuating their round fullness. Desire pulsed through him.

Jesus, would you stop already?

"Let's try this one." She slid the edge of her fork into the cake, a cream-covered strawberry sliding out. "It's my favorite." The Montana sapphire studs glittered in her ears, and her lush mouth curved into a smile. His dick went hard.

He accepted the fork, but even when the cake and cream hit his tongue, he couldn't taste a thing. Because the only thing in his mind, heart, and body was the primal, urgent need to taste *her.*

All that teenage longing came roaring back. He wanted her more than ever. And not because she was beautiful and had a body his hands were dying to explore, but because every single cell in his body yearned for her.

And *this* was why he'd never come back to Snowberry. He didn't want to yearn for the things he couldn't have. Didn't want to wait for his mother to give him a crumb of her attention. Didn't want to be around these people who'd only ever looked at him with disgust.

"What do you think? Delicious?" Daisy's voice yanked him out of the negativity.

And he was damn glad. Because his past didn't matter anymore. He was a man now. He'd made his way in the world. And he had a chance to be that man around Daisy. His gaze on her mouth, he said, "Hell, yes."

But when her eyes flared, and he registered her surprise at his tone, he turned to the stage.

"Who's playing tonight?" *Calm the fuck down.*

"Trapped. They're a Calypso band from Missoula. They play here maybe once a month or so."

"Cool."

"Cooper Hood!" A dude with chin whiskers and a man-bun approached the table, both hands clutched over his heart. "I cannot *believe* I get to meet you. I love Blue Fire."

Daisy scowled at the guy. "You're such a pain in the ass, Jason." She gave Cooper an exasperated look. "I told him to leave you alone, but he's obviously decided to ignore me." She rolled her eyes. "Cooper, this is Jason. To be fair, he plays a wicked bass."

"Hey, man." In a V-neck T-shirt and worn skinny jeans, Jason smiled broadly, reaching out to shake Cooper's hand enthusiastically. "You're my role model. No lie. You probably don't even remember me, but I was in the music program, too." Some other guys came up behind him, and

Jason stepped aside to make room. "We're the Kneeknockers. Anyhow, I just wanted to meet you and tell you how cool I think you are. I love your sound, and I'm not kissing your ass when I say that. I mean, seriously, Blue Fire's on a whole other level than anything else out there right now."

"Thank you." Cooper stood. "Glad to meet you." They shook hands.

Just when he thought they'd leave, Jason's smile turned mischievous. "How glad?"

"Jason." Daisy's tone held a warning.

"Sorry, Daze. I've got one shot, and I'm taking it." He turned to Cooper. "We want to play for you tonight."

"Okay?" He glanced at the stage, not seeing the problem.

"Jason, no." Daisy got up, smoothing her hands down her skirt. "Trapped is playing tonight."

"I already talked to them." Jason's smile was triumphant. "They're going to let us do a short set."

"Really?" Daisy gave him a challenging look. "And who's singing?"

His smile faltered. "Daisy, come on." He tipped his head toward Cooper. "*Blue Fire.*"

All at once, everything clicked into place. "Is this *your* band?" Cooper wanted to hear her sing.

She nodded.

"Play. I want to hear you."

"See, Daze," Jason said. "He wants you to."

When she hesitated, Cooper reached for a strand of that silky, dark hair and wrapped it around two fingers. "I do."

Her lips parted, and her features turned pink. "One song."

"Trapped said we could do three," Jason said.

Daisy shot him an intractable look.

"Fine." Jason clapped his hands together. "Two songs."

"One."

Cooper had to smile at the force she put behind the single syllable.

"Fine. I'll take it. One song." Jason turned to his bandmates. "Let's do this."

The guys left, practically tripping over each other like a pack of puppies to get to the stage.

"I'm only giving into those weirdos because you asked." She didn't sound happy.

He tipped her chin, so she'd look at him, and the moment their gazes collided, the energy between them crackled and sparked. Emotion rushed him hard, expanding in his chest until he couldn't take a full breath. "Sing for me."

"When you look at me like that..." She let out a shaky breath. "Okay, then." Her smile burst free, and a rush of happiness tore through him. He wanted to grab the back of her neck, haul her over to him, and kiss that beautiful, sexy mouth.

He wanted to get her alone, finally get his hands on the soft skin of her luscious body.

Instead, he broke their heated stare and nodded to the stage. "Show me what you've got."

As Jason adjusted the mic stand, feedback from a microphone screeched. The other guys strapped on their guitars and took their places on keys and drums.

"Hey, guys." Jason's energetic stage presence immediately silenced the room. "I know we're not scheduled to play tonight, but I asked my buddies from Trapped if they'd do me a solid. As everyone in Montana probably knows by now, Cooper Hood from Blue Fire's in the house." The last three words came out low, deep, and loud, like a DJ introducing an act. The audience burst into applause. Boots stomped, and all eyes turned to Cooper.

He'd never once had the attention of the townspeople on him in a positive way. Even when he'd performed in high school, there'd been boos and snickers mixed in with half-hearted applause. So, sitting there, taking it, made him itchy.

You like me now? Now that I'm famous? He didn't want to go there, though, so he just smiled—at least he hoped it came off as a smile.

"I couldn't pass up the chance to play for him," Jason said. "You understand, right?"

"We can hear you any night," someone shouted.

Someone else called, "Trapped!"

"Yeah, yeah," Jason said in his good-natured way. "Two songs, okay?"

In her flirty dress and red cowboy boots, Daisy took the stage, grabbing the microphone. "*One* song." She turned to the crowd. "Hey, y'all. Thanks for letting us crash the show. Let's see if we can make it worth your while."

When she beamed a mischievous smile, the crowd lit up with fist-pumps, whistles, and shouts. She turned to her band, called, "A-one, a-two, a-one, two, three, four," and then the music exploded.

Cooper sat back, mesmerized by her performance. She'd had pipes as a kid, but she hadn't had this confidence, this command of her audience. She held the rapt attention of every person in the room. Even the wait staff stopped, arms loaded with plates, to watch her.

Her powerful voice—as big as Maria McKee's, clear as

Natalie Merchant's, and with the perfect pitch of Eva Cassidy—belonged on platinum-selling CDs. He had no idea why she was in hotel management instead of rocking stadiums around the world. The band played a rip-roaring brand of rockabilly that had the entire audience rocking out.

A prickle of awareness at the back of his neck prompted him to turn toward the weight of someone's stare.

Slider. Adrenaline shot through him.

The red-haired man stood in the doorway of the café. The same age as Cooper's mom—forty-eight—his weathered skin made him look at least a decade older. Years of drug use had clearly taken their toll.

Cooper's senses narrowed, and he examined the man more closely. *Do I look like him?* They had a similar build —though Cooper was taller and more muscular. And, of course, he had dark hair—not red. Honestly, he didn't see much of a resemblance at all.

But he was less compelled by a genetic link than the man's reaction to seeing him.

Am I your son?

Do you want me to be?

At that moment, Daisy hit a powerful note, and he turned back to her. She held it, her hips swinging side to side, and then, with a crash of drums, the song ended.

With thunderous applause, the audience shot to its feet.

After thanking Trapped and the audience, Daisy jumped off the stage, her dress flaring up to reveal smooth, womanly thighs. *So fucking sexy.* People rushed her, surrounded her, but she kept her sights on Cooper as she made her way to him.

Fantasy blurred with reality. He'd imagined this exact scenario countless times as a kid. Daisy coming off the stage, her gaze fixed on him, as she headed right into his arms with a smile so luminous it made her glow. Excited to see him, not even caring about anyone else in the room. No one else in the world mattered but him. *Them.*

The memory—the yearning—held him in a chokehold.

When she reached him, she looked radiant, expectant. And he knew she wanted him to hug her. She seemed to hold herself back, waiting for him to make the move. And if he were a different kind of man, he would. He'd pick her up, swing her around, and whisper in her ear that she'd done a great job, tell her how sexy she'd looked up there, how she'd owned everyone in the room. His hands could almost feel the curve of her ass cheeks, and he wanted to squeeze them so badly he forgot to breathe.

The moment stretched a little too long…until it passed, and she dropped into the chair beside him. They stared at each other, him so swollen with unnamed emotion he thought it might burst out of his skin. He had to find words. A gesture, anything to let her know she'd brought down the house.

"That was…" He swallowed. "Amazing."

She stared at him, her features flushed and glowing with the high of performing.

He had to give her more. "*You're* amazing." It struck him then that he was behaving just like the boy who'd loved her from afar. Who hadn't felt worthy of her.

He couldn't have her—for Christ's sake, he was leaving town on Sunday—but he didn't have to behave like that dirty kid.

And so, he reached for her hand, brought it to his

mouth, and kissed her palm. He didn't say anything, just held her gaze, and when she smiled softly, he knew he'd given her *something*.

An angry shout silenced the chatter in the room. A glass shattered. Daisy jumped out of her seat as Slider reached for a man sprawled across a table, grabbed the front of his shirt, and hauled him up. His arm cocked back.

Right before it launched, one of the bikers Cooper recognized from the auction got Slider in a bear hug from behind. Slider jerked violently, his legs kicking out. "Get off me."

Daisy bolted, and Cooper popped out of his seat to catch up with her.

"Dammit, Slider," she shouted. "I told you not to show up here drunk."

Slider, cheeks mottled red, shot Daisy a foul look. "How 'bout you teach your customers to show some respect?"

Cooper, along with men from nearby tables, surrounded the scene.

"Do you want to press charges?" she asked the man, just getting up from the table.

The guy smoothed his wrinkled shirt. "Nah. I'm okay. Just keep scum like him out of here."

Daisy turned back to Slider, hands on her hips. "Swear to God, the next time you show up here drunk, I'm calling the sheriff."

The biker released him but kept a hand on Slider's biceps, as he led him toward the door.

Slider whipped around. "Unless I become famous, right? Then I'm welcome here?" He sneered at Daisy.

"Everyone likes him now that he's a big shot rock star, huh?"

It was less the man's words than the attention of everyone in the café that sickened Cooper.

"Hey, man," someone said. "Don't talk about your kid like that."

"He's not my kid." He straightened, pointing a finger at Cooper. "I took a paternity test, man. Ask your mom. She's been lyin' to you."

The bowels of hell belched, emitting licks of flames that engulfed Cooper.

The eyes of one hundred Snowberry residents burned holes right through his clothes, singeing his skin.

"Damn, Slider," someone said.

"Why you gotta say that here, man?" one of his friends said.

The café was silent, the only sound the roar of a leaf blower in Cooper's mind. He couldn't feel his feet, his hands, or his heart. He just stood there, awash in shame and filth. And then Daisy slid her arm through his and pulled him against her warm, soft body. She tugged on him like she wanted him to follow her.

But Cooper wasn't going anywhere. Not while they all felt sorry for him.

He didn't need their pity.

Forcing his body into a relaxed pose, he said, "Well, that's a relief." He kept his gaze on Slider. "Don't have to worry about any gingers falling out of the family tree."

Daisy tipped her head against his shoulder, her body shaking with silent laughter. No one else in the café held back. They burst out laughing.

With a careless smile, he gazed down on Daisy. "Want

to get out of here?" He gave a quick salute to the patrons. "'Night all."

As the Camaro sped down 191, wind whipped his hair around his face. The bite in the night air collided with the anger that kept boiling up. How long had his mom known? Why had she kept the truth from him?

This is my childhood. Right here. This endless frustration over his inability to control anything that had to do with his mom. She lied. She manipulated. She stole.

She did whatever served her needs in the moment.

The tires ate up the asphalt, and the headlights illuminated the reflective lane divider. Daisy slowed to turn into Blue Sky. Pulling into a large parking lot framed by several apartment buildings, she eased into a space and cut the ignition. The engine ticked and music from the different buildings made a crazy cacophony of sound. "You got a plan, handsome?"

"I want answers."

"Are you going to bang on her door and demand them?"

He slowly turned to her. "No." He smiled because that had pretty much been his plan.

"Good, because I'm not sure how well that'll work with someone who's spent her life hiding in booze and pills."

He couldn't argue with that.

In school, his anger had gotten him suspended plenty of times. He didn't put up with the cracks about his drug addict mother, his dirty, ill-fitting clothes and unwashed hair, or his free lunches. He'd shut them up with his fists.

But that had stopped the day he'd found Mr. Walker

in the principal's office, offering him a spot in the music program. And from there, it didn't take more than a couple of comments about his "enormous" talent for all the bullshit of high school to fade away. He'd taken to that music room like a guitarist set free in Willie's American Guitars. Instead of worrying about who looked at him funny or what people were saying about him, he poured all his energy into learning how to play.

He'd discovered a path out of Snowberry.

"You want to know why I stopped fighting in high school?"

She shifted towards him, lifting a knee onto the seat. "I do."

"One day, Mr. Walker asked what success looked like to me." That had been a great fucking question. "Up until then, I'd had some vague idea of going to college. Maybe music would pay my way. I didn't really know, but that question formed a picture."

"What did you say?"

"'I want to be a rock star.'" He checked her reaction—didn't want to sound too cocky—but she just looked amused. "Mr. Walker didn't laugh. He just nodded and said, 'Then from now on, every time one of those boys says something you don't like, picture yourself on stage at Madison Square Garden.'" He liked the next line best. "'And picture the bully in coveralls with a broom and a dust pan, his flask tucked into the back pocket.'"

He wouldn't tell her that the image of Hunter Blackstock's sons as janitors of Snowberry High School had served him well over the years.

"I don't know why I just told you that story. Except to say that I'm not that angry kid anymore. I'm not going to blow up at her." He glanced at the apartment buildings. People stood on balconies, smoking, drinking, and laughing. He'd already texted his mom to tell her he was on his way—though not why—and now he texted again.

Cooper: I'm here.

Time to go.

When they met in front of the car, Daisy punched her keypad, and the orange lights on her Camaro flashed. Threading through the parked cars, Cooper searched for the address his mom had given him. "She's in Building C. Three-nineteen."

"That one." Daisy nodded to the one in front of them.

His stomach squeezed into a fist. Perspiration popped out on his forehead. He could tell himself it didn't matter, that he didn't need a father, but it wasn't true. It did matter. It just did.

Passing under a portico, he pulled the door open for Daisy. Every step he took led him closer toward the answer he needed to put his paternity to rest once and for all.

Just as he took that first step up the staircase, Daisy reached for his hand, clasping it, and something in him broke.

It mattered because of all the things he didn't have as a kid—food, shoes that fit, an actual bed—a dad was the only thing he'd ever truly wanted. And because it was Ronnie they were talking about, he had a feeling that whoever was a 99% match on that paternity test wasn't going to be a good guy.

And there you have it. That's what he feared most. Slider, he could accept—*he's all I've ever known.* But someone else—someone *worse*? A wave of fear rolled through him, making him nauseous.

When he tried to let go of Daisy's hand to head up the

stairs, her grip tightened. She met his gaze with a steadfast expression. *We got this.*

And it hit him hard. He was dragging this beautiful woman into his ugly mess.

Isn't this the whole reason you couldn't have her in high school? He'd refused to expose her to the ugliness of his life. He opened his mouth to tell her not to come with him, but she tugged on his hand, launching them up the stairs. "Let's go."

The hallway smelled of cheap beer and old gym socks. As they walked down it, a door opened, and a girl wearing nothing but a towel bolted out, laughing as she nearly ran them down. "Sorry." Giggling, she dove inside a room and slammed the door.

"Cooper?" His mom waited for them outside her unit. With a stoic expression, she watched them approach, her body tense and fidgety.

"Hey." He couldn't keep the hostile edge out of his voice.

As familiar as his mom looked, she felt oddly foreign to him. Over his childhood, he'd had glimpses of her sober, of course, but those times hadn't been a whole lot better than when she'd been high. Sober, she was irritable, like she wanted to claw off her skin. She smoked, had a short fuse, and couldn't seem to cope with something as simple as opening a jar.

"Hey, Miss Hood." Daisy leaned in for a hug.

His mom's arms remained at her side, her body stiff. As soon as Daisy let go, his mom turned toward the door. "Well, come in."

She had the kind of furniture found in a cheap motel. A couch that obviously pulled-out, considering the flap of cream-colored sheet hanging out the side, an old-school television on a low TV stand, and a small kitchen table with two chairs that had woven straw seats and backs. A plastic salt and pepper shaker and a low stack of paper napkins sat right in the center of the table. The place smelled of canned pasta.

"SpaghettiOs?" Cooper said.

His mom tipped her head. "What?"

"You had SpaghettiOs for dinner."

"Oh, yes." She looked confused. "They had a sale. Ten cans for ten bucks."

"Yeah, so…" The fight had gone out of him. This woman—his mother—was hanging onto life by her fingernails. How could he attack her for lying to him when she'd been a junkie for two-thirds of her life? He turned to Daisy. "You want to sit down?"

"Sure." As Daisy stepped past him, her scent fluttered like a scarf behind her, tickling his senses with her subtle femininity. He hated himself for bringing her here.

"Sherry says you're on tour with your band?" his mom asked.

His mom typically didn't chat, so he figured she *really* didn't want to talk about it. "That's right."

"You mad I called off the contractor?"

Okay. Not doing small talk. Just as he opened his mouth to cut to the chase, Daisy came up beside him. His anger settled with the brush of her silky hair on his arm.

"We got a lot done today, Miss Hood."

His mom winced like she'd stepped on a shard of glass. "Just call me Ronnie. No one calls me Miss Hood."

"Sure. I think you'll be happy with your new house." Daisy was pure, positive energy. "We visited the site today with an architect—"

"You did?" His mom eyed him warily as if she didn't believe he'd go through with his offer.

He reassured her with a curt nod.

"We went over a bunch of ideas," Daisy said. "But Cooper really liked the log home option best."

Actually, he'd put down a deposit. It was a done deal. But he appreciated Daisy's gentler approach.

His mom's gaze kept flicking to him like she was assessing his reactions.

"It's the quickest way to get you into your new home," Daisy said. "You can choose the lay-out, but we really liked a two-bedroom, one-bath cabin with a nice-size living room and kitchen. It's cozy and just perfect."

"Can't you just fix up my father's place? It'd be a lot cheaper." She addressed him.

"Nothing to fix," Cooper said. "There's no insulation, and the wood's rotted. It has to be torn down, but you can build on the same site. I've got a flight out tomorrow, but I set up as much as I could today." He didn't have time to play games. "Look, I've already put a deposit down on the log cabin package, and the vendors will bill me directly. Just pick out what you want, and they'll take care of it."

She drew in a sharp breath, her eyes turning glassy. "Thank you. I…it's not easy living here."

"It might be harder living alone on that property." Isolation and boredom seemed a good recipe for getting wasted.

"It's better than here." She gestured to the balcony—barely wide enough to hold one metal folding chair. Music filtered through the sliding screen, along with the occasional shriek of laughter and honk of a horn. The pleading look in her eyes weakened his anger. "I know you don't have to do this for me, but I appreciate it." She rubbed her hands together, twisting them so roughly it looked painful. "Okay?"

"Okay." As he looked at her, he wondered if he was supposed to feel love for his mother. But he didn't. He felt…affection, he supposed. Mostly, he just felt hopeful she'd stay clean.

But Cooper needed answers. "So…Slider. He told me."

"You saw him?" Her spine stiffened, and her gaze narrowed.

"Tonight."

"What'd he say?" The hard edge to her voice intimidated people. Made her seem strong, righteous, but he knew better. Her bottom lip trembled, and her chest rose and fell in quick beats.

"He told everyone in the Sugar Bowl that he took a paternity test—and failed. At least where I'm concerned."

Fear crimped the skin around her eyes, and for the first time in his life, he saw her not as a mother but as a frail, vulnerable woman. "Bastard." She hugged herself.

"Forget Slider. I've been here twenty-four hours. You've had plenty of time to tell me yourself."

"I have to *work*. The resort closes down for two months at the end of October, and then again in April. And who's going to hire me for those two months? I need the money."

No more excuses. "Who's my father?"

He saw the moment her spirit broke. Her shoulders sagged, and her features wilted, making her look like a houseplant that had gone a few days too long without water. Jerking open a drawer, she pulled out a lighter and a pack of cigarettes. She shook one out and lit it.

"Don't smoke around us."

She took a deep drag, held it, as she walked out to the narrow balcony. Smoke swirled into the air, whisked away on a breeze.

"He said he took the test a while ago," Cooper said.

When she tugged on her leggings, he noticed a hole at the knee.

"When did he take the test?" *How long have you known?*

The hand holding the cigarette trembled, but it just pissed him off because she'd never been able to handle anything. All she had to do now was give him a name, and she couldn't even do that.

"Mom." *Who the fuck is my father?*

"Years ago." She took a deep drag, the orange tip flaring.

Material rustled, and then Daisy grasped his hand. Her warmth seeped through his skin and into his bones, calming him down some. "More than four years ago?" *Before you got clean? Or after?*

"Yes." She turned away from him and blew smoke out into the night.

"You've always known, haven't you?" *You lied to me my entire life.*

She let out a shaky breath. "I was with Slider for twenty years."

"You weren't with him, Mom. Jesus, you're not still chasing after him, are you?"

"No, of course not. That's been over a while now."

Images flashed through his mind. His mom clinging to Slider, begging him to stay. Putting on make-up when she knew he was coming and trying too hard to be fun when he was around. Crying for days when he'd disappear.

"My *point* was that Slider and I were on and off for twenty years, but I was with other guys."

Strangely, relief loosened his joints. It seemed better not to know than to find out his father was someone else's husband or one of his teachers. "Are you saying you don't know? Because that's fine. It doesn't matter. I just want to know once and for all."

She let out a shaky breath, looking at her bare feet, the blue polish chipped.

Dread rumbled under his skin. If she wasn't telling him, then it had to be bad. A judge, a former mayor. Mr. Tandy. *Who?* "It's not that big a deal. I'm twenty-eight, for Christ's sake. I'm not going after anybody for child support. Just tell me."

Daisy's fingernails lightly traced circles on the scar on his forearm. Her kindness was unbearable.

"*Mom.*"

She snapped out of it. Determination set in her eyes. "It's Hunter Blackstock. Okay? You happy now? Your dad's Hunter Blackstock."

Chapter Five

HE'D KNOWN NOT TO COME BACK HERE. ALL THIS rage, this wild frustration—it defined his childhood. He'd broken free of it in college, found his outlet in music, and his family in Blue Fire.

And the moment he came back to this fucking hellhole, all the ancient feelings rose up and pulled him back under.

Good thing he'd gotten the house project going because he was never coming back here. He was done.

"You must have so many questions." Daisy's soft voice in the quiet of the car should've been soothing. Instead, it grated on his nerves.

He had *one*. "Did you know?"

She tore her gaze from the road. "Me? How would *I* know?"

Anger rose off his skin like steam. "Did *everyone* know?" All those years he'd thought people avoided him because of his dirty clothes and his mom's shitty behavior. But maybe they'd known he was Hunter's bastard kid.

Jesus, he couldn't stand to be in this car, in this town, one more second. Fuck his mother, fuck all of them.

"Cooper, I—"

"Did your mother know?"

It took her a moment to respond. "I don't think so. If she did, she never said a word."

Awareness lit up his mind like fireworks over the Hudson River. *This* was why the Blackstocks had confronted him that day. *Keep your filthy hands off her.* It had never made sense why they'd worry about him spending time with Daisy.

He'd been sixteen when they'd pulled their Jeep into the rest area, shocking the hell out of him. He'd had no idea what they wanted, but as usual, his body had geared up to fight. And he would have. He'd have fought all three of them right there on the side of the road.

But they'd leveled him without lifting a finger. "Keep your filthy hands off Daisy."

His body had burst into flames. He'd thought he'd hidden his feelings for her, so to have these guys—the coolest kids in town—know his secret…had mortified him.

"Fucking druggie," one of the twins had said before getting back in the Jeep.

Ethan, the oldest, had lingered. "I see you around her, man, I'm serious, I will fuck you up."

"Try it, asshole." Cooper's tone might've held venom, but he'd been shaking as he'd said it.

He'd never understood why they'd hated him since he'd kept to himself.

Now he knew. He was the town's dirty little secret.

The moment she pulled into the parking spot in front of her cabin, Cooper reached for his seatbelt.

"Hang on a sec." She reached for his arm. "She didn't know. No one did, and I'll tell you why I'm so sure. As a kid, I didn't have a babysitter, so every day after school I'd sit at a table in the bakery and drink my cocoa, eat my snack, and do my homework. I was like wallpaper to everyone. And I know that because they'd talk in front of me, say things they never would've said in front of a kid. Seriously, I heard all the gossip. The week Mrs. Turner's husband cheated on her with the lady who owned the jewelry store? I was home sick. Every day she'd meet her best friend for coffee and go over every detail of what he'd done, the evidence she'd found, how she was treating him since she'd found out." She touched his chin, so he'd look at her. "I would've heard something as big as Hunter being your dad."

His impulse was to bail. Because he didn't know who to trust. But when he looked into her kind, honest eyes, his anxiety settled. He believed her. So, he turned his hand in invitation. She responded immediately, and their fingers entwined. He took his first full breath since finding out.

"Also, I've known the Blackstocks my whole life. There's not a chance Hunter would ignore his child." She let out a huff of indignation. "He wouldn't have let you go hungry."

Doubt stirred, unearthing a chill that made him shudder. She couldn't know that for sure. She just couldn't.

"I don't know if you want to hear this, but…" She squeezed his hand. "I see it."

"See what?"

"The resemblance."

No, I don't. His thumb flicked the catch on the seatbelt, releasing him. He threw open the door and got out of the car. Filling his lungs with cool, clean mountain air, he tipped his head back and scrubbed his face with both hands.

Her keys jingled as she flipped them around a finger, and her cowboy boots crunched over gravel as she approached him. "I mean, look at your body. You have the same physique."

"Okay." He couldn't wrap his head around it. How could he be related to the Blackstocks?

Related? How about *brothers?*

It didn't make sense. He couldn't be more different from them. They'd all been three-season, varsity, record-setting athletes. He played guitar. They were like royalty in this town. He'd been a total outcast.

She touched his bare arm, right beneath the sleeve of his T-shirt, and gazed up at him. "I know it seems crazy right now, but it's not a bad thing, being a Blackstock."

"I'm not. Not really." Even if it were true—and he wasn't a hundred percent sure about that—he'd still leave town tomorrow, and that would be that.

Knowing his paternity wouldn't affect him in any way.

"Well, yeah, you are." She said it matter-of-factly. "It might take a minute or two to sink in, but when it does, I'm telling you, it's not gonna suck."

He was done talking about it, so they headed up her walkway in silence. When they reached her porch, he said, "You've got to promise me something."

"Okay."

"Don't say anything to them."

Confusion furrowed her brow. "If that's what you want."

"It is. For now, let's keep it to ourselves." He stepped aside so she could unlock her door.

"Well, on a super positive note." She pushed the key into the lock and turned it. "Slider's not your dad."

"I don't have a dad."

Her features fell. "No, I know you don't. But you *do* have a father. Look, I won't say anything, but you should know family means everything to the Blackstocks. When they find out, they're not going to let it go. They're going to…well, I don't know what the *guys* will do, but Hunter won't take this lightly."

"Daisy." *This isn't going to have a happy ending.* "It's possible Hunter's known all along. The man has a family. A wife, kids. He wouldn't want to blow that up."

She shook her head. "No, I'm telling you. I know him. He'd have claimed you if he'd known you were his boy."

Hunter Blackstock's *boy.* Jesus, the idea that he could've grown up in a normal family, had clean clothes… meals where people sat at a table and talked about their day…it gutted him.

He thought back to high school. Had there been any indication Hunter might've known?

If Daisy saw the resemblance, then others must have, too. Had Hunter looked at him and wondered? The man *had* slept with Cooper's mom.

"Don't let this drive you crazy. If you want answers, talk to Hunter. And if you're not ready to do that, talk to your mom. She owes you the truth."

"My mom's not all that familiar with the truth."

With her voice almost a whisper she said, "I can't believe I never saw it before. Your hair might be darker, but it's the same texture as theirs." She reached up and ran a hand through it, her fingernails igniting a trail of sparks across his scalp.

Goddamn, how she lit him up. He closed his eyes to savor the brilliant sensations.

"But none of them has your marble eyes."

"Marble?" *What does that mean?*

"I've only ever seen that color in marbles. Don't you notice people staring?"

"No one stares at me." Or if they did, it was because he was in Blue Fire.

"Oh, please. Don't play coy with me. Everyone stares at you. They always have."

"They stared at me because my clothes didn't fit, and I smelled like a dumpster."

She fought back a smile. "Not because you were the hottest guy in school? *Right.* And your body? Come on, Coop. You've got the body of a warrior. Just like your brothers."

"Okay, we're not calling them brothers. I'm not…"

"Yeah, I know. You're not there yet. And if you leave tomorrow, you might never be."

"Daisy." He cupped her chin to make sure she understood. "I'm leaving."

"I know." Her hand closed around his wrist. "But it doesn't have to be tomorrow."

Jesus, when she looked at him like that—her features softened with desire—she made him want things he couldn't have. He closed his eyes, inhaling her scent, holding it in his lungs.

He pulled away. "It does. I have a job to do, and there's nothing more important right now than finding an opening act." He wouldn't let his bandmates down. Not for the Blackstocks. Not even for Daisy.

"Postponing it a day or two won't change anything. Why don't you leave Monday instead?"

"I've got till then to come up with a band. Besides, you're only thinking about how my mom's news affects me. If you're right and Hunter doesn't know, I'll be dropping a bomb in the center of his family. I'm not dropping it and then jumping on a plane to Austin."

"Yeah, that makes sense." But she seemed disappointed.

As they stood so close in the shadows of the covered porch, the connection between them alive and vibrant, Cooper realized his desire for her had changed. His attraction wasn't that of a kid with a painful, unrelenting crush. He was a man who wanted things from her he didn't have time to explore. "I should go. Thank you for everything. Today…tonight…" He shrugged.

"I'm glad I could be there for you."

He should go, but the potent energy between them kept his boots rooted. "Are you dating anybody?" He had no business asking, and yet he waited for her answer with as much anticipation as finding out his paternity.

"No. I mean, it's Snowberry. The dating pool's not that big. And if you break up, you're stuck in each other's faces the rest of your lives. I had two boyfriends in college, and I dated a little when I took my first job in Blue Sky but going out with tourists grew old quickly. What was the point?" She looked away. "I think I'm just at an age where I'm not going to waste my time hanging out with someone who doesn't excite me." And then she let out a shaky breath. "If it doesn't feel like this" –she wagged a finger between them—"then why bother?"

A fireball of heat rocketed through him. His heart thundered. He stepped closer and cupped her elbows. "What exactly does *this* feel like?" He shouldn't have asked. Because as surprising as it was to learn about her interest in him as a kid, it didn't have the same impact as feeling her body heat up, watching her lips part, and her eyelids lower.

"It feels…" Her tone held a hint of whimsy. "Inevitable."

When her fingertips touched his chest, electricity raced across his skin. As he leaned into her, his rational mind blurred, his mouth drawn inexorably to hers. Her raspberry-pink lips, close enough to kiss, elicited a fierce pang of desire that struck so deep and wide his heart ached.

"Cooper." She reached up and cupped the back of his neck, and with a tug, she bridged the distance, joining their mouths. Just the barest contact sent a shiver of the sweetest, most perfect burn down his spine.

He'd never wanted any woman the way he wanted Daisy Charbonneau. And when her fingers gripped the hair at the back of his neck, he had to have her.

The moment he closed his mouth over hers, she leaned into him, holding him in place as though she feared he'd stop.

But he couldn't. And when he licked into her mouth, their tongues touching, lust punched him. He went completely, painfully hard.

Daisy. This is Daisy. Her scent enveloped him, and her hair feathered over his arms, his hands. Like everything else she did, she threw her whole self into the kiss, and when she shifted closer, pressing her curvaceous body against his, he thought he'd go up in flames. His palms spread wide on her back, needing to touch every inch of her at once. With firm pressure, he slid them down— slowly, so he could feel the rise of her ass. When he had her cheeks in his hands, he couldn't resist giving them a lusty squeeze, drawing her closer just to feel the pressure against his cock. She moaned. Fuck, Daisy *moaned*, her body melting into his.

A bark of laughter from the path ripped them apart. He took a step back. "*Shit*." The cool of the evening air snapped reason back into him. "Sorry."

Her fingertips touched her mouth, and she looked disoriented.

"I'll, uh, I'll let you go." He turned and jumped off the two stairs of her porch. But with each step he took away from her, the more frantic he became. Because this was it. He'd leave in the morning, and he wouldn't see her again. He stopped at the end of the walkway and found her stepping into the warm yellow light of her house. "Daisy."

She leaned against the frame, her hand resting on it like it had on his chest.

Haloed in the warm light, she looked soft and round and so fucking beautiful. He would never forget the way she'd moaned in his arms. "Goodnight."

She nodded, pushed off the frame, and disappeared inside her home.

He needed to crush this wild energy. Between his mom's news and that kiss—*Jesus, that kiss*—he was completely fucked up. He needed to get his head out of Snowberry— his past—and onto his tour. And that meant getting the hell out of town.

As soon as he got back to his room, he'd switch to an earlier flight.

In fact, why bother staying here? Might as well head into Bozeman now. He'd head to the airport first thing in the morning and get on a standby flight back to Austin.

He heard laughter and quiet conversation up ahead. As he rounded the bend, he found a group of people in front of his cabin, the women in party clothes, big hair, and cowboy boots, and the men in jeans and button downs.

"There he is." Carrie Levitt parted from them. "Cooper Hood. It is *so* good to see you."

The girl who'd led him into the textbook storage room in tenth grade and gave him his first blowjob wrapped her arms around him, brushing her lips across his cheek.

Daisy's scent lingered in his senses, and for one wild moment, he had the impulse to push Carrie away. But then he remembered he was leaving. That he and Daisy weren't—and would never be—together, and so he let Carrie pretend a familiarity they'd never had.

He drew back to greet the others. "Hey, how's it going? You guys heading out to a party?"

"We brought the party to you." Carrie tapped her finger to his chest. "I can't wait to catch up." She shrugged her eyebrows suggestively and then gestured to the others. "You remember James and Luke, right? And these are some friends of mine from college."

One of the women lifted a shopping bag. "We brought some goodies."

The tallest, a blond with a rocking body, stepped forward to trace the licks of flames inked onto his collarbone. "I *love* Blue Fire. Seriously. I have all your albums. Maybe you can sign something for me?"

Two. They'd put out *two* albums so far. But who cared? They'd brought him a party. "You bet."

"Let's do this," Carrie said.

As soon as he let them into his cabin, the music from an iPod dock kicked on, drinks were poured, and the women started dirty dancing together. *This is perfect.* Just what he needed.

He thought about Daisy, her smile, the look in her eyes that made him feel like a superhero, and he smashed the image into little pieces.

Daisy was Snowberry, and Snowberry was over.

After washing her face and brushing her teeth, Daisy brought her mug into the kitchen and rinsed it under the tap. She usually slept like a log, but after Cooper's kiss, her heart had yet to settle back into a normal rhythm.

She'd tried to read, even made herself a cup of chamomile tea, but the image of his face right before he'd kissed her kept popping up, pumping a fresh burst of excitement to her heart.

He'd looked so...rapturous. Like kissing her would take him to Nirvana.

And then when he *had* kissed her? *God.* No one had ever kissed her like that. And the way he'd grabbed her ass like he was one second from lifting her off the ground?

If people hadn't walked by, would he have taken her right there on the porch? She closed her eyes to relive it, and there it went again, that fiery wash of sparks.

She smiled because she totally would've let him. When was the last time she'd felt this way around a guy? Sure, she'd had some decent sex. She'd even thought she'd loved Garrett sophomore year. But no kiss had ever made her lose her mind.

Damn him for being so stubborn. For refusing to stay in town just a little longer. He didn't get that he'd won the family lottery.

A knock on the door pulled her out of her thoughts. "Be right there." She wasn't about to open the door in her tank top and skimpy cotton sleep shorts, so she hustled down the hall to her bedroom and grabbed a hip-length cardigan. Shoving her arms into the sleeves, she hurried back to the door in her bare feet.

She peered through the window to find a towering wall of muscle on her porch. Ethan Blackstock gave her a chin nod, his expression troubled.

The impact of Cooper's edict hit her right then. She worked with these guys every day. How was she supposed to keep a massive, life-altering secret from them?

She opened the door. "Hey, Ethan."

Of all the brothers, this one would have the hardest time with the news. Where the twins seemed to accept their dad's passion for music, Ethan seemed the most hurt by it. And not just that he'd missed out on their games in high school because he was performing, but that he hadn't taken care of or developed the rental cabins, which had once been the only source of income from the property.

If Ethan hadn't initiated the resort plans, she didn't know what would have become of the Blackstock Ranch. Not many people wanted to rent worn-out cabins from the nineteen-sixties.

Wrapping the sweater more tightly around her, she stepped aside to let him in.

"Sorry to come by so late, but I saw your lights on." He smelled like wood smoke, so she guessed he'd been at the nightly bonfire the ranch held for its guests.

"No problem."

"Just wanted to find out if you'd asked him." He looked cautiously hopeful.

"I did, but he said no. He doesn't want to cut short the

band's family time to fly out here and perform at the festival."

Disappointment weighed on his sturdy frame, but he gave a deep, accepting nod. "What about him? Will he do it?"

Some people thought that, because an injury had forced his early retirement from the NFL, Ethan wanted to replace his glory days with this fancy resort, but they were wrong. Ethan was all about family. He wanted to do what his dad had failed to do—give them a sustainable living on their land. "I'm sorry, but I couldn't ask him." *And I can't tell you why.*

"Because of tonight?"

She froze. She'd been so caught up in Cooper she hadn't even considered the fact that the news had already spread. Damn Slider for making his announcement in the Sugar Bowl, where half the town congregated on a Saturday night.

She couldn't lie to Ethan any more than she could reveal Cooper's secret. So, how was she supposed to word it? "He's heading back to Austin tomorrow to find an opening act to finish out their tour. It's just not the right time. I'm sorry."

"Damn. I'd thought we lucked out."

Oh, you lucked out all right. You just might never know how. Because Cooper was awesome, and the Blackstocks would be lucky to have him in their family. "I'm not going to let us down, Ethan. Believe me when I tell you I'm going to come up with a Plan B that'll be even better than a Shout! reunion." *I have to.*

"The thing is," he began. "If Mickelson or his friend back out because of this…" He shoved his hands deep into the pockets of his jeans. "If we don't have enough share-holders, we're going to have a shortfall of equity."

A chill skittered down her spine at his ominous tone. "Yes, I know. We won't be able to build the lodge. But I'm going to do everything—"

"No, Daze. We need investor money for the lodge, but we also need it to cover the money we spent on infrastructure. The cabins don't do that."

Anxiety started a drumbeat at her temple. "If we don't build the lodge, Ethan...what exactly are you saying?"

His shaky exhale foretold disaster. "If we don't get the investor money, the bank will call the loan."

"Are you telling me they could take the ranch?" He wouldn't have done that.

But she could see from the fear in his eyes that he had.

"I had no choice. Look, it's not going to come down to that. I won't let it. We've got a smart plan, and we're close. Damn close. If Stuart hadn't bailed on us, we'd be right on track. But he did bail, and we need a Hail Mary."

And Cooper could be their Hail Mary.

Any other time she wouldn't hesitate to press Cooper to play the festival for them, but this weekend? *Tonight?* He might have honed his stoicism well over his childhood, but tonight his pain had seeped out of every pore.

She couldn't imagine what Ronnie's news meant to him. It was so much more than finding out she'd lied or that the man he'd always thought was his father wasn't.

Tonight, the dirty, angry outcast had learned he was a prince. And it struck her that *that* was why he didn't want to tell his half-brothers. He didn't want to see their revul-sion when they found out he belonged to them.

Oh, God. She couldn't bear knowing he was all alone in his cabin with his pain and fears. She wanted to tell him until it sank in just how worthy he was of being a Blackstock.

She couldn't do that, of course. He didn't want that.

But the Blackstocks losing their *land*? It was unthinkable.

And she wouldn't let it happen. "Trust me to come up with something, okay? I know it seems like Cooper's the only answer right now, but he's not."

"Yeah." Ethan rocked back on his heels. "Okay." With his hand on the doorknob, he glanced over his shoulder. "How'd he take the news?"

This is what I love about him. Underneath that hard-ass mountain man persona was a deeply caring man. "I think he's a little weirded out right now, which is understandable."

Ethan stepped out onto the porch. "Can you at least ask him if he knows of a band that would play? He's got connections. We'll show them a good time out here."

She smiled. "Absolutely."

He gave her a hint of a smile. "You're good people, Daze. There's no one else I'd rather work with." The door closed behind him with a soft snick.

She could ask, but that didn't mean Cooper would deliver. And no matter what she told Ethan, the truth was —they had no Plan B.

After a fitful sleep, a shower, and a quick cup of coffee, Daisy pulled on her leggings and ballet flats and hurried out the door. She'd try to catch Cooper before he left town.

She had to ask for his help, but she also wanted to make sure he was okay. All night long, every time she'd start to drift off, she'd imagine him alone in his bed, eyes open in the darkness, trying to make sense of a mother who, even when sober, didn't care about him. Of the startling news that he belonged to a family. A family that could've saved him from the hunger and deprivation of his childhood. From the bullying and shame.

It killed her to think about what he must be going through.

Fear that he might've already left hastened her steps. She didn't know if he'd arranged a car to the airport, but she wouldn't mind driving him. It would give them a chance to talk.

Up ahead, she heard conversation and the sharp click of heels on the asphalt path.

"Where can I get a massage on a Sunday?" a woman said.

She heard a smacking sound, followed by a squeal. "Come back to my place, baby," a man said. "I'll give you a massage."

"Don't you ever take a break?" that same woman asked.

"Oh, my God, that was the best night," another woman said. "I'm so bummed he's leaving."

"I'm just happy we got a night with him. I lit up my Snapchat."

"Hey, can we get a cinnamon roll and coffee from the Sugar Bowl before we head back to town?"

As Daisy rounded the bend, she recognized Carrie Levitt among the group heading away from Cooper's cabin. Reality hit like a punch to the gut.

He hadn't been alone. He'd been *partying*.

While she'd lost sleep worrying about him, he'd been with *Carrie*.

But she was the manager of the resort, so she slapped on a smile. "Morning."

God, he'd kissed her like he wanted to crawl inside her and never find his way out. But it hadn't meant anything to him.

Of course not. He's a rock star. His reputation as the last playboy left in his band wasn't some image fabricated by a publicity team. It was him.

It made her sick to think he'd kissed Carrie with the same passion.

The most popular girl from high school, the bitch who'd tormented Daisy for years, squinted against the early morning sunshine. "Daisy?"

"Hey, Carrie. You guys have a good night?"

"The best." Carrie had a suggestive glint in her eye.

Her high school nemesis hadn't been the prettiest girl, but she'd had confidence. If she'd only ignored the kids who weren't on her level, Daisy might not have cared. But Carrie always had a cutting—though not particularly intelligent—remark that got a kid right where she lived.

"Have a great day." She waved to them as they cut across the grass to the parking lot.

After they'd disappeared, she let the disappointment crash through her. What a fool. She'd gotten way too invested in Cooper Hood.

And here I was going to drive him to the airport—as if I have time for a trip like that.

Pulling her phone out of her tote, she scrolled down to the last group text with the Blackstocks and sent a new message.

Daisy: Let's brainstorm a Plan B. What's a good time to meet?

"Daisy?" Cooper shut the door behind him, pocketing

his wallet.

She shouldn't care that he'd spent the night with Carrie. His mom was a wreck, his bandmates were in New York, and he was by himself in the town that had never given him a break. So why wouldn't he have partied last night?

Because he could've been with her. And he'd chosen Carrie instead.

He stopped in front of her, his black T-shirt accentuating his cut physique, his worn blue jeans molding around his taut thigh muscles. "Are you okay?"

"Of course. Well, a little stressed." *I couldn't wait to see you this morning because I haven't felt this excited over a guy since…well, you.* "Listen, Stuart's left us in a terrible bind. There's more at stake here than he realizes. I thought about it all night, and I know you have to get back to Austin, but I need to ask you for a favor."

"Daisy, I can't ask—"

"I know that. I just want you to talk to your friends in other bands, your manager, your label, anyone you can think of who'll play the Huckleberry Festival. With Mickelson Media coming, we can give them amazing exposure, and they'll get a pretty awesome vacation out of it." When nothing registered on his features, her mind kicked into overdrive. "We have something pretty unique here. This ranch—*resort*—offers year-round outdoor activities. We're an hour away from Yellowstone National Park. We've got world class rappelling, fly fishing, hiking—"

"Daze. I know."

Of course, he knew. He'd grown up here. She wanted to dive into the bushes. She'd been so frazzled that she'd turned into a manic tour guide. Because, come on, her childhood crush had just had an *orgy*. "I need your help."

"I already put out some feelers last night."

She snorted. Like he'd thought about her problem last night while Carrie Levitt was swinging naked from the antler chandelier in his cabin.

"What?" He seemed confused.

"No, that's great. Thank you. I appreciate that. Anyhow, I should go. It was great seeing you." She'd almost turned away—almost—before she caught one last glance at him, and the moment their gazes met, that connection snapped into place, and she saw him. Really saw him.

And what she saw was not a man exhausted and sated after a wild Saturday night. No, she saw a man who looked utterly lost and...alone. And all her anxiety and jealousy fizzled out.

They'd had a great day together. A great kiss. But in the end, he was still a rock star. She was wired for roots and commitment, while he'd escaped an ugly past through a nomadic existence.

She sucked in a breath. "I'm sorry." Then let it out. "I'm freaking out right now, talking a mile a minute. I just have so much on my mind."

"I'll do my best to come up with something."

"Thanks. I appreciate that." She should go. Turn away and go back down the path. But her stupid mouth opened. "Do you have a ride to the airport?"

"I can get a ride from the resort. Or Carrie, I guess. She offered to take me. Either way, I'm good."

Heat rushed up her neck. She could've ended things with dignity, but no, she'd had to take one more shot at spending time with him.

Time he didn't want. "Perfect. Okay. So." *Go.* "Bye."

Chapter Six

As the sedan drove under the Blackstock Ranch sign, Cooper pressed the button to close the window. He'd had enough of the pine and sage of Snowberry. Pulling up his phone, he reread the text his mom had sent him.

Mom: Slider would've left me if he'd known the kid wasn't his.

The kid. *That's fucking me you're talking about.* He stared at the text, waiting to feel something, but her words had anesthetized his heart.

He'd known his mother hadn't cared about him but hearing her say it sliced deeper. It eliminated room for doubt.

Or hope. He hadn't had much of it, but he'd obviously had some. Otherwise, her total detachment wouldn't bother him.

The weight of the driver's eyes in the rear-view mirror got his attention. "Did you want to stop at the Sugar Bowl before we head to the airport?"

"The Sugar Bowl?" *Why would I do that?*

"Sorry, I thought you were from here."

He didn't get it. "I am. Was."

The driver shrugged. "It's Sunday. Everybody gets one of Ms. Char's cinnamon buns."

"I'll pass. Thanks." Would Daisy be there?

He hadn't liked her hurt expression when he'd told her about Carrie's offer. But she'd been stressed enough—she didn't need to take a couple of hours out of her day to take him to the damn airport.

Why was he worrying about this shit? He was leaving, getting back to his life. And, Jesus, did he want to get the hell out of this town.

Stupidly, he looked at the screen again.

Mom: Slider would've left me if he'd known the kid wasn't his.

His mom had written this while sober. She'd had a clear head.

Hurt seeped in.

"Just the airport, then?" the driver asked as he hit 191.

"Yes."

But as the man flicked on the turn signal, as he checked in either direction for oncoming traffic, Cooper felt a tug. If he left now, the unanswered questions would eat away at him. *Did Hunter know? Did* everyone *in town know?* And he didn't want to be plagued with anger and frustration. He wanted to leave all of it behind.

"Actually, can you take me to Blue Sky first?"

Perks of being a rock star: the manager had no problem giving up his mom's location in the resort. Of course, later, when Cooper came back down, he'd talk to the guy about that.

The elevator landed, the doors parted, and he stepped out to see a housekeeping cart about a third of the way down a long hallway. His temper rose, and his body girded for a fight. He was done going easy on her. When had she ever considered his feelings?

And this was his last chance to get the answers he deserved, so fuck it. He'd get them. Whether she was on the job or not.

A glance out the picture window overlooking the mountain gave him a view of the cables from the Hidden Peak Tram swooping from the summit to the back of the hotel. He watched parents slide onto the moving seats, while their two young children waited for the next chairlift. The older of the two started to get on, but the younger one hesitated. With the parents motioning and shouting, the older kid pulled on his sibling's arm, but the kid just grew more resistant. A worker quickly guided the kid onto the seat.

Living in a tourist town, he'd watched scenes like this one all the time. Families taking pictures in the gazebo on the town green or sitting on picnic benches with box lunches from the Sugar Bowl. He'd always been on the outside looking in.

But he'd *had* a family. Jesus fucking Christ, if his mom had handled it differently, he could've been part of those scenes. It burned like acid in his gut.

That's why you're here instead of at the airport. To purge the nasty shit once and for all.

He spun around and headed down the hallway, ready to confront his mom. But when he reached the cart parked outside the open door of a guest room, he heard mumbling. Leaning in, he spotted her. In a pale blue uniform with its starched white collar, she rested a hip against the dresser, a pencil in one hand and a sheet of paper in the other. Forehead creased in concentration, she whispered, "*Three* bath sheets, *three* hand towels, *three* wash cloths." She looked into the bathroom, her finger bouncing as she counted. "One, two, three, one, two, three, one, two, three." Pulling the pencil from her ear, she made a checkmark on the paper.

Her walkie talkie squawked. "Ronnie?"

She startled, as though caught in the act, and dropped the pencil. Grabbing the walkie-talkie, she said, "What?"

"Three-nineteen said they asked you for water bottles and you told them to call room service."

"Yeah, so?"

"They asked you for water. Get it for them."

His mom hooked an arm across her stomach and gazed out the window. "They're supposed to call room service for that."

"Jesus, Ronnie. Just do it."

"I have to finish this floor by one o'clock. How can I do that if I have to go down to the kitchen and pick up water bottles?"

"Get them their damn water."

His mom lifted a handful of hair off the back of her neck and pulled hard. "Fine, but don't crawl up my ass if I can't get the floor done on time." She tossed the walkie-talkie onto the bed. "Bitch."

With a furtive look around the room, she picked the pencil off the floor. Her teeth sank into her bottom lip as she grabbed the list and mouthed something Cooper couldn't decipher. Then, she approached the coffee and tea station. With a shaky hand, she counted the row of tea packages. She seemed to lose count and had to start over. "Shit."

All his anger, all the frustration, just crashed in on itself. Watching his mom so flustered by a simple task made him finally understand. She'd started using drugs in high school. That meant she'd bypassed the period of life where she should've become independent and self-sufficient. If she couldn't handle restocking the tea and coffee bar, she sure as hell couldn't handle raising a kid.

Cooper moved into the room. "Hey, Mom."

She startled, clutching the list to her chest. "Cooper?" The way she looked at him made him feel more like a vice cop than her son. "What're you doing here?"

Gently, he pried the list out of her hands. "Tell me what's left to do, and I'll take care of it while you get the water."

Her eyes went wide, and she gestured around her like the parts of a 747 engine were strewn haphazardly around the room, and it was up to her to put them back together. "You don't know what to do."

He scanned the list. Seemed pretty straight-forward. "I'll give it a shot."

"This is a fancy place. I have to make swans out of hand towels. I have to put the soap in the dish. You can't just set it out on the counter."

"How about I leave the hard stuff for you? While you're out, I can restock the mini fridge and coffee basket."

Shoulders relaxing, she exhaled. "Yeah, okay. That would be good." Handing him the pencil, she gazed up at him with a wary expression.

Was she expecting to see disgust? Anger? At the moment, he had neither.

Because right then, he realized that the battle going on inside his mom was harder than anything he'd ever had to endure in his life. "Go on. I got this."

She nodded and took off.

Daisy was right. His mom couldn't handle the house project. He could imagine her in Home Depot with a wall full of toilet seats to choose from, a ceiling crowded with light fixtures, and completely losing it.

It wouldn't work. And, as much as he wanted to be in Austin looking for a band, he didn't need to physically be there to do it. He could do it from anywhere. So, he'd stay.

In Snowberry.

For two weeks.

He'd do as much as he could during that time to get her house built, and then he'd hand it over to Daisy. In exchange, he'd play the Huckleberry Festival.

And how ironic was that? He was helping out the very family he had the power to destroy.

As Cooper kneed open the door, he shoved the key card into his front pocket and pushed into the cabin. House-keeping hadn't had a chance to clean yet, so it still reeked of beer and clashing perfumes. He'd picked up as much as he could before checking out, but he'd barely made a dent in the mess Carrie and her friends had made.

Luckily, he had this place for two more nights. After that, though, he was screwed. With the festival two weeks away, every town within driving distance was booked solid.

Maybe he could rent a house? He'd rather stay in Bozeman anyway. The less time he had around the Black-stocks, the better.

Unzipping his bag, he pulled out his toiletry kit and tossed it onto the bathroom counter. Turning back, he nearly slammed into a massive body.

Hands came down on his shoulders, and the imposing figure held his gaze with striking intensity. Cooper stared into the eyes of the man who might be his father.

A range of emotions flickered across Hunter Blackstock's features—confusion, hurt, curiosity—until awe won out. The man looked…happy. Proud, even.

With unruly salt and pepper hair—though predominantly salt—and a thick beard and moustache, Hunter looked every bit a rockabilly musician. The western shirt stretched across broad shoulders, and the frayed hem of ancient black jeans dropped over scuffed black cowboy boots. His Adam's apple bounced with a deep swallow. "Son."

The word ricocheted inside his skull like dart pellets in a tin pan. "Don't know about that yet." He pushed past him.

"I do." While the man's voice sounded confident, his expression was fraught with concern.

Cooper moved into the living room. Hands on his hips, he faced the picture window, where a green lawn sloped down to the river. "Did she call you?"

"Your mom?" He barked out a bitter laugh. "No."

"Then who?" But the roar of betrayal blasted through him because who else knew, other than Daisy? What, the moment he'd left town, she'd run and told Hunter?

"Word got around pretty quick last night. Soon as I heard about it this morning, I came right over. It's got to be me."

"It really doesn't." He was an asshole, plain and simple, for thinking Daisy would do something like that. He *knew* her. She wouldn't. But it was hard to think clearly with his brain so rattled. "My mom was pretty messed up back then. Not sure how reliable her information is."

"She's not wrong about this."

Confused and frustrated, Cooper folded his arms across his chest. "I don't get it. You dated my *mom*?"

"No." His cheeks turned ruddy. "We didn't date."

"Look, no offense, but I've run out of patience. Can you just spit it out? Because your son and I are the same age."

With a careful expression, he nodded. "Your mom and I…got together once. And I was single at the time."

His abrupt honesty dismantled Cooper's armor, exposing the little boy in him who was looking at his father for the very first time. The shock of it had him taking a step back and sitting on the arm of the leather couch.

"Why now, though?" Hunter said. "Sounds like Slider took the test years ago. Why's she coming out with it now?"

Who cared about the timing? But it didn't take him long to process what Hunter was actually saying. Right when the Blackstocks were about to turn their ranch into a world-class resort, Ronnie Hood revealed her son's paternity. A burn of mortification swept through him.

This guy thought his mom wanted to stake some kind of claim? Cooper had only been around her for five minutes before he'd realized she was hanging by a thread. She was in no way capable of masterminding some scheme to get a piece of the Blackstock pie. "I can't speak for my mother, but I don't want anything from you."

"Okay." Hunter looked confused.

"And I don't want anyone to know. It doesn't go further than this room."

Hunter rubbed the back of his neck. "I can't lie to my boys."

Invigorated, he got up. "I'm only in town two weeks, and I've got a job to do. I don't want to cause trouble for you and your family."

"You are my family." He looked so sincere. "If it's true…Cooper, I'm your father. That matters to me."

If it's true…did that mean he wanted proof? "I'm not interested in a paternity test. There's no point. Like I said, I don't want anything from you. I'm twenty-eight. It's a little late for the whole father-son thing. And it's not like I'm ever coming back here."

"Cooper…" The man looked like he was trying to rein in his emotion. "I *want* you to come back here. You're my son. You're part of us. Me, my wife, and your brothers."

Noise roared in his head. A father. Brothers. Fucking hell. How was this happening? He was being offered a *family*. Yesterday, he was an only child with a neglectful mom. And now, all of a sudden, he had a father, brothers. *Blackstock* brothers. "Slow down, okay? Just…I'm not sure I want any of this."

Was that flinch of emotion…was that hurt? *Fuck.* This wasn't going well. He didn't want to hurt the guy, but Cooper couldn't see himself ever being involved with them.

His head was going to explode. How did any of this make sense?

It occurred to him just then how different Hunter was from his sons. Where Hunter was quiet and a little awkward, they had the confidence of men who'd never once doubted their place in the world. The kind very few people possessed. Likely borne out of the incorruptible bond the three of them shared. The brothers knew they had each other, and they didn't need anyone else.

Plus, owning all that land had to have ingrained a

sense of invulnerability in the family. They could endure a zombie apocalypse with all the caves, healthy soil, and water on their land.

Cooper might not want to disrupt the man's family, but he did want answers. One in particular. "I need you to be straight with me. Did you know? All this time, did you know I was yours?"

"No." The man sounded appalled at the very idea. "I wondered. Of course, I wondered."

"You wondered but never bothered to find out."

Hunter's head snapped up. Pure honesty shone in his eyes. "You bet I asked, but your mom told me you were Slider's." Interest sparked in his eyes. "And I believed her up until the day I saw you in the hallway at school." He tugged on his beard. "I was there to help with the music program, and I saw this big kid walking to class. A bunch of football players slammed into him. They should've knocked the kid into the lockers, but he held his ground." He widened his stance and bent his knees, as if to reenact what the kid had done. "I saw his expression and…." He shook his head. "I saw myself in him. In *you*. It was you."

Cooper didn't remember that particular moment, because it was one of many. "We don't look anything alike."

"Of course, we do. Me, you, my boys, we've all got the same height, same body types. Your hair might be darker, and your eyes are blue, but the nose? The jaw?" He stood taller. "But that's not what I'm talking about. When I saw you in the hallway that day, it wasn't your physical features I noticed. It was the look on your face, the set of your shoulders. Quiet, fierce. The way you fought back—you wouldn't let them get away with that shit." He shook his head. "I saw *me*."

"So instead of demanding a paternity test, you just shrugged it off?" Why was he pushing? Nothing would change the outcome. *Let it go.*

"You bet your ass I demanded it. As soon as I finished up with the class, I went straight to her cabin. She was pretty strung out back then, but she was adamant. Insisted Slider was your dad." He drew in a breath. "Look, I'm trying hard right now not to badmouth your mom. You know better than anyone what she was like. But she was your legal guardian, and there was nothing I could do. And you left town before you turned eighteen."

"Yeah." Everything he said made sense. He couldn't argue. "Okay."

Hunter watched him for a long, tense moment. "I was cheated of you. Of raising my boy. And I'm so damn sorry."

Cooper stood there, hollowed out, nothing but an erratic heart beating in a tin drum. He took short breaths, not enough to fill his lungs, and he grew light-headed. Swallowing, he forced himself to fill the awkward silence. "It all worked out in the end." Stupid, empty words that sounded as limp as a paper straw wrapper.

Hunter took a few steps toward him. "I'm proud of you. Damn proud of the man you've become." Moisture shone in his eyes. "I would've liked to watch you grow up."

Cooper felt stripped bare. His emotions, raw and bleeding, threatened to overwhelm him. The little boy in him, the one who'd desperately wanted Slider's attention— a pat on his head, a smile that said *That's my boy*—ached to take what this man offered.

But there'd be no happy ending here. Hunter's wife and sons wouldn't welcome Ronnie Hood's kid into their family. Besides, what did any of this matter? He'd be back on tour in two weeks. After that, the band would hole up and write new material, then spend months recording it before going out on tour again—the next one would likely be international.

Hunter dragged his hands across his cheeks and blew out a breath. "Damn glad I caught you. I heard you were heading out today."

"Change of plans. I haven't told Daisy yet, but I'm going to perform at the festival. And since I'm working on a project for my mom, I'll be staying in town until then."

Happiness bloomed on the man's features. "Is that right? You're here for two weeks?"

"Not *here* exactly. Your resort's booked, but yes, I'm in town until the festival."

"Stay with me and Crystal."

What? Hell no. "Thank you, but no. I'll find something."

"The boys all have their own places, so it's just the two of us in that big house. Plenty of bedrooms."

Cooper wouldn't change his mind.

Hunter came closer. "You're my son. My boys are your brothers. You can choose to hold off on letting them know, but *we're* going to get to know each other. We've all been cheated out of something beautiful, and we're going to correct that starting right now."

Something beautiful. The two simple words dissolved a whole layer of his formidable outer shell. "You have any idea what this will do to them? Jesus, their dad had a kid with another woman. You slept with two women at the same time."

He winced. "I'm not hiding you or my actions."

"Look, I'm here to do a job, and that's the only

thing on my mind. While I'm here, maybe something will come of this"—he gestured between them—"and maybe it won't. But right now, let me take care of my work."

"You mean for the festival?"

"No, *my* work. Our opening act blew up, and I have to find a new one to finish off our tour."

"I can help you with that." Hunter grew energized.

He wished it were that easy. "I need one by tomorrow morning."

"I can make a few calls and in half an hour get a dozen bands out here to audition for you. In fact, why don't we do that right now? We've got the stage built for the festival so we can start this afternoon." Taking a step closer, Hunter ran a hand through his unruly hair. "But *I* need to know my son."

The depth of emotion in Hunter's voice sank deep under Cooper's skin. It left no room for doubt. And it fucking gutted him.

This is my father.

And he wants me.

But he shut it down. "I'm not looking for rockabilly bands. Or bands that play local clubs. Besides, I've got a few contenders already, just nothing that's a slam dunk."

"I listen to your music. I know what you're looking for."

"You do?"

"Of course. You're the kid from the music program who made it big. You bet I checked it out." He seemed impressed. "I like your sound. And I can think of three bands off the top of my head that might work for you."

"Like I said, my guys in Austin are on it. They've got at least three bands of their own."

"Yeah? Let my three face off against yours." Hunter's mischievous smile broke through the tension.

And just then, a brilliant plan snapped into place. *Oh, hell, yes.* "Get out your phone, old man." He pulled his out of his pocket, hit Emmie's speed dial, and smiled. "It's *on.*"

Cooper followed the vanilla and honey scent to Daisy's office.

"Would you do that?" he heard her say.

He stopped outside the half-closed door. The hallway was lined with framed architectural drawings, topographical maps, and photographs of the ranch—caves, waterfalls, moose, bear, and pine needles frozen into icicles. A kind of beauty he'd never noticed as a kid growing up in these mountains.

"I'd love that." She paused, obviously on the phone.

No one had been at the front desk, but maybe he should go back and wait in the reception area.

"Yes, definitely. Either of those artists would be great."

Sounded like she was still looking for an act to headline the festival. *Good.*

"Great. Let me know the moment you hear back from either of them. Thanks so much. Yep. Bye."

Just as he was about to knock, he heard, "Yes," in a whisper that restrained what he suspected was a shout of happiness. He could just see her overcome with happiness, her eyes sparkling, and he wanted it. Wanted to feel it on his skin like sunshine. It was exactly why he'd hovered around her in high school, to stand in the wake of that pure and honest joy.

And by some strange twist of fate, life had given him the opportunity to hover for another two weeks.

Rapping on the open door, he pushed it wider. "Daze?"

She looked up from the mess of papers on her desk. A pink flush rose across her cheeks, and she tilted her head in confusion. Her gaze went immediately to the bottom of her computer screen.

And then she jumped out of her chair. "Oh, my God. What happened? Did Carrie bail on you?" She snatched her keys off the desk. "I'll take you to the airport right now." She swung around the desk in her pretty halter-style dress and gold sandals.

"No, no. It's cool. I'm not going to the airport."

"I don't understand." As she came closer, the full skirt of the dress swished around her legs.

"I changed my flight. I'm staying."

"Here? You're staying in Snowberry?" Those blue eyes tried to read him. "For how long?"

"Two weeks."

Happiness lit her features. "Are you serious? You're staying the whole two weeks?"

"Yeah." Cupping her elbows, he bent so they were eye level. "Daze? I accept your proposition. I'll help with the festival if you'll take on my mom's building project."

She started toward him, looking like she was about to throw herself into his arms. But she stopped herself, and he didn't know why. "That's great, Cooper. Thank you. When you say help with the festival, you mean headline it?"

"Yes." He drew out the single syllable because that wouldn't be the highlight of the event.

But before he could say another word, she said, "Oh, to hell with it," and pressed her voluptuous body against him, giving him the hug she'd only a moment ago withheld.

His body went haywire. Part of him hummed with the sweetness of her touch—just enjoying the fuck out of holding her in his arms. But another part was clanging and churning with the awareness of her breasts, the warmth of her hands on his back, and the now-familiar scent of her hair.

"Thank you so much." She pulled away. "I just got off the phone with The Desperados' manager, and she's got two artists in mind, but neither has a name nearly as big as yours." She sighed. "I can't tell you grateful I am."

He had to force his thoughts back on the situation. "I'll play if you want, but I've got a better idea. Something that'll work for both of us."

Her expression turned hopeful.

And damn, but he did not want to let this woman down. "What do you think about hosting a Battle of the Bands?"

"I'm not sure. Explain it to me."

"There's not a chance I'm going to find a band that's ready to come on tour with us by tomorrow morning, but I do have a bunch of acts I'm interested in. So, why don't we turn it into a competition? I pitched the idea to our manager, and she loves it. She's already run it by the label. They're down for the attention we'll get with an event like this. And I think your investors will like it, too, because the winner gets to tour with Blue Fire. And since it'll take place during the festival, you've got the attention you need right here all three days—not just one night." He waited for a reaction. "What do you think?"

"I think it's perfect."

"Good. I'm glad you like it."

"I can't believe it. This is ten times better than a Shout! reunion." She dragged her fingers through her hair, catching it in a ponytail and doing that thing where she twisted it and somehow kept it in a bun. "God, I was dreading having to tell Mickelson that Stuart bailed." She blew out a breath. "I'll still hold off on telling him, though, just until we work out all the details. But we have it. We have our Plan B."

No lie. It felt good knowing he'd helped her.

"You don't know what this means to us." She stuttered out a laugh. "It's stupid, but I'm just so happy you're staying here for two whole weeks."

The way she looked at him…. *Fuck.* Two more weeks with her.

Leaning in, he whispered her name, meant as a question but coming out more a plea. Her answer came in the tilt of her chin, the parting of her lips.

So, he took it. He took her mouth, covering it with his, and she opened right away. That warm, wet, softness stirred the ember deep inside of him that glowed only for her. Everything that was Daisy—her scent, her hair, the pure abandon of her kiss—ignited the desire he'd banked for so many years. And the moment their tongues touched, sensation rocked him, and all his restraint dropped away.

He pulled her hard up against him, thrilled when her hands slid up his chest and wrapped around his neck. As their tongues tangled, she made a needy sound that matched the chord playing inside him, and it made him wild.

Until she tore her mouth away. "Do you kiss Carrie like this?"

"What?" What did Carrie have to do with anything?

"I've never kissed her in my life." Carrie might've gotten off by giving him head in the storage room, but he'd had no interest in pretending it was anything more than what it was: her fucking around with the bad boy and him getting his base needs met. "Why would you ask something like that?"

"This morning...I saw her..."

"Daisy, trust me. I've never kissed anyone the way I kiss you." He brought his mouth back to hers—barely touching. "And I'm going to steal as many of them as I can in the next fourteen days."

"Cooper." She got up on her toes and licked the shell of his ear. "You don't have to steal anything."

Sensation danced across his skin. He drew her mouth back so he could pour all that desire into the kiss, telling her with his body what he couldn't say in words. As the kiss deepened, his chest tightened with a sweet ache. *This is Daisy. I'm kissing Daisy.* And nothing in his life had ever felt so good, so perfectly right.

She wrapped her arms around his back and slid her thigh between his, pinning his hard, throbbing cock between their bodies.

Jesus. He grew ravenous for her. Her hands, her mouth, her tongue showed him she was just as hungry. Out of his mind, he caressed down her back until he gripped her firm, round ass. She sucked in a breath, moaning in a purely sexual way, and all conscious thought shut down. Driven by raw need, he lifted her, turned, and walked her back to the wall. Her legs banded around his hips, and a thrill shot through him when her back met resistance, allowing his cock to grind against her stomach.

Their hips rocked hard, their mouths fed off each other's, and their hands gripped and squeezed whatever flesh they could reach. The tingle heating the base of his spine warned he was close to losing it.

In a glimpse of clarity—he shouldn't be making out with her in her office—he considered pulling away, but then she said, "Cooper, oh, *God*," and he was gone. Just gone. His boot kicked out and slammed the door.

Tugging the knot behind her neck, he pushed the straps off her shoulders, exposing all that creamy skin. He kissed the tops of her breasts, mounding over the strapless bra. Her back arched, and her hands fisted his hair. He lowered the cups, exposing her lush, full breasts. Wild with need, he cupped one and licked the nipple.

She made a strangled sound, her legs tightening around him, hips arching into him. "*Cooper.*" She gasped. "Oh, my God."

His mouth closed over her nipple, his tongue caressing, stroking, and then he reached under her dress and found her panties.

When he ran his hand along the gusset, she bucked, moaning like a woman desperate for release. And *Jesus fuck*, there was nothing he wanted more than to watch Daisy come apart at his touch. His finger slid under the lace of her panties, sought and found her slick heat, and she writhed against him.

While his tongue lavished attention on her nipple, his finger found the hard little bead that made her gasp and twist in his arms. She gripped his shoulders so hard he felt the bite of her fingernails.

"Oh, God, oh, God, oh—"

"She in?" a deep voice said from the hallway.

Cooper's mouth left her breast, and he started to withdraw. But when he saw the desperation in her eyes, he rubbed her clit until her eyes closed, and her lips parted in a silent O. "Damn, Daisy." His quiet tone held reverence. "You're magnificent."

And then her body seized with ecstatic release.

"Nah, I got it." The male voice came closer. Sounded like Ethan. "Thanks."

Quickly adjusting the cups of her bra, Daisy tipped her forehead to his cheek and sighed. He set her down, lifting the ties of her dress and knotting them behind her neck. She smoothed her skirt with one hand and her hair with the other, just as someone knocked on the door.

"Daisy?"

She looked at Cooper, eyebrows lifting. *Do I look okay?*

Tucking a lock of hair behind her ear, his palm brushed across the soft skin of her cheek. He gave her a nod to let her know she was perfect.

Just as the door opened, Daisy stepped toward her desk. "Hey, Ethan. Come on in."

The oldest Blackstock entered, mouth open, ready to speak. His jaw snapped shut when he saw Cooper. "Am I interrupting?"

"Not at all." Her smile didn't quite reach her eyes.

"You look…are you upset?"

There wasn't a man alive who could look at Daisy just then and not know exactly why she looked flushed and slightly disheveled, her mouth still swollen from kisses.

"Just the opposite," she said. "I'm actually incredibly excited."

And *he'd* been the one to give her that pleasure. The caveman in him wanted to throw an arm around her and claim her in front of Ethan. But he'd never embarrass her that way, so he stood there cool and composed, hoping no one could hear the wild beating of his heart.

"We've got our Plan B. And it's awesome." She

gestured to Cooper. "Cooper's going to run a Battle of the Bands competition, and the winner gets to tour with Blue Fire. Isn't that amazing?" She waited for a response that didn't come. "I haven't told Mickelson yet, not until we work out the details, but he's going to flip out over this." She turned all that sunshine on Ethan, but he wasn't smiling. In fact, he seemed pissed. "What's the matter?"

"We're not hosting a Battle of the *Bands*. That's not the level of entertainment we're looking to provide."

"And what level would that be?" Cooper would be damned if he'd let Ethan steal her happiness.

"The one where people bring water bottles filled with vodka and hide blunts in their dreads. We're not looking to host garage bands. That's not going to interest Mickelson."

"We're not talking about *garage bands*." Daisy sounded appalled. "These are bands good enough to open for Blue Fire."

"What kind of crowd did you think Shout! would bring?" Cooper asked.

"Professionals." Ethan's tone sounded terse. "Their fans have grown up. They've got enough money to vacation at the kind of resort we're building here. They're not going to get drunk and into fights." He looked to Daisy. "How's a Battle of the Bands going to impress our investors?"

Daisy was about to speak when Cooper faced him. "You can't seriously think a Shout! reunion's going to bring the well-heeled, wine-tasting crowd. They're raunchy rockers. Their drummer was arrested for pissing into the audience."

"They brought Mickelson and a new investor," Ethan said. "That's all I care about."

"Ethan, Blue Fire's a Grammy-winning band," Daisy

said. "Derek and Slater have been on the Ledger List for two years in a row—they're on a whole other level. And not only do we have their lead guitarist here for the festival, but he's running a competition to discover the next big thing. Come on. We'll be running our own *America's Got Talent* here in Snowberry."

"I get it," Ethan said. "But I'm not convinced it's the best way to go."

"Do you really think I'd pitch an event featuring garage bands to Mickelson?" Daisy asked. "But that aside, we have less than two weeks to pull this off. Do you have a better idea than inviting *established* bands—bands that're close to getting signed by record labels—to compete for a shot at opening for a Grammy-winning, chart-topping rock band?"

"It's not for me to decide," Ethan said. "We'll discuss it at the next board meeting."

The tension left her body, and Daisy smiled. "Sure. We'll do that. Now, would that be ribs at your dad's house or a fried chicken picnic at Eagle's Landing?"

Ethan shot her a look that said, *Cute*. "I'm meeting my brothers for coffee at the Sugar Bowl. You want to join us? That can be our brainstorming session."

"Absolutely." She walked him to the door.

Once he was gone, Cooper said, "Is he going to cause problems? Because I can't screw around here." He knew Ethan's rejection had less to do with the idea itself than with Cooper's involvement. "This thing's in motion. I've got my Austin guys on it, and Hunter's setting up auditions."

She grew interested. "Hunter? Have you talked to him?"

He nodded.

"Hold on a minute. You talked to Hunter? This is huge. How did it go?"

"It went fine, but let's talk about this event. I've got a lot of people waiting for me to give them the green light on this."

"I promise it won't be a problem. We'll pitch it at the meeting, and the guys will love it."

"Ethan doesn't."

"It's not that. It's just…there's a lot more at stake for him than you realize. But don't worry about it. He'll come around. Now, let's go pitch your idea so we can get the ball rolling."

He'd do her a favor and *not* go. She'd have a better shot without him there.

Chapter Seven

Noon on Sunday, the Sugar Bowl café was hopping. On the bakery side, crowds bunched together to ogle the display cases. A line threaded out the door for her mom's pastries.

Daisy sat in a booth with Ethan and the twins in the bustling café that took up the rest of the large, low-ceilinged building.

"Hi, sweetheart." Her mom set a basket down. "How's it going, boys?"

Immediately the scent of cinnamon and sugar-fried dough filled her senses. "Hey, Mom."

The brothers slid out of the booth to greet her. Daisy got a kick out of watching her mom swallowed up by the brawny men who patted her back and teased her about the flour on her cheek.

Daisy had grown up with these guys. From the time they were little kids, they'd gotten off the bus with her at the bakery. With Hunter busy with his music, and their mom working in Bozeman, her mom had offered them hot chocolate and a snack while they did their homework and waited for a parent to pick them up. In many ways, they were her brothers.

The moment they sat back down, all three reached for the golden brown churros.

"They're like a pack of wolves," her mom said with a teasing tone.

"Thanks, Ms. Char." As Nash bit into the fried dough, his eyes closed in pleasure. "Damn. So good."

"You're welcome. Enjoy." Her mom headed back into the kitchen.

Remi, Nash's twin, chewed. "It's like she puts cat nip for people in it." He perked up. "Is that a thing? Cat nip for people?"

With a coffee pot in hand, a waitress came up to the table. "Can I get you guys anything else?" Her voice came out all breathy as she looked at Remi.

The brothers grinned. Nash pulled the lemon wedge off the rim of his iced tea and tossed it across the table, where it hit Remi's cheek.

"Fucker. Cut it out." Remi swiped the moisture with his fingers before answering the waitress. "We're good. Thanks." As he whipped his napkin out from under the silverware, his powerful biceps flexed.

It took a moment for the waitress to tear her gaze away. "Okay, well, just let me know." She turned to leave. Hips swiveling, she glanced over her shoulder.

But the guys weren't looking. Remi was too busy lobbing the lemon right back at Nash, who caught it easily.

"So," Daisy said. "Great news. We've got our Plan B. Cooper Hood"—the memory of his touch sizzled through her, but she forced herself to stay on point—"the lead guitarist of Blue Fire, is going to run a three-day competition."

"Okay." Sounding doubtful, Remi reached for his coffee mug.

"Cooper Hood." Nash shook his head. "Never saw that one coming."

She had. She'd seen his passion, his total dedication in the music program. What she hadn't seen was this rock star persona. Leaving Snowberry had freed him to become the man he was meant to be.

And that man had kissed her with fierce passion. *God.* Had she really just done that with him in her *office?* "He dedicated himself to learning—not just how to play guitar but how to read music and understand composition. I was there. I saw. No one took music more seriously than Cooper." It had been his ticket out. Damn, she was proud of him. "Not only did he have a natural talent—"

A shock of awareness sped through her when she connected the dots. His natural talent came from Hunter. Their *father.* And she couldn't say a word about it, so she busied herself with opening her notebook. "Anyhow, he needs an opening act to finish out his tour, and we need an event strong enough to keep Mickelson Media interested in us. That brings us to the Battle of the Bands."

Nash and Remi held matching skeptical looks.

"The winner gets to tour with Blue Fire."

"Can we pull it together in two weeks?" Remi asked.

"We've already got a jump start. Cooper and your dad have bands lined up and ready to audition. We've got the stage and sound technicians. So yeah, we can do it, no problem." She set both palms on the scarred wood table-top. "With Blue Fire's name behind this event, plus the power of their record label *and* Mickelson Media? We're golden. What do you think? Everyone on board?"

"We don't know if Mickelson's interested," Ethan said.

"I'll talk to him tomorrow morning. But if he's in?"

"If he's in, then yeah," Remi said. "Sounds cool."

"What about logistics?" Nash said. "How does this affect our current plans? Food, traffic, toilet facilities, security. Are we equipped to handle this many bands and their roadies and fans?"

"It's not that different from what we've always done," Daisy said. "Only instead of random bands performing throughout the festival, they'll be competing against each other. Besides, we planned on Shout!, and they have a huge following."

"True." Nash didn't sound convinced.

"But even before Stuart bailed on us, I'd already ordered more Port-a-Potties and talked to the electrician about extending the lighting on the property."

"It's not just about Port-a-Pottie pump-outs," Ethan said. "It's the increased risk of broken arms and heart attacks, the parking and traffic issues. Look, nobody wants this event to be successful more than I do, but we can't screw up. And we don't have time to think through and accommodate all the mitigating circumstances."

"I could hire an event coordinator I know," Nash said.

"That would work," Ethan said.

"Someone you're boning?" Remi asked. "Or someone we have to pay?"

"I'm not *sleeping* with her," Nash said. "I've hired her the last two years for my office holiday party."

"Then it's an expense we can't afford," his twin said.

"We'll cover it," Ethan said. "Better safe than sorry."

Affection rushed through her. She loved working with

these guys. They were honest, genuine, good people. And they always took the time to think through issues and make smart decisions.

"Thank you." She gave him a warm smile. "So, if we have the event coordinator, are you all in?"

Remi sat forward, setting his arms on the table. "I'm in. But it doesn't change the fact that we still come off looking like assholes."

"Agreed," Nash said. "Everyone who bought a ticket and made reservations with us? They're going to get here and find out the concert's moved to Blue Sky, and we're hosting a Battle of the Bands instead." His expression said *Not cool.*

"Take that up with Stuart. There's not a damn thing I can do about that." She reached into her bag for a pen. "At least the people who planned their vacations around the reunion concert will still get it. They can't slam us for not delivering. And without a doubt, Stuart sucks, but I'm not going to spend another minute thinking about him. I'm going to put on the best damn festival I can and hope the investors see that we're an awesome tourist destination."

"I like your attitude, Daze." Remi balled up the paper wrapper from his straw and rolled it between two fingers. "You're the best."

"You only say that because my mom gives you free churros." She grabbed one from the basket and shook it at him. She laughed when he snatched it out of her hand and took a big bite. "Okay, moving on. We need judges. And it can't be any of us since we're hosting it. Thoughts?"

"You thinking local?" Nash said. "Business owners?"

"No way." Remi put one end of the straw in his mouth and aimed it at Nash. "We go large. How about Miss Montana?"

"Thinkin' with your dick again," Ethan said.

Daisy wrote it down. "Actually, I think that's a great idea. How do we get a hold of her?"

"Can't be too hard. I'm on it." Remi shot out his spit ball.

Nash clapped a hand to his cheek. "You fucknut. That's disgusting."

"Pay attention, man." Ethan leaned forward. "We've got to settle this."

Wiping the soggy wad of paper off his face, Nash sat up and reached over to Ethan. "Here, let me put his saliva on *your* face. See how you like it."

Ethan grabbed Nash's wrist before it touched him, twisting it away. "I assume Cooper will be one since the winner's going to open for his band?"

"I haven't talked to him, but yes, I'm sure he'd want that. So, that's two."

"But isn't he inviting some bands?" Remi said.

"He's inviting lots of bands," she said. "He doesn't know any of them."

When Nash settled back down, he rubbed his napkin on the damp patch.

"You know who'd be good?" Ethan's interest made Daisy happy. He was on board. "Buddy Mercer."

"Oh, yeah, that dude's awesome," Remi said.

"The rodeo clown?" Daisy wrote his name alongside the other two. "That's a good one. I like it. So, that's three. We either stop there or add two more. Can't have an even number." She looked to Ethan. "What about your NFL friends? Would any of them come out here for this?"

"I could ask."

"You realize we have to pay all these people," Nash

said. "So, now we're talking about an event planner *and* judges. This is going to add up."

"We don't have a choice," Ethan said. "You know that."

The guys turned somber.

"I could talk to some of the guys I work with," Nash said. "Get some money together."

"No." Ethan balled up his napkin. "Thank you, but you know where I stand on that."

Nash had offered to go to his friends in the tech industry before, but Ethan wouldn't build the resort with pity money. He'd only do it with shareholders. A portfolio of wealthy investors from all over the country would guarantee well-heeled ambassadors promoting the project. That wasn't something well-meaning friends and family could buy.

Daisy believed in this project with all her heart, and not because she had a five percent ownership in it. The ranch sat on prime recreational land—over a thousand acres backing up to the Bitterroot Mountains and bisected by the Gallatin River. The property offered just about every kind of outdoor activity imaginable.

"We don't have to pay them cash," Remi said. "We can give them spa days or adventure weekends."

"We don't have a spa," Ethan said.

"Once the resort's built we will," Remi said.

"No, I bet we can get away without paying them." Daisy jotted the idea down. "This event will be good exposure." *If Mickelson Media's still on-board.* God, she hoped so.

"True." Ethan sat back when the waitress refilled the coffee mugs.

"So, Nash you'll talk to your event coordinator. Remi, you'll get a hold of Miss Montana?"

"With pleasure." Remi reached for the last churro, just as Nash snatched the basket away. He threw his twin a look that said *Really?* Nash smiled.

"And Ethan, you'll find Buddy and talk to some of your football friends?"

"Sure."

"Hey, Daze, are you going to enter?" Remi asked.

"Me?" She tore open a sugar packet and tipped the contents into her mug. "Of course not. The bands entering are one step away from a contract with a major label."

"Yeah, but you're awesome." Nash took the last churro. "You bring the house down every time."

"Thank you. But I can't take a serious band's spot, you know? This could make someone's career. I already have mine." She tapped her pen on the notebook. "Okay, give me a few more suggestions."

Nash's phone buzzed, and he read the screen. "I gotta go." He reached into his back pocket and pulled out his wallet. He tossed several bills on the table.

"Hang on. We're not done." Daisy didn't like the edge in her voice. Now that the idea had become a reality, she had to actually pull it off.

Nash slid out of the booth. "We'll think of some more judges."

She shook her head. "Guys, I'm pitching this idea to Mickelson tomorrow morning. I'm not going to tell him we've got some vague ideas."

"She's right," Ethan said.

"I have to pitch a complete package. So, give me a few more ideas, and let's line up everyone as soon as possible."

"Cooper, Miss Montana, Buddy Mercer, and some thick-necked NFL goon." Remi flashed his older brother a smile.

"Nice recap," Ethan said. "But that's an even number, and we'll need alternatives in the likely case that one of them says no."

"You know what we should do?" Remi said. "Whoever scores the biggest name judge gets Eagle's Landing."

Nash froze. Ethan stopped chewing.

Of all the thousand plus acres of spectacular Blackstock land, there was one section so beautiful, so perfectly situated at the top of the valley, that everyone coveted it. But which of the brothers should get it? And they didn't want to use it for the resort. It was too special. Too unique.

"But it has to be A-list-actor-big." Remi seemed oblivious to his brothers' reaction. "Not some no-name third string quarterback who wants to come out here and hook up with Miss Montana."

"We're not giving up that land over a stupid bet," Ethan said.

"So, what're we gonna do with it?" Remi said. "Just let it sit there? Someone's got to build on it—let's just pull the trigger already."

Ethan sat deceptively still. "I've got a hell of a lot more on my mind right now than who gets Eagle's Landing."

Fear jolted her. Because if they didn't pull off this event, not only would her mom and godfathers lose their savings, but the Blackstocks could lose the land altogether. She wanted to reach for his hand and promise him everything would work out, but she couldn't.

She didn't know what would happen, only that she'd

do everything in her power to make the festival a smashing success.

"Well, there's not going to *be* a lodge if we don't get the money," Remi said. "So, what's more important than the outcome of this event?"

"Come up with another incentive," Ethan said. "We're not giving Eagle's Landing away to someone who comes up with another judge."

"Not just a judge," Remi said. "Someone with name recognition. Come on, Buddy's great, but it's not like Mickelson's going to know who he is. What better incentive than Eagle's Landing?"

Nash glanced up from his phone. "I have to go. Are we done here?"

"One more judge," Ethan said. "Come on."

Movement out the window caught her attention, and she turned to see Cooper on the town green surrounded by his entourage. Carrie Levitt stood right beside him. With his shoulder-length dark hair gleaming in the sunlight, his inked body, the leather bracelets and rocker swagger, he sucked every thought and worry out of her mind. All she could see was him. She could still feel his hands on her ass, his lusty squeezes.

Watching his easy banter with his fans reminded her of all the images she'd seen of him in the media over the past few years. He was in his element. He loved his life.

Of course, he doesn't want to be in Snowberry.

A couple of teenagers raced over to him, waving their phones. He nodded, and then one of the girls pushed up against him for a selfie. Carrie ducked behind the duo, photobombing them.

"That him?" Nash asked.

"Yes." Flustered, Daisy turned her attention back to the table. "That's Cooper."

Ethan leaned over to see out the window. "You sure we want to mix with him?"

"Why wouldn't we?"

"Because we can't afford any fuck-ups."

"He's *helping* us."

Ethan tipped his chin, and Daisy turned to see even more people surrounding Cooper. "All I see in the press about him is drugs, booze, and groupies."

"Are you serious? The guys in Shout! are *still* in the media for drug and domestic abuse arrests, and you didn't have a problem with them. Blue Fire had one band member with a drug problem, and they fired him. The whole reason they're looking for a new opening act is that the last one was out of control. What's your problem with Cooper?"

Ethan and his brothers shared a look.

"What? Just say it."

Ethan let out an exasperated breath. "He was a druggie, Daze. Everyone knew that."

"Drugs? Are you…what in the world are you talking about? I was around him almost every single day in the music program for four years. He didn't do drugs."

"Daisy." Ethan's tone brooked no argument. "He did."

Nash looked up from his phone. "We saw."

"You saw him do drugs?" Her tone let them know she didn't believe them.

"Yeah," Remi said. "We did."

"Okay, this is ridiculous. You are so wrong about him that you're pissing me off. Cooper's a good guy." On the lawn, Cooper held his coffee cup aloft, as he smiled for more selfies. "You should be thanking him for saving our asses." She tossed her pen and notebook in the tote and nudged Ethan to get out of the booth. "Not badmouthing him."

"Hey, where are you going?" Remi asked. "I thought you wanted more judges?"

"I'm going to save him."

Ethan got out. "Not sure he's looking to be saved, Daze."

"He has work to do, and he's too nice to say no to his fans." She hitched the tote onto her shoulder. "You guys make those calls to the judges, think of a few more, and then we'll meet back up tonight."

"Barbecue at my place?" Ethan said.

"Perfect. See you then."

With a wave to her mom behind the bakery counter, Daisy headed out into the bright sunshine and dashed across the street to the green. When she saw Cooper with his arms wrapped around blonde twins, letting them each press a kiss to his cheek for the camera, she slowed.

What Ethan said had stung, but he'd called it. Cooper didn't need saving from something he so obviously enjoyed. *Okay, forget it.* She pulled out her phone to text him that she was heading back to the resort. *Carrie* could give him a ride when he was ready.

"Daisy?" The mayor called out in his raspy voice as he jogged toward her.

"Hey, Stuart." He was the last person she wanted to see.

His bombastic energy rattled the air around her. "Hey, how's it goin'? Wanna make sure we're all right."

She glanced to the picture window of the Sugar Bowl, where the Blackstock brothers laughed together. "I'm busy Stuart. Did you need something?"

"I do, yeah. I need you to get me a list of all the guests who bought tickets to the show. I got a buddy, owns a limo business. He's gonna get us a bunch of party buses. That way, we can run all the guests out to Blue Sky for the concert. We'll stock 'em with champagne, give everyone the VIP experience. Great idea, right? Party buses?"

As if she'd help him. She dug into her bag for her keys as she headed to the car. "I've got my own event to worry about, so you'll have to handle the arrangements for your concert."

Energy bristling off him, he stepped in front of her. "What event are you talkin' about?"

"We're hosting a Battle of the Bands."

He noticeably relaxed. "Yeah?" His tone said, *Really, Daze? That's lame.*

But that was good. She didn't want to get him riled up about it. Knowing him, he'd view her event as competition and then go around badmouthing it. "See you later, Stuart. I've got a ton of work to do."

"Well, hang on. You still need to figure out a way to let your guests know about the party buses. You could email 'em or put up flyers."

"I don't know who bought tickets to your show. I only know who books a room at the ranch."

"Yeah, okay. So just put up some flyers."

"Since the ranch isn't hosting the event, we won't be putting up flyers. But you can do it." She gestured to the town hall corkboard and started to move around him.

"Don't be a bitch."

A shock ripped through her. She spun back around. "Don't you *ever* talk to me like that. You made this mess, and it's yours to clean up."

"You're right, you're right. I'm sorry." His tone softened slightly. "But you gotta know, it's not like I wanted it to go down this way."

"I don't care what you wanted. I only know you let us down." Though, truthfully, she liked Cooper's idea so much more.

"Yeah, well, it is what it is, and now we gotta deal with it."

"I'm dealing with my end, and you're going to have to deal with yours. Get your manager to help."

"I don't like you bein' pissed at me. You know, the only reason you want the show at the ranch is to drum up investor money. Well, my friends have money. I'll get 'em to donate. Give me a figure and I'll make it happen."

She didn't have time for Stuart's nonsense. "I'm not interested in donations." Just as she turned away from him, she noticed a big, tall rock star striding toward her.

Cooper looked like he was going to knock Stuart to the ground, whisk her off her feet, and carry her to his lair. And that intensity—the clear intention to protect her—just did something to her. Something primal that called up every feminine instinct she had.

"Hey." Cooper looked between them, a determined air about him. "What's up?"

She wanted to throw herself into his arms and whisper, *Can we go back to my office and finish what we started? Only maybe start from the beginning?* Instead, she focused on business. "The meeting went well. We got the green light."

Behind him, the fans had dispersed, except for Carrie who kept an eye on Cooper. Was she waiting for him? Did they have plans? Just as jealousy started its ugly twist through her, it hit her that Cooper was with Carrie *again*. After he'd taken Daisy up against the wall in her office, he'd gone right back to another woman.

Are you a slow learner or what?

He did the same thing last night. He'd kissed her like a lover on her porch, and then he'd spent the night with Carrie and her friends. So what if he hadn't *kissed* Carrie—he'd still been with her.

He was *still* with her.

Rock star, remember?

What a fun vacation this must be, so many willing women. And she couldn't even be angry with him because she'd thrown herself at him from the very start. Telling him about her crush, touching him every chance she got. *Coming apart in his arms in my office.*

She felt completely stupid that she'd handed over the reins to the sixteen-year-old girl that still lived inside her and still crushed on Cooper Hood.

Well, she'd let her teenage self out to play for a bit—and it had been *good*—but she was done. "Okay, fellas, I have to get going." She focused on Cooper. "I assume you'll get a ride back on your own?"

"I'm with you, cinnabun." Cooper gave her his easygoing smile.

Cinnabun? She wanted to tell him what he could do with his nickname, but she didn't. Because it was cute. And she liked it.

And there she was, losing her head again.

"See you later, Stuart."

Just as she and Cooper were about to take off, the mayor said, "Well, hang on a sec. So, what all's involved in this Battle of the Bands?"

A Jeep sailed by, and someone shouted, "Cooper Hood." Cooper waved. "We'll have six bands competing for the top prize of opening for Blue Fire's national tour."

"Really?" Stuart's nostrils flared as he gave a forced

smile. He eyed Daisy meaningfully as if she'd misled him. "You gonna modify your permit for that?"

Oh, no, you don't. She wouldn't let him throw a wrench in their plans. "I *can*, but it's not necessary. We always have bands playing throughout the festival. You know that."

Stuart nodded. "Sure, sure. As a musician myself, I love the idea." He looked thoughtful. "'Course as mayor, I've got to put on another hat. These aren't local bands, right?" He smacked Cooper's shoulder. "You're not gonna have Earl and the Stingrays openin' for you." He snickered. "So, these bands you've got comin' are from out of town? Bringin' fans, roadies, that kind of thing? Makes me think about security, waste management. Food, lodging. Stuff like that."

Damn him. Lodging could be a problem. "We've got that figured out." Well, they would. They'd handle everything. "I'm going to write up an article for the paper, so I'll be sure to put out the call for local homeowners who want to rent out rooms or garage apartments. It won't be a problem."

"The bands I'm inviting will be coming in buses and vans," Cooper said. "They won't want to pay for hotels."

"Good point," Daisy said.

"And their fans won't bother coming all the way out here, considering they get to see them play in their hometown every week. So, it should be pretty chill." While his features remained completely relaxed, Cooper's gaze sharpened. "We're not changing much. Just doing what we can to keep the event on the property. Isn't that what you all wanted?"

Daisy could tell Stuart got Cooper's message by the way his lip started to curl into a sneer. "We'll leave it in the hands of the Zoning Commission. They'll evaluate your new proposal." Stuart gave a sleazy smile. "I'm sure it'll go your way."

Zoning commission? That would take weeks. "We don't have time for that, Stuart." Which he obviously knew. "We're already adding some fencing and more Port-a-Potties. We're addressing all the concerns."

"Do you consider traffic issues on 191? Different crowd for a Battle of the Bands. We gotta consider emergency personnel, vending issues. But let's not sweat it right now. Let the commission do its job. I'm sure it'll all work out."

"*Stuart.* We've been hosting the Huckleberry Festival for years, and we've done a great job. You've praised us in the past for how well we've run it. We're even hiring an event coordinator this year to make sure everything runs smoothly."

"Then what're we talkin' about? You shouldn't have any problems with the commission." He slapped Cooper's shoulder. "Hey, sorry we didn't get a chance to jam. You leavin' today?"

Cooper shrugged. "Thought I'd stick around. Since I'm helping with the event."

The mayor's smile faltered. "You're playin' the festival?"

Oh, this is good. "He's going to be the MC." The idea had just come to her, and she liked it a lot. Way better than him being a judge.

The flash of ugliness in Stuart's eyes set her into action. "Listen, we've got a ton of work to do if we're going to pull off this event. We'll see you later."

"Well, now, don't get too deep into it. Not 'till you hear from Zoning."

"We're not worried," Cooper said. "They're going to be

real happy with the private security we're hiring." He waved to Stuart over his shoulder as they headed off to the car.

"Did you just lie to the mayor?" she asked quietly.

"Nope. You know Carly Demetrios?"

"Of course." *Whale's daughter*.

"She and her mom stopped to take a picture. They wanted to know how long I was in town, and I told them about the event. She started asking questions."

Daisy liked where this was going. Whale's wife was a cop.

"Said she could get us some off-duty cops to help out."

She smiled. "That's brilliant." But then she thought of the cost.

"What just happened?" he asked.

"What do you mean?"

"The light went out of your eyes when I mentioned the off-duty cops."

"Oh, no, it's just…it's a great idea, but it might be too expensive."

"I got this."

"No. Absolutely not. You're not paying for anything."

"It would give me great pleasure to shut Stuart down. I don't like the way he looks at you, talks to you, or treats you."

And this was why she lost her head around him. "Thank you." Her impulse was to touch him, but she stopped herself. Did he treat Carrie with this kind of consideration?

"Coop. Wait up."

Speak of the she-devil. Blonde and blue-eyed, Carrie was a boldly sexual woman. And she partied hard. The ideal woman for a rock star.

They both turned, waiting for her to catch up.

"Why do you look at her like that?" Cooper asked.

"Because she's a bitch."

His eyes widened in surprise.

"You seriously don't remember her in high school?" she asked.

"I'm sure we have very different memories."

Carrie waved, as she sashayed over to them in her jean skirt and flip flops.

"She was horrible to me. I developed early, and in middle school, she called me Boobalicious. And then in high school…" Really? She was going to share her ugly high school stories about his hookup? "Never mind. It's ancient history."

Daisy hit the keypad and unlocked the Camaro. "I've got a bunch of work to do right now, so go ahead and hang out in town if you want."

He seemed concerned. "What do you have to do?"

"A bunch of things."

"Like?" He sounded impatient.

"Well, first, I have to do is come up with some more judges. As soon as I have them, I'll write the article for the paper. I want to have as much impact as possible."

"Hey, there. Where you off to?" Perspiration shone on Carrie's forehead.

"We're working," Cooper said, and not all that nicely.

"I'm heading to the ranch," Daisy said. "But you two can hang out."

"I got him." Carrie gazed up at him, a promise in her blue eyes. "I'll bring him back later."

At that moment, Daisy *hated* that she'd let him touch her. Because for the next two weeks she'd get to watch him touching all kinds of women.

Okay, she hadn't *let* him do anything. She'd wanted everything they'd done. No regrets. She'd made out with the guy she'd fantasized about for a good four years. *Leave it at that.*

"I'm going with Daisy." All the playfulness had left his voice. "I'll be working with her for the next two weeks, so I'll see you around, Carrie."

Wait, what just happened?

For a moment, Carrie looked like he'd slapped her. But she recovered quickly. "Let me give you my cell number. When you take a break, we can go for a hike or have dinner. We'll find something to do."

"That's okay." Cooper got into the car. "See you around."

Chapter Eight

Daisy checked her rearview mirrors before pulling away from the curb. "Why'd you shut her down like that?"

"She was a bitch to you."

"Yes, in *high school*."

"Nobody puts baby in a corner."

She laughed. "Oh, my God, rock stars don't quote *Dirty Dancing*."

"Do you know how many women I live with? I can't grab a cold one from the kitchen without passing through a living room filled with women bawling their eyes out over some rom-com. And forget high school, Carrie ignored you today. That's not cool."

Her body warmed at his sense of loyalty to her. Made her want more from him than he could ever give. "Hey, we don't get many celebrities around here. You can't blame her for going for the gusto."

"The town'll be filled with rockers in ten days. She can grab her gusto then. I'm not interested in Carrie."

"Ah. So, you're a one-and-done kind of guy. Got it."

He reared back with an almost comically shocked expression. "What's that supposed to mean?"

"Never mind." *Stop making him uncomfortable.* "Look, you're here for two weeks. I don't want it weird between us just because we had a little nookie in my office. It was…"

"It was what?" His tone held a challenge.

"It was nothing."

"You didn't sound like it was nothing."

"Cooper." She smacked his shoulder.

"What? If it was nothing, I didn't do it right."

"Oh, you did it right. You did it better than…" *Shut your trap—God!* "My point is that you're here for two weeks, and I don't want you uncomfortable around me when you're…"

"When I'm what?" He didn't look the least bit amused.

"I'm totally cool with you—"

"Having nookie with other women, yes, I got it." Why did he sound angry?

"We had a little flirtation. Got it out of our system. Now we can just be friends." She felt his gaze but wouldn't look at him. He didn't need to see that she was full of it.

"You kiss your friends like that?" he asked.

"No. I'm not saying…God, why are you…" She let out a huff of breath. "I'm trying to make this easier for you."

"So, I can hook up with Carrie." He shook his head.

"And others. Your friends were pretty worn out when they left your cabin this morning."

"And 'worn out' is a euphemism for satisfied sexually?" He tipped his head back and blew out a breath. "So, that's what I did last night. I had an orgy."

"Didn't you?"

"Daisy, I'd just had the kiss of a lifetime with you. Did

you really think I'd go from that to *Carrie*?" He shot her a look. *Are you serious right now?* "And that I'd touch you like I did in your office the morning after an orgy?" With both hands, he scrubbed his face. "Don't you get it? I fucking respect the hell out of you."

Eight simple words, carried by bluebirds, then draped around her like a shawl. Nobody had ever made her feel so special. "I'm sorry. I shouldn't have jumped to conclusions." *But thank you for telling me what that kiss meant to you because you just filled my soul with the glow of a million blazing stars.*

"Look, I like you," he said. "Probably more than I should, and I would hate if things got weird between us. I also don't think you and I can have *nookie* and then pretend like nothing happened. We've got some serious work to do while I'm in town, and if we're going to pull it off, we need to stay focused. Let's just keep things in the work zone."

Why did that sound as satisfying as gluten-free bread? Or sugar-free cookies? No-salt pancakes, for God's sake.

But she thought about her mom and her godfathers, about the ranch being leveraged, and she realized Cooper was right. She couldn't afford any mess-ups, and if a kiss and one humping session turned her inside-out, what would sex with him do?

"You're right." When the Blackstock Ranch sign came into view, she flicked her turn signal. "Okay, then. Back to business. As I mentioned, we have to get judges. Remi's going to call Miss Montana, and Ethan's looking into a rodeo clown who's really popular around here. He's also going to ask some of his football friends. We thought you could be one, but I like the idea of you as MC better. Which means we need at least two more. And they need to have huge name-recognition which, given that we're talking about a Battle of the Bands in Snowberry, Montana, seems insane." Her tone said, *Amiright?*

"Someone like the governor?"

"*Exactly* like the governor. God, Cooper, that's perfect because the Blackstocks contributed to her campaign." Excitement bubbled through her, washing away her silly romantic issues. She ignored the death glare from her inner teenager because she was a woman, the manager of a ranch that she was trying to turn into a five-star resort. And she had an amazing event to plan. "Do you even realize how you've saved us? I don't want to think where we'd be if you hadn't come home this weekend."

Without thinking, she reached for Cooper's hand, curled her fingers around it, and squeezed. She smiled at him, wanting to share the moment, but the look in his eyes—the *longing*—only reignited that damn spark.

She pulled her hand back.

She *had* to stop touching him.

Laughter and conversation drifted over the fence, and the lights from Ethan's backyard cast a yellow glow on the dew-dampened lawn. As usual in the mountains, the air held a chill that made Daisy wish she'd worn a sweater.

Cooper had been quiet for most of the walk over. But then, he was about to have dinner with his *brothers*. Not that they knew about it. Worse, he'd have to pretend Hunter was nothing more than a guy helping with the Battle of the Bands.

"This is going to be weird, isn't it?" It seemed wrong not to tell them.

"Yep." He glanced ahead as if imagining the scene on

the other side of the fence. "But I'm here representing my band and my label, and the only thing I want to focus on is pulling off this event. I don't want any distractions right now."

Two weeks was a long time to hold onto a secret of this magnitude.

"Daisy." Just outside the gate, he grasped her arm. "I'm serious. I don't want you saying anything."

"I know that. I wouldn't do that to you."

"But you were thinking about it."

She broke into a scowl. "How do you read me so well?"

"I've spent a lot of time watching you."

She leaned in and gave him a saucy smile. "And now you've done more than watch. You've actually kissed me."

His nostrils flared, and the air crackled around them. "Daisy."

"What?" She kind of liked riling him up.

"If we're going to keep things uncomplicated, you can't say things like that."

"What, things like kissing?"

He drew in a breath, gazing somewhere over her shoulder. "Yeah, Daze. Like kissing."

"We're just talking about it."

"I don't think you get it." His gaze swung back to her with a directness that startled her. "I've wanted you for more than half my life."

She drew in a sharp breath, her heart singing. *I want you, too*. But just as she leaned into him, he released her. "Come on. Let's get through this dinner."

"Sure." She took one step, and the leather sole of her sandal slid on the damp grass. Cooper caught her upper arm before she ass-planted.

Catching her around the waist, he pulled her up against him. "I got you, cinnabun."

The heat of his body chased away the chill, and her senses opened up to the unique scent of him.

He unlatched the gate, holding it open for her.

"We don't have to stay long." She passed through.

"Doesn't make a damn bit of difference. It'll only be awkward if they know who I am. Otherwise, it's all business."

She walked ahead of him along the narrow stone pathway that ran along the side of Ethan's cabin and opened to his backyard. An ex-girlfriend had placed fairy lights along the fence and gazebo. The white light reflected off the colorful glass garden stakes she'd placed around the perimeter of the lawn, making them wink and sparkle.

Nash, tall and striking with his broad back and thick hair, manned the barbecue beside a beautifully put-together woman.

"Hey, Daze." The screen door snapped shut, and Remi came out with boxes of crackers and cans of cheese.

"You're kidding me, right?" Daisy pulled a can from under his arm.

With a lazy smile, the adventure guide set the food down before grabbing a bottle of beer out of the cooler by the back door. "You said to bring cheese and crackers."

"Thanks for holding the door open, asshat." Using his bare foot, Ethan nudged the screen open. After dumping hamburger and hot dog buns and bottles of ketchup, mustard, and relish on the sturdy picnic table, he turned back to close it. "Is that squeeze cheese? I love that shit." He grabbed a can, unwound the protective seal, and popped the top off. Tipping his head back, he squirted a string of bright orange cheese into his mouth.

"I haven't had that since I was a kid." Nash grabbed a box of crackers and neatly opened it. He held one out for Remi, who squeezed out a blast of cheese. "More."

"There's not that much in here."

"It looks like a bird shit on his cracker," Ethan said.

Remi held the can to his mouth, trying not to crack up as he sprayed the cheese. His twin tried to grab the can, but Remi twisted away.

"There's one can for each of us." Ethan tossed one to Nash.

Daisy reached for a cracker. "When I said cheese, I meant something nice. Like Brie."

"Brie tastes like dirty underwear." Remi took a pull from his beer bottle.

"I'm not going to ask how you know what dirty underwear tastes like," Nash said.

Noticing Cooper's silence, Daisy stepped back to include him. "Guys, you remember Cooper Hood."

"Hey, man." Nash reached out a hand. "Good to meet you."

"We lucked out that he happens to be in town this weekend," she said. "He's totally saving our bacon with this event."

"I've got my own reasons." Cooper shook Remi's hand. "Glad they align with yours."

"Let me introduce you to our event coordinator." Nash turned and waved his friend over.

The tall, elegant woman set down the tongs and made her way over to the wooden deck. The moment she caught sight of Cooper—all big, hot, and inked—her gaze lingered. A tendril of possessiveness wound through Daisy, as she watched color flood the woman's cheeks on her approach.

"This is Laura Kincaid," Nash said. "She's agreed to take on our project."

"So nice to meet you, Laura," Daisy said. "Thanks so much for working with us on such short notice."

"I've been coming to this festival since I was a little girl," Laura said. "So, I'm thrilled to be part of it. Nash caught me up on the situation with Stuart, but I'm hoping you can give me a better sense of how the competition will be run."

"Absolutely." Daisy reached for Cooper's arm. "But it's his brainchild, so I'll let him answer."

"We'll have a total of six bands," Cooper said. "Three play Friday, the other three on Saturday. They'll start at noon and finish up at seven, in time for the main show to begin at eight." He waited while everyone nodded their agreement. "At the end of each day, the judges will choose a winner. And then, on Sunday, the two winners will battle it out. Sound good?"

"Sounds terrific," Laura said.

"So, what's the next step with you?" Ethan asked the event planner.

"I'll need to sit down with you guys and go over your plans. It's possible you've already got everything figured out, so the least I can do is give you the confidence that no monsters are going to pop up. And the most I can do is fill in any gaps I might find."

"She's got enough experience with big events to know how many Port-a-Potties and food stalls we'll need," Nash said. "That kind of thing."

"Speaking of which," Daisy said. "This morning Cooper talked to Whale's wife about security, and she's going to hook us up with some off-duty cops."

When all eyes turned on Cooper with appreciation,

Daisy smiled. *This is so good.* Working with Cooper would lay the groundwork for accepting him into their family. They'd see he was a really good guy.

"Off the top of your head," Daisy began. "Is there anything you can think of that we need to consider?" She needed to hit the ground running Monday morning.

"Honestly, I've always been a little nervous about the river." Laura gestured toward the house, which sat a quarter of a mile from the Gallatin. "I don't know if you've considered it in your development plans, but it might be a good idea at some point to put up some fencing, keep the kids and pets safe."

"I'm adding some already, but you're talking about the entire length of it?" Daisy didn't know if they could pull that off in two weeks.

"Along the festival grounds, yes. You've hired me to make sure your revised permit gets approved, so I'm looking at every possibility. Temporary fencing is just one safety precaution Stuart can't get you on."

"Can't believe that bastard did this to us." Nash headed back to the grill to flip the burgers and hot dogs.

Laura set her beer bottle on the table. "I'd also like to get started on some press releases." Her gaze flicked over to Cooper. "When can the three of us get together and work on them?"

Daisy couldn't help glancing at Cooper to get a read on his response to the beautiful woman, but his demeanor didn't betray even a hint of interest. "I've got calls to make in the morning." She reached for Cooper. "What do you and Hunter have planned for auditions?"

"Actually, he's trying to set some up tonight," Cooper said. "My Austin friends are already talking to the bands I liked, seeing if they want to come out here."

Affection swept through her. She *loved* working with him. He was on top of everything. "So should we meet mid-morning?" she asked Laura.

"Perfect."

Yes. She was just so flipping happy. While the others carried on the conversation, she turned toward Cooper, shutting them out. "We're actually going to pull this off."

"We are." He gazed down at her with a sweet expression. "Not gonna let you down, Daze."

He had no idea the power of those words. They delivered an equal rush of warmth—because, of course, she wanted to believe him—and frustration because people let each other down all the time. She'd much rather rely on herself, and then if people came through on their promises, awesome, but if not, she had everything covered.

But the way he looked at her—the message in his eyes that said *I know what you're thinking and you can just stop. I've got this* —told her he really did understand.

Sometimes she had to remind herself how little she knew him, because her heart, her soul, felt powerfully connected to him.

"Okay." Ethan's voice snapped through their personal bubble like a whip. "Next on the agenda. Judges."

"I sent an email to the Miss Montana website," Remi said. "But I have a buddy who went to the same high school as her, so I've asked for her contact info, just in case the organization takes too long getting the message to her."

Daisy was relieved that they all seemed to understand the urgency. "That's great."

"Buddy Mercer's on board," Ethan said. "Joe's brother is the Stock Contractor for the Rodeo Circuit Board, and he got a hold of him for me."

"Seriously?" Daisy said. "I didn't know that."

"I'll talk to the governor's office tomorrow." Nash aimed his spatula at Cooper. "Good idea."

Remi elbowed Cooper. "So. Blue Fire."

Expression wary, Cooper nodded. She didn't know if he simply didn't trust these guys or if he couldn't look at them without thinking of his secret.

"Did you guys know Blue Fire won two Grammys this year?" She wanted to ease his discomfort.

"Daze." He just shook his head.

Nash nodded appreciatively from the grill. "That's cool."

Remi gave a chin nod to his twin. "He doesn't listen to rock."

Ethan joined them. "But only because he can't hear anything over the sound of his latest girlfriend."

"Don't start," Nash said.

"What?" Remi said. "You think because you live in the woods, no one can hear? Believe me, people on the space station can hear her."

"Okay, we're not talking about this." Nash stabbed a barbecue fork into a hot dog and transferred it to the ceramic platter.

"Sorry, Nash, but Remi's not wrong." Daisy bit back her laughter. "I've heard her, too."

Nash shook his head and turned his back on them.

"Seriously, dude," Remi said. "I came by to drop off those kiwis. I was standing on your porch." He tipped his head back, hands caressing in circles over his chest, and made high-pitched over-the-top orgasmic sounds.

Ethan started cracking up. Nash turned and watched them for a long moment before giving Cooper a chin nod. "They're not used to women making sounds during sex."

"Oh, hey."

Everyone turned to the familiar voice.

With a canvas grocery bag in one hand, Hunter closed the gate behind him. "Sorry I'm late." He saw Cooper and stopped abruptly. "You're...I thought..." His gaze moved slowly over each of his sons, concern etched on his brow.

"What's up, Dad?" Remi lifted his beer in salute.

"Just in time." Nash handed the platter of burgers and hot dogs to Laura and then reached for an empty plate. "Dinner's ready."

But Hunter watched Cooper carefully. "I thought you didn't want to tell them."

Cooper stiffened, shooting the man a look of warning.

"Tell us what?" Remi looked between his dad and Cooper.

"No, it's good." Hunter must have misunderstood Cooper's message. "I'm glad you did. I want them to know." He approached his sons, his features wrought with trepidation. "You guys okay with this? I know it's a lot to take in, and I'm sure you have questions. I'll answer them. I'll tell you anything you want to know."

Oh, God. "Hunter."

At her tone, he jerked toward her.

"We're talking about judges." She turned to the brothers. "Any more ideas?"

Ethan stalked closer to his dad. "What do you want us okay with?"

"Dad?" Nash lowered his beer.

"Jesus." Cooper glared at Hunter. "Not now. I *told* you."

"Told him what?" Ethan snapped out each word.

Hunter pulled in a sharp breath. "I'm sorry." His gaze

shifted between the brothers. "I thought…you're here with them. I assumed…"

"What?" Ethan asked. "Just say it."

Oh, dammit, dammit, dammit. This is not the way for them to find out.

Underneath Cooper's anger churned a desperation that absolutely killed her. How could she help him? Obviously, she couldn't put the horse back in the barn, but she had to do *something*. "I think maybe Cooper and I should give you guys a chance to talk."

All at once, Cooper straightened, his shoulders pushing back. "*I'll* leave." He gave a curt salute.

"Hang on, son." With a stricken expression, Hunter grabbed his shoulder and pulled him back.

"*What* did you just call him?" Ethan said.

Daisy braced for the impact.

"He didn't mean it like that." Remi laughed, but his gaze flicked from Hunter to Cooper. "Right, Dad?"

Resignation hit Cooper's features, and with a nod, he gave Hunter the go-ahead.

The tension lifted from Hunter as he announced, "He's my son."

All three brothers startled as if a gun had fired. But, honestly, thank God Hunter had sounded proud to be Cooper's father.

Laura touched Daisy's shoulder and leaned in. "I should go." She gave it a pat. "Let's talk tomorrow."

"Okay." But she couldn't tear her attention off the family.

With a quick wave, Laura headed toward the gate.

"How about you explain what the fuck's going on?" Ethan looked between his father and Cooper.

"He's my son. Your brother."

"Got that the first time you said it," Ethan said. "Now, how about explaining it?"

Remi stood there, the badass wilderness guide nowhere in sight. He looked like a little boy hiding in the corner as his parents fought.

Hunter gave Cooper a warm, supportive smile. "I just found out this morning."

"You found out Cooper Hood's your *son*?" Nash asked.

Accusing stares landed on Cooper, and Daisy shifted closer to him. "Guys, Cooper just found out, too."

"Is that why you're helping us with the festival?" Ethan asked. "Because you think you're a Blackstock now?"

Cooper jerked away from Hunter's touch. "I'm not a Blackstock, and this doesn't change anything. The only thing I care about is the competition."

"Okay, hang on," Hunter said. "Look, we're all a little shocked. Cooper and I haven't even had a chance to wrap our heads around it."

"How do you know it's true?" Nash asked.

All attention turned to Cooper. His dark hair and pale blue eyes didn't immediately link him with his half-brothers but seeing all of them together left no doubt at the shared genetic material.

"His mom told him," Hunter said. "But it doesn't matter because I know it's true."

"You can only know it's true if you were sleeping with two women at the same time." Ethan's lips curled in disgust. "You cheated on Mom?"

"You slept with the drug addict?" Nash asked.

"She's clean. She's been sober for four years." Cooper's stance told them to back off. "So, watch how you talk about her."

"How do we know if she's telling the truth?" Remi said. "He could be—"

"He's mine," Hunter said.

Daisy couldn't stand them attacking Cooper. "This is just as much of a surprise to Cooper. You know what happened last night, so you know he just found out."

All three brothers stood stiffly, obviously battling between anger, confusion, and hurt.

"Did you cheat on Mom?" Remi asked.

"No." But Hunter's confidence flagged.

Cooper finally broke away from the group. "I'm gonna let you guys work it out."

"Wait," Hunter called. "Hang on, okay?"

Cooper looked at the wall of Blackstock brothers. "This is none of my business." He strode away from the group.

Daisy took off after him. He needed to know this wasn't his fault, that if he gave them some time to wrap their head around it, they'd come around.

But the moment he unlatched the gate, he turned back to her. "No." He leaned closer. "This went exactly as I knew it would, which is why I didn't want them knowing. I'm not here for family or relationships or anything of this shit. I'm here for business. I don't want to be mean, Daze, but leave me alone."

As much as she wanted to go after him, she knew he needed time to process everything that had happened. She whirled around to the brothers. "Shame on you for making him feel like some dirty secret."

Ethan's features remained impassive. Remi looked wild, like he had no idea what to do, think, or feel.

Nash just stared at his dad. "How did this happen?"

"Your mom..." His jaw shut, and he looked down at

his boots. "Your mom and I were in the same band. We weren't dating, but we…"

"Hooked up." Ethan's tone was flat.

"Yes. We were on the road a lot. We…liked each other. But we weren't together. And one night after a gig, Ronnie…approached me." He swallowed, looking out to the lawn.

"Jesus, Dad, just say it," Ethan said. "We're not kids."

Hunter let out a breath. "She was waiting for me when I got off the stage. She was eager, and I was a twenty-three-year-old with a lot of adrenaline running through me after a show. It happened one time, and frankly, I forgot about it. I didn't even know her." He blew out a breath, raking fingers through his thick, white hair. "And then a couple months after that, your mom found out she was pregnant." He paused, looking thoughtful. "We'd known each other a long time. We were close. So, we got married." He looked to Ethan. "I wanted to do right by you."

"When did you figure out about Cooper?" Nash asked.

Hunter's gaze settled on the wall of trees just beyond the fence. "I saw him in the hallway at school. I wondered —there was something about him—so I went to see his mom, but she swore he was someone else's."

"Slider," Nash said.

"I started paying more attention to him, but with that dark hair and those strange blue eyes, I didn't…I wasn't sure. It ate at me because he sure as hell doesn't look like Slider." He clapped a hand at the back of his neck. "Your mom and I talked about it and decided we needed a paternity test, but Ronnie wouldn't do it. And Cooper wasn't eighteen, so our hands were tied. Of course, by the time he was the right age, he'd left town."

"This is so fucked up." Remi snatched the grapes off the platter, plucked one off, and lobbed it over the fence.

"Yeah, it is. But he's my *son*."

Tension snapped through the men. They rarely saw Hunter so stern. So unyielding.

"And he's your brother."

No one said a word.

"And as hard as this is, I expect you to treat him like one."

Chapter Nine

"Now I know why you're staying out there for two weeks," Ben said.

With a party raging in his cabin, Cooper had holed up in the bedroom so he could check in with Emmie, let her know where things stood with the competition. But his friend, the band's drummer, had grabbed the phone. "Yeah, to find a band."

"She's hot."

"Who's hot?" Cooper had to shout over the loud music. "I don't know what you're talking about." Sitting on the edge of the mattress, he listened to the laughter and conversation on the other side of the wall. He should be out there. As soon as he hung up, he'd join them. Shake off this foul mood.

"Your blonde hookup."

Blonde? Cooper grabbed his laptop from the nightstand and touched the mousepad. "I'm not here for some chick." Maybe one of the selfies he'd taken today with the tourists had gone viral. He couldn't imagine why. They'd all been pretty tame.

Opening up the Beatz website, he found a picture of himself on the homepage.

Blue Fire's Cooper Hood parties off the grid.

Surrounded by women, he smiled into Carrie Levitt's camera phone. She had her hand on his chest, her puckered lips on his cheek, and a look in her eyes that declared her *Property of Cooper Hood.*

The post had nearly a million views and a hundred thousand comments. He scanned the top ones to learn that he was apparently banging an old high school flame.

Carrie had obviously taken the shot the night before and sent it to the music industry news site.

"I'm not with her." Had Daisy seen it? There was nothing he could do about it if she had.

"Yeah, well, it looks like you're having a good time out there."

His mind flashed back to the horrified expressions of the Blackstocks when their father had revealed the truth. As if it sickened them to know Cooper was part of their sacred family. "Sure."

"So now that you've got this Battle of the Bands thing teed up, you don't need us to come out there?"

"I never asked you to come out here."

"I know that. Em just thought...never mind."

"No, what're you talking about?" He'd kept Emmie informed so she wouldn't worry. Had he unintentionally upset her by telling her about Stuart's shenanigans? "I've got this under control, man. It's all good. And you finally get time with Lee. I wouldn't even think about cock-blocking your ass."

"Appreciate that, man. It's just that before you came up with the idea for the competition, Em said you were gonna fly back to Montana and perform solo. I thought maybe you wanted us to come out and play with you."

"Hell, no." He wasn't that much of a selfish prick to cut short their break and work an event with him.

"Yeah, okay." Ben sounded strangely disappointed.

"So, how's it going?" He needed to snap out of this shitty mood. "Having a good time?"

"You should be here, but yeah, it's chill. Eating, hanging out, fucking."

He heard a woman shout, "Shut up," and then Ben said, "What? I'm not gonna lie to my best friend."

He liked that. *Best friend.* He liked that a fuck of a lot. Things were changing. He'd worried their friendship would suffer now that Ben and Lee, the keyboardist's sister, had gotten together. With Ben's party days behind him, where did Cooper fit in? "Look, man, I'll let you get back to your girl."

"Yeah, sounds like you've got a rager going on."

Last he'd seen, two women were making out on the coffee table, while a bunch of guys took videos with their phones. The music was so loud it sounded distorted through his bedroom wall. "Livin' the life, man."

"Now that you got things set up, you could fly out here," Ben said. "Hang out with us before you go back for the competition."

The desire to be with them flew up so sharply it hurt. But he had work to do. Bands to audition, arrangements to be made. It wasn't in the bag yet.

And no matter how much he hated this town, he couldn't ignore the drag of resistance when he thought of leaving. Because…*Daisy.* He wasn't ready to leave her. Not yet. "There's too much to do to get this thing off the ground."

"Okay, but if you want to come home for a few days…I'd even change your sheets."

"You had sex in my *bed*?"

Ben burst out laughing and ended the call.

"Fucker." Cooper smiled. Yeah, he wanted to hang with his bandmates, but he knew what it felt like to be the only single guy in a town with a four-digit population.

And yet here he was alone, locked in his bedroom, instead of out there partying.

Frankly, he'd only let them in because he hadn't wanted to be a giant asshole when he'd come back to find a dozen people hanging outside his cabin waiting for him.

Well, and because he'd still been reeling from the guys' reactions to Hunter's news. Of course, he'd expected it, but that didn't make actually experiencing it any easier. So now, instead of auditioning bands tonight, Hunter would have to deal with the grenade Slider had lobbed into the middle of his family.

What a mess. How did he get them to forget about the paternity issue and focus on the event? He'd have to convince them he didn't want anything from them. He just wanted to get through the festival and back to his life.

The life he'd had before Daisy had charged into it.

Daisy and all her kindness, her generosity and fierce spirit. For all the shit that had happened since he'd come to town, she was the one bright spot. And tonight, he'd pushed her away.

Leave me alone. He'd treated her badly. He had to fix it.

He got off the bed. It would be bad enough when she saw the picture of Carrie plastered all over him. He didn't want another one going viral with yet another woman. He never wanted to hurt Daisy.

Time to kick everyone out.

He opened the bedroom door to total chaos—people dirty-dancing, throwing back shots, snorting lines. He'd find the docking station and kill the music.

"Oh, hey, man." Some guy he'd never met grabbed him. "Daisy's here to see you. She's at the door."

Of course. Let's just slap a pickle on my shit sandwich. Thick with the humidity of too many bodies in motion, the living area smelled of beer and pizza. He pushed through the crowd to get to her.

Just as he passed the kitchen, he found a woman on the counter. One guy poured vodka on her stomach, while another sucked it out of her belly button.

Jesus Christ, it's Carrie. When did *she* get here?

And then, he turned to see Daisy, standing there amidst the drunken revelers, looking fresh and beautiful in her lavender sundress and silver sandals, her filmy wrap fluttering around her from the breeze coming in the open door. Awareness bloomed across his body.

He wanted this woman on a cellular level. It wasn't any one thing—it was *her*. Something in him recognized her. *My woman.*

When she spotted him, she didn't smile. Just waited patiently until he reached her. "Hey. Can I talk to you a sec?"

He nodded, ushering her outside and closing the door behind them. The cool air snapped him out of his funk. "What's up, Daze?" He tried to read her features, but she'd pretty much shut down.

"Hunter's—"

He held up a hand. "I don't want to hear about it." And he didn't. It was their family drama. Not his.

"—got two bands ready to audition at the Sugar Bowl right now."

"Why the hell didn't he tell me?"

"You don't have a ride, so I told him I'd come and get you. I assume you want to go."

Everything in him expanded, fresh air seeping in so he could breathe again. Having a purpose energized him. "Yeah, of course." Being around her made him happy.

A shriek of laughter came from inside the house. "You're welcome to bring your friends. I don't mind getting an audience reaction to their sound."

"I think you know they're not my friends. And, no, I don't want them to come." He shoved his key into his jeans pocket.

"You're going to let them party without you?"

"They won't even notice I'm gone."

Leaning against the wall with his arms folded across his chest, Cooper couldn't take his eyes off her.

On the Sugar Bowl's stage, Daisy belted out a Lone Justice song. Damn, that woman could sing. Her band had taken the stage after auditions ended, so they were just having fun. But there was just something about her—her positive energy, her beauty that glowed from within. Daisy was fresh air and wide-open Montana skies. She was sunshine and community.

That's exactly what she is. Community. She's everything that's good in this town.

He had to smile. No matter how many leather bands he'd worn or guitar picks he'd gone through, no matter how much money in his bank account or new ink that covered his skin, he was still just the boy who wanted Daisy Charbonneau.

She held onto the final note, taking it places most singers couldn't reach—except maybe Axl Rose. The moment the song ended, everyone broke into applause, whistling and stomping their feet.

As soon as Daisy and her bandmates left the stage, they clustered together at the bar. Standing on her toes, she hiked up on the counter to reach for something. When she came back down, she had a jar in one hand and a bright red cherry in the other. Her gaze drifted from the conversation, searching the room until it landed on him. And then her pink lips closed around the cherry, and she pulled it from the stem, licking the juice from her lips.

Blood rushed to his cock, making it throb. His body burned. His heart raced.

He wanted her. More than when he was a kid because this time, he'd gotten to really know her.

Hunter came up to him. "So, what did you think of the bands tonight?"

He tore his gaze from Daisy. "I liked the second one a lot. The first one probably wouldn't fit with our crowd."

"A little too country?"

"A little too quiet."

"Huh. I like them." Hunter seemed surprised.

"They're talented, but they don't have the stage presence for big stadiums."

"I guess I can see that. So, the second one's in?"

"Probably, but I don't want to commit to anyone yet. Let's get a list of possible contenders together and send their demos to my band, so they have a say in it. I'm all set with the bands in Austin, so once we finish these auditions, we'll look at all the talent and go from there."

Hunter nodded. "Sounds good. I've got three more acts coming in tomorrow, and then two more on Tuesday. Not bad, huh? The worst problem we've got is having too many to choose from."

We. What a strange word in the context of Hunter Blackstock. "Yeah, it's looking good." A surge of hope ran through him. He might just pull off this event.

"Listen, Cooper. I'm sorry for letting the cat out of the bag like that. When I walked in and saw you all together, I just…"

"It's done. I wish you hadn't done it, but we need to put it on the back burner and focus on the competition."

Hunter didn't look happy about that, but before he could respond, a whiff of honey and vanilla floated around him.

"Hey, you two."

Cooper gazed down into Daisy's bright blue eyes. "Hey." And tried like hell to ignore his body's response to her.

"You did good." Daisy nudged Hunter with the back of the hand that held her beer. "I liked both of those bands."

The Kneeknockers gathered around. "So, what do you think, man?" Jason asked with a goofy smile. "Think we're good enough to score a spot in the competition?"

"Jason." Daisy's tone held a warning. "That wasn't an audition. That was us having *fun.*"

"Ah, come on. I don't see why we can't toss our name into the hat. We're good enough." He looked to Cooper for a response.

"You are." Cooper couldn't deny it, but…Daisy coming on tour with him? The idea was equally terrifying and thrilling.

"So, what do you say?" Jason said. "Can we be one of the six?"

"Jason, stop." Daisy sounded pissed.

"We're not making any decisions until after everyone's auditioned," Cooper said. "But I'll put you on the list." He turned to Daisy. "If that's what you want."

Jason pumped a fist, and the drummer said, "Hell, yeah."

"You guys, hello?" Daisy said. "I'm not touring with you, so if you enter this contest, you'll have to find a new singer."

"We don't have another singer," the drummer said.

"Come on, Daze," the lead guitarist said.

She didn't look the slightest bit tempted. "I'm building the lodge."

"*You* won't be building it." Jason gave her a challenging look.

The lead guitarist touched her shoulder. "You told us as soon as the money comes in, you're good to go. You've got everything set up as far as construction."

"And it's not like you're the contractor."

"Talk to Ethan," the drummer said. "He wouldn't hold you back."

Daisy looked offended. "This isn't about Ethan. I'm a *partner*. And this isn't some job. It's my career."

"Yeah, but Daze," Jason said. "This is the opportunity we've been looking for."

"You know I want that for you, but it's not the opportunity *I've* been looking for. Talk to Lia. Maybe she'll be interested."

"At least sing for the competition, okay?" Jason said. "We'll figure it out after that."

Cooper didn't see any point in discussing it. "Guys,

you can't compete with one singer and then take another on tour. Whoever wins needs to be ready to hit the road. If you're looking to replace your lead singer, that's not you." They looked like he'd just killed their one and only chance at success. He knew exactly how they felt. Blue Fire had struggled for years before Emmie, their manager, had opened the right doors for them.

Which gave him an idea. "You can't enter the competition, but what about headlining the event?"

"What does that mean?" Jason brightened.

"The competition ends at seven, right? So, what if you guys take the stage at eight?"

"Which night?" Jason looked like he could barely contain his enthusiasm.

"Can we get Saturday?" the drummer asked. "That'll have the biggest turn-out."

"How about both nights?" Cooper said.

"Are you serious?" Jason turned to the others. "Do you know the kind of exposure we'll get? The media's going to be all over this event. Holy shit."

Cooper glanced over to find Hunter beaming at him. And it gave him the strangest sensation—like the ground had turned to fog, and he couldn't quite gain traction. It took a moment for him to grasp what it was: he'd made his father proud.

He let it seep in. Seep in deep. And it gave sustenance to the tiny seed of hope that lived in the heart of him—the little boy who'd just wanted Slider to pat his head and say *Good job*.

He was twenty-eight and getting that pat for the first time. And, stupid as it sounded, it felt good.

"Are you going to play with us?" Daisy said to him, bringing him back to the conversation.

"Nah, we'll let this be about Daisy and the Knee-knockers."

"No, man, seriously," Jason said. "We want you to play with us."

"We'll see how it goes. If you want me to join in for a few songs, no problem. Sound good?"

"Sounds amazing." Jason turned to his band, and they high-fived and fist-bumped.

"Thank you, man," the drummer said. "This is so cool."

"Thanks for the opportunity," the lead guitarist said.

Cooper remembered when Emmie had gotten them into their first big festival. It had changed their lives. *Pay it forward.*

Daisy looked at her watch. "Oh, damn. I've got to go." She looked up at Cooper. "Do you mind if I drive you back to the resort now?"

Where was she going at nine o'clock? "I can walk."

"You're not walking on the Gallatin Road at night. Hunter?"

"I got him," Hunter said.

"Great, thanks." She looked to her bandmates. "Lock up for me?"

"You got it, Daze." Jason followed her to the door. Wrapping her in his arms, he whispered something in her ear that made Daisy push away with a smile. Before she could leave, another band member pulled her in for a hug.

Cooper had no idea what was going on. Needing to make sure she was all right, he headed over, reaching her just as the others left. "I'll walk you to your car."

"Oh, no, that's okay." Her voice sounded funny. "I'm not going to my car. Goodnight."

Were those tears glittering in her eyes? "Daze."

But she was gone.

"Let her go." Jason came up behind him.

"Why's she upset?"

"It's her birthday."

"It's *what*?" Why had no one said anything? He'd been around her the whole weekend and not once had anyone mentioned it. Not at the Blackstock barbecue, not even at the Sugar Bowl among her closest friends. "So, where's she headed?" And why the hell was she sad? "I don't get why no one's celebrating with her."

"That's how she wants it," Jason said. "Always has."

The keyboard player joined them. "She's going up to her mom's. It's just a Daisy thing."

"She was *crying*."

The guys shared a silent exchange, and then Jason said, "Her dad's kind of an asshole. It's…" He pulled his phone out of his pocket. "It's nine o'clock, so she's obviously not going to hear from him."

"Drives her crazy, not knowing if he's going to remember or not," the keyboard player said. "So, she tries not to make a big deal out of it. She and her mom have their own private celebration. That's how she wants it."

"What's with her dad?" Cooper asked. "Why doesn't he call on her birthday?"

"Oh, he'll call," Jason said. "He'll call tomorrow or the next day and apologize because he missed it."

"And he'll have some great story to tell about why," the keyboard player said. "Like he met some movie star who brought him back to her trailer, or he took a wrong turn and wound up in a nudist colony in the middle of Texas Hill Country. You're so into his story you forget he fucked up."

"So, you're telling me the whole damn town knows,

and not a single person wished her a happy birthday? No one gave her a damn present?"

"That's how she wants it." Jason sounded a little defensive.

Hunter's big hand landed on his shoulder. "Her mom's got her."

"All right," Jason said. "Let's get this place cleaned up and shut down."

The band members dispersed, but Cooper didn't move, unable to get past the way everyone just let Daisy leave with tears in her eyes.

"It's always been like this," Hunter said. "Her dad's a project manager, so half the year he's waiting for a call, and the other half he's off in Texas or North Dakota, or wherever the job is. He makes a lot of promises, but he rarely comes through."

Yeah, Cooper got the picture. "So, she's upstairs right now with her mom?"

"Yep. Just like every year."

Maybe they were all used to it, but it didn't sit right with him. They'd all been together in the Sugar Bowl. They could've done *something*. Jesus, everyone should celebrate Daisy.

But what did he know? He'd been in town for a weekend. Who was he to second-guess her? "Okay, well, guess I'll head out."

"Let me grab my Fenster," Hunter said. "And we'll get going."

"I'd rather walk, but thanks."

"You sure?"

"Positive." He gave the group a chin nod.

He headed out the door into the chilly night, flexing his hands and trying to get a handle on this need driving him to climb the stairs to her mom's apartment and join the party, so it was more than just the two of them.

But if she'd wanted a party, she'd have one. Daisy didn't play games. *Her mom's got this.* He'd have to trust the guys who knew her a whole lot better than he did.

Stepping off the curb, he turned back to check out the town. Living in Eden's Landing, on the tip of Long Island, he was used to towns that rolled up their carpets at eight, but Snowberry on Daisy's birthday just seemed sad. The town green should be lit up, a band playing in the gazebo, people going nuts on a portable dance floor, and a folding table heavy with a huge birthday cake and presents.

He glanced up to her mom's apartment, expecting to see lights and movement, but the windows were dark, just one flickering yellow light behind a gauzy white curtain.

Okay, this is just fucked up. Nothing was going on up there. Heading to the bottom of the stairs at the side of the building, he noticed the door to the apartment had been left ajar. He'd take a quick look inside, make sure everything was okay.

In the two days he'd been in town, he'd watched Daisy work her ass off for the ranch and for his mom's building project. She'd even taken the stage twice for her band, after working all weekend.

Instead of ignoring it, everyone should step in and make a big deal out of her birthday so she wouldn't have time to even think about her dick of a father.

At the top of the stairs, he peered into the apartment. Daisy reached for a knitted blanket folded over the back of the couch and spread it across her sleeping mom.

The room was well-kept, no frills, with basic, inexpensive furniture. A small cake with unlit candles sat in the middle of the kitchen table.

Her mom worked six days a week. Up at some ridiculous hour to get the bagels and croissants made, her day didn't end until the café closed. Tonight, Daisy's band had asked her to audition, and her mom had fallen asleep before she could celebrate her daughter's birthday.

Backing away, he pulled his phone out of his pocket and found Hunter's number. He punched in the digits but didn't hit send until he reached the sidewalk.

The man answered on the fifth ring. "Hey, change your mind? I'm just heading to my car."

"I need a favor."

"Anything."

"Can we have a party at your house?"

"Are we talking about Daisy?"

"Damn right." His mind raced ahead, making plans. "Get your sons over, tell them to bring party snacks. You know any of her godfathers?"

"Of course, but Cooper, I'm not sure she wants this."

"Maybe, but she deserves it. Tell her godfathers to stop at CVS and pick up a bunch of presents. Doesn't matter what. Just stuff she can open. Chocolates, paperbacks, hair things, whatever they can find. And wrapping paper. And tape. And bows and shit. I'm going back to the café to see if her band's still around. How much time do you need? I can keep Daisy busy for, I don't know…is half hour enough?"

"Give me an hour. Some of her godfathers live in Bozeman." Hunter had a smile in his voice.

"Good. See you at…" He checked his watch. "Ten-fifteen."

"Cooper?"

"Yeah."

"Daisy's real clear that she doesn't want a fuss."

"That's because she doesn't know what a fuss feels like."

After tucking her mom in, Daisy went to clear the table. Her mom had set out two plates, two linen napkins, two porcelain tea cups, a matching pot, and a strawberry cream cake.

But instead of clearing, she flicked a match across the striking plate. Bringing the flame to one pink candle, she watched the wick flare to life. Then she leaned into the faint heat source. *Happy birthday to me.*

When she closed her eyes to make a wish, Cooper appeared with his sexy and—can she say adoring?—smile. *Yeah, that's what his smile feels like.*

Until he'd come to town, she'd thought she had a good life. She loved her work with the Blackstocks, loved her godfathers and her mom—even her dad. Yeah, he hurt her —a lot—but she knew in his own way he loved her. And, besides, he was the only father she had.

Maybe she'd just gotten complacent. Somewhere along the way, she'd stopped hoping for more. More attention, more…love.

Spending time with Cooper, though, had shattered the complacency, allowing her decadent, delicious, *passionate* side to seep out of the cracks. To yearn for things she couldn't yet name. And it wasn't his rocker swagger or the lonely boy hidden in the depths of his eyes. It was *them*. Their sizzling connection. Cooper read her like no one else ever had. He looked out for her. He… excited her.

Of course, he was leaving, so nothing would happen there. Well, maybe he'd opened her up to possibilities.

After he left, she'd make it a point to date more. Join dating apps.

Please. She knew better. It was *Cooper* who roused her inner sex kitten.

Daisy blew out the candle.

Her mom sighed, and Daisy's heart leaped with the hope that she might've awakened from her nap. But she only rolled onto her side, drawing up her legs and clasping her hands under her chin.

On the coffee table Daisy noticed a jewelry box sitting in the middle of a square of wrapping paper. Scissors and a tape dispenser sat to one side, a bottle of beer on the other. Clearly, her mom had been in the middle of wrapping when she'd decided to close her eyes for a bit.

Love for her mom grabbed hold of her heart and squeezed. No matter how many hours her mom worked, she'd always made Daisy feel special and loved.

Plucking the candles out of the cake, she licked the whipped cream off the bottoms. Her mouth watered at the sight of all those juicy red strawberries. So, she cut herself a thick slice and dropped it onto her great grandma's porcelain dessert plate. Grabbing her tote, she scanned the room one last time to make sure everything was all right and quietly shut the door behind her.

As she headed down the stairs, she wondered what piece of jewelry her mom had found for her. Had she bought something at the farmer's market? She'd have to wait until tomorrow to find out.

Adrenaline slammed her as she noticed the hulking figure of a man waiting at the base of the stairs. It took a moment to make sense of the breadth of those shoulders, the length of that dark hair, and the black boot resting on the stair above. "Cooper?"

"Hey." His deep, sexy voice burrowed under her skin and heated her blood.

"What're you doing here?"

He didn't say a word, just kept his gaze on her, capturing her in a thick, sultry web of attraction and intimacy.

If she swayed forward, she could press her mouth to his neck and breathe in the clean scent of his long-sleeve T-shirt and the subtle spice of his shaving cream.

He reached for a lock of her hair, wrapped it around two fingers, and rubbed. "Happy birthday."

Pleasure rushed through her. "Oh." The guys must've told him. "Thank you."

But then she remembered the party in his cabin. Carrie on her back, her shirt gaping open. Did Cooper even remember rejecting Carrie that morning out of solidarity with *her*?

It didn't matter. There was too much at stake to get caught up in figuring out a man who'd only be in town for two weeks. She started to move around him, but his hands caught her hips.

See, this was why she found him so confusing. He had a party going on his cabin, and yet here he was giving her that possessive grip that drove her wild. They were at eye level, so she got to see his handsome face up close.

"Have you had cake today?"

She lifted the dessert plate. "My mom made me one. I'll have some with her tomorrow, but I couldn't resist taking a slice."

"You shouldn't have a *slice* of anything. You deserve a whole damn birthday cake. With candles and the whole town singing 'Happy Birthday.'"

"Oh, come on. I'm too old for that."

"No, you're not." He pulled a box of birthday candles from his back pocket. "Now, all we need is a cake."

"Where did you get those?"

He cracked a grin. "The Sugar Bowl. Now let's see about that cake."

"I've got this. We can share it on the ride back to the ranch."

"You're not sharing, Daisy. Not today."

"Nothing's open."

He cocked his head. "Could have sworn your mom owned a bakery."

"You want to break into my mom's bakery?"

"I don't need to break in. The guys left it open for me. After they scrounged up the candles."

Yeah, Daisy liked her life. She loved her family, her town, her job. But Cooper Hood opened up a whole other side of life she didn't even know she'd been missing. He indulged her. He celebrated her.

And tonight, she was going to bask in the center of his attention…and forget all about the party in his cabin.

Chapter Ten

SEATED AT A SMALL CAFÉ TABLE IN THE CORNER OF the bakery, two espresso cups and a chocolate mousse cake between them, Daisy flicked a finger across the flame of the votive candle.

"The oil industry's volatile." She tipped her cup, letting the dark liquid slosh first to one side and then the other. "My dad goes through periods with no income, so when an opportunity shows up, he has to take it."

"That probably sucked as a kid."

She sat back in her seat, wiping her finger on the napkin. "It did." Everyone liked to blame her dad's flakiness on the nature of his career. They must've thought it would hurt her less to frame it that way. They were wrong. And she appreciated that Cooper didn't bother pretending. "I always understood that my dad had to make a living, but I got sick of the broken promises. How many times can a girl pin her hopes on someone, only to have him fail? I finally made him stop making plans. I told him just to show up when he could. It's easier on me that way." She leaned in as if telling him a secret. "You want to know the turning point?"

He leaned in, too. "Yes." Golden candlelight warmed his masculine features.

"I was twelve. My dad had been home for months, and it was awesome because he'd spent a ton of time with me. But summer was coming, and my mom needed to make sure I had plans. I was too old for a babysitter, so for the first time, she let me go to camp. A lot of kids around here go to Steven's Ranch in Idaho, and I'd always wanted to go, too. It was expensive, but my parents were willing to go in on it together, so I finally got my shot. It's a big deal because this camp fills up for the following year at the end of each summer, so I had to go on a wait list. But I got in."

Right at that moment, people were slurping shots out of Carrie Levitt's belly button in Cooper's cabin. She glanced up to find his attention riveted on her, and he didn't seem the slightest bit antsy.

And it made her feel soft and warm that he'd rather hear her sad story about summer camp than be at that party. "I can't even tell you how excited I was. My mom and I made all these trips into Bozeman, so I could get my trunk and toiletries and the right hiking gear. I checked off every item on that camp list like I was going on the space shuttle."

Picking up her espresso spoon, she scraped the inside of her cup and tasted the cinnamon-flavored foam. "Then, a few weeks before school let out, my dad took me to dinner at the Roadhouse. He and his friends were swapping stories about the open road, and all of a sudden, he looks at me and goes, 'Girl, there's a whole world out there you need to see.'"

She found him smiling at the way she imitated her dad's loud, exuberant tone.

"All the guys shared their stories of bear and wolf encounters and sleeping in tents under the night sky, the strange terrain of the Badlands and the Jackalopes they sell at Wall Drug, and I was just enthralled."

"I can imagine."

"Right? And like I said, he hadn't worked for the better part of a year, so he figured what better time to take his daughter on a road trip? And it was perfect because everything I'd bought for camp was exactly what I'd need for our trip. So, yeah, long story short, I gave up my spot at camp to spend the whole summer traveling with him."

"He took a job?" His lips pressed together in anger.

She nodded. Wow, all these years later, it still stung. "Yep. Two weeks before we were scheduled to go, he got a job in Texas. Of course, he had to take it. He'd been out of work for almost seven months at that point."

"No luck getting your spot back at the camp?"

"Nope. But it wasn't the kind of thing where I could be angry with him. He *had* to work. And he was upset, too. He hated disappointing me. So, he swore up and down that no matter what, he'd be home for my thirteenth birthday. He'd take a few days off work, and we'd camp in Yellowstone." She lowered her head and blinked, refusing to cry over something that had happened fifteen years ago. "He didn't even call to cancel. He just…forgot." Emotion rushed her hard. *Dammit.* She'd long ago accepted her dad for who he was.

Or had she? She kept telling herself she had but look how upset she'd gotten over the dead battery.

She swiped under her eyes. She was just tired and stressed and hated her birthday. "So, anyhow, that was it. I told him never to make promises again, and for the next couple of years, my mom and I took a special birthday trip together, just an overnight somewhere. But then…I don't know. I went off to college, and her business expanded, and we stopped traveling. But we did keep the tradition of celebrating my birthday quietly, just the two of us."

"Did you ever wish he'd change his career? For you?"

"You bet I did. All my friends' dads had jobs here or in Bozeman. Why couldn't he find one? Worse, my dad's friends in the biker club were all just as free-spirited as he was, but they settled down. They became accountants, lawyers, mechanics, IT guys. The club changed, but my dad didn't. So, yeah, I wished pretty hard for him to settle down, too. But I'm lucky because my mom made it clear it's not me. It's him."

"He only came to some of your shows, so I always wondered about him. He seemed like one of those cool dads."

"Oh, yeah. My dad's the life of the party. And luckily for him, he never stays in one place long enough for you to hate him for not putting his dish in the dishwasher or leaving his clothes on the floor instead of the hamper." She dropped her spoon on the saucer and sat back. "Listen to me. I sound like my mom. Whatever. My dad doesn't like to be tied down, and he doesn't do well with desk jobs and regular hours."

Cooper gently dragged the tines of his fork across the cake's gooey chocolate ganache frosting. "I think I'm only just figuring out now that my mom's just another asshole out there trying to make her way. Having a kid doesn't make someone wise or even caring. People just are who they are."

"You're absolutely right about that." She pushed aside

her cake plate and reached for his hand. "Thank you, Cooper. For making this birthday special."

"You're welcome."

The series of bear claws took up most of his forearm, disguising the scars. But when she traced the ink with the tips of her fingers, she felt the ridges and valleys of his skin. "I remember when this happened. Not the details— no one ever said—but I do remember all the fuss that was made over it."

He shifted his chair, so he sat sideways to the table. "There was no fuss. I was out of school for ten days, and when I came back, life went on as usual."

"Remember my perch." She tipped her head to the bar stools facing the picture window in the bakery. "Things got pretty heated over the neglected kid who got mauled by a bear. They talked about what they could do to help. It almost got people to call Child Services on your mom."

A flare of interest lit his eyes, and she thought he might ask questions. Instead, he tilted his chair back so it was up on two legs. "It didn't. Some people came to interview me, but that was all."

"Do you wish they had?"

"Taken me from her?" His gaze wandered to the stage, and he didn't speak for several moments. "No." He brought his chair back down to the floor. "I had the music program, and that changed everything."

She tapped the scar. "How'd it happen?" Wildlife encounters were common enough that no one had questioned his injury. But now, after touching his scarred arm, she understood the bear had *mauled* him.

"Sleeping in the woods."

"Like camping out?"

His gaze flicked up to hers. "Sure."

The turmoil in his eyes told her it wasn't about pitching tents, s'mores, and ghost stories. It was getting away from what was happening at home. Her heart ached for that little boy. "Did you do that a lot?"

He nodded, obviously uncomfortable. "You saw how small the cabin was. My mom…entertained a lot. It got loud." He pulled at his bottom lip. "Her friends liked to mess with me. Thought it was funny."

Her heart clenched in pain. She couldn't stand to see him hurting, so she changed the direction of the conversation. "When did you get the tattoo?"

"Sophomore year of college. Derek—he's our bass player—was in getting ink. One of the artists noticed my scar." Creases appeared on his forehead. "It was weird because that was the first time anyone had ever asked me about it. No one here said a thing."

"They were scared of you. You were scary."

"I didn't scare you."

She smiled. "No. You didn't scare me. And that's the thing. If they'd known you the way I did, they'd have loved you."

His phone buzzed, and he glanced at it. "Okay." His demeanor changed. "We should get going." He got up abruptly, gathering their plates and forks.

"Is everything all right?"

"Sure. It's late. We want to be ready to hit the ground running Monday morning."

Was it a text from Carrie? She had to be wondering what was taking him so long.

The hit of jealousy hurt more because it was mixed and shaken with embarrassment. He'd felt bad for her that she was alone on her birthday, so he'd made this sweet gesture.

But what he really wanted was to throw on his rocker cape and get back to his real life.

When they reached the turnoff to his cabin, Cooper tapped his knuckles against the window. "You mind dropping me at Hunter's?"

"Now?" A glance at the dashboard clock showed it was nearly ten-fifteen. "Hunter might keep weird musician hours, but Crystal works in Bozeman. She gets up early."

"Yeah. He wants me to pick up some demos." He talked to the window. "We're trying to figure out who we're going to invite for auditions."

She didn't blame him for being uncomfortable. "If you're worried about running into his sons, don't be. They definitely won't be there this late on a Sunday night."

"Not worried. After what went down at the barbecue, I doubt they want to hang out with their dad right now."

"You're probably right about that." Staying on the main road, she drove into the denser woods at the back of the developed property. When the ranch-style home came into sight, she ate her words about it being too late for a visit. All the lights were on. And when her headlights flashed on metal, Daisy realized cars were parked haphazardly everywhere. She recognized Jason's VW van. "What's going on?"

"Some of the bands auditioning tomorrow needed a place to crash tonight." He was still talking to the window. "Maybe they're jamming." He unbuckled his seatbelt. "Want to come in with me?"

"I'm pretty beat. I'll just see you in the morning, okay?" Honestly, she was wrung out and confused. Disappointed that her dad had forgotten to call her—for God's sake, they'd talked on the phone *two days* ago—embarrassed to know Cooper had thrown her a pity party just because she was helping him with his mom's project—and jealous that she-bitch Carrie was waiting for him in his cabin.

As soon as he got out of the car, he held onto the doorframe. "Sure thing." He tapped his fingers on the glass. He wasn't leaving.

"You okay?"

He thumbed his lower lip. "Yup. Fine."

It occurred to her that Crystal hadn't been at the barbecue. "Are you worried about Crystal?"

"Yeah." He nodded deeply. "I really am."

If he hadn't bolted, he'd have heard that Crystal had known about him. "I get that." She wanted to suggest he get Carrie to go in there with him, but he didn't deserve that. He hadn't done anything wrong. And he was in a crappy position, thanks to Hunter. She shifted into park and cut the engine. "I know her well. I'll come with you."

"Thanks. That would help me a lot."

She swung around the front of the car. He probably expected Crystal to come flying at him on a broom, blaming him for destroying her family. Or to not let him step one foot inside her home. "She's a good person."

"I hope so." He reached for her hand. "I'm just glad you're with me."

Gah. All her resentment and self-pity turned to mush. *Poor guy.* This had to be hard. Of course, she'd go in there with him.

Under a sky ablaze with glittering stars, they walked up the stone path, music from the house floating out the open windows. Hunter routinely had jam sessions, and this one sounded like a hell of a lot of fun.

Right before she reached for the doorknob, Cooper squeezed her hand. "Oh, and Daisy?" When he leaned in, she got a whiff of his masculine scent.

She took in the strong line of his jaw and the sexy curve of his lips. The smile in his eyes loosened something inside her. "Yes?" Her voice came out tissue-thin.

And then he kissed her. Just a soft press of his mouth on hers.

Oh.

With a swipe of his tongue across her lips, he licked inside, giving her a lovely, lingering kiss before pulling back. "Happy birthday, beautiful."

Vaguely, she thought about the magic associated with the number three. Because she'd just gotten her third kiss from him, and it fluttered through her on fairy wings.

He opened the door and then, with a wicked smile, said, "You go first. Wouldn't want anyone mistaking me for a burglar."

So, he really was worried about how people would treat him now that the truth had come out. Grabbing his hand, she swept right into the house. She'd make sure they treated him right.

"Surprise!"

Holy crap. The foyer was crowded with people wearing party hats and waving noise-makers. The Blackstocks, her band...her *godfathers*? Everyone rushed toward her, engulfing her with hugs, kisses, and an endless round of birthday wishes.

"Thank you. Oh, my God, you guys, thank you so much."

Crystal handed her a champagne flute. They tapped their glasses together. "Happy birthday, sweetheart."

"Thank you. I seriously had no idea. None." Still overwhelmed, her heart beat wildly. 'How…when…" She laughed. "I don't understand."

"Your rock star gave Hunter a list of things to do." Crystal's gaze settled on Cooper standing alone by the door, and her smile faded.

"Is this awful for you?" Daisy said. "I don't want to make you uncomfortable in your own home."

"Oh, no. We've had a while to get our heads around it." Pain gripped her features. "It's just so upsetting. If only we'd known, we'd have taken him in. Of course, we would have. Hunter *told* that woman, but she absolutely refused to take a paternity test." Tears shone in her eyes. "I don't know how she can live with herself."

"I don't think she's doing such a good job of it."

"Right." The older woman hooked an arm around Daisy's shoulders. "This is a conversation for another day."

"Where's my girl?" Whale swept her off her feet, making the champagne slosh out of her glass. Laughing, Crystal grabbed the flute.

As he carried her deeper into the house, Daisy noticed the dining room table, normally loaded with sheet music and instrument cases, now held bowls of chips and pretzels, bottles of soda, and stacks of red Solo cups.

The moment Whale set her down, Remi caught her around the waist and hugged her. "Happy birthday, Daze."

"Thanks, Remi."

Suddenly the music cut off, and Hunter plunged into the Beatles' "Birthday Song" on his grand piano. People started scrambling for instruments and, before long, the house rocked with the driving melody.

In the joyful mayhem, she'd lost sight of Cooper. He hadn't left, had he? She knew he didn't feel like he belonged.

He belongs with me.

When she found him leaning against the built-in bookcase, watching her, she headed over. Up on her toes, she spoke into his ear. "You're a terrible liar."

"And yet the expression captured on about a dozen camera phones tells a different story."

"I don't know how you pulled this off."

"It was easy." He gave her an affectionate smile. "Everyone loves you, cinnabun. They want to celebrate with you."

Emotion jammed in her throat. "Yeah." It was all so amazing, but what really stood out was that *he'd* arranged it for her. "Thank you."

"I'm just glad you're not pissed about all this." His gaze took in the room, crowded with people, food, and presents. "They said you didn't want any attention."

"I want it from you."

Cooper: This is fucking weird.

Cooper hit send. From his perch on the arm of the sofa, he and Emmie had been texting back and forth while Daisy opened her gifts.

Emmie: It's only weird because there are no nymphs for you to party with.

Cooper: Got a cabin full of them waiting for me right now. Smiling, he sent it just to provoke her.

Emmie: And I think it's sweet that instead of being with them, you're with Daisy. She added about a dozen heart emoticons.

Cooper: Just throwing a party for an old friend, Em.

Emmie: Seems to me your work is done. If you wanted, you could scamper on back to the festival of nymphs.

And then a second text came in right after it.

Emmie: Unless you're actually...I don't know... exactly where you want to be? With Daisy?

Well, no, he wasn't anywhere near Daisy, and he wasn't having fun. Everyone else was, though. The house was alive with music, laughter, and clusters of deep conversation, and just like he had when he was a kid, he sat apart, watching.

He was a man now—their equal in every way—and yet he still separated himself.

Which only fed their perception that he didn't belong. That he was Ronnie Hood's son, and he had something to be ashamed of. But he didn't.

He never had.

A crowd gathered around the piano as Hunter played and various people with guitars and violins, flutes and tambourines, jammed with him. Cooper was a musician, and a damn good one, so why was he sitting on the arm of the couch?

Getting up, he scanned the instruments leaning against the wall and picked up a banjo. As he approached the group, he saw Daisy standing on the other side of the gleaming black baby grand, singing her heart out. She lifted a hand off the Dobro to wave him over.

Energy surged through him, and he joined her, joined *them*. Before long, he'd picked up the beat from Jason's autoharp, the bongos, and the various guitars.

And it hit him hard. He was jamming with Hunter— his *father*—and Daisy—the woman he'd crushed on from afar. What a fucking trip.

He'd never played rockabilly before, but it was a hell of a lot of fun. When he tuned into Daisy's lyrics, he realized she was making them up as she went along.

Fourteen days and fourteen nights
That's all I got to get it right
Fourteen days and fourteen nights
Girl, get out the way 'cuz he's worth the fight

When the song ended, the room went silent. Everyone stood there locked in a moment of surprise and awe. Cooper swiped the perspiration beading on his hairline, and then applause, hoots, and laughter exploded.

"That was unbelievable," Whale's wife said.

"Hey, you should start a band," someone called.

Smiling, Daisy set the Dobro in its stand and then walked right into his arms. Jason smacked his back and said, "That was fuckin' awesome, man."

When the applause died down, and people went back to talking, Daisy stayed with him, arms locked around his waist. As she looked up at him, attraction flooded him. He'd never felt this way for someone before—he didn't know what to do with it. He wanted to hold her hand and make her scrambled eggs, lie on their backs in the tall grass and talk about their day. He wanted…more than he'd ever thought he could have.

But when her look turned sultry, affection shifted into something deeper, darker, and his blood started to heat. Jesus fuck, he wanted to kiss this woman, lose himself in all her softness. Lightly, he touched her chin, aligning their mouths.

"All right, Daisy," Whale said.

She flinched and whipped around to her godfather.

With a smile as big as his belly, Whale clamped his hands on his wife's shoulders. "Got to get my old lady home so she can get up early and make me a nice, hot breakfast."

The petite cop rolled her eyes. "Daisy's had your kale and blueberry smoothie, old man. Quit pretending you're some scary old biker."

"All right, I'll walk you out," Daisy said. "Thank you, guys, so much for coming.

"You shoulda seen your face when you opened the door," Whale said as they made their way through the crowd.

As Cooper turned to set the banjo in its stand, he caught Ethan watching him with a concerned expression.

Oh, Christ. What now? Frankly, he couldn't care less about the guy. He wasn't trying to take his place in this family, so the dick could just fuck off.

It was time to get going. First, though, he'd thank Hunter for hosting the party at the last minute. He pushed his way through the crowd of musicians surrounding the piano. "Hey, man."

Hunter stood from the bench and shook the extended hand. "Heading out?"

"Yeah. Big day tomorrow. Thanks for hosting the party. I hope it wasn't too much of an inconvenience."

"Not at all. Happy to do it." The man gripped him a little too long, looking like he wanted to say something. But Cooper didn't want to hear it. It had been the longest, strangest weekend of his life, and he actually looked forward to Monday morning, when he'd go into work mode. "Let me know when you've got the next round of auditions set up."

"Will do." But Hunter seemed determined to speak his

mind. He stepped closer, clapping a hand on Cooper's shoulder. "Happy I got to play with you. Real special for me, son."

That word. *Son.* It hit him like a shock of cold water each time the man said it. He stuttered out a laugh. "You've got to stop doing that."

Hunter nodded with a smile in his eyes. "Or maybe you've got to get used to it."

"Yeah, maybe. All right, I'm out. Thanks again." He started off, eager to get the hell out of the Blackstock house when Ethan intercepted him.

Clean-shaven, broad-shouldered, the man looked every bit the NFL powerhouse he used to be. "Hey. We got some calls about a party going on in your cabin."

"I'm heading there right now. I'll shut it down." Cooper moved to step around him.

But Ethan blocked him. "Already did that."

"Good. Then we've got no problems."

"Look, man, we're working hard to build this place into a resort, so—"

"Yeah, I get it. You don't want my type around."

"If by your *type* you mean big celebrity rockers, then we sure as hell want you. And when we get to phase five, the time-share homes, then you can throw all the parties you want. In the meantime, I'm going to ask you to tone it down."

"Not an issue. I've only got the cabin until Tuesday."

Ethan cocked his head. "I thought you're in town through the festival."

"Your resort's booked. I have to find somewhere else to stay."

"Ah. Gotcha."

Cooper gave him a chin nod. *We done?*

"Coop." Daisy waved at him from the entryway.

He saw the moment Ethan registered her expression—there was no mistaking her interest in Cooper—and a powerful sense of protectiveness rose in him. He didn't want anyone souring this fresh, new bud of a relationship. He wanted it all for himself, all long as he could have it.

Ethan gave him a thoughtful expression. "Have you seen this?" He pulled his phone out of his pocket and swiped the screen until he found what he was looking for.

Cooper recognized the Beatz website. Once again, the homepage displayed a photograph of him partying, this one taken tonight. *Blue Fire's Playboy Extraordinaire Hits Up the Hometown Honeys.* As he'd let those people into his cabin, a woman had jumped on his back, holding out her phone to capture them with their faces pressed together. Cooper looked exactly as he'd felt. Surprised, and not in a good way.

Anger and unease twisted through him. "What's your point?"

He nodded toward Daisy. "I get this is your lifestyle, man, and it's none of my business. But Daisy? She's working her ass off to turn this ranch into a five-star resort. And not just because it's her job, but because she cares about this town. About her mom. It would hurt her reputation to be seen in the tabloids with you."

The stink of shame wafted up from where he'd buried it a decade ago. And it was so familiar, so unwanted, Cooper wanted to scrub it off. But he got it. Starting next week, the press would be crawling all over this place. They didn't need to see Daisy hanging out with him, depicting her as a groupie fucking a rock star.

But he'd be damned if Ethan would tell him what to do. "I wouldn't do anything to hurt her." He leaned in, lowering his voice. "Now, I let you fuck with my head when I was a kid, but it's not going to happen this time around."

"Fuck with your head?" Ethan looked incredulous. "You were a drug addict. All we did was tell you to stay away from her. She didn't need that shit in her life."

"What the hell are you talking about? I never touched drugs." Not in Snowberry. Not once.

Ethan looked at him like he was a disgusting piece of filth. "We saw." He gestured to the floor. "Whippets all over the place."

"*Whippets?* You think I did whippets? You asshole. My mother was a raging drug addict. Do you really think I'd touch anything when I lived with that insanity?"

"We saw it. Those canisters were all around you."

"It was a fucking *rest area*, genius. I'm sure plenty of people used that picnic table to drink and get high. But *I* was walking home from school—yet again—and the sole of my shoe came off. If it wasn't humiliating enough to rummage through a garbage can looking for string or wire or some kind of cord, imagine how it felt when the three of you assholes jumped out of your Jeep and told me to stay away from Daisy." He had to restrain himself from thumping the bastard's chest. "I'm in town for two weeks." He kept his tone low, grave. "Stay the hell away from me."

Cooper brushed past him. To avoid Daisy and her bandmates at the front door, he cut through the kitchen. He was done. Just fucking done. He headed out the sliding glass door to the backyard.

Tromping through a thick fog across dew-soaked grass, he found his way to the path at the side of the house. *Fucking hell.* They'd thought he was a drug addict. Now he understood the nasty looks they'd given him over the years.

Throughout his teens, he'd wanted only one thing: to get the hell out of town. He'd kept his eyes on the prize—a music scholarship—to pave the way for his future.

That same urgency coursed through him right then. He wanted out of this damn town. Tomorrow he'd find a place in Bozeman. Get some distance from these people.

But with each step he took away from the house, his anger burned off, leaving nothing but the familiar smoke of loneliness that had clung to him throughout his childhood.

They'd thought he was a *drug addict*. They still thought he was the same fuck-up, only dressed better. It didn't matter that he'd graduated UT with honors. That he and his band had worked their asses off until they'd finally hit the big time.

He was nothing but Ronnie Hood's loser son. *That's all they'll ever see.*

The tight knot of anger in his chest made it hard to draw a full breath.

And on top of everything else, Ethan was right. Cooper couldn't be with Daisy. The only single guy left in Blue Fire meant the paps went out of their way to get shots of him partying. His actions fed the media beast, and a single photograph with them in a compromising position would tag her as a groupie.

He'd hurt her reputation not just within the context of the resort but her community.

So, thanks, Ethan, for the lethal shot right through the heart of my teenage fantasies.

Except his heart didn't thunder around her because of his memories. It was the woman she'd become. The beautiful, strong, sexy, caring woman he'd gotten to know. She was magnificent.

And Cooper couldn't have her.

Hitting the asphalt walkway, he stomped the dew off his boots. Of course, he couldn't have her. He was leaving in two weeks. Why was he even thinking about it?

He'd rent a house in Bozeman. That way he could turn up the volume on his parties. No worrying about other hotel guests shutting him down. Yeah, that sounded good.

It sounded great.

Chapter Eleven

"Cooper?" *Daisy*. The one voice in the world that had the power to rip off his bravado and reduce him to that sad-sack little kid who'd wanted too much. "Wait up."

He closed his eyes, torn between his insatiable desire to be with her and the need to make a clean break. Being around her and not being able to have her was pure torture. But of course, none of this was her fault, so he waited for her to catch up.

Her sandals slapped against the pavement, and low-level clouds spattered mist, dampening her dress, so it clung to her curves. "What're you doing?"

"Heading back," he said.

"Yeah, I see that. You left without saying goodbye."

Dammit, she was so beautiful, her spirit so fierce. *Keep it business.* "With the two-hour time difference, I have to get up early to check in with Emmie. When will you talk to Mickelson?"

"Can you give me a few hours—say, midday? I'd like to get confirmation from our judges. I'd feel a lot more confident if we could get one or two high-profile people."

"He'll have some good connections of his own."

The smile that broke across her features made his body hum. "That's a good point. I wanted to deliver him a package that would bowl him over, but he might want to get involved once he hears our plan."

They walked in silence for a bit, and he could see her working through something. "What's going on, cinnabun?" He found it impossible to be strictly business around her.

"I saw you talking to Ethan."

That's why she came after me? "Yeah? So?"

"So, he upset you."

"I'm a big boy. I can handle Ethan."

"I know. But if he said anything about the paternity thing—"

"I don't care. What he says or thinks has no impact on me. None." As they passed under a lamp, beads of mist glittered in her hair like yellow diamonds. She walked close enough that the back of her hand brushed his, and each pass sent sparks shooting up his arm. "Forget about the Blackstocks, okay? Let's end your birthday on a good note."

"You're so damn stubborn." She glanced behind her, in the direction of her car, but kept pace with him. "I do have some good news, though. I figured out a solution to your lodging problem."

"Yeah?" So had he.

"You can move into my cabin, and I'll stay with my mom."

This woman. She was the best person he'd ever known. "Not kicking you out of your home, Daze."

"Oh, don't worry. My bedroom at my mom's place is fully intact." She smiled. "It still has my Green Day and Weezer posters on the wall."

So many of his fantasies had centered around her bedroom—the perfect intimacy of the two of them in her bed—but he'd never had a clue what it looked like. He smiled at the image she'd given him, even if it came ten years too late. "I appreciate the offer, but I'm all set." They'd reached the junction where he'd veer left to get to his cabin, while she'd go straight to hers.

But instead of continuing, she stopped. "What does that mean?"

"I'm going to rent a house in Bozeman."

"That's forty-five minutes away."

He knew that. "Okay?"

"I need you here."

"No, you don't."

"What about auditions? And all the decisions we'll have to make? It's a lot more work than you realize. And I can't have you forty-five minutes away."

"A lot of emergencies come up when planning a Battle of the Bands?" he said.

"I wouldn't know. I've never done one before. But I run events in the summer, and things go wrong all the time. I can't afford mistakes."

"Neither can I. But I'm not kicking you out of your house."

"I want you there." She reached for his hand and drew it to her chest. "I want you here."

He knew he should go. Get his ass back to his cabin and away from temptation, but his feet wouldn't move, and blood roared in his ears. He just wanted to be near her.

It started to drizzle, and he felt the light patter on his skin. "You're getting wet, Daisy. Just go. We'll talk in the morning."

Slowly, she shook her head.

"What?"

"I've got you figured out, you know."

"Yeah?" He gave her a bored, almost patronizing look, all while sensation ripped across his skin. Because she cared. And this fierce woman caring about him—fuck, was this what had drawn Slater to Emmie? Derek to Violet?

Because it was potent, and he could see how much a man would give up for this kind of connection.

"You act like you don't care. Like you're just some rocker looking for the next party. And at first, I bought it. I mean, the parties in your cabin, the selfies of you and Carrie." She shrugged. "I bought it, but at the same time, it confused me because I couldn't make sense of how you looked at me, how you *kissed* me when I knew you had Carrie spread out on your kitchen counter."

He hated that she'd seen that. "I didn't invite Carrie. I don't want her."

"I know that." A slow smile spread across her lovely features, and with each second that ticked past, she seemed to bloom, her every petal unfurling right before him. "I get it now. Because you're here with me. Everyone told you I like to spend my birthday alone with my mom, but you didn't listen. You went with your gut. And your gut told you to do this for me. To celebrate me. I see the way you look at me, Cooper Hood." She stepped closer with a confident gleam in her eyes. "You yearn for me."

"I don't yearn, Daze." He tried to make it sound like he was humoring her.

Because yearning was the one thing he couldn't bear. It

had been the driving force behind him leaving town. He never wanted to feel that bottomless, gaping ache for things he couldn't have.

"For me, you do. I've got your number now. You want me as much as I want you. You're just too afraid to act on it."

"I'm not afraid to act on my attraction to you—obviously." The memory of taking her up against the wall in her office made his blood sizzle. Damn, if she didn't live in Snowberry, if he thought she'd ever consider moving, he wouldn't give a damn about the paparazzi.

Because he wasn't stupid. It was crystal clear to him that Daisy was one of a kind.

Maybe even the only woman for him. If he believed in shit like that.

But she'd never leave. "I'm going to my cabin now." Still, he didn't move. Standing under a lamp, he was caught in the magnetic pull of their bodies. He wanted to lick the rain drops off her sweet raspberry lips, lick into that hot mouth that had welcomed him so hungrily in her office.

"Okay, handsome, I'll see you in the morning. But starting Tuesday night, you're in my house." She placed her hands on his shoulders and whispered in his ear, "I want you to sleep in my bed, on my sheets, so after you're gone, I'll imagine all the things we should have done."

"Daisy...Christ. You're the most..."—*beautiful* —"frustrating woman I've ever known. Do you really want to start something with me when—"

"Yes."

He stopped short, swallowed. Reminded himself she wasn't used to the press. It wouldn't occur to her that their every action would be recorded and posted online.

"Hanging out with me is only going to get you into trouble."

"How so?"

If he told her, she'd just say she didn't care. So, he pulled his phone out and opened up the Beatz website. He showed her the latest image of him. "Because this is going to be you. And I know you don't want to be seen with Blue Fire's man whore."

A flash of shock turned into anger. "So *that's* what Ethan said."

"It's not about Ethan."

"I saw him show you his phone. He told you that you'd ruin my reputation if we got involved. Have I got it right?"

"He didn't have to tell me. I know from my own experience. The media will be out here in full force for a Blue Fire event. Obviously, they're going to get shots of me. And it's not only them." How could she not see the problem? "You saw the picture Carrie sold. It went viral in an hour. It'll happen the rest of my time here. So, let's just work on the Battle of the Bands. That's what we both need to focus on." And he was right. Everything he said was exactly right.

"Okay, Cooper." She shook her head like she thought he was a complete doofus. "You want me but not enough. Got it." She took off, waving over her shoulder. "'Night."

Every step she took tightened the cord that bound them. He started to panic. Because one of the things that drew him to her was her honesty. That was Daisy. No games, no manipulations, no second-guessing.

And what did he give her in return? The sense that he didn't really care either way?

She deserved better than that. "I want you." His voice

boomed in the foggy night. "Of course, I fucking want you." In a few steps, he caught up with her. "But not at the cost of your reputation."

"Thanks. Glad you're in my corner. But no one, not Ethan, not the media, not even you, is going to tell me how to run my life."

And another thing about her that turned him on? Her fierce inner strength. Fuck, that was hot. He needed to touch her, to pull her up hard against him, feel the press of her breasts and breathe in the scent of her hair. Dammit, she made him so fucking hard. "You make me crazy."

"No one gets to tell us what to do or how to behave. We're adults. We make our own choices." Her expression said, *And I choose you.*

She tipped her head back, those beautiful eyes gazing at him with so much desire. Taking a step forward, she slid her hands up his chest, warming his skin and filling his senses with her fragrance. Clasping her hands behind his neck, she said, "Sometimes I just ache for you."

"Okay, you're not even trying here."

She pressed a kiss to his chest, and then rubbed a circle over it. "I want to kiss your heart and make the pain go away. I want to crack you open and let all the ugly fly out and then close you back up with my mouth, kissing you until you're healed and whole."

"Jesus, Daisy. Enough. I mean it. I'm fine. I'm whole. I don't need *anything*." But he did. He needed her so badly his skin felt tight.

"I want to pour all my respect and desire and passion over you until it smothers every single memory from your past, and all that's left is pure happiness."

"Oh, fuck me." He hauled her to him and took that mouth that wouldn't shut up. His body went up in flames, as she licked inside, pulled at his hair, and shifted closer to him. "*You* make me happy."

When she moaned into his mouth, his arms tightened around her waist, holding her in place, so she didn't disappear into the fog. Desire like nothing he'd ever felt before burned through him.

She kissed him like a lover, like they were alone on a lazy Sunday morning, the sun filtering in through gauzy curtains, with all the time in the world to learn each other's mouths, bodies, and pleasure points. She felt so good—*no, perfect*—in his arms, their tongues tangling, her fingers sifting through his hair.

It was a slow build, an inexorable spiraling of need in his body. Each sigh, each shift of her hips, each gentle tug of his hair, struck the flint until it all combined to ignite the raw, primal imperative to *fuck*.

He had to have her. *Now*. Dragging his hands down her back, he gripped her ass through the thin fabric of her dress and lifted her. Wrapping her legs around his waist, she rocked against his painfully hard cock. Moving over him with short, rhythmic rolls of her hips, she cried out, a sound so erotic, so desperate, he didn't think he could stand another moment without being inside her.

Just as he carried her off the path, she pulled away. "Wait. You…you haven't been with Carrie?"

Carrie? "No." Hadn't he made that clear? "I haven't been with anyone."

"It's just…she was there again tonight, and…"

"I haven't touched Carrie or anyone else. I'm not an asshole. I'm not going to use a woman's body when I'm thinking of someone else. That's too shitty even for me."

Her features softened, and she gripped the back of his neck, pulling him to her mouth. Her kiss turned voracious. She moaned like nothing had ever felt so good, and the sound enflamed him.

The world narrowed to the soft, slick heat of her mouth, as he backed her up against the trunk of a towering pine, pinning her in place in the darkness of the forest.

"Oh, God, Cooper." Her hand pushed between their grinding bodies, reaching for the waistband of his jeans. Fumbling, she opened the first, then the second button. And then those feminine fingers closed around his cock. Her fist tightened, and she gave a hard tug.

Electrified, he thrust into her hand. "Dammit, Daisy. I can't...*fuck*." Everything about her—from her tight grip on his cock, her scent filling his senses, to her sensual moans—incited his lust. She was his catnip, his kryptonite, the switch that lit him up.

When her thumb ran slow circles around the head, desire exploded. He needed friction, or he was going to lose his mind. He needed the slick grip of her feminine core around his straining cock.

Jesus, he had to stop before he took Daisy up against a tree. *What was he doing?*

Do you want a shot of Daisy grinding on you to go viral?

Just as he slackened his hold on her, ready to set her down, she wriggled free. And then, with a wickedly lustful smile, she got down on her knees and peeled his jeans off his hips.

"Daisy." His voice held equal parts warning and desperation.

He tried to grab under her shoulders to pull her up, but she'd wrapped her hand around the base of his cock as her tongue swiped around the head. The burn of intense arousal ripped along his nerves, and when her mouth closed over his cock, he felt the jolt of sensation down to the soles of his feet.

"Daisy, stop."

"No."

"Someone might—" The incredible suction, the flick of her tongue just under the head, made him sizzle. "Fuck." He caught a fistful of that gorgeous hair, and the flare of guilt for taking her so obscenely in public died out when she moaned, leaving no doubt how much she enjoyed giving him this pleasure.

Jesus, the feel of her hot mouth sucking his cock was unlike anything he'd ever known. And then, when he looked down to see that thick, dark hair, that perfect mouth wrapped around him, everything intensified, and way too soon, his body started tingling, the pressure to release so great he couldn't hold back.

But coming in her mouth seemed too filthy, and he needed more of her, all of her. In a frenzy, he pulled out and hauled her to her feet. He had a vague awareness that the bark of the tree would hurt her back, so he spun her around, flipped her dress up over her ass, and jerked her hips back. When he saw her hands on the tree trunk, when she pushed back and squirmed against his cock, he lost it. He was about to push inside her when the last remaining bell of reason chimed. "Condom."

"I'm on the pill." She sounded breathy, urgent.

"I'm clean. You sure?"

"Oh, God, yes."

And with that, he eased inside her and shuddered at the feel of her slick, clasping heat.

His body trembled with the utter elation of being inside Daisy. Every sound she made—each cry, each plea —*Oh, God, Cooper, Oh, God*—drove him out of his mind.

And the way her ass popped up each time he slammed home, as if to pull him in deeper—*oh, fuck, yes.*

"Daisy, I'm gonna come." But he was taking her with him, so he cupped her breast and pinched her nipple. Slid his palm down her stomach, letting his fingers delve into the slick heat between her legs. When his finger brushed over the hard nub of her clit, her body bucked, and she gasped.

"Cooper. Oh, God. Oh—" She slammed back so hard her elbows locked, and her body shook. She threw her head back as she let out a shuddery cry.

That was it. Everything in him coiled so tightly it hurt to hold back, and then he burst, as euphoria set him free. With her ass jammed hard against him, he gripped her hips, slamming into her, the relief so intense a shower of lights exploded behind his eyelids. "Jesus." Nothing had ever felt so good.

A bark of laughter on the path slammed him back to earth. He stilled at the sound of footsteps and quiet conversation. In silence, Daisy pulled up her panties and smoothed her skirt. Cooper jerked up his jeans but needed several tries before his trembling fingers managed to button them.

The voices passed. Reality rushed in and slapped him with a cold hand.

Someone could have seen Daisy on her knees giving Cooper Hood, lead guitarist for Blue Fire, a blowjob.

The cool night air chilled the perspiration on his skin, and he filled his lungs with the pine-scented air. Just as he opened his mouth to speak, his little spitfire whacked his chest.

"Not one word, Cooper Hood. Get it through your thick head that my reputation means more to me than it does to you. And while I'll always protect it, I'm still going to live my life. And before I'm a partner in the resort, a daughter, and a friend, I'm a *woman*, and this woman had more fun in the last ten minutes than she's had in a year. So don't you dare ruin it for me."

Her hair tousled from his hands, her lips swollen from his kisses, she gazed up at him with a wildly sexy and formidable expression that held no room for argument. "Now, let's go back to my cabin and do it all over again."

A cool breeze washed over him, teasing gooseflesh along his arms. Cooper awakened to find himself in a distinctly feminine bedroom.

Beside the ottoman lay a pair of worn, red cowboy boots—one tipped over. Running a hand lazily over his chest, he thought of Daisy in that flared skirt, her bare legs. *Damn.* He'd licked those thighs last night, held her ankles in his palm as he'd slid into her, all that dark hair spilled across her sheet.

A sting of awareness sped through him. *I slept with Daisy Charbonneau.* Twice. The first time almost hadn't counted because he'd been as frenzied as a teenage boy losing his virginity. But the second time…his body tingled at the memory…the second time he'd given his hands the run of that luscious body.

Given the nature of his life on the road and living in his bass player's farmhouse, he didn't spend the night with women. He didn't wake up in the morning and lounge around, didn't linger with quiet conversation.

So, waking up in Daisy's bed, smelling her vanilla and honey scent in the sheets and on his skin, made his body hum. He'd never—not once—considered turning his fantasy of being with her into reality.

But I did it. He almost couldn't believe it, but it was better than anything he'd ever imagined.

With a jolt, he remembered it was Monday. Time to launch their event. They needed to hit Town Hall as soon as the doors opened for business so Daisy could file her revised permitting paperwork.

He swiped his black boxers off the floor—smiling at the memory of Daisy yanking them off his hips last night —and hit the bathroom. When he finished, he followed the aroma of coffee into the kitchen to find Daisy in her pajama shorts, bare feet, and a flimsy cardigan with over-long sleeves. As she scraped butter across toast, he stood back to watch her hair shimmy with the exertion.

She must've sensed him because she glanced over her shoulder. Her jaw slackened, the knife lowered, and she gaped at his chest as he approached.

No one made him feel as robustly masculine as Daisy. Her gaze took a slow climb down to his dick, where the blood had already begun to pool, and then back up to his pecs, higher still to snag on his mouth. When she reached his eyes, a sheepish smile bloomed, and she turned back to her toast. "Morning."

He'd never been happier for the fitness training Violet had imposed on the band back when she'd been their minder.

He came up behind her, wrapped his arms around her waist, and nuzzled her neck. "Morning." Her slightly damp hair and fresh, clean scent told him she'd already showered. Her head tilted back, exposing her neck, and he pressed his mouth to the fluttering pulse point.

Her arms went up and around his neck, holding him

to her, and she lifted her mouth to greet his. Kissing him, she turned in his arms until their chests were pressed together.

His hands slid down to her ass, hitching her up against him. "You feel good."

Her fingers scraped into his hair, and she sighed into his mouth.

Reaching under the elastic of her shorts to cup her bare flesh, he kissed her deeply, hungrily, and then lifted her onto the counter. He pushed her thighs open, jerked her ass to the edge, and stepped between her legs. Pushing aside the sweater, he shoved the tank top up over her bare breasts.

Jesus, look at her. A rush of tenderness for this beautiful, sexy woman nearly took out his knees. She gave herself to him so completely, holding nothing back—it filled him with awe and affection so profound it almost hurt. He pushed those bountiful mounds together and licked first one nipple and then the other, back and forth, sucking and licking, until she writhed against him, back arching, hands braced on the counter behind her.

"Cooper."

He kept his mouth on her as one hand lowered to peel down her cotton shorts. She lifted first one hip, and then the other, so he could pull them off and toss them aside. The moment he slid a finger into her slick heat, her thighs fell open, and her head tipped onto his shoulder. Hot little pants of breath hit his neck.

He teased her slick core, drawing lazy circles around her clit, and when she released a slow, sensuous moan, affection darkened into white-hot lust. *That's it.* Scooping her off the counter, he carried her to the couch, where he set her down only long enough to push down his boxers.

She threw off her sweater and tank top and straddled him in all her naked glory.

"I'm greedy for you." Still, he forced himself to slow down. With her eyelids heavy with passion, her lips still wet from his kisses, and that long, thick hair shiny in the morning light, she was the most beautiful woman he'd ever seen.

Getting up on her knees, she grasped the base of his cock and gave him a sexy smile. And then, holding his gaze, she lowered herself onto him, sheathing his rigid cock in her tight, wet heat. She started to move, but he clamped his hands on her hips.

He had so little time with her. He needed to savor every moment. "Wait. Let me..." How did he say it? That he couldn't believe he got to be with her? That he needed to hang onto every moment—clip some small piece of it to his heart, like a photograph in a locket?

"What is it?" She smoothed the hair off his cheeks.

Too many emotions scrambled his mind. Lust, affection, yearning, fear, everything just raced headlong into a fiery crash and shut down his ability to reason. Lifting her, he brought her down at the same time he punched his hips up.

"Oh, God." She tumbled forward. With her hands on the back of the couch, her sweetly scented hair closed around them like a curtain.

Fuck, she smelled good. She felt good. Planting his feet on the wood floor, he powered into her, her sounds of pleasure whipping him into a frenzy. But it wasn't enough. He needed more. "Let me see you."

She leaned back, hands on his thighs, as she watched where their bodies joined. *Fuck, that's hot.* Her breasts bounced, her hips rolled, and it drove him into a state of mindless, sensual ecstasy. She reached a hand between them, surrounding him, so that his cock felt the brush of her fingers with his every stroke. "Daisy. Oh, *fuck*."

Her lustful moan let him know she was barely hanging onto her sanity. He batted her hand away, rubbed her clit —so fucking slick—and sucked her nipple into his mouth, lashing it with his tongue. As she cried out, her fingernails digging into his shoulders, his climax barreled through him. "Ah, Jesus, Daisy…" It was too much. Her touch, her hair, the look on her face as her climax whisked her into its vortex. "*Fuck*." Sensation exploded, and he came so hard it electrified his skin.

Daisy slowed, still rocking, a lazy smile forming as she let out a long, satisfied sigh.

"Let's never stop doing this, okay?" She cupped his cheek, giving him a slow, sexy kiss.

He pushed her hair aside to get better access to her mouth.

But she pulled away with a regretful sigh. "Town Hall."

"Right."

She got off him, stretching her arms over her head. The arch of her back thrust her breasts out.

As spent as he was, desire still crackled under his skin. "If you don't put some clothes on, you'll get your wish." *We won't ever stop doing this.*

"Fine." With a laugh, she scooped her sweater off the floor. "I'm going to grab *another* shower. I've already eaten, so the toast and coffee are for you."

Body still humming, Cooper got up and quickly put on his boxers. By the hearth, Daisy had a basket of cinnamon-scented pine cones. Between that and the brewing coffee, the cabin felt cozy. Like home. And for a guy who had zero interest in any kind of domesticity, his level of comfort here came as a surprise.

He liked tour buses and hotel rooms. He liked the never-ending party of life on the road. At Violet's, he often got restless. *So, what's different here?* He only knew there was nowhere he'd rather be than in Daisy's kitchen eating the toast she'd prepared for him.

A knock on the cabin door had him jerking away from the counter. As if he'd been caught in her house.

"Daze?" *Ethan.*

Great. Well, he wasn't about to hide. He grabbed the jeans he'd left on the floor and the black T-shirt he'd tossed on the back of a chair as he and Daisy had raced to get naked the night before.

Dressed, he opened the door, letting in the cool morning air. "Yeah?"

With a set of car keys in his hand, Ethan's surprise gave way quickly to displeasure. "Where's Daisy?"

Saying she was in the shower would imply an intimacy he didn't know if Daisy wanted to reveal. And until he talked to her about it, he wouldn't embarrass her.

"Those hers?" He snatched the keys out of Ethan's hand.

"What're you doing here, Cooper?"

Cooper didn't like the accusation in the guy's tone. "I'm—"

"Oh, hey, there, Ethan. Come on in."

Both men turned to see Daisy in a pretty white sundress with a red belt and matching red cowboy boots. She wheeled a small suitcase behind her. Ethan pushed past Cooper and stepped inside.

"I know you want to get to Town Hall first thing," Ethan said. "So, I drove your car over."

"That's so nice of you. Thank you. We were just heading out."

"Remi and Nash'll start making calls after they get back from their run." Ethan's gaze lowered until he hit Cooper's bare feet. He turned a questioning eye on Daisy.

"Cooper's staying in my cabin."

Ethan's features hardened. "Are you sure that's a good idea? This place is going to be crawling with press. I don't want our message to get lost in this one." His finger flicked between Cooper and Daisy.

Even though Ethan was right—who Cooper was fucking would grab far more attention than a band competition—Cooper still wanted to tell him it was none of his damn business.

But Daisy breezed past them both to grab a file folder off the kitchen table. "Don't be a knucklehead. The whole town's booked for the festival, so when Cooper told me he was going to stay in Bozeman, I told him he could take my place. I'm staying with my mom."

Ethan didn't look entirely convinced, but at least he didn't argue.

"Okay, I'm ready." She looked to Cooper. "You need a few more minutes?"

"Yeah." He headed back into her bedroom to grab his boots.

"You need me to come with you?" he heard Ethan ask.

"Nah, I got this. When I hand over the papers, I'm going to point out that we're not making any major changes. Hopefully, that'll be enough to convince them they don't need an actual zoning meeting. It all just depends on what Stuart told them."

Cooper sat on the edge of the mattress, tugging on his boots as he listened to them talk.

"Okay." Ethan said. "Let me know how it goes."

"I will."

After the cabin door shut, Daisy's heels clacked on the wood floors. She stood in the doorway, watching him tie up his laces. "You angry I lied?"

"No." He understood. Daisy *shouldn't* be associated with him.

"Good." Her chin dipped with a naughty smile. "This is going to be so much fun."

Get the hell out of my store.

Fourteen years had passed, and that damn voice still hadn't faded.

Cooper stood at the entrance to Tandy's Grocer, feeling just as sick as when he'd run out with a bag of beef jerky stuffed in the side pocket of his backpack.

He'd been so damn hungry, though. They'd had no neighbors out at the hunting cabin, and he couldn't cop a free lunch from school because of spring break. So, when his mom hadn't come home on that fourth morning, he'd hiked into town, marched into the store, and asked for a job.

Tandy had looked at him like he was a junkie with a needle hanging out of his arm. Told him he couldn't hire a fourteen-year-old. With all those customers watching him, Cooper had hustled away, but the smell of peanuts had stabbed a knife of pain into his stomach, and he'd gone light-headed. As he'd raced past the beef jerky display, he could taste the salty, teriyaki flavor, and the punch of hunger made him lose his step.

He'd crouched, pretending to tie his shoe, while he wrestled with the terrible impulse to steal. His skin had broken out in a clammy sweat, but he hadn't seen an alternative. So, he'd gotten up, a bead of sweat trickling down his spine, and looked around. The coast had been clear. But at the exact moment he'd reached for the bag, Mrs. Kerrigan had turned her cart down his aisle.

While she'd read the ingredients on a bag of Chex Mix, he'd gone for it. Yanked the jerky off the rack and stuffed it into his backpack. He'd darted out of that store, anxiety raising the hairs at the back of his neck. Waking up to a bear taking a swipe at him was nothing compared to the abject terror of getting caught by Mr. Tandy.

The old man's voice had been louder than God's. "Cooper Hood!"

Cooper hadn't even turned around. Just as he'd pushed out the door, he'd heard, "You get the hell out of my store and don't come back."

He hadn't. Nor had he ever stolen anything again.

More importantly, he no longer needed to. He pulled open the door and stepped inside to find the layout had changed. Fourteen years ago, there'd been a diner counter with five red soda fountain-style stools on the left side. Now, a wall of refrigerators had replaced it, packing every kind of beverage known to humankind. The cramped aisles had widened, and bins of bulk candy and nuts replaced the dusty fake plants that used to be the end cap.

"You want anything?" Daisy stood in front of the refrigerator.

"I'll take a water, thanks." His voice sounded too loud like he was challenging Ed Tandy to come out of his office and face him.

But Tandy had been a middle-aged man back then, and he'd looked pretty old at the auction, so maybe he'd retired.

What the hell did he care if the fucker still worked there? He couldn't hurt Cooper anymore.

With an armful of water bottles, Daisy approached him. "After we drop off the paperwork, let's stop at the Sugar Bowl. All we had this morning was toast, and I'm starving. You want a bagel?"

"Nope. I'll grab something here." He quickly scanned the aisles, his gaze settling on a familiar sight. "A bag of jerky." Or twelve. He could afford the whole case.

Daisy scrunched up her nose at his choice. "You could always just peel off the soles of my boots, slice them up into strips, and soak them in teriyaki sauce."

"But then I'd worry about your feet."

"Har."

"Daisy?" That booming voice had everyone turning to watch Ed Tandy charge out of his office and stalk her like a hunter toward his fear-paralyzed prey. "Daisy, glad you came by. I wanted to talk to you about—" He stopped talking when he noticed Cooper. "Cooper Hood."

"Mr. Tandy." He offered a hand, hoping the man would keep his mouth shut.

Get the hell out of my store.

The big, beefy paw gave him a firm shake. "Heard you were in town." The way he took in Cooper's tats and long hair made him feel like that dirty kid all over again.

"Yep."

Daisy stepped closer. "Cooper's helping us with the Huckleberry Festival."

But Tandy didn't seem to be paying attention to her. "Heard you play in a rock band."

"You heard right."

"You plan on taking the stage with the mayor?"

"No, sir, there's been a change of plans."

"Shout! bailed on us," Daisy said. "They're playing at the Blue Sky Amphitheatre instead, but Cooper saved our butts by coming up with an even better idea. We're going to host a Battle of the Bands."

Mr. Tandy glowered. "You're bringing in more than one rock band?"

"That's right," Cooper said.

"Not just rock," Daisy said. "We've got a nice mix of jazz, rockabilly, and country rock, too."

Mr. Tandy's bushy eyebrows moved closer together the more she spoke, and it became clear to Cooper the old man didn't give a damn about the festival. Cooper's involvement pissed him off.

"You can stop giving me that look. I'm not going to steal anything." He dug into his pocket, pulled out his wallet, and thrust a twenty dollar-bill at him. "That should cover the jerky and the handful of Bic lighters you didn't know I took when I was eleven. We square?"

Tandy just stared at the bill. And then his features split in a grin. He barked out a laugh. "Oh, I knew about the lighters all right."

"Yeah? Well, thanks for not chasing me out of the store that day." He took the waters from Daisy and set them on the counter, along with his bag of beef jerky. "We'll just pay for these and go."

Heading behind the counter, Mr. Tandy tapped the register a few times. He peered through fingerprint-smeared glasses as he held the water bottle under the scanner until it beeped. "Battle of bands, huh? Think it'll bring in even more tourists than that crazy old band of Stuart's?"

Oh, Christ. He meant more people like Cooper, with

whippets at their feet and white powder under their nostrils.

But before he could defend himself, the old man went on. "Sounds like it'll bring in a lot of business for us." He peered over the glasses, his gaze shifting from Daisy to Cooper. "Appreciate you young folks working so hard to give a kick to our economy." He reached under the counter for a bag.

"No bag, thanks." Daisy collected the bottles.

Cooper grabbed his jerky and stuffed his wallet into his back pocket.

Just as he turned to go, he heard that deep voice. "You turned out even better than I expected."

Anger flashed through him. "Considering you expected me to wind up in prison, that's not saying much."

The man's jaw went slack. Christ, the last thing he wanted to do was embarrass Daisy, but he hated how the same people who'd shut him out when he was a nobody suddenly admired him now that he was famous.

So, really, fuck him. Fuck everyone in this town who knew what his life had been like in that hunting cabin and had done nothing to help him. "Let's not pretend you thought I was anything other than a piece of shit back then, okay?"

Mr. Tandy's shoulders pushed back. "Piece of shit? Oh, hell, no. I admired you."

"Yeah? Is that why you yelled at me in front of the entire store? Jesus, did you think I *wanted* to steal? Did you think I was some bored kid who got a thrill out of grabbing something and making a run for it? Well, I wasn't. I hated it. But that time? When you made a scene in front of everyone? My mom hadn't been home in four days. I'd eaten my last can of corn, and I was goddamn hungry. I was *fourteen*."

He expected to see a hint of shame on the old man's features, but Mr. Tandy stood strong. "Did I call the cops?"

"No."

"That's right. I called you out publicly. Knew it would burn you pretty bad. Bad enough so stealing wouldn't become a solution to your hunger problem. Did it work? Did it stop you from doing it again?"

Cooper gave him a begrudging chin nod.

"Then I don't regret what I did."

"You stopped me all right. Put the fear of God into me. I nearly pissed in my pants."

Daisy smiled with that sparkle in her eyes. "Okay, boys, good talk. But Town Hall opened fifteen minutes ago, and that makes us late."

Chapter Twelve

"*PUBLIC NUISANCE*?" HEADING OUT OF TOWN HALL, Daisy slammed the lever on the door. Sunlight exploded in her eyes. "What is the *matter* with him?" She held the door open with a foot, while she dug into her tote for sunglasses. "We *always* have noise. We *always* have traffic. It's a damn festival."

Cooper strode past her, aviators already on. She stopped searching to take him in. Good God, the man was hot. His powerful chest filled out the worn Van Halen T-shirt, and his biceps flexed and bulged as he pulled his phone from his back pocket and gave the screen a swipe.

How *in the world* was she supposed to act like his business partner when she wanted to lift his shirt and lick his tattooed stomach?

Uh, because of *Stuart.* She found her sunglass case. "Why would he sabotage our event? He's the *mayor.* It doesn't make sense."

"He wants all the attention on him."

"Okay, but his audience hasn't changed. They bought

tickets. He's still going to have the same show regardless of the location."

"Doesn't matter. We'll have one running at the same time."

True. And with someone from Blue Fire on board, it could easily be just as good as—if not better than—a Shout! reunion.

After the building's air conditioning, the midmorning sun warmed her skin as she hurried down the steps. She slid her sunglasses on. "I'm going to kill him."

"Don't bother. You saw that lady's face. Once you explained the situation, she got it. She's on your side. I doubt she'll even bother taking it to the Zoning Commission."

She let out a breath, slowing down. "You're right. I'm letting him get to me."

"Well, sure. He's fucking with us." When he held her gaze like that, the whole world faded away until it was just the two of them. Sparklers went off in her chest. But he just cleared his throat and looked away. "What's next on the list?"

"The guys should be making their calls to the potential judges right now, so while I'm waiting to hear back from them, I need to get that article started for the paper." They stepped off the curb and headed for the green.

"Should we make some calls of our own?" he asked. "In case they don't come through?"

"Oh, they'll come through. In typical Blackstock fashion, they've turned it into a contest. Whoever scores the biggest-name judge wins Eagle's Landing."

"What's that?"

"It's the best parcel of land on the property. It sits like a huge shelf against the mountain and overlooks the entire valley. You can see the ranch, the Gallatin River, the town, and then just mountains forever. It's amazing."

A group of excited girls headed toward them, and it sucked because she wasn't ready to share him. She wanted him all to herself. God, they were intense together. Sex had never felt like that before.

What *was* this connection between them?

She obviously couldn't let personal feelings keep him from fans, though, so she turned to them. But instead of his usual open demeanor, the lazy smile that lured fans over, Cooper tucked his head down and kept walking, effectively shutting them out. Almost comically, the girls came to a hard stop and then turned away.

What was that all about? She'd never seen him turn away from fans.

"Maybe they should leave it alone," he said. "Not everything needs to be claimed and conquered."

"Don't you know them at all? They're the most competitive bunch of guys I've ever met. And that piece of land is the bone they've been fighting over their whole lives. "

"So, they'll give it away over a stupid bet?"

Now would be a good time to tell him. But she couldn't betray Ethan's confidence. "All summer long, we've had investor weekends. Wine tastings, fly fishing, art shows. We have a very clear number of shareholders we need to make a go of this resort. And this weekend—"

"It's the last one. I get it. But having a big-name judge isn't a make-or-break situation for the competition."

She stopped, holding his gaze. "This weekend is make-or-break as far as the *resort* goes."

The moment he got her meaning, he gave a curt nod.

"Anyhow, we're meeting with the event coordinator to

go over press releases at eleven. And then some lighting and fence people are coming by."

"Sounds like you've got a busy day."

"I do." She wondered at his playful tone.

"Probably not a good time to bring it up."

"Bring what up?"

"How much I want to kiss you."

Heat exploded in her chest and spiraled out along her limbs. "I…" She burst out laughing. "Cooper?"

"Yeah?"

"I appreciate the whole badass rocker vibe. Believe me, I do. But, boy, you don't give anything away." Her thumb hit the keypad to unlock her car. "It's all I can do to keep from climbing onto your lap and licking your tattoos, and there you are, all cool as a cucumber, making me feel like you're not thinking about me at all." Just as she stepped off the curb, he grabbed her upper arm.

"Daze."

"Yeah?"

"Which ones?" His voice went tight and growly.

She wanted to lift those shades up to see his eyes. She could read everything in them, and she really wanted to see his hunger for her. "Which ones what?"

"Do you want to lick?"

Oh, dear God. That deep voice, the carnal intentions, just thrilled her. "Do I have to choose? Or can I take my time licking all of them?"

"Pull over." Cooper knew this stretch of highway, and the dense stand of trees hiding the river had a narrow enclave.

Her car would be well hidden from the highway and the fishermen.

She didn't even hesitate, just checked her rearview mirror before easing off the road. The moment she put the car in park, they reached for each other. Her hands cupped his cheeks, and their mouths met in greedy possession. When their tongues touched, electricity lashed through his body. Everything about this woman…her positive spirit, her fierce loyalty, her soul-wrecking kindness…slayed him. Just fucking slayed him.

With the shadows of the forest cocooning them, he let himself sink into her feminine softness. He traced a path down the petal-soft column of her neck to the rise of her breasts. He cupped them, giving a gentle squeeze. The ripe fullness, the beaded nipple, lit a fire at the base of his spine.

Her hand fell to his lap, the heel of her palm rubbing his erection. She tore his buttons open and grasped him through his boxers.

A phone buzzed, ripping through the haze of lust. They pulled apart, foreheads still touching, their breaths hot and mingling. With a sigh, Daisy reached for her phone in the cupholder.

She read the screen. "It's Ethan. There's trouble."

As they turned into the Blackstock Ranch, Cooper steeled himself for the bad news. *Better get Cooper over here.* What did that mean?

"Can you hand me the lipstick in the zippered part of my tote?"

"Don't bother." Her mouth, pink and swollen, was still

wet from his kisses. "You won't be needing it while I'm in town."

"*Cooper*." She pressed her thighs together. "You realize in about two seconds I'm supposed to get out of the car and pretend like we're just business associates, right?"

After they crossed the river, they entered a hive of activity. Guests walked toward the main building for breakfast or workouts, workers unloaded white tents in the meadow, and golf carts whirred along the paths.

Hard to think of her as a business associate while her scent still clung to his shirt, and his palm remembered the weight of her breast. "Don't care what's on the agenda today. You and I are having a private lunch meeting."

"Oh, I love when you get all bossy." Smiling, she parked alongside the workers' trucks. She killed the engine. "Wish I'd worn my pretty lingerie."

"Don't give a damn what you wear. I'm just going to get you out of it anyway." As he reached for the handle to open the door, Cooper clocked the beat-up Toyota Corolla. Dread smacked him like a dead fish. What the hell was his mom doing here?

Daisy came around the front of the car and waited for him to get out. "What is it?"

He got out, his pulse ticking like a bomb. "My mom."

She struck off across the scrubby grass. "Let's go see what's up."

White fabric from the tents dotted the meadow like deflated balloons, and silver poles gleamed in the bright sunlight. In the clearing ahead, the Blackstock brothers stood side by side, a wall so formidable Cooper couldn't see who or what they faced. But he knew.

Raised voices had him picking up his pace. And then he saw Hunter. The normally quiet man's features were red and damp, his movements jerky, as he yelled at Cooper's mom.

"Shit." Cooper raced ahead.

With a cigarette burning in one hand and an arm crossed over her stomach, Ronnie Hood scowled at something in the distance.

"Answer me," Hunter said. "I have a right to know."

Ronnie looked up at Cooper's approach. The hand with the cigarette gestured to the crowd surrounding her. "Not here. Not in front of everyone."

Hunter's eyes went wide. "You came *here*. What did you think would happen?"

"I wasn't looking for you." Cooper hated that tone. Mean, hard, and ice cold. It was the voice of his childhood whenever he'd asked for anything.

"Well, lady, it's my property, so it can't be much of a surprise that you found me." Hunter's eyes widened when Cooper showed up. He blew out a breath.

But Cooper could only focus on his mom. "What's going on?"

"I'm looking for Slider."

"Oh, Christ. *Mom*."

"Not like that. I'm pissed at him for telling you about the test. That you found out about…" She jerked her chin towards Hunter. "*Him*. He didn't need to let it out like that."

"Would I ever have found out if he hadn't?" Hunter asked.

His mom took another hit off her cigarette and looked away in disgust. "That's why the kid came to town. So, I could tell him."

The kid.

Cooper let the two words—as inanimate as drumsticks

—careen through his body until they landed on the bruised bed of his heart. It shouldn't hurt. He should be used to her disregard.

"You're supposed to be at the building site." He'd arranged a meeting with the contractor to go over the building plans. Even though Cooper had chosen a specific layout, he wanted his mom to add the details that would make it her home. "Isn't that more important than talking to Slider?"

"That's where I was going. But a friend of mine texted, said she saw him working here." She tilted her head toward the meadow. "And he hasn't returned my messages, so I came to let him know he's an asshole."

Cooper stepped between her and the Blackstock men, his shadow looming over her. "Forget about Slider." He said it low, even though he knew everyone could hear him. "Focus on the house we're building."

"I *am*. I just want to give him a piece of my mind."

That had been his mom's problem all along. No impulse control. She had the maturity of a teenager.

"Well, I'd like to give you a piece of *my* mind." Hunter's voice trembled with anger.

"Dad," Ethan said.

"No." Keeping his focus on Ronnie, Hunter speared a finger at Cooper. "He's twenty-eight years old. Twenty-eight. And I just found out about him? He grew up with *nothing*." He spread his arms, opening them wide to indicate the whole of the property. "When I could've given him everything."

Her expression remained belligerent. But Hunter couldn't know that his reproach would only harden her. He wouldn't get that she didn't have the capacity to care.

"I would've given him a home...food." He jerked a hand to his sons. "A goddamn family."

The little boy in Cooper rejoiced—he'd imagined this scenario a thousand times. A big strong man—clean, groomed, kind—would kick in the door and rescue him from Ronnie and her strung-out friends.

But the boy also knew that provoking Ronnie would lead her to say things no one would believe a mother could say.

"I thought he was Slider's." She bit out each word.

"Bullshit. You might've wanted him to be Slider's, but you knew. Look at him. Of course, you knew." Hunter shoved both hands in his hair like he was trying to keep the pieces of his fractured skull together. "Jesus. I can't believe you're standing here giving me attitude. You kept my son from me. You kept him from a decent life." His pleading tone belied his aggressive stance. "He's twenty-eight years old, and I can't make it up to him. I can't make up for those years he lived in filth, poverty, and neglect."

"Okay." Cooper grabbed Hunter's arm and pulled him back. "That's enough."

"No, it's not. It's not nearly enough." Hunter's voice rose, more desperate. "It makes me sick to think my son grew up thinking no one cared about him. Jesus, how could you have done that when I was *right here*?"

"I said that's enough." Cooper stepped in front of his mother. "She's in a different place now."

"You can't defend her." Hunter stepped back, stunned. "You just can't."

Up until their first keyboard player had blown up his career, Cooper had assumed his mom had chosen to live the way she had. That getting loaded, trading whatever they owned for her next hit, selling her body for drugs, had been her choice. But, as an adult, he'd lived through enough with his bandmate to understand the terrible clutch of addiction. He'd come to understand it had been beyond his mom's ability to control.

He kept his body a barrier between his parents. "Nobody chooses to live the way she did. It's harder to be a junkie than it is to live a normal life."

"I don't give a damn how she lived. It's you I care about. *You* didn't have a choice, and that's what I can't get over."

"But it *is* over, and I'm fine now. She has a disease, and she's fighting like hell every day to stay sober. So let it go." He moved toward the block of Blackstocks, herding them away from his mom. "You've said your piece. Now leave her to get on with her life. She's building a better one now."

"No, *you're* building one for her," Hunter said. "What's she doing for you?"

Remembering what Daisy had said, Cooper flashed a look at his mom. He didn't need her to feel shitty because she had nothing to give her son. "The only thing I want her to do. Stay clean. Let that be her only fight right now."

"Everything okay here?" A police officer in a khaki-colored uniform approached, reading the situation.

It just keeps getting better. Anticipating his mom's response, Cooper cut the guy off before she had a chance to make things worse.

But it was Ethan who stepped forward and reached out his hand. "How's it going, Zach?" The men shook firmly.

The cop peered around him to see Cooper's mom who, instead of trying to prove she wasn't causing trouble, looked angry and defiant. "Ronnie."

His mom's chin tilted higher. "I didn't do anything."

The tension in the cop's body told Cooper the man had plenty of experience with Ronnie Hood. "Got a call about trespassing."

"Ms. Hood's here with her son," Nash said.

Zach shared a brief but meaningful look with Ethan, who gave a barely noticeable nod. After a moment, the cop eased back. "Okay, then." With a sweeping look of the meadow, he said, "Getting ready for the festival, I see. Looking good."

"Yep," Ethan said. "Everything's right on track."

"Thanks for coming by, Zach," Hunter said. "Sorry to waste your time."

"No problem." He took off back to his idling cruiser.

His mom dropped her cigarette on the stubby lawn and ground it with the toe of her hiking sandal. Her features turned sour, so before she could unleash her venom, Cooper said, "Let's get to the property, Mom. I want you to look at the floorplans, see if you want to make any changes."

He cupped her elbow, forcing her along. As he headed off, he glanced back to Hunter. "Text me as soon as you're ready to start auditions."

"I've got a band coming in from Washington, so it won't be till later this afternoon. Might as well do them all at the same time."

"Sounds good." As he passed Daisy, she gave him a supportive smile. But he just looked away.

He guessed she got it now, why he couldn't have dated her back in high school.

Shitty way to prove his point.

The sun hid behind an enormous cloud, chilling the air. "Well?" Daisy waited for Ethan to finish reading the text message. Everything hinged on the answer.

He slid out of the car. "He's in." A rare smile broke across his handsome features. "The governor's in."

Remi let out a whoop. "Fuck, yeah."

Daisy clutched the car keys to her chest. "Oh, thank God. This is really going to happen. We're going to pull this off." She wanted to hug Cooper, thank him for coming up with these brilliant ideas, but she hadn't heard from him since he'd gone off with his mom several hours ago.

The three of them headed toward the building. "Do we still need Mr. Walker?" Remi asked.

So far, everyone had accepted their invitation and, thankfully, once they heard about the media exposure, they'd all waived their appearance fees. "We've only got three judges, but even if we had ten, I'd still ask him. This town wouldn't have a music program without him, and I want to honor him with the role if he wants it." She knew Cooper would agree.

Ethan held the front door open, and Daisy and Remi walked into the high school. Glass cases towered on either side of the wide and bright foyer. The Blackstocks were represented by trophies, framed photographs, and plaques for their achievements over many, many years. Ethan's were for football, of course, and the twins had loads of commendations for snowboarding and skiing. Nash had also lettered in wrestling, though his brother had refused to shove his face into "some guy's sweaty balls."

They headed down familiar, cool hallways, getting closer to the sound of rock music. For as long as she could remember, Mr. Walker had offered music classes through the Parks and Recreation Department. She'd taken them, but mainly because it had given her time with Cooper over the summer.

Remi stopped, smiling wickedly outside a door. "Ah, man. The memories."

"Of the textbook storage room?" Daisy didn't get it.

Remi shared a look with his brother, both of them smiling. "Melissa Sawyer."

Ethan scowled. "She's two years older than you." But Remi just held onto his smug grin. "Bullshit. You never got with Mel."

Remi laughed and moved on. "Whatever you want to tell yourself."

Melissa Sawyer had been valedictorian of their class. She was gorgeous, popular, athletic, and about the nicest girl Daisy had ever known. She could totally see Melissa hooking up with hot, naughty, and rugged Remi.

She took advantage of her moment alone with Ethan. "Hey, I wanted to thank you for diffusing the tension when Zach showed up."

He looked uncomfortable. "The way Cooper stuck up for his mom…I thought that was cool."

She'd liked that, too. Of course, she'd agreed with everything Hunter had said—who wouldn't?— but she'd admired Cooper for understanding his mom's limitations. "To be honest, I worry that you guys will blame him for what your dad did."

Remi slowed until they caught up with him. "My mom says she and my dad weren't together when dad and Ronnie hooked up."

"Is she upset, though?" Daisy asked. "To know her husband has a kid with another woman?"

"She's not." Ethan sounded surprised. "She said my dad talked to her about his suspicions from the start."

The music grew louder, and it was nothing like her memories of music class. It was boisterous rock. "I just hope you keep in mind that he's as innocent in all this as you."

Ethan's expression shut down. "The only thing I care about is him pulling off this event."

"There wouldn't *be* an event without him." They'd reached the music room, and in an attempt to make her displeasure clear, she swept inside only to come to an abrupt stop. The brothers crashed into her from behind.

Facing the classroom, Cooper sat on a stool with an acoustic guitar on his lap. His fingers flew over the fret, his long hair covering his cheeks and bouncing with his exertions.

The entire class of a dozen or so kids rocked out to AC/DC's "You Shook Me All Night Long." Some played instruments and shouted the lyrics, but everyone moved with the hard-charging tune.

"What the hell?" Remi looked amused.

"This is Mr. Walker's summer class?" Ethan asked.

She loved it. Absolutely loved it. "This is Cooper." What a shame he only showed the world his party-boy persona.

Mr. Walker approached them with his arms open. "Daisy. What a lovely surprise." He drew her in for a big, warm hug.

"Hey, Mr. Walker." She turned to include the guys. "You know Hunter's sons, Ethan and Remi?"

"Of course. Nice to see you." The men shook hands. "Did you come to see our famous visitor?"

"We didn't even know he'd be here." The kids were utterly captivated. Not by the rock star but by the music. "He's amazing." She'd never seen a group of kids so into music.

"He is. He stopped by to say hello, and within minutes he had them in his thrall. Come in, come in. He brought snacks." Mr. Walker led them to a table loaded with pale pink bakery boxes from the Sugar Bowl, jugs of lemonade, and cartons of milk.

"Cooper brought all that?"

Mr. Walker nodded, obviously pleased...and proud.

Remi immediately grabbed a crawler. His foot tapped, and his head nodded in time to the beat.

She leaned close so Mr. Walker could hear her over the music. "Did Cooper have a chance to tell you about the Battle of the Bands?"

"He mentioned it briefly. Sounds like a good idea."

"It's going to be great. We're looking for judges. So far, we've got Miss Montana, Buddy Mercer—"

"The rodeo clown?" His eyes glittered with delight.

She nodded, smiling. "And the governor."

His eyebrows shot up in surprise.

"And we're hoping you might join us, too."

A smile enlivened his features. "Well, isn't that something? I'd be honored. Thank you. Thank you for thinking of me." He looked to Cooper with pure pride. "Having him stop by for a visit...and now this? It's wonderful. Really wonderful."

"Daisy Charbonneau," Cooper's deep voice called over the music.

The room quieted down. "Gonna need an alto for this next song." He turned to the class. "Who wants Daisy up here?"

The kids shouted and shook their tambourines, everyone urging her to join in.

Laughing, she grabbed a guitar from its stand and dragged over a stool.

Cooper leaned toward her. "You game?"

She was game all right. She was game for everything with him.

And that was the whole problem. Because she had no idea how she was supposed to keep from falling in love with him.

In the four days he'd been living with her, Daisy had let Cooper drive her car exactly zero times.

So, when he reached around to open the door, his chest brushing up against her back, she gave him a foul look. "No one but me has ever driven my car."

"Sounds like it's time to shake things up." He placed his palm on top of her head and gently pushed. "Get in."

"You going to tell me where we're going?" Reluctantly, she settled into the passenger seat and tugged on the seatbelt. The car smelled absolutely delicious. Warm bread. And something else—spicy spaghetti sauce?

"On a date." He shut her door and got in on the other side. Jamming the key into the ignition, his eyes glittered with lust as he stared at the dashboard. "Let's see what you got, baby."

She whacked him. "Cooper."

He burst out laughing. "I'm kidding. I'm not all that into cars."

"Great. Then let me drive." But it was hard to stay too annoyed with him when he filled out that dark suit so nicely.

She'd never seen him dressed formally—not in the press and certainly not in Snowberry, but it looked good on him. The starched white collar of his dress shirt and the burgundy and gold tie looked sharp against the deep navy of the jacket.

He'd asked her to wear a dress, but she hadn't thought he'd meant cocktail dress. Restaurants were pretty casual in this area. Given the take-out bags in the backseat, though, it didn't seem like they were eating out. "You look really good. Like, *really* good. Like good enough that we don't actually have to go anywhere."

Instead of responding, he reached into the console and took out a small, clear box.

Inside rested a perfect pale pink orchid wrapped in a white satin ribbon. "What's this?" Her voice was a whisper. The pieces came together in her mind.

"It's a corsage, cinnabun." He pulled it out. Tossing the box into the backseat, he reached for her hand.

"But why?"

Sliding the stretchy band over her hand, he settled it around her wrist, turned over her palm, and placed a kiss in the center of it. "Because that's what the cool kids wear to the prom." Checking behind him, he put the car in reverse and backed out.

"You're taking me to the prom? In August?" She ran the soft petals across her cheek. "It's so beautiful." Tears stung, and her throat closed.

"Ten years and four months ago, you invited me, but I didn't hear you. I'm hearing you now, and I'm saying yes." He turned toward her. "Thank you for inviting me, Daisy. There's no one else I want to go to the prom with."

. . .

Her high school gym looked—and smelled—exactly the same, except for the flashlights Cooper had set up haphazardly on the bleachers, pointing to the ceiling. There must've been fifty of them. His laptop played a Nickelback song, but they were laughing too hard to actually dance.

"Okay, that's it. I can't stand that song." Cooper stepped away to change it.

"But they were huge in 2007." She couldn't believe how hot he looked with his shirtsleeves rolled up to his elbows, exposing his tan, inked forearms. "I'll bet you liked them just a little."

"I didn't." When Rascal Flatts' "My Wish" came on, he pulled her into his arms. "Besides, I only want to dance if it's a slow one." His arms enveloped her, his big hand taking hold of hers and pressing it over his heart.

God, he smelled good. Not just his freshly-showered scent or the hint of cologne clinging to the shirt, but *him*. "Where'd you get this?" She tugged on the fabric at his back.

"Borrowed it from Nash."

"Nash?"

"I asked Hunter if I could borrow something of his, but he said I was more Nash's size. So, I picked it up from his house on the way back from Mr. Walker's class."

"I can't believe you did all this. It's amazing."

"It's kind of lame, actually, but Mr. Walker and I were talking…" Color flooded his cheeks.

"You told him about us?"

"Not exactly. He said he'd noticed the same spark between us today as when we were kids."

Oh, she liked that.

"I couldn't have asked you out back then. I guess you

understand that now. But he made me wonder what would've happened if I had."

Honestly, they couldn't think about what-ifs. Especially, since life had brought them back together. "You wouldn't have wanted your life to turn out any differently." *Right?* She sought an answer in his eyes, but he gave away nothing. "You love your life."

"I do."

"And you have no interest in settling down?"

He shuddered but with a smile. "God, no."

Ouch. His absolute certainty stung. Not that she'd thought they'd wind up together or anything. That would be ridiculous, considering they hadn't even been together a week. *Been together? You've been sneaking around.* But it might've been nice if he were so swept away by her that he couldn't imagine living without her.

Hey, there's nothing wrong with a rich fantasy life. "What is it about being a rock star that appeals to you? I mean, obviously besides the nookie."

"If I answer that, I have to turn in my keys to the rocker clubhouse."

"But you're not a rock star right now. You're Cooper Hood, my date to the prom. My friend." She brushed her lips across his cheek, up to his ear. "My lover."

"You already know I'm going to cave. I can't keep anything from you. But, please, go ahead and work me over."

She ran her palm over his hard, round ass, felt the muscles tighten, and gave him a squeeze. "Talk."

"I'd rather fuck."

"Cooper." She pinched a cheek.

Never letting her go, his hips shifted away. "Fine, but

just so you know, you've gotten more out of me in one week than my bandmates have in ten years."

You have no idea how happy that makes me.

He pulled her closer, resting his chin on top of her head. "First of all, I'm completely unapologetic about my lifestyle. We worked hard for this level of success, and I'm having the time of my life. But I was an outsider for a long time. Eighteen years of no one wanting anything to do with me. Because I was dirt poor, people thought they could say whatever they wanted. To them, I was an ugly sofa or a mangy dog. But the moment I strapped on a guitar? Famous or not, people idolized me. And there's something pretty powerful in that kind of attention. I'm not stupid. I get that they want me because I'm in a band. I know the minute my star fades, they'll forget about me and move onto the next guy with ink and a Fender. But while I've got their attention, I'm going to ride it out. I'm going to eat up every last bite."

"It doesn't get…old?"

He brushed a lock of hair off her shoulder. "Nah, I haven't had it that long."

She shouldn't push—he'd been perfectly honest—but she couldn't help herself. "You don't want something more meaningful?" *Ever?*

"I get meaningful from my band. What I have now? It's all I could ever ask for." The song ended, and she started to pull away, but he tightened his hold. "Hang on. I've queued up a bunch of nookie-bait songs."

"As if you have to work for it."

He gave her a devilish smile just as RBD's "Tu Amor" came on.

"You sure did your research." She'd forgotten most of these songs.

"Damn straight." His hands lowered to her ass, and he drew her up against him. "See, now, I wouldn't have done that move back in high school."

"It's a good one."

"I had you on a pedestal back then."

"Where's the fun in that?" *I like you better now.*

He kissed just under her ear, sending a wave of goosebumps along her arms. "What about you? What do you want?"

"I'm pretty basic. I want to fall crazy in love with a man who's madly in love with me. Who gives me babies. And I want to raise them here around my family and lifelong friends."

"I thought you said you don't date guys from Snowberry?"

"I don't...." She had to smile the moment she got it. "Houston, we have a problem." *Talk about setting yourself up for failure.* To avoid his gaze, she rested her cheek on his chest. "My college roommate once said something that really hit me. She said your first boyfriend is usually your dad. How your father treats you sets up your expectations for future men. I guess I'm doing a bang-up job of making sure I don't get hurt."

"Daisy?" He tipped her chin and pressed a soft, warm kiss on her mouth. "Don't let your dad steal your future from you. That's what Mr. Walker taught me a long time ago. You deserve to have all your dreams come true."

Yeah, she did. But what if *he* was her dream come true?

Chapter Thirteen

DAISY STARED AT THE MASSIVE HOLE IN CABIN TEN'S wall.

The festival starts in four days. I don't have time for this. "How on earth did this happen?"

Harold, the head of maintenance, crouched in front of it. "Roughhousing, most likely. The family had four kids." He stood, knees cracking. "See the back of that desk chair?" He rolled it around so she could see the support bar. "Kids probably pushed each other around in it, slammed it into the wall."

"That hard?"

Harold shrugged. "It's just wallboard. Got it right between the joists."

The next occupants had requested early check-in. "This seems like more than a patch-up job. How soon do you think you can get it fixed?"

He shrugged. "I can have it ready to go in a couple of hours."

Oh, good. "Thank you so much, Harold. I know you're doing the job of ten people right now."

"Says the woman who's busting her butt to turn this place into a resort." He gave her a meaningful look. "It's going to be a god-send for this town. For my family. Besides, you folks treat me right."

"We couldn't do any of this without you." They headed to the door. "All right, I have to run." She had fifteen minutes to get the punch list and site map to the event coordinator, who needed them for today's deliveries. "Thanks again." As she stepped outside, she found Cooper approaching with a package wrapped in foil.

Sunlight gleamed on his dark hair and glinted off the silver pendants hanging around his neck. Hard muscle flexed beneath worn jeans, and a sexy smile curved lips that had explored every inch of her body. They'd had the best week together. Somehow, they combined the passion of secret lovers with the intimacy and ease of a couple who'd been together for years.

"Hey." Her heart sang with joy at the sight of him.

And then gave a sharp twist. *He's leaving in six days.* She'd tried so hard to keep her expectations in check. To keep it fun. But times like this, when happiness bubbled over at just the sight of him, she knew she was in big trouble.

"Morning." His naughty smile told her he remembered how she'd awakened him. And how he'd thanked her in the closet when she'd tried to get dressed. "Everything all right?" He nodded toward Cabin Ten.

They'd done a great job of hiding their relationship, so the contrast between their blasé public interaction and their insatiable bedroom antics was pretty funny. *Oh, did I say bedroom?* How about her office, her car, the maintenance shed by the pool—*and let's not forget that picnic table down by the river. That was hot.* "The usual drama. You wouldn't believe how people treat hotel rooms." She pointed to the foil in his hand. "What's that?"

"You left without breakfast this morning, so I made you a croissant sandwich."

Heat rushed up her neck, burning to the tips of her ears. Sometimes, she had a hard time reconciling the bad boy rocker with this incredibly sweet and thoughtful man. She just…God, she just *liked* him so much.

"It's nothing like your mom's, but I heated it up. I know you like the croissant crunchy."

Oh, screw it. She threw herself into his arms. Yes, she heard the laughter floating out the window of Cabin Eleven. She was aware of the running shoes slapping the asphalt as a guest ran by. But she didn't care. She was crazy about him. Breathing in his freshly-showered scent, she had to wonder why everything was so amplified with him —her heart, her senses, *everything*.

"It's just a sandwich." But his arms tightened around her, and he dipped his face into her hair.

Oh, God. Realization knocked the breath from her lungs. *This isn't some fun summer fling. I'm not playing out my teenage fantasy.*

It's so much more. Her heart seized with joy and fear. It pounded with hope.

Because she'd fallen completely and totally in love with him.

Calm down. It doesn't change anything. He's still leaving in six days. Lifting up on her toes, she cupped his cheeks and drew his mouth down to hers.

Because trying to keep from getting hurt wasn't working. She was already in too deep. So, while he was here, she'd go all-in. She'd love him with everything she had.

His response was immediate. He licked into her

mouth, hugged her so hard he had her up on her toes. Kissing Cooper felt like stepping off the edge of the world. She lost all sense of time, place, and purpose. He kissed like there was nothing he'd rather do. Like he was put on this earth to love her. She pressed closer to him, wanting to feel the strength of his powerful body against hers. But it wasn't enough. She couldn't get close enough, go deep enough. Her soul ached for more. Her hands went under his shirt and caressed up that hard, hot, muscled back.

A door slammed.

She jerked away. "I, uh…" It took a moment to return to her body. Where did she have to be right then? "I should go. I have to meet Laura." She started to pull away from him, but his grip tightened.

He shook his head, one side of his mouth curling in a mischievous look. "You're not gonna kiss a man like that and run, are you?" He grabbed her wrist and towed her into the empty cabin, quickly shutting the door and locking it.

"I don't have time…"

As his tongue made a slow slide across his bottom lip, he cupped her breasts, his thumbs flicking across her nipples,. "No?"

"Maybe a minute." Her pulse fluttered in her throat.

"Turn around, Daisy."

Energy shot through her so fast she tingled. On jittery legs, she turned to face the wall.

Her eyes closed at the feel of his big hands gripping her ass and squeezing. Lowering his face into the slope of her shoulder, he gently bit the tendon. "Can't get my fill of you."

The back of her dress whooshed up, and he jerked her hips back. Pushing her panties down, he bent as he lowered them to the floor, and she stepped out of them. On his way back up, he bit one cheek, his hands on her thighs. "You're so fucking sexy."

He slid a finger into her wet heat, sending a shock of sensation throughout her body. "So fucking wet." With his other hand, he unbuttoned his jeans and lowered his boxer briefs.

He slid his cock along her wet core, rocking back and forth with unbearable slowness. Each brush against her clit hit a bolt of lightning. "Cooper." Her voice sounded shaky and weak. "I want you so much."

He angled her ass higher and pushed inside. God, he felt good, filling her so completely. After a deliberate jerk of her hips against him—*stay here*—his hand caressed her stomach until he captured her breast. "Cooper. Oh, God." The pinch to her nipple lit the fuse, making both pleasure bases connect in a fiery collision. Her body jerked, and he must have taken it as his signal because his pace quickened.

He leaned over her, his mouth at her ear. "You make me crazy."

She kept her ass tilted and pressed back to meet his thrusts because she didn't want his hands to leave her breasts. Each moan, grunt, and intake of breath slipped right into her bloodstream, making her hotter, wilder.

He swiftly unbuttoned her shirtdress, pulling it open, and yanking down the cups of her bra. The palm of his hand scraped across one nipple while his fingers tweaked the other, ratcheting the tension until pleasure reached a crescendo. Ecstasy ripped through her with a force that sent her reeling. He grabbed her hips, pulling her back onto his frantic thrusts.

And then he held her tightly to him, his hips

punching in short, powerful snaps. He shouted with his release, before sagging against her, his breath hot in her ear.

With his body wrapped around hers, he nuzzled her neck. "Did I make you late?" He backed away to pull up his briefs and jeans.

She adjusted her bra and buttoned her dress. "I'll just explain that my man needed a good seeing-to."

He smiled. "Damn, right. And maybe next time you won't get your man all stirred up when you don't have the time to finish what you started."

"Well, don't make your woman a breakfast sandwich."

He turned away, a faint blush tingeing his cheeks. "It's just a croissant. Slice of cheese and a fried egg. Some Canadian bacon."

She didn't have Canadian bacon in her refrigerator, which meant he'd made a special trip to the store. For her. Because she hadn't had a chance to eat breakfast. "Says the man who equates domesticity with death."

He shrugged. "Hey, I can do anything for two weeks."

His cavalier attitude landed like a swipe across her tender heart, so she looked down at the buttons her trembling fingers tried to manipulate. He batted her hands aside. Unaffected, he had her put back together in a snap.

Grabbing her breakfast, he led the way out the door. "Besides, I kind of like playing house with you."

She hated how easy it would be for him to walk away and not look back. But of course, that had been his plan all along. She was the one who'd gotten in too deep.

But, come on, the way he looks at me—like I'm the sexiest, most delightful creature on the planet? What chance did I have?

If he gave her the chance, she knew she could love him so hard she pushed out all the pain of his childhood. She could fill every day with love, laughter, happiness, and cinnamon buns. God, she could see that future, feel it deep inside.

But that's not what he wants. Maybe in a few years...*oh, stop it.* Who cared about the future when her heart was on the line today?

"The Austin band that got in last night wants to rehearse," he said. "So, Hunter and I are going to offer everyone a time slot on the stage."

He waited for her to respond, but she was having a hard time stuffing her feelings back into the professional box. "Okay."

"I'll come get you before the first band plugs in."

"That's okay. I don't need to be there for rehearsals."

The back of his hand brushed hers. "What can I do to help?"

"Help what?"

"I know you'd come to rehearsals if you could, so I'm guessing you've got too much going on. What can I take off your plate?"

You can stop being so damn kind. "No, you're right. I do want to see them. Text me when they're ready to go." She had him for six more days.

"I'll come get you." He leaned in close enough to whisper. "So, I can add one more kiss to my collection."

She'd take all the sweetness he had to offer. "Sure. I'd like that."

They'd reached the fork in the road for him to go to Hunter's and her to continue on to her office. "You okay?" He handed her the sandwich.

"Of course. I have a lot on my mind."

"Let me know what I can do." He brushed his mouth over hers. "I'll see you later."

She watched him walk—okay, swagger—away until he turned and flashed a cocky smile. *Bastard.* He knew what he did to her. Shaking her head, she smiled and waved him away.

"Hey, sweetheart."

Daisy looked over to see her mom parked at the side of the road bordering the meadow. Surprise at seeing her gave way to relief when she sank into her arms. "What're you doing here?"

Her mom gestured to the vendor tents. "We've got some issues with our space." She smoothed Daisy's hair. "You okay? You look a little flushed. I can't wait until you're able to hire more people. You've got way too much responsibility here."

"I love it." And she did. She loved her job. Not just running the resort but helping design its expansion. *Good reminder.* She loved her job as much as Cooper loved his. Switching roles, if she'd been on tour with him for two weeks, and her time was coming to an end, she'd be just as excited to get back to her job and community.

"I know you do, angel. You just looked a little sad, that's all."

She couldn't keep Laura waiting, not with the deliveries they had coming, but she really needed to vent. "Cooper's leaving in six days."

Her mom reached to tuck a lock of hair behind her ear. "You've gotten close."

"Yeah, we have. I…" *I love him. And I can't have him.* "I've never felt this way before."

"What way is that?"

"Myself." As soon as the word popped out, she felt the

solid truth of it. "I'm totally and completely myself around him." But there was so much more. "He makes me laugh. He takes care of me." She lifted the breakfast sandwich. "I left without eating this morning." Peeling back the foil, she peered inside. "So, he brought me this. He made it for me."

Her mom's features softened. "That's sweet."

"He's *so* sweet. And he's strong. And fun. And determined, and talented, and loyal. And he just seems to *like* me. You know? The way he looks at me, it's like he finds everything I do adorable or sexy or impressive." *It's intoxicating. Of course, I fell in love with him.*

"So, what's the problem? His tour's only three months."

"Mom, I told you he's not coming back here. He lives in New York with his band. After the tour, they'll work on new material and then go into the studio."

"Well, you could both try to be a little flexible. Could you go on tour with him?"

"He wants to be a rock star. He doesn't understand why his bandmates settled down. Believe me, he wouldn't want me on tour cramping his style."

"That was before he met you. Talk to him about it. Maybe he's feeling the same way."

Hey, I can do anything for two weeks. "No, he isn't."

"You don't know that. Let me ask you this. If he wanted you to go, would you?"

Her heart leaped, but she quickly realized it was the part about him asking. Because it would mean he loved her, too. But the tour part? "No."

"Hm. That didn't sound convincing. Maybe while you're still young and unattached, you could do one crazy thing. Hit the road and tour with a rock band. It's only three months. Your job will still be here. And you'll get more time with the man you're obviously developing feelings for."

And then what? He'd go back to New York, and she'd come home. And what would she have but some memories and a trashed heart?

Wait, why was she even considering it? He didn't *want* her to come with him. And she couldn't go. "I can't leave here."

"What if you could? What if you talked to Ethan, and he gave you his blessing to take a three-month leave? Would you go?"

"Maybe right after college, I would have, but I'm almost thirty. I love what I do. I love that what I do *matters*. It's way more satisfying to me than performing. The only reason I'd go is to spend time with Cooper."

Her mom looked at the breakfast sandwich. "His feelings for you might be stronger than you realize."

"I can't believe you're encouraging me to do something so reckless. What if you'd met someone you were crazy about when you were my age? You were pretty much at the same point, turning the bakery into a café and a job into a career. Would you have just up and left it? Taken off for three months?"

Her mom smiled knowingly. "I did that once, remember? And you know how it turned out."

Like Cooper, her dad had made it clear he didn't want to settle down. He'd loved his freedom, loved the open road. Pregnancy hadn't changed him, and neither did having a baby.

Listen to what a man says. He means it.

"Thanks, Mom. That's just what I needed to hear."

• • •

"Sorry I'm late." Daisy breezed past the receptionist. "Is Laura here?"

"Not yet." Miranda reached for some papers on her desk. "Hang on. Got a few things for you."

Grabbing the pile, Daisy briefly sorted through them. "Thanks for printing out the site map."

"Also, Nash agreed to give up his cabin."

She'd figured he would. "Fantastic. Let's get housekeeping in there right away. I want that place to sparkle. Fresh flowers, sheets, comforter." Mickelson had gotten one of the *Entertainment Update* anchors to be a judge. The woman just needed a place to stay in the sold-out resort.

"Also, the power's out on the lower meadow. Got some complaints from the vendors."

Ah. That's why Mom's here. "Call—"

"Already called the electrician. He can't come till tomorrow morning, but it's only Monday. We're good."

Electrical issues for an outdoor event were never good. "Call him back, please. We need him out here today. As soon as possible. And if he can't come today, then let's find someone else."

"He said not to worry about it."

"Does he know what the problem is?"

Miranda shook her head.

"Then he needs to come out right now. We can't take the risk."

"On it." Miranda reached for the phone.

Daisy pulled an envelope out of the pile. "What's this?"

Miranda glanced up. "Not sure. It was delivered about an hour ago."

Daisy checked the return address. "The Gallatin River

Authority?" Hiking her tote higher on her shoulder, she unsealed the envelope and pulled out the letter.

You are hereby ordered by the Gallatin River Authority to immediately cease and desist preparations for the Battle of the Bands *event scheduled to take place at the Huckleberry Festival August 12, 13, and 14 at 6475 Gallatin River Road, Snowberry, Montana, until such time as an environmental impact statement covering the Gallatin River Watershed has been submitted to the GRA and you have obtained the necessary permit from the GRA under Montana statute B20-1986.*

Fear clamped down on the bundle nerves at the back of her neck, squeezing so hard it sent a wave of nausea through her. "Oh, God."

Miranda lowered the phone. "What?"

She couldn't believe it. "What has he done?" He'd shut them down. The event was *four days* away. It would take months to get an environmental impact study done. "Ethan!"

He popped out of his office. "What's going on?"

"Stuart." She waved the letter. "He did it. He killed our event."

Ethan snatched it out of her hand and scanned it. "Mother*fucker*." He tossed the letter on the desk. "He's not getting away with this."

"He already has. In order to file a claim, he had to submit proof that we're harming the river. They have no choice but to investigate."

"We'll talk to them. Just like you did at Town Hall. They'll see the stunt Stuart's trying to pull."

"He's not *trying*. He's done it. He's forced them to go

through the process." *Okay, think. Think.* She had to calm down long enough to get her head clear. She had to figure something out.

And then it hit her. She had proof of her own. "Hang on." She charged into her office.

Ethan followed. "Talk to me."

She pulled open the top file drawer and plucked the legal-size accordion folder from last year's festival. Propping it on her desk, she sorted through it. *Come on, come on.* Where had she put it?

"Daze?"

She didn't even look up, just kept flicking through the papers. "We host the festival every year. And every year we schedule bands to play. The only difference this year is we're calling it a competition."

"The media coverage's going to bring in a lot more people."

"And we've planned accordingly. I'm telling you, between me and Laura, we've covered every possibility. I'm going to put a file together documenting everything. I'll show them the list of bands that played last year so they can see it's close to the same this year. I'll show them the fencing I've installed to keep people away from the river. The added security and waste management. I'll show them I've already considered the impact."

"We, Daisy. We're in this with you."

Finally, she looked up at him. "Of course. I know that." But she didn't. Not really.

Because people let her down all the time. Like her dad and Stuart. They were *in* this situation because of the mayor. She'd learned a long time ago she could only count on herself.

But, of course, the Blackstocks weren't like either of those men, and it wasn't fair to lump them all together.

His hand came down on her forearm and gave her a reassuring squeeze. "He's not going to win. Don't forget my aunt's the director of the GRA."

"The family tie's only going to make it harder on us. She can't be seen doing favors for you. I don't know what charges Stuart filed against us, but your aunt's duty is to protect the river." Didn't she have all these files on her computer? She quit searching and sat at her desk.

"What about the environmental assessment we had done when we presented our resort plans to them?"

She broke into a smile. "*Yes*. It was two years ago, but I'll definitely put it in the file." The tightness eased in her chest. If the GRA had approved their plans to build a huge resort, why would they have a problem with a three-day festival?

Her fingers stilled on the keyboard. "I just don't get it. Why is he doing this? He should be worrying about his own concert. The world's waited years for a Shout! reunion."

Ethan faced the window overlooking the woods. "The only thing we've got over him is the media attention. He's got a small dick. Maybe he can't stand that we've got *Entertainment Update* coverage and he doesn't."

"That's got to be it." She'd been so preoccupied with her own event she hadn't noticed any press for his.

Ethan pulled out his phone and started tapping the screen.

"What're you doing?"

He lifted a finger. After a moment, he said, "Hey, Aunt Bev. It's Ethan." He listened for a moment. "Good, good. How about you?"

Daisy paced to the window that took in the wildflower meadow at the base of the mountain.

"Listen, we just got your notice shutting down the Battle of the Bands. Given we're four days out from the festival, we need to talk to you or someone on the board right away." He went quiet, listening. "Right, but we've always had bands playing, and this year we've taken extra precautions to protect the river, but if you need us to implement any additional compliance measures, we'd like to get a jump on them right now. Let me know when it's good for you to meet."

She turned back to him to see his expression.

"I appreciate that. Talk soon." He ended the call, shoved the phone in his pocket, and pulled in a sharp breath. "She's going to look into it and get back to me."

"Even if she agrees to meet with us, she still has to present our rebuttal to the board." She glanced at the Snowberry Volunteer Fire Fighter calendar tacked to the wall. "Which doesn't convene again until September 8." A month after the festival.

"Let's take this one step at a time. Pull together whatever you've got, and then we'll go talk to her."

"On it."

"We got this, Daze." Just as he reached the door, he said, "In the meantime, we carry on like nothing's happened."

Cooper entered her office, looking between them. "What's going on?"

She dreaded telling him the news. "Apparently, Stuart's silence didn't mean he'd given up his vendetta."

He pushed past Ethan. "Which means?"

"He filed a complaint with the Gallatin River Authority." She saw the flinch of surprise. "And they've issued a cease and desist order on our event until an investigation can be done."

His features hardened. "They can't take him seriously."

"They have to. It's an environmental impact thing. They're required to investigate."

"My aunt's the director of the GRA," Ethan said. "She's looking into it."

Cooper noticeably relaxed. "So, we're okay." He let out a breath. "You should've started with that."

"Actually," Daisy said. "It makes it worse. She can't just make her family's problem go away. The board has to look into the matter and then call for a vote."

"Don't worry," Ethan said. "We'll figure it out."

Cooper looked down at his boots, brow creased in concern. "Well, that's the thing. It's my problem, too." He started for the door.

"Hey," Ethan called. "Where're you going?"

"To talk to him."

"No," Ethan said. "You're not. That'll only antagonize him."

Daisy had to agree. She got out of her chair and came around the desk. "We have more than enough evidence to support our side. We just need to present it to Ethan's aunt."

"But she still might have to go through a process."

Ethan gave him a curt nod. "She might."

"Then I'm going to talk to him."

"We're handling it," Ethan said.

Cooper stepped right up to him. She had to admit that witnessing two equally determined men face off was pretty spectacular. They might have been Highlanders meeting on the battlefield. "There's not a chance in hell I'm going to hope that you figure this shit out. There's even less of a chance that I'm going to call my manager and tell her I failed to deliver on my promise."

"No matter what happens, you've got a band for your tour," she said. "You can choose any one of the bands we're auditioning."

He gave her an implacable look. "My label's interested in the *event*. Without the media attention, some random band we choose means nothing to them. They'll go with their original choice, and that's not acceptable. I'm not going to let my band down when they're counting on me to pull this off."

She loved that this event mattered as much to him as it did to her. With the enormous responsibility she felt for her mom, her godfathers, and Joe's personal investments, it just meant the world to her that she had these warriors fighting with her.

"I hear you." Ethan's tone seemed more conciliatory. "But before we go and kick his ass, let's try meeting with my aunt first, okay?"

The word *we* sent a jolt of awareness through her. For the first time, Ethan had included Cooper, and he wouldn't have done it if he didn't respect him.

Hope bloomed. Ethan had just taken a step toward accepting his half-brother.

Unfortunately, Cooper seemed as uninterested in a connection to his family as ever.

As a child, she'd believed in her father whole-heartedly. With every hit of disappointment, she'd pop back up like an inflatable bop-bag. Until the summer he'd bailed on their state park adventure, and then she'd given up. Her heart couldn't take anymore.

But everyone had let Cooper down. Other than Mr. Walker, no one had been there for him. He'd saved *himself* by getting good grades and learning to play music so well he'd earned a scholarship to a top university.

So maybe he didn't place a whole lot of value in family or community. Not until they'd truly proven themselves like his band had.

"Yeah, okay." The tension in Cooper's shoulders eased. "If you can get this meeting set up today, I'll hold off."

Tuesday morning, Cooper stood at the kitchen counter, the coffeemaker burbling, and waited for Emmie to answer the phone. He could picture the early morning chaos in Violet's farmhouse kitchen, Mimi's hands wrapped in oven mitts as she pulled a decadently rich coffeecake out of the oven; Derek pressing Violet up against the counter and whispering in her ear, coaxing out that shy smile; Lee, perched on Ben's lap, sketching a dress for her fashion design class and shoveling cereal in her mouth.

An ugly snap of pain tore through the pleasant images because he was interrupting their vacation yet again. He had to tell them about Stuart's latest trick. While he'd make sure things didn't go sideways, he couldn't blindside them if they did.

"Coop?" Emmie answered. "How's it going?"

"It's okay. Just wanted to let you know we're meeting—"

"*Hey.*" Emmie's voice sounded distant. "Give me my phone."

"Coop?" Slater came on the line.

"Yeah, man."

"Now's not a good time. Lilah Dove had a rough night

—she's teething—and Emmie's burning it at both ends. You get me?"

Fuck. "Yeah." He hated giving her more to worry about when the whole point was to handle this *for* her. "But she's not going to have peace of mind until I fill her in, so put her back on the phone and let me give her a quick update."

Slater sighed. "Make it real quick. I just got my daughter down for a nap, and that means Emmie's got less than an hour to rest."

Cooper smiled. Three years ago, their lead singer, with his GQ good looks and movie star charisma, had been the focus of their fans' attention. But he'd kept himself aloof and closed off to everyone, including his bandmates. Meeting Emmie had changed all that. So, hearing him talk about his daughter? It was crazy how far that man had come.

"Talk to me," Emmie said.

"Daisy sent the file yesterday, so the director's had a chance to go over the reports and receipts, everything that proves the Blackstocks have addressed environmental issues."

"Good." Her relief came through the line.

"And we're meeting with her this morning." *Three* days before the festival began. Jesus, he had to pull this off.

"Does she have the authority to act without a board meeting?"

"Generally, no, she doesn't. But if we can convince her Stuart's claims are without merit, she might be able to toss them out." He braced for her next question. Because he knew her. She left nothing to chance.

"And if she won't toss them out? If the family tie forces

her to be transparent and go through the process? Then what?"

He could give her a bunch of promises, but they'd be empty. Life wasn't fair, and people didn't always listen to reason. And he didn't fuck with Emmie. "Then I pull out my wild card."

"Which is?"

"Irwin." Their A&R rep at the label was the most powerful man in the industry.

She let out a huff of exasperation. "Irwin doesn't have time to deal with this petty crap."

"It'll take one phone call to Shout!'s manager to end this bullshit. All Irwin has to do is say the word, and suddenly the guy can't book his bands anywhere."

"Look, I know he's the obvious answer, but he's everyone's obvious answer. And, frankly, the reason he likes working with me is because I don't bother him every time something goes wrong."

Shame pierced like a splinter under his fingernail. "I'll make sure it doesn't come to that." But he wouldn't hesitate to go there if necessary.

"How about if I—" The connection got muffled. "*Slater.*"

"Angel, you trust Cooper?" he heard Slater ask.

"Of course, I do."

"Coop, you got his?" Slater said into the phone.

"I do."

"Excellent. My wife's going to get some shut eye. Give us a call after the meeting."

"You got it."

And then he heard Slater say, "You've got ten seconds to get up those stairs before I carry you. And, woman, I will carry you."

Emmie's squeal of laughter let him know Slater had followed through with his threat, and then the line went dead.

"Good news?" In her sleep shorts and tank top, hair disheveled and not a drop of make-up on her beautiful face, Daisy made her way into the kitchen.

Every. Time. Every single time he saw her, heard her voice, or got a whiff of her scent, he took a hit. A wallop of emotion so intense he needed a moment to recover.

When he was a lonely kid, Daisy had captured his imagination. But as an adult, she'd claimed his heart. And he only had five more days with her.

A chill stole across his skin. *Five* days.

After that, he'd never touch her again. Would never wake up to her body jammed up against him, hear her joyful laughter, or watch her neck arch as she came apart in his arms.

He lunged for her, got his hands on her ass, and scooped her off the ground.

"Cooper!"

Nuzzling her neck, he filled his lungs with that scent that drove him right into the heart of *them*. "I want more."

Her fingernails scraped across his scalp, pushing the hair away from his face. "Can you be more specific?"

"More kisses." *More time with you.*

He pressed his mouth to hers, licking inside. It fired him up, knowing in five days he'd quit getting to feel her hands in his hair and her arm across his chest in the middle of the night. He kissed her so she'd remember him. He squeezed her to let her know she'd ruined him for this freedom he'd once valued above all else.

Her legs wrapped around him, and she shifted lower to tease his cock. "Someone's frisky this morning."

If she thought it was about sex, he wasn't being real enough. Because Daisy Charbonneau was magnificent, and he needed her to feel that down to her very soul. "I want you."

She smiled against his mouth. "You have me."

But only for five more days. He backed her up to the wall between the pantry and the kitchen door and kissed her as if he had one last chance to let her know how he felt. "I want to see you."

She wriggled her arms free, pulled her tank top off, and tossed it. Flicking her hair aside, she pressed her shoulders to the wall, baring her luscious breasts to him.

"You're perfect." His fingertips traced her collarbone, his tongue licking a trail from her neck down to the crests of her breasts.

She cupped them for him, pressing them together so he could worship both nipples with licks and gentle pulls. Moaning, her hips rocked restlessly.

The way she responded to him made him crazy. He needed his hands on her body right the fuck now. Setting her on the counter, he shoved aside the toaster and the coffeemaker. A glass toppled over. He covered her breasts with his palms, nipping the tips that peaked between his fingers. He needed to feel her wet heat, so he reached into her panties. He only got one finger into her slick folds before she pushed him away. "Cooper. God. Wait." While she shed her bottoms, he yanked off his jeans and kicked off his boxers.

The moment she repositioned herself on the counter, she grabbed hold of him, ready to guide him inside. But he needed to get closer, skin to skin. He lifted her and carried her out of the kitchen. In his haste, he nearly tripped on the rug in front of the hearth, but he caught himself, and she clutched him more tightly.

Kicking open the bedroom door, he laid her down on the bed where he'd kissed and licked and discovered every inch of her soft, warm skin.

Her tousled hair covered one eye, her lush lips were parted, and her body trembled with need. A dark erotic heat grabbed hold of him, and he nudged her knees apart, grasped his cock, and pushed inside her.

She clung to him, hands on his back, heels digging into his ass. He loved it. Loved how it felt to sheathe his achingly hard cock in her tight, slick heat.

He angled his hips just the way she liked, and she rewarded him by arching her neck. With each pass over her clit, she gasped. *Jesus mother of God*, he'd never seen anything so beautiful in his life as Daisy lost in erotic sensation, taking her pleasure from him. It hit him hard the way she let herself go so completely—the trust she had in him. It made him want to make it so good for her. So she'd never forget them. *Him*.

Her breasts bounced, and her cries filled the room, and everything about the moment—him in Daisy's cozy cabin, sharing this kind of intense intimacy—coalesced into a throbbing, burning rush of sensation so powerful it shook him to his core. Tension built fast and hard. Too fast. He never wanted this moment to end.

When his spine tingled, his body racing toward the inevitable, he reached where their bodies were joined and found the hard bead that would release her from the spiraling tension.

Her body jerked, twisted, and her legs relaxed their hold around his hips. She planted her feet on the mattress and lifted her hips, jamming their bodies together. "Oh, God. *God*."

Nothing had ever turned him on more than wild Daisy, features wrenched in passion, hips grinding on him each time she slammed home. "*Cooper*."

He needed her. Needed her so fucking badly. Gripping her ass, he drove into her again and again, faster, harder. Her body tensed, as she shouted his name, writhing and coming all over his cock.

Lost completely in her, he pumped furiously. Nothing in his life had ever felt so good, so right. Electricity flashed across his skin, and heat flooded him. The tension in his balls burst, as he went into freefall. Pleasure took hold of him, a relentless, airless, timeless euphoria he didn't want to ever end.

But of course, it did. He collapsed on top of her, quickly rolling to the side, sparing her his full weight. He drew her against him, and they lay quietly together. Idly, she stroked his arm.

He watched her fingers trace each tattooed bear claw. "Do you mean to touch that scar all the time?"

She eyed it curiously, then tipped her chin to gaze at him through mussed hair. "No. Mostly, I just like touching you."

Another joybomb went off in his chest, releasing a fresh wave of desire and heat. "But you're always touching this one."

Her fingertips caressed his scar. "I don't mean to." She lifted his arm, brought it closer to examine it. "I guess I just hate that it happened to you. That you were alone in the woods, face to face with a bear. I hate it so much."

Time to get going. He popped up. "We live in the

mountains, Daze. Everyone's had a wildlife encounter." He snatched a fresh pair of boxers from the dresser.

"I know." She sounded like she wanted to say something more.

He could finish the sentence for her. *But it happened because your mom neglected you.*

"It just…it hurts my heart."

"I'm going to hit the shower." He headed into the bathroom. "Can't be late to the meeting."

Her bare feet slapped the wood floor as she came up behind him. "What did I say?"

He flicked on the lights and hit the faucet. He didn't even wait for the water to heat up, just stepped inside and ducked his head under the cold spray.

The water transitioned from warm to hot, making his skin tingle at the rapid change in temperature. Closing his eyes, he leaned forward until his forehead hit the tile.

"I don't feel sorry for you, you goof." Daisy, in all her naked glory, stood outside, one hand holding the shower curtain aside.

He reached for the soap.

"I've had feelings for you since I was a kid." She stepped into the stall and grabbed the soap from him. Lathering up her hands, she set it back on the hanging rack and caressed his shoulders, his arms, all the way down to his fingers. Clasping his hands, she gazed up at him. "You're a fool if you think my heart didn't hurt for you when you got mauled by a bear." Releasing her grasp, she placed her soapy palms on his stomach, making slow, sensual circles up his ribcage and then around his nipples, hardening them to sensitive peaks.

Those warm hands skimmed lower. Reaching between his legs, she gently soaped up his balls, sending a roar of desire through him and making his cock ache for the pressure of her hands. When she gripped him, he sucked in a harsh breath.

Her eyes flared, and she tightened her hold, her soapy hands twisting and tugging.

He grabbed her wrists. "I'm not that kid anymore." *Don't see me like that.*

"I know that." Her earnest gaze implored him to believe her.

Breaking her grip, he lifted her arms and held them against the wall. Water streamed down her breasts, and he licked a droplet off her beaded nipple. "Then don't look at me like I am."

She twisted out of his hold and pushed back on his chest. "Maybe you're used to women who want to be with you because you're a rock star." Grabbing his arm, she showed him his scar. "But I like you because you're the man who turned a terrifying experience into art." Letting him go, she pushed the wet hair off her face. "The man who defends his not-very-nice mother. The man who threw me a birthday party after everyone told him not to. Celebrating me like that...it just put an end to this stupid game of chicken I play with the father who can't be bothered to remember his own daughter's birthday. I'm with you because you make me feel things I've never felt before —the least of which, I can promise you, is pity."

She reached for the shampoo. "Now, we can't be late for this meeting, so let's get a move-on."

Cooper liked women. A lot. And he wasn't clueless. He knew he liked them because of the show they put on. They gave him their wild energy, their fun spirit, so they could be the one to turn on a rock star. He never stuck around long enough to see any other side of them.

But Daisy had a lot of sides—he'd gotten to see many of them. And there wasn't a single one he didn't like. Feisty, fierce, kind, loving, angry, sad, insulted, everything about her made him admire, respect, and want her.

He swiped the bottle out of her hands, popped the top, and poured the creamy pearlescent liquid into his palm. Setting it back on the metal rack hanging off the faucet, he rubbed his hands together and dug his fingertips into her thick hair, massaging her scalp until the shampoo lathered. He moved in slow circles with a good amount of pressure, increasing it when her eyes closed and she leaned into him, dropping her forehead to his chest and moaning.

"Can you do this every day?"

This *is what the guys have. This is why they gave up the rocker lifestyle so readily.*

They got the girl that made them feel this way every day of their lives.

They were lucky sons of bitches.

Because they'd never had to choose.

If Cooper wanted Daisy, he'd have to give up the band and live in Snowberry.

And do what? Teach music?

And if he wanted his band...his true family...well, he'd do exactly as he planned and leave on Sunday.

Chapter Fourteen

HAIR STILL WET FROM HIS SHOWER, COOPER STOOD at the kitchen counter, going over his notes for the morning's meeting. Stuart had made their event sound like Woodstock, so he'd let the director know that festivals these days were run like NFL games, with the same attention to medical services, crowd control, and overall safety.

Outside he heard deep voices—probably just tourists heading out on a hike. Daisy was running late, so he poured her coffee into a travel mug, added a good amount of milk and sugar, and then stirred it just how she liked.

Just to reinforce his point, he'd checked Blue Fire's concert demographics and discovered they had a fairly affluent fan base. So, not the type to pour vodka in water bottles and start fights like Ethan had suggested. Besides, their event wasn't taking place on a farmer's field or even at a concert venue. It involved travel expenses like hotels and rental cars. The only people who'd come were the ones with disposable income. Not the ones who followed garage bands.

The unmistakable sound of horse hooves clopping on

the asphalt path distracted him, and he looked out the living room window. He didn't see a damn thing.

But the bark of laughter outside his door was unmistakable. The Blackstocks.

What the hell? They were all supposed to meet at the office at nine. That was twenty minutes from now.

One of them knocked on the door. "Cooper? Coop!"

In a white sundress splashed with bright red cherries, Daisy rushed out of the bedroom, her scent whirling around her.

"Cooper!" Another voice joined the first.

He shot her a look. *How do you want to handle this?* They'd hid their relationship well, but it would be impossible to get around the fact that they both had wet hair and bare feet at eight-forty in the morning.

This was her world, her relationships. He'd play it however she wanted.

She ignored him, going straight to the door and opening it. "Hey." She looked beyond them. "Oh, for heaven's sake. What're you guys doing? We have a meeting this morning."

Cooper came up behind her to find Remi and Nash astride two of the biggest motherfucking stallions he'd ever seen. Between them, they held the reins of three other massive beasts.

"My aunt and uncle are at their place in the woods," Ethan said. "We don't want to mess up their vacation over this, so we're going to them. And the only way in is to ride."

"Good way to distinguish us from Stuart," Daisy said. "Okay, let me change real quick." She turned and disappeared into the house.

"You ready to go?" Ethan looked down at Cooper's bare feet.

Fear streaked through him. *How do I get out of this?*

One of the horses stomped a foot and reared its head, whinnying. Remi spoke some dark magic, and the Satanic beast settled.

"Get some boots on, and we'll head out."

Ethan just expected Cooper to climb on the back of one of those things and know what the fuck to do. "I'll meet you there."

Remi laughed, and Cooper shot him a death glare.

"There're no roads to my aunt's cabin," Nash said. "The only way in is by foot or horseback."

Of course. Well, this meeting was between the resort owners and the people trying to protect the river. The lead guitarist of Blue Fire had nothing to do with that discussion. Besides, he'd already gone over his points with Daisy, so she could deliver them.

She had just as much at stake. She wouldn't fail. "Cool. Let me know how it goes."

Ethan cocked his head. "You're coming with us."

"You guys have to prove you're protecting the river. I don't have anything to add."

"Bullshit," Remi said. "It's your event."

"You need to pitch your idea," Nash said. "Stuart put ideas in her head."

"You convinced us about the type of people this event will draw," Ethan said. "Do it for her."

Cooper felt their nod of approval like breaking the surface of water after he'd been under too long. Like he could take a full and deep breath for the first time since he'd come to town.

"Okay." Daisy squeezed between him and the doorframe. She placed a hand on his chest and gazed up at him with concern. "You want to get your boots on?"

Did Daisy know she'd just claimed him? Cooper wasn't going to wait around for their reaction. "Sure."

But she stopped him before he could slip back into the house. She held his hand and faced the brothers. "I know I can trust you guys to keep my business private."

"Of course, Daze," Remi said.

Cooper watched Ethan, who gave an impassive nod.

So, they were cool with it? He didn't know what to make of that, but okay. He'd left his boots by the door, so he stepped back inside and jammed his feet into them. Tying the laces, he came outside and closed the door behind him.

Remi lifted the reins of a black horse the size of an SUV. "I saddled up Rigamarole for you."

Wild black eyes said *I'ma fuck you up, asshole.* The monster pawed at the dirt, steam shooting out his nostrils. *Okay, not really.* But damn, that beast looked sinister. "Knew I should've rented a damn car."

The guys burst out laughing.

"Told you there're no roads," Nash said.

"Besides, riding's more fun." Ethan headed over to his horse.

Perspiration stuck his T-shirt to his chest. Cooper had to come out and say it. "I don't ride."

All eyes turned to him.

"You're from fucking Montana," Remi said. "Of course, you ride."

"He's been gone a while," Nash said to his twin.

"Ten years," Ethan said.

Remi's smile had a devious edge. "It's like riding a bike." He held out the reins.

When the hell would he have ridden a horse? All those years of summer camp he never went to? Or on the ranch he hadn't grown up on? But the way they were looking at him—clueless, expectant—he obviously had to spell it out. "I don't know how to ride."

"Ah. Gotcha." Nash looked to his twin. "Maybe give him Angus instead?" The other horse, the white one with brown spots, looked like he'd rather be out in a field noshing on grass and flicking his tail.

"He'll be fine on Rigamarole," Ethan said. "Angus is Daisy's horse."

"He's not *my* horse." Daisy head toward Angus. "He and I just have a special bond. Right, my love?" She caressed his muzzle and whispered things Cooper couldn't hear.

But it sent a flush of heat through him because she'd done that same thing to him, stroking his belly, licking the shell of his ear while letting him know just how much she liked what he was doing to her.

"I'll ride Rigamarole today." She moved away from the nicer horse to take the reins from Remi.

"Let's go," Remi said. "Aunt Bev makes the best biscuits you've ever tasted."

"This is a meeting," Nash said. "You better not have asked her to cook for us."

"I don't have to ask," Remi said. "It's a morning meeting. I guarantee she's made us biscuits."

Nash gave him a pointed look. "She's on vacation."

"If she's not pulling biscuits out of the oven when we get there," Remi said. "I'll groom the horses myself when we get back."

"Deal." Nash slid a sly look to Ethan.

"That means *you're* grooming them if I'm right," Remi said.

"Everyone heard you, sunshine." Nash held the reins out to Cooper. "Let me adjust the stirrups." He swung a leg off his horse and dropped to the ground. "Come on. Say hello to Angus."

Cooper did not want to do this. But as they approached the horse, Nash said, "No worries. It's an easy trail ride to my aunt's house."

As Nash unbuckled a stirrup, Daisy headed over to the Clydesdale-sized brute. "Okay, Rig." She rubbed his hindquarter. "Let's do this."

Cooper watched her every move. She put her foot in the stirrup, grabbed onto the pommel, and then swung herself over the back of the demon beast. Snugging her ass in the saddle, she flashed him a big smile.

"All right," Nash said. "Get on up."

Cooper couldn't think of anything he wanted to do less than get on that damn horse, but Ethan watched him with a look that said, *You gonna wuss out in front of your girl?*

Now or never. Cooper reminded himself that he was riding the nice one, so he reached for the pommel. The horse nickered, flicking its tail.

With the reins in his hand, Cooper lifted his boot into the stirrup and swung over. The horse skittered, making him think he'd been too aggressive with his mount. He needed to calm down, so he didn't freak his horse out.

Heart pounding, he sat in his creaking saddle, boots slotting into the stirrups. Nash made quick adjustments and then got up on his steed. Before Cooper could get his bearings, the others struck off, and as they'd promised,

Angus followed their lead without a bit of guidance from him.

This isn't so bad. His horse ambled along as they moved off the path and onto the trail behind the cabins.

Ethan took up the rear. "Angus is a gelding."

"Okay?" Cooper had no idea what that meant.

"He's chill, and this is an easy ride. But in case the guys decide they want to have some fun"—which Cooper took to mean *brace, they're about to let loose*—"and Angus decides to catch up with his buddies, remember to sit back hard on your ass. Don't pull on the reins, don't fight him, just sit back and put all of your weight on your ass."

Cooper's stomach twisted. Ambling he could handle, but the *fun* part? *No. Just…no.*

"Keep your heels down in the stirrup," Ethan said. "And your body leaning forward. Move with your horse."

The good news was that no one seemed interested in *fun*, enabling Cooper to relax a little. The hot sun bore down on him, and he breathed in the pine-scented air. The Blackstocks might've viewed the mountains as a playground, but his childhood had felt like living in the zombie apocalypse.

Riding on this early morning in August, though, Cooper saw it through different eyes. And for one moment, he allowed himself to imagine exploring the ranch with his half-brothers. Snowboarding, skiing, fishing, hunting…becoming part of their pack. What would it feel like to have a sense of ownership of this land? Roots in this town?

It wouldn't happen, of course. These guys had a lifetime of shared experiences. But he couldn't help wondering what might've happened if his mom had let him live with Hunter instead of using him as a ploy to convince Slider to stay.

The narrow trail gave way to a meadow, and just when Cooper thought maybe this riding thing wasn't half bad, Remi kicked his heels, and his horse shot ahead. With a whoop of joy, Nash followed after him.

Oh, shit. Here comes the fun part. Daisy glanced back at him with a look that asked, *You okay?* What was he supposed to say? *No. Get me off this thing?* So, he just nodded, like he didn't give two shits that he was about to be thrown off a horse onto the hard-packed dirt of a dry meadow.

A moment later, her behemoth exploded like a bullet. Angus took it as his cue to get moving, though he didn't have quite the same fire as the others. He trotted, making Cooper's teeth clack. But it's okay. It might not be comfortable, but he wasn't flying like the other three horses. But then—*oh, fuck*—Angus jolted forward. Instinctively, Cooper's thighs tightened, and he grabbed onto the pommel. His ass lifted and slammed back down, his balls slapping against the hard leather seat. It started to fucking *hurt*.

He tried to look ahead, see how the others managed to seat themselves, but he might as well have been inside a blender for the way the world kept jostling. So, he focused on Daisy's hips, her easy movement in the saddle.

Why am I bouncing? How did he get the animal to cut it out?

From behind, he heard Ethan's shout. "Sit your saddle."

"I'm sitting." What the hell did that even mean?

"Catch the horse's rhythm."

"I don't know what the fuck you're talking about."

Ethan laughed. "Keep your heels pressed down, your body leaning forward. Move with your horse."

Trying to ignore his aching ball sac, he focused on Daisy. Her hips rolled with the horse's movements. He pinned himself to the seat, moved his hips, trying to find some kind of rhythm. It wasn't working.

Wait—there. He got it. And just like that, he wasn't popping like a corn kernel in a hot pan. But about two seconds after he figured out how to *sit his fucking saddle,* they'd re-entered the forest, and the horses resumed their lazy gait.

"Ah, Jesus, Cooper," Ethan said. "Your horse is farting."

Cooper turned back to see Angus's tail hitch up as shit squirted out the ass. "What's the matter with him?"

"I don't know," Ethan said. "Jesus, it stinks. He must've eaten something bad."

"Dude, I can smell it from up here," Nash called. "Move ahead. Let Coop take up the rear."

"No, Ethan, stay back there," Daisy called.

Another load dropped out. "You gave him extra oats, didn't you?" Ethan sounded pissed.

"He was hungry." Remi threw his head back and laughed so loudly it echoed in the forest.

"You asshole." Looking like a gunslinger out of a Clint Eastwood western, Ethan shot out of line, squeezing between the brush and Cooper's horse, and overtaking the lead.

"Nash," Daisy called, indicating he should take up the rear.

But even before Nash could respond, Angus expelled a poof of foul air so odious Cooper had to hold his breath.

"Sorry, man," Nash shouted. "I'm not breathing that

shit in." The moment his horse shot ahead, Angus bolted. With Ethan leading the way, all the horses galloped along the trail.

Cooper's body rocked back so hard he nearly fell out of the saddle, but his hands grabbed the pommel. Clutching it, he leaned forward, his thighs clamping around the horse, and he held on for dear life.

Lazy gelding, my ass. Angus ran as if the hounds of hell had been unleashed behind him. Cooper's thighs strained from their grip on the horse. When he heard warrior cries from the guys, he chanced a look up ahead and saw them riding free, their hair flying in the wind, their bodies moving in perfect rhythm with their horses' gaits.

It looked fun. It looked wild. And he wanted it. Daisy's long, dark hair streamed behind her, and she had an arm up, punching the air.

Easing his grip, he slowly sat up, thighs relaxing. The ride became less jarring and…better.

And then, with a hand on the pommel, his hips moving in rhythm with Angus's gait, he was riding. Wild and free. His smile stretched so big and wide it was just embarrassing.

The trampling of hooves on hard dirt, the blur of pine trees streaked with sunlight, and the rush of wind over his skin…yeah, it was exhilarating.

When the forest gave way to a clearing, the horses slowed, and the riders dismounted. Everyone laughed and chatted as they led the beasts toward a white-fenced pen. The sliding screen of a large A-frame home slapped closed, and Cooper turned to find his high school guidance counselor on the deck.

That's their aunt? She must've retired and taken on the role at the GRA.

"Do me a favor and tie them up inside the paddock, boys," she called. "That Rigamorale's an escape artist, and I don't want to be chasing him down through the forest."

Cooper followed the others, as they slid the bridles off the horses, haltered them, and tied them to the fence.

"Aunt Bev." With the grace of an athlete, Remi grabbed the top of the fence and leaped over. He raced up the stairs of the deck, catching his petite aunt in a bear hug.

The years had been kind to the woman who'd been tasked with making sure he graduated. With her chin-length hair and slender figure, she looked very much the same. Each of the brothers engulfed her small frame, but she patted their backs as if they were still little boys.

Keeping one arm around Ethan's waist, she held the other open for Daisy.

When Cooper realized he was watching them from inside the pen, he notched his boot on the lowest post, jumped over the fence, and marched over to them. "Ms. Gonzales."

Shielding her eyes from the sun, she looked up. She seemed to take his inventory—his long hair, the riot of colorful ink on his body, and his bracelets.

It was a painful, tense moment until Daisy stepped in. She reached for his arm and pulled him closer. "Mrs. Gonzales, this is Cooper Hood. He—"

The woman clapped both hands over her mouth and burst out laughing. "Oh, for goodness' sake. Look at you. *Look at you.*" She wrapped her arms around him, but he kept his at his sides. Yeah, years had passed. And, yeah, he'd turned out all right. But he wasn't all that interested in making nice with the counselor who'd handed him a bunch of brochures for technical schools. He hadn't had a problem with the schools, but it had pissed him off that she'd never believed in him.

Of course, he'd skulked in the shadows, shoving football players into lockers, and fucking popular girls in supply closets, so he couldn't blame the administrators for their low expectations. But still. They'd never protected him from the bullies, so he wasn't going to pretend like it hadn't happened.

She pulled back, holding onto his arms. "Cooper Hood." She said it warmly.

"Ms. Gonzales." *Oh, whoa. Hang on.* She wasn't just his former guidance counselor. She was his *aunt.* It felt like his joints were held together at the small of his back, and someone had just yanked the strings. He looked at all of them from this new perspective.

Aunt. Brothers. Family.

Yeah, not there yet.

"Well, come on in. I hope you're all hungry. I'm just taking the biscuits out of the oven." Her gaze sought out Remi, and she pointed at him. "I made an extra batch for you. Consider it your own private stash."

"That's awesome, Aunt Bev. Thank you." Remi gave an exaggerated smirk to Nash. "Hey, man. When you're grooming our horses, can you be sure to pick the shit out of Castle's hooves? Some of Angus's diarrhea got in there real good."

Nash muttered something and whacked his twin with the back of his hand.

"What was that?" Remi said. "Aunt Bev, did you hear what Nash said?"

But their aunt was already inside, checking on the biscuits in the oven.

The guys barged right in, chairs scraping on the

linoleum floor as they sat around the table. Remi guzzled orange juice, and Ethan conferred quietly with Daisy.

The yellow linoleum floor might as well have been an alligator-filled swamp for all Cooper could do to get his legs to cross it and join the others at the table. Still standing at the sliding glass door, he watched Bev slide a hand into a quilted red and white-checked oven mitt and pull a cookie sheet out of the oven. She set it on a trivet and smiled at him. "It's so good to see you, Cooper. I'm real proud of you."

Right. "Guess I didn't need those tech school pamphlets after all, huh?"

She gazed up at him with concern. "Did it feel like an insult when I gave them to you?"

The sincerity in her eyes made him back down. "Nothing wrong with technical school." To be fair, she'd given him college brochures and grant applications, too. But back then, only the pamphlets had stood out.

"It doesn't sound like I communicated well. What I meant to do was give you hope. To show you a way out." She let out a heavy breath. "Lots of kids have trouble at home, but most of them don't rise above it. They're taught at a young age that life will beat them down and people can't be trusted. When I handed you those pamphlets—I think that was, what, ninth or tenth grade? I wanted you to see a way out. That's all."

"Did you give any of the Blackstocks pamphlets to vocational schools?"

"You bet I did. Ethan, I wasn't worried about. He's always been driven and focused. But Remi?" She turned to watch, as he lunged across the table and snatched an apple out of Nash's hand a moment before his twin bit into it. "He was wild. Sure, he was a star athlete, but how many athletes find success after high school? That boy needed to see options beyond the physical." She turned back to Cooper. "My job wasn't to tell you what to be when you grew up. It was to give you hope, direction, and guidance. I'm sorry if I didn't deliver that message to you."

"You may have, but I was only hearing one thing at that time in my life."

"Well, I can certainly understand that."

"Aunt Bev?" Remi called. "Biscuits ready?"

Time to get on with the meeting and breakfast. He didn't need to hold everyone up with his bullshit.

"Hold your horses, Remington Blackstock." Bev started piling the biscuits in a basket.

"What can I do to help?" Cooper asked.

"You finish this, while I get the other tray out of the oven."

But she didn't leave. She watched him for a moment. "You were smart, quiet, but anyone could see how you took everything in. I guess you had to be that way to survive." She gave a soft smile. "But music, that's where you shined. In our meetings, Mr. Walker couldn't stop talking about your talent, your focus, your…intensity."

"What meetings?"

Her expression turned tender. "We were so worried about you. I don't know how many times we met to figure out how to help."

"Nobody helped me." He hated how aggressive he sounded. He didn't feel sorry for himself, and yet he knew he sounded like he did. "I'm sure everyone thought I'd turn out to be a druggie like my mom." Now that he knew why the Blackstocks had confronted him in the turn-out, he wanted to know if everyone had made the same assumption about him. "Or that I was dealing at school."

"One thing I can tell you, teachers see everything. We know who sells drugs, and who's taking them. We know who's bullying, and who's being victimized. We see it all." She looked him right in the eyes. "No one thought you'd turn out to be an addict. You never got near drugs or the people who dealt them. You kept to yourself, worked hard in school, and didn't take crap from anybody. We didn't know how you'd turn out—we certainly never imagined you'd be a *rock star*—but we did marvel at your strength of spirit. And that's why we decided against calling Child and Family Services."

His senses went on alert.

"Sure, we came close. I can't tell how many times we decided enough was enough, that it was time to get you out of that house."

"But?"

"But you were doing great. Your teachers reported outstanding performance. You spent hours after school in the music room, and you were in the top one percent of students grades-wise. Ultimately, we decided we didn't want to risk putting you into the system. You were doing so well on your own...what if you wound up in an even worse situation? And I promise you, we knew how alone you were." She leaned closer. "When you were real little, lots of people tried to help. We had a drive at church. Put together food, clothes, gift certificates. But...I don't want to speak badly of your mom, but I suppose you're old enough now to know she didn't want any of it. I'm sure you can figure out why. She needed her isolation." She touched his arm, gazing up at him with pride in her eyes. "I'm sorry we couldn't help you, but I'm so proud of you for doing it yourself."

"I, uh..." He tried to find words—*thank you, okay,*

good to know—but he'd gone numb. Hearing that they'd cared, talked about him, tried to help…that his mom had *refused* their help…it just left a mess of broken impressions inside him.

Later, he'd figure out how to piece them together. Now, though? "We should get to work."

They'd left the meeting with Ms. Gonzales's promise to get back to them as soon as she had an answer. With everything they'd presented, it seemed impossible she'd follow through with an investigation, but they'd have to wait and see.

In the meantime, just as they'd arrived back at the Blackstock stables, the contractor had texted to let Cooper know about the early log delivery. Thanks to the cancellation of another job and the man's relationship with Daisy, Cooper would actually get to see the construction of his mom's house. He and Daisy had jumped in the car to meet her at the site.

The scritch of a match against the striking surface drew Cooper's attention. The end of his mom's cigarette flared orange, as she took a deep drag and held the smoke in her lungs.

He glanced over to see the crew unloading pine logs from a flatbed truck. The contractor, speaking with a few of his guys, watched his mom's every move. "Better not smoke out here, Mom."

Tilting her head back, she exhaled and then leaned into Daisy's Camaro. She came out with a Coke can and made a show of flicking the ashes into it. After a moment, she gestured to the cement foundation of her future home. "Thank you."

Cooper heard her, but it didn't compute. Those two words didn't normally come with an expression of such distaste.

"I feel like shit, you know?" Her gaze flicked over to him. "Forty-eight years old, and I'm taking a house from my son."

"Happy to do it." And he was. It meant a lot to give her a permanent roof over her head.

His fingers flexed, the tips brushing over the back of Daisy's hand. She glanced up at him with a question in her eyes. "Thank *you*," he said quietly.

"For what?"

"Making this happen."

"You're welcome. I'm glad it's worked out so well. And now you'll have peace of mind when you leave to finish your tour."

"You know what I'm gonna do?" His mom shoved her cigarette butt into the can and gave him a smile.

The shock of it flashed across his skin. He honestly couldn't recall the last time she'd smiled at him.

She headed to where the porch would eventually be erected. "Plant peonies here. Red ones. Dark red. It's what my dad used to do for my mom. I was just a kid, but I remember." She stared at the ground, lips pressed together, forehead tensed in concentration. "I don't remember much of her, but I remember the peonies."

A profound sense of satisfaction spread through him. In his entire life, he didn't think he'd ever seen his mom genuinely happy. Elated when things were going well with Slider, yes. But content? Never. The most he'd hoped to give her was security but making her happy was an unexpected bonus.

Daisy leaned into him and lifted onto her toes. "You're

doing a wonderful thing, Coop." She wrapped an arm around his waist. "You're such a good man."

He got close to her ear. "If you knew the bad things I plan on doing to you when we get home, you wouldn't say that."

The tip of her nose rubbed his earlobe. "Sure, I would."

Chapter Fifteen

As they stopped in town on their way back to the ranch, an idea occurred to her.

Daisy wondered if her mom would be interested in opening a satellite bakery in the new lodge. Imagine that —fresh croissants for breakfast, luscious desserts. What a hit that would be.

"I thought we were getting coffee?" Cooper asked as they walked right by the Sugar Bowl.

"We are." Not many people knew the reliquary museum sold the best coffee in Yellowstone County.

A few blocks off the green, the museum was housed in the historic district. Right out of an old Western movie, the street had wooden boardwalks and iron hitching posts. Though weathered, the original business advertisements could still be seen on the sides of the buildings.

The museum stood out because the curator, Lia Bloom, had painted it turquoise blue and hot pink and covered it in old street and animal crossing signs.

As Daisy climbed the two steps to the boardwalk, she

turned to see Cooper taking it all in. "You're going to love this place. It's the coolest coffee house you've ever seen."

"Sounds good." When he opened the door, cowbells clanged, but he stopped, his gaze fixed on the exterior wall.

"What is it?" she asked.

"Look at this map."

Someone had carved a crude map into the wood with the tip of a knife. His fingertip traced the groove from the post office on Main Street to Hell Roaring Trail. "This is probably a hundred and fifty years old."

Cooper touched the letters G.B.

Ah. Now she got it. "That's Galen Blackstock." Your great-great-great-grandfather. *Wow.* "He was one of Snowberry's original settlers." She gestured to the mountain ranges surrounding them. "This land's pretty much unworkable, so when people were moving out west, they visited but kept on going. In the 1800s, the government gave acreage away for free. Galen traveled all the way across the country for that free land." She hoped he remembered how the town had teased the Blackstocks at the auction about Galen's infamous thriftiness because now it had personal meaning. "And the joke is that even though the land was nearly useless, Galen took whatever he could get his hands on. And a few years later, when the government upped the offer of free acreage, desperate to get people to settle here, there was Galen, at the head of the line, snatching up as much as he could."

"So, in all these years, only Ethan's grandfather did something with the land."

"That's right." In the fifties, he'd built rental cabins. Their popularity died out thirty years later when families lost interest in their worn-out cabins in the woods.

"And now Ethan's trying to turn it into a fancy resort."

She didn't like his tone. "Yes, so he can keep his family together. They couldn't live off the cabin rental income, so they had to come up with something else. They wanted to figure out a way to make a living off their land, but also to invigorate the local economy, so people like my mom don't have to work their asses off during tourist season to survive through long stretches of winter."

His features were unreadable.

"There's so little opportunity in this town, Cooper. And this resort will make it possible for people who grew up here to actually stay. Or come back when they want to raise a family around friends and parents and siblings." She didn't like his impassive expression. "Some people like it here. They *want* to come back."

His gaze slid to hers. "I get that."

"You know, I've been holding back because it's none of my business, but your time's running out, so I'm just going to say it. We can talk about Galen and Hunter and Ethan like they're some people we know in town, but the fact is they're your *family*. Galen Blackstock, one of the founders of Snowberry, is your ancestor. Hunter's your *father*. And you're making a big mistake pretending they're not." She stepped into the museum. "You've got five days left. It's not too late."

She headed right to the counter, the warped wood floor creaking with each step. The historic house smelled strongly of roasted coffee beans, with undercurrents of old paper, sweet tobacco, and the mustiness from the vintage clothes displayed on mannequins.

As Cooper took it all in, she followed his gaze from one display case to another. Antique weaponry, taxidermy animals, clothing from every era of U. S. history, cutlery, and liquor bottles. Relics from Snowberry's history crammed into every square inch of the house.

"This place is wild."

She smiled at the awe in his tone. "You probably don't remember Lia Bloom—she was a few years younger than us—but this is her baby. When the last mayor threatened to close the museum because of budgetary concerns, she stepped up to run it. Of course, it's not a paying job, and she has to make a living, so she turned it into a coffee shop. She sells some of my mom's pastries, too."

"Doesn't that drive business away from your mom?"

"Maybe it drives business *to* her. If you like it, you'll go to the Sugar Bowl for more."

The way he looked at her—*dear God*—it made her all warm and fuzzy. He grabbed her hand and yanked her to a shadowed corner.

He gazed into her eyes, looking a little wild. "Look, it's just…it's a lot to take in."

"You mean the Galen Blackstock stuff?"

"No. Well, yes. But everything. I talked to their aunt this morning—"

"*Your* aunt."

"Yeah, okay. My aunt. She said some things. I don't know. It's just a lot to take in. My aunt, riding out with…"

Say it. Call them your brothers.

"Ethan and his brothers, meeting my…aunt." He blew out a breath. "But you're right. I've only got five days left."

"You can come back. After the tour's over, you can spend Thanksgiving here."

"I spend it with my band." His tone lacked his usual certainty. "I've spent the holidays with them for ten years. Before them, I didn't have holidays."

She wanted to suggest he try starting new traditions with her, with his blood family, but she wouldn't do that. They'd only been hanging out for a couple of weeks. She didn't stand a chance against ten years with the guys who'd given him the only sense of community and family he'd ever known.

"I didn't come here for any of this." A touch of sadness underscored his frustration.

"No, I know. But it's what you got."

"It's what I got." He drew in a breath. "I guess I don't know what the hell to do with it."

She could understand that. "You finally got everything you ever wanted as a kid, only now you're an adult, and it doesn't fit into your life."

He gave a sad smile. "That's exactly right."

"You know what I think?" She didn't wait for an answer. "I think you should focus on the one thing you've become really good at."

"Music?"

"Nope. Kissing me."

A smile broke through his troubled expression. He lowered his mouth to her ear, his hand resting on her ribs, his thumb stroking the underside of her breast. "I wonder how many more I can fit in."

She leaned into him. "Well, you're kind of an over-achiever, so I suggest you shoot for at least ten a day until you leave."

"Why put limits on it? Given all the places I want to kiss you, they might add up."

She tugged him deeper into the corner. "Could you be more specific? Like, for example, where would you start?" Her voice became a whisper.

"Best to start at your toes. Just so I don't miss a spot."

When his thumb brushed over her nipple, her toes curled in her boots. "And then where?"

"Think I'll kiss all the way up to the back of your knee, then come around to the inside." He reached between her legs and stroked the spot he had in mind on her inner thigh. "Kiss you right here."

"And then? Where would your mouth go after that?" She took his hand and put it right between her legs.

"You make me so fucking hard." Fingers teasing her through the gusset of her panties, he sucked on her earlobe.

A high-pitched voice shot through the quiet of the museum. "*You got to not talk dirty, baby.*"

They shared a smile of recognition. Prince's *Kiss*.

Heels clacked on the stairs, as Lia descended, her ears covered in old-school headphones. Carrying an armful of small, colorful bottles, she didn't even notice them tucked away in the shadowy corner. She opened a curio cabinet filled with antique atomizers and set the bottles on a shelf. "*If you want to impress me.*"

Daisy reached between them and stroked his erection through his jeans. "Don't listen to her. Talking dirty totally impresses me."

Cooper pressed into her hand, and she rubbed him more firmly. He lowered his mouth and took hers in a deep, hungry kiss.

The moment the kiss turned feral, she eased back from him to find Lia with a feather duster dancing in front of the cabinet.

Cooper touched her chin, bringing her attention back to him. With a desperate look in his eyes, he said, "Let's lose count. I want so many kisses I can't keep track."

Her body screamed, *Yes, all the kisses*, but her heart didn't know how much more it could take. What he didn't understand was that every kiss drew her in deeper. What happened after the last kiss, when she was so lost in him, she couldn't find her way out? Was she just supposed to watch him leave? See him in the media getting on with his life as a rock star? How was she supposed to handle seeing pictures of him surrounded by other women, stealing kisses meant for her?

When Cooper stepped out of the little enclave, Lia startled. "Oh." She tore off the headphones. "You scared the crap out of me." Setting down her duster, she came over to the coffee counter. Her turquoise blue T-strap wool shoes with a hot pink bow across the top clacked on the floor. "Hey. You guys here for coffee?"

"We are." As they approached, Daisy smiled. "Lia, this is Cooper Hood. He grew up here."

"I know who he is. Jase can't stop talking about him."

"Jason's her boyfriend," Daisy said.

"Nice to meet you, Lia." His big hand swallowed up her much smaller one.

"I can't believe Snowberry made a rock star. It's just so surreal, you know?" Lia moved behind the counter. "And you know Jase thinks you're the bomb. You're totally his idol."

"I've heard him play," Cooper said. "He's good."

"Oh, that would seriously make his day. So, can I get started on your coffees to cover the fact that you caught me feather-dusting to Prince?"

Daisy laughed. "Sure, skinny latte for me."

"Cappuccino."

"Your voice. My God, it matches the hot package." Lia shot her a look that said, *How can you stand it?*

All Daisy could do was smile because the acoustics in

this cramped, old house made Cooper's voice sound even deeper and sexier.

Lia wiped down the spigots of the cappuccino machine. "You realize Jason's never going to forgive you for not entering the competition."

While she said it jovially, Daisy knew the truth. Jason *was* devastated to miss out on this once-in-a-lifetime opportunity. "He's known all along that I sing for fun. It's not my real life."

"Oh, I get it. Believe me. He's stuck on the fact that it's only three months, but I told him *I* wouldn't want to go away for that long. I have responsibilities here, a job, a life. I mean, for him, I'd do it. Because I love him and I want him to have his shot playing stadiums, but I get why you can't, for sure." She smiled at Cooper. "He wants your life."

"Then he might want to get out of Snowberry," Cooper said.

Lia glanced at him over her shoulder. "That would mean leaving me."

"You won't leave?" Daisy sincerely wanted to know. Not many people their age stayed in town.

"Nope. My sister just had her first baby, and I'm not going to be that faceless aunt who sends a card on her birthday. Besides, I have everything I could ever need here. The mountains, my family, this museum. Jason...well, for now." She shrugged. "Who knows what'll happen with his career."

Daisy knew Jason well. What he lacked in talent, he more than made up in energy and drive. But she didn't know what he was willing to sacrifice for his dreams. It would be awful for Lia to give up her life in Snowberry, only to have Jason dump her once he started touring and caught the rock star fever.

"This place is amazing." Cooper scanned the artifacts. "Where did all this stuff come from?"

"Give me one sec."

As the steam machine gurgled and whirred, Cooper wandered over to a display case of copper and coal deposits, uncut and unpolished sapphire and agate, and lava rocks.

When Lia finished, she poured the hot milk into mugs. "It started with a few display cases in Town Hall. But they had storage rooms filled with dusty donations at the Historical Society, so the council decided to open a museum." After shaking out the foam to create hearts, she came around the counter to hand them their drinks. "Since I've taken over, I've put out notices in papers and on bulletin boards, so I'm getting tons of donations. Mostly, it comes from estates."

"It's cool." Cooper looked away from a mounted bison head, war medals dangling off the horns. "You don't get paid for this?"

"No, but I'm finding ways to make a living doing it. I was a history major, so to me all these things are stories." She smiled. "Jason doesn't get it, but I'm like Daisy. Family, my roots, my community, that's the heart of my life. For him, he just wants to know what fame tastes like."

She looked at Cooper like she wanted answers. *Is it as good as Jason thinks it'll be? Is it worth leaving me behind?* Daisy wanted to tell her that it didn't matter what Cooper said. If a person had a restless spirit, he wouldn't settle down, no matter how many promises he made. Jason hadn't hit the road to follow his dreams, and he was nearly thirty, so maybe he just fantasized about it.

She headed down a hallway, noticing changes in some of the other rooms. "You've been busy this summer." It seemed Lia had arranged the rooms into collections.

"There's so much more I want to do, but I'm only breaking even at this point. Once I open the gift shop, I hope to be self-funding."

"How much do you need?" Cooper asked.

Daisy stilled. He wouldn't have asked if he didn't intend on donating. And it just seemed like the town's reliquary museum would be the last place he'd want to support. Lia strode over to a short metal filing cabinet next to an antique scroll-top desk. Withdrawing a file folder, she pulled out a spreadsheet and handed it to him. "These are my projections."

Cooper scanned them. "The town won't give you *this*?"

Lia looked indignant. "Stuart won't even consider it. He acts like this place is some little pet project of mine, but I keep telling him it isn't about me. It's about preserving our unique history. I'm just a curator of this town's heritage." She pointed to the wagon wheel hanging on the far wall. "That was in Mrs. Barker's old barn. After she passed, her kids rented dumpsters and started loading it with 'junk.' I asked if I could look through it. You can't believe what I found." She pulled a key out of her pocket and opened the lid of a glass case. "Look at this. These are love letters from Jedidiah Barker to his wife Heloise that go all the way back to 1847, when he came out here during the gold rush."

"Why's this one framed?" Daisy pointed to the burnished gold frame.

Lia lifted it out of the case. "Because it's beautiful." She pressed it to her chest, arms folded across it. "Jedidiah grew up on a small farm in Illinois. He'd watched his parents struggle to feed twelve children, and he wanted a better life. He had big dreams, and while he loved Heloise with all his heart, he didn't think he could be the man she needed if he didn't try to fulfill them. He begged her to come with him, but she wouldn't leave her family. She also had another suitor, a wealthy guy, and while she didn't love him, she trusted the future he offered. I don't have the letters she wrote to Jedidiah but judging from the passionate plea in this one"—she turned the framed letter towards them—"it's clear she questioned whether she could trust her heart to a man with such wanderlust."

Lia read the letter out loud.

My dearest Lo,

It is because I know my heart that I can ask you to come with me. I know if I had stayed for you—and you know I surely would have if you hadn't given me hope that you would consider joining me—I would have died a little each day having to work the same uncompromising land I have worked since I could hold a hoe. I would have wished and dreamed until all that wonder hardened into resentment. You surely own my heart, my dearest Lo, but my soul seeks adventure and is driven to explore this glorious country to realize whatever potential I might possess. And I ask you to consider this: if you stay, if you marry Lawrence and stay in that town and tread those same streets, never having seen any other color of dirt, will you become everything you could ever be?

I can do this on my own, but you are my heart, and my life is not complete without you in it. Please, Lo, please trust me. I will not let you down.

Eyes shining, Lia set the frame back in the case, closed

it, and locked it. "She did come, obviously. And they had eight children." She drew in a shaky breath. "He died two days after she did. Of a broken heart."

It was a poignant story, sure. Heloise had followed her heart and made a wonderful life with her man. But frankly, the woman was lucky it had turned out so well. Because she'd given up a lot in the hopes that her relationship with Jedidiah would last. Had she ever seen her parents, aunts, uncles, cousins, or siblings, again?

"Hey." Cooper tipped her chin. "It had a happy ending."

It pissed her off that he didn't get it. While Heloise had built a whole new life, a part of her had forever ached for the ones she'd left behind. "It's great that she saw this *glorious country*, and I'm glad it worked for her and Jedidiah, but what if it hadn't? She'd have given everything up for a miserable marriage in a harsh world without the love and support of her family."

"Well, she obviously found a new community," Cooper said. "And with eight kids, she made a family of her own."

"Yes," Daisy said. "But she left behind her sisters, her mom, dad, grandparents, best friends, the teachers she'd known her whole life."

Cooper didn't back down. "His point was that sometimes you have to leave home to realize your potential."

"I get that. Of course, I do. I left home to go to college. I spent my junior year in Italy. But ultimately, I made the choice to come home, to realize my *potential* around the people who matter to me. And there's not a chance I'd give up my life to follow some guy."

"Heloise had *some guy*," Cooper said. "And his name

was Lawrence. She chose to follow her heart, whose name was Jedidiah."

Lia's eyebrows shot up, and she bit down on a smile that said *He got you there.*

Her heart flipped over with surprise at this window into his romantic side. But still. "It was a different time. Heloise's singular purpose was to get married and have children. In *this* time, women have careers. They build whole lives that *include* families. If she'd had a career she'd worked hard to build, that she loved, maybe she wouldn't have followed after some restless guy. I'm glad it worked out for her, but what if she'd given up everything only to find his heart was as restless as his feet?" They just stared at each other, neither backing down.

"Maybe you can't paint every man with the same brush." He said quietly but firmly.

Oh. That…Her jaw snapped shut. *That's a low blow.*

"I don't know whether you guys are fighting or writing a song together but speaking about giving up careers." Lia turned their attention to an Ethan Blackstock shrine. His Seahawks jersey hung on the wall, along with photographs of him scoring a touchdown. She even had the shot of his career-ending injury. He'd been sacked during the Pro Bowl, and a photographer had captured his face in anguish as he lay on his back, cradling his knee to his chest.

Dammit, Cooper was right. She did start with the assumption that people would disappoint her. In fact, Garrett had broken up with her because she'd been too self-sufficient. Once, after waiting half an hour for him to show up, she'd gone ahead and moved herself into her new dorm. It had taken her five trips to lug her belongings across campus. Turned out he'd seen her moving, and he'd been angry that she'd assumed he'd blown her off. He'd said he was sick of her assuming the worst of him.

So, yeah, maybe he hadn't broken up with her about the whole self-sufficient thing.

And maybe it was time to retire that stupid brush she painted people with.

"I have some of your family's stuff, too," Lia said. "If you want to see."

For a moment Cooper just stared dumbly at her. And then shock burned through the numbness. "*My* family?"

"There's only ever been one Hood family here. Was your great-great-grandfather Asher Hood?"

Cooper swallowed, jammed his hands into the pockets of his jeans, and said, "Yes."

"Come with me." Lia led them into another room. "I'm putting all the tools and industry-oriented artifacts in here." She reached for an old piece of pipe. "This is from the original water lines they put in. Asher Hood was part of that."

"My great-great grandfather put in the water lines?"

Lia gave him a warm smile. "He did. I have his name in the company ledger."

Silence weighed heavily in the small room. Dust motes spun and danced in the bright sunlight streaming through windows with glass so old sections of it were melting.

Cooper's fingers brushed across the pipe with a strange kind of reverence.

"You didn't know how far back your family went here?" Daisy asked.

Cooper shrugged, a gesture that made her realize she'd embarrassed him. "My grandfather died when I was young. I barely knew him."

Which meant his mom hadn't even given him *that*, his

family history. And suddenly, taking him for coffee in the reliquary museum had turned into a blessing.

"I've got something else to show you." Lia led them down a long hall filled with framed vintage photographs. She tapped the glass of one of them. "This is Asher and your great grandfather. James, I believe."

Daisy glanced at the sepia-stained photo of two men outfitted in bulky fur coats and trapper hats, each toting a rifle. Cooper stared transfixed.

She and Lia shared a look, in awe of this moment when Cooper came face-to-face with his roots for the first time.

"Maybe you can ask your mom if she has anything else," Lia said. "Even if it's just pictures, I'd love to have them. I'm trying to get as many news articles and family photographs as I can."

Wouldn't that be something? Discovering a hidden trove of Hood history?

Cooper tore his gaze away. "Other than essential household stuff and clothes, my mom never kept anything."

She couldn't help glancing toward Lia, who looked as stricken as Daisy felt. But she knew he didn't want their pity, so she turned everyone's attention to the picture. "You look just like them." And then she smiled. "Well, if you take away the bison pelts and trapper hats."

"Do you have anything else?" he asked Lia.

"I can't think of anything, but there's still so much to sort through."

Daisy pulled out her phone to check the time. "Okay, I've got to get Cooper back to the ranch. He's got a meeting with the sound engineer. Let me just pay for our coffees." She dug into her tote, but Cooper held up a hand. As he reached for his wallet, Lia shook her head.

"Forget about it. I got to make Cooper Hood a cappuccino. It's my treat. And it was totally worth it 'cause I got to show you around the museum."

"I appreciate that," Cooper said.

"Thanks, Lia." Daisy led the way out. As they left to the clatter of cowbells, she had to shield her eyes from the bright sunlight. The air smelled like sage and pine, and she slid on her sunglasses. "We should come back and look around the Blackstock room."

"No time."

"We'll make time." She slid her sunglasses on. "Did you know they have Galen's bagpipes? Can you imagine?"

Cooper's boots struck the weathered wood of the boardwalk.

"I mean, they came with him from Scotland in the late eighteen-hundreds. Your great-great-great-grandfather played them."

He stopped. "Daisy, ten days ago, I found out about Hunter, and it shocked the hell out of me. But it's worn off, and now it's just interesting information. Good to know whose DNA I got, but that's about it."

Liar. "Okay."

"The only thing I care about is hearing from Bev that we're good to go. If not, if the board wants to do some kind of formal investigation, I'm going to have to do something that my manager won't like. Because we will have a Battle of the Bands. And for the rest of my time in this town, that's all I'll be doing."

"Well, that and kissing me."

His smile cracked the tension between them. "Fuck, yeah, cinnabun. Not gonna miss out on my kisses." His tone gentled. "But there's no time for me to become a son or a brother, okay? You have to let that go."

"They really like you."

"They like me because my name and this event are bringing Mickelson Media out here." He resumed walking.

"No, they like *you*. As a person. They admire you."

"Daze, I mean it. Drop it. This idea you have of us becoming one big happy family, with me coming here for the holidays, is never going to happen."

The slap of his words had her heart cowering. "Don't say that. I get that it won't happen now, or even tomorrow or the next day. But at least be open to the possibility. You *can* come back here."

"I don't *want* to. Okay? I don't want to come back here. I like my life. I *want* to be a rock star, and I already have a family. The roots might only be ten years old, but they're just as important to me as..." He gestured behind him to the museum, now two blocks away. "As all that."

His brow furrowed in concentration, they walked in silence. "The only reason I'd come back here is for you." He looked ahead. In half a block, they'd be back in the heart of town. "I like you. And it's not like when I was a kid, and I had you on a pedestal. Because now I've had my hands all over you." His nostrils flared, and he tipped his head back. "Fuck, Daisy. Now that I know you, I understand why my bandmates gave it all up."

Her breathing turned shallow. Her heart thundered. But she knew—she *knew*—the inevitable end to his train of thought. The dreaded *But.*

"But my life isn't here."

It could be.

"And I don't think you want the kind of relationship

where we see each other a couple times a year when our schedules happen to line up."

No, she didn't.

"So please stop trying to show me how great this town is, how deep my roots go. Let's not turn this into something it's never going to be."

"I'm not *trying* to show you anything. You can't turn around in this town without bumping into your roots, and I happen to like that. I took you to that museum for the best coffee in town, and the fact that you can look at your family history and not be moved by it, not want to learn more, is beyond me."

She grabbed the back of his shirt, pulling him into the alley behind the vet's office. She didn't need paparazzi getting shots of her yelling at him. "And you know what else? I think you're a fool if you don't take this amazing opportunity—this *gift*—that's been given to you. So what if you're twenty-eight? I mean, turn the situation around. If one of the guys in your band told you he'd just met his real dad, but that he didn't care, that he was just going to ignore the news and continue on with his life, what would you say to him?"

Her unwavering gaze demanded an answer, and she appreciated his thoughtful expression. After a moment, he blew out a breath. "I'd tell him he'd be an idiot to blow off his family."

Affection rushed her. She loved his honesty, his openness, his *humility*. "And the girl he ran into? The one he'd crushed on in high school but never asked out? What would you tell him to do about her now that he finally had a chance to be with her?"

I could love you so hard.

He winced. "That's a tougher one. I'd ask him if he

thought there was any way to make it work." He slid his arms through hers. "I'd ask him what it feels like to kiss her. If it had ever felt that way with anyone else before." His hands settled at the small of her back. "I'd tell him to get as many kisses as he could, just to be very sure, because he might never get kisses like that again."

Preparations for the festival had gone into overdrive. Trucks and vans were parked haphazardly around the meadow, as vendors set up their booths and workers hauled tools and cables.

It might've been a warm August day, but inside her car, Daisy was on fire. "It's a good thing I like wearing dresses."

Cooper's big hand cupped her thigh, his fingers idly caressing the sensitive skin. Every now and then, his thumb brushed the juncture between her thighs, sending a shock of electricity through her. To anyone watching as they drove past, it looked like he was gazing out the window. Meanwhile, her body pulsed with need.

Something caught his eye, and he sat up straighter. "Don't stop."

She didn't know what he was talking about until she noticed Ethan waving her down. She eased off the accelerator.

"Drive."

She thrilled at the intensity in his voice. "I can't ignore him."

He peeled her hand off the steering wheel and placed it over his very hard cock. "You can."

God, he felt good, so hot and hard. Reflexively, she squeezed.

He sucked in a breath. "Floor it."

Hitting the brakes, she laughed as Ethan approached the car. "Hey."

Ethan leaned in. "Hey, how's it going?" He gave Cooper a chin nod.

"Great." Guilt flickered through her for sneaking off with Cooper mid-morning three days before the festival started, but not enough to stop her. Because she was going to steal every moment she could with him. "We're grabbing a quick lunch before—"

"There'll be nothing quick about it," Cooper said in a low voice.

She wanted to whack him, but instead of drawing attention, she acted like he hadn't said anything. "Cooper meets with the sound engineer, and I get back to my office."

Ethan nodded. "Just heard from my aunt." He looked to Cooper. "We're good to go."

Oh, thank God. "Are you serious?" *Thank you, thank you, thank you.*

Even though he tried to rein it in, she recognized Ethan's relief.

"We did it." She reached for Cooper's hand, and they shared a smile.

He pulled his phone out of his pocket, glancing up at Ethan. "So, we're good?"

"I can't think of a damn thing he can do to stop us at this point," Ethan said.

Cooper opened his screen and started tapping.

"When this is over," she said. "I want everyone to know what Stuart did. In the meantime, I'm pulling out all the stops. I mean it. This is going to be the best event this town has ever seen."

"Damn straight." Ethan pushed off her car. "Listen, we're still not getting electricity to the left quadrant of the meadow. Might have to bring in another electrician."

"I've got some guys I can call. Let me—"

Ethan held up a hand. "We're on it. Mario's going to try one more thing. If that doesn't work, he's calling his cousin from Bozeman."

"I'll talk to him," Daisy said.

"Not necessary. Go have lunch. We'll meet after that."

"I don't need lunch as much as I need electricity."

"I got this. Get something in you, and I'll see you at the office." Ethan fought a smile and headed off.

Daisy punched the accelerator. "He knows."

"Knows what?"

"That 'lunch' is a euphemism for sex." *Get something in you.* How mortifying. Her tires crunched over gravel as she eased into her parking spot.

"Daisy, we're actually going to eat lunch right now." He was totally serious.

"Yes, but that's after I have my way with you, and he knows that." She cut off the ignition, her heart so full she didn't think she could take much more sweetness from this man. No one had ever looked out for her the way he did. Her mom loved her and had done her best to take care of her, but she worked so many hours she didn't have much left to give at the end of the day. And her godfathers had families of their own. Hers was a close-knit community, but she'd never felt claimed until Cooper. "I love the way you take care of me." She opened the door so he wouldn't see all the emotion spilling out of her, but he grabbed her arm.

"If things were different, I'd take care of you every day."

"Don't say that." She didn't want to hear what they'd never have.

"I just did. And I meant it."

The heat and sincerity in those pale blue eyes had her lunging for him, ready to climb onto his lap and kiss him so deeply he'd figure out he couldn't live without her.

But his hand connected with her collarbone, jarring her. His gaze shifted just over her shoulder. "Paparazzi." He punched his seatbelt lock and opened his door. "House. Now."

A burst of adrenaline had her shouldering the door open. She hustled to meet Cooper in front of her car, trying to remain businesslike when lust flooded her body and made her limbs shaky.

"Laney, Pete." Cooper ambled up the walkway to the porch, giving the photographers his lazy-lidded smile.

"Hey, Cooper. Any chance the other guys will come out here?" Pete asked.

"Are you saying I'm not enough for you?" Cooper placed both hands over his heart. "You hurt my feelings, Pete."

"Coop, are you and Daisy an item?" Laney asked.

Cooper smiled. "She's got more sense than that."

She hoped they couldn't see her trembling hands as she stabbed the key into the lock, twisted it, and kneed the door open.

A hand on her lower back, Cooper nudged her inside. He knocked her tote onto the floor, bent his knees, and lifted her. Pressing her to the wall, he kissed her hungrily, his hands squeezing her bottom, hips rocking into her.

"Bedroom." Even though they kept the curtains closed, she didn't know what lengths the paps would go to get a shot.

When he lowered her to the floor, her knees buckled, so he wrapped an arm around her waist. "Fuck it." Lifting her in a fireman's hold, he carted her down the hallway.

The moment he dropped her onto the bed, he reached underneath her and unzipped the back of her dress. Pulling off the ballet flats, he kissed the arch of each foot before tugging on the hem of the dress. She slipped her arms out and lifted her hips, and he whisked the dress out from under her.

He traced the black satin ribbon woven through her pale pink lace panties. "I'm taking this pair with me." Peeling them off, he tossed them onto the floor.

"Oh, my God, you're not taking my underwear as some kind of souvenir of your time here."

His fingers stilled, and he watched her with an unreadable expression.

"Well, I'm sorry, but when you leave, it's going to suck. *You'll* be off on your grand adventure, new cities, new people, but I'll be here. Remembering you in my bed. In my shower. In my kitchen." *In me.*

Placing a knee on the mattress, he straddled her, grabbing under her arms and dragging her up to the pillow. With her wrists in his hands, he drew them over her shoulders. "It won't be easy to leave you." Lowering his face into her cleavage, he inhaled. "I've got five days left, and all I can think about is breathing you in, taking you so deep into my lungs I trap you inside me. Touching you until I never forget the way your skin feels. The sound of your voice, your smile, the way you look when you come…I want to swallow you whole, so you'll be with me wherever I go."

Oh, God. She squirmed beneath him. "Take off my bra. I want your mouth on me."

A simple flick freed the back clasp. He peeled the straps down her arm, tossing it on the heap of clothing he'd made. His hot mouth covered her, the swirl of his tongue making her back bow.

She loved the soft, silky feel of his hair brushing over her skin. Lying under him naked while he remained dressed made her feel vulnerable, sexy, *wanton*. It made her want to be naughty. Scooting down the bed, she unbuttoned his jeans and shoved them down his hips. When his cock sprang free, she saw he'd gone commando. She clasped him at the base and licked around the head.

"Fuck, Daisy." He reached behind his neck, grabbed the T-shirt, and yanked it off, baring hard muscle and tan skin. All that ink gave him a hard edge that excited her—especially since she got to see the softer side of him. "Hang on." Pushing off the bed, he yanked off his boots and jeans and then climbed back over her. Taking his cock in his hand, he brought it back to her mouth. "Yeah."

With his hands braced on the headboard, his hips rocked, as he watched his cock slide in and out. He groaned. "Fuck, yeah. So good, Daisy."

She gripped his ass, guiding his thrusts, her tongue flicking up and down his length.

When his eyes rolled back in his head, he pulled out of her mouth. Shoving a hand under her bottom, he took her with him when he rolled onto his back. "Want to see you. All of you."

With her thighs straddling his waist, she ran her hands up his chest, her fingers sifting through the smattering of hair and circling the soft skin of his areola. She pinched his nipples, and his big hands gripped her ass. "Now."

Lifting up on her knees, she reached between them to grasp his cock and then eased down on him. Sensation bloomed and flowed through her...so sexy, so delicious. "Cooper," she whispered.

His strong arms took control of her rhythm, moving her up and down on him, and his tongue licked out, flicking across her nipple before his mouth captured her breast, surrounding her with all that slick heat. Each time she slammed down, a shockwave of electric heat sped through her, driving her out of her mind.

His strength and passion were such a turn-on, the way he worked her on his cock, punching his hips up so hard and fast like he was desperate for her. The rough, relentless friction made her feverish with lust. "Cooper, oh, oh, *God.*"

Perspiration glistened on his skin, as he watched her with such intensity as if nothing mattered more than her pleasure. The tendons in his neck strained, his biceps bulged, and it was all bearing down on her too fast. She pushed off his shoulders, arching her back, and bracing her hands on his muscled thighs.

In a rush, he sat up. "I fucking love the way you lose yourself." He buried his face between her breasts.

Her hands cupped the back of his head, holding him there. "God, Cooper. This isn't losing. It's finding myself. Right here, right now, this is me. When I'm with you, I'm everything I've ever wanted to be."

"Don't say shit like that, Daisy. Jesus." With his palm on her back, he turned her over onto the mattress. His mouth covered hers, his tongue seeking, as his knees pushed her thighs wider, and he guided himself back inside. For one moment, his eyelids fluttered closed in a look of pure bliss.

His powerful hips drove into her—again and again— winding her up until she needed to break to keep her sanity. And then he shifted, his pubic bone scraping over her clit. A rush of heat tore across her body so fast the soles of her feet tingled, and then release hit, sending her streaking through a timeless, brilliant-white universe. Her legs stretched, her toes curled, and her neck arched off the pillow.

"*Daisy.*" He slammed into her once, twice, three times, and then a fourth. He cried out, as he pinned her hips to the bed. And then he collapsed beside her, scooping her up and burrowing his face into her neck.

Oh, God. So good.

Damn this man. He'd *ruined* her.

Chapter Sixteen

THE WIND WHIPPED COOPER'S HAIR ACROSS HIS EYES AS the dirt bike careened down the hill. When the trail bottomed out, he found himself swallowed up in a cloud of gritty dust.

Up ahead, he caught sight of Daisy, swinging a leg off her bike. Tugging the elastic out of her hair, she ran her fingers through it. And when she tipped her head back to take in the last of the sun's rays, a satisfied smile on her beautiful features, his entire world narrowed to her.

The festival started tomorrow. That meant he had three days left. Three days to savor every moment, even if it meant dirt biking with the Blackstocks.

"*Cooper.*"

"*Brake.*"

His attention snapped back to the trail—only to realize he'd run out of it. With a row of dirt bikes coming up fast, he reflexively squeezed the brake levers. The bike jerked hard, sending him airborne.

"Oh, shit," someone called.

"Cooper," Daisy cried.

In those seconds when his body flew over the head of the bike, he had one thought: his tour. If he injured his hands, arms, wrists, or fingers, he was out. And instead of helping, he'd only add to his band's problems.

With the ground rushing up at him and no time to think, he tucked in his elbows, drew up his knees, and curled to take the hit on his shoulder. At the moment of impact, he forced his body to roll with the momentum, winding up on his back, looking at a cloudless sky. The blow knocked the air out of his lungs, and he closed his eyes while he waited to breathe.

Daisy's hands landed on his chest. "Are you all right? Cooper? Is he all right? You guys, he isn't moving."

"Give him some room." *Hunter.*

Am I hurt? He flicked his wrists, clenched his fists, and tried to lift his arms.

"Shit, man." Sounded like Remi. "Is that a convulsion?"

"He plays guitar." Hunter crouched beside him. Funny, in the short time he'd known the man, he'd become familiar with his scent, particularly the pine and patchouli of his beard oil.

"He's going back on tour in *three* days. Oh, my God, is he hurt?" Daisy smoothed the hair off his face.

He wanted to tell her to leave it. Let him hide behind the curtain just a little longer.

Because he felt like a complete idiot for crashing.

"And that right there's your paternity test." *Remi.*

"Shut up," Daisy said.

The guys wheezed with laughter, but Daisy sounded upset, so he cracked an eye open.

Her features softened, and she leaned in. "Are you

okay?" Her mouth was close enough to kiss—if he had the energy to lift his neck off the ground.

"Yeah, cinnabun. I'm good."

"Seriously, man, only Dad would wipe-out like that," Ethan said.

"That's just embarrassing," Remi said. "I'm not claiming him as my brother."

Cooper smiled at that.

Daisy sat back on her heels. "Let's get him up."

But he didn't need their help, so he held up a hand in warning. He'd do it at his own pace.

"You okay?" Hunter gestured to his hands.

"Think so."

"Nice tuck and roll, dude," Remi said.

Cooper sat up, body aching. "Yeah, well, I've been researching how to be as manly as you big, rugged mountain guys. Thanks a fuck of a lot for including me."

Everyone broke out laughing, and the connection snapped into place. They might not be family yet, but there was something between them. A start.

Not that he knew what that meant. *Or where I go from here.* He supposed he could keep in touch with them through social media. Email or text with Hunter.

"Come on." Hunter went for his bike. "Let's get the grill fired up."

With a mischievous gleam in his eyes, Remi grabbed Cooper's bike by the handlebars. "I got this, pretty boy."

Ha ha. Cooper pulled it away. "Fuck off."

"You sure? You're gonna need both hands to get your balls to drop back down."

Cooper gave Remi—his brother—*half*-brother—a shove.

As they headed to Hunter's to stow the bikes on the

hanging rack in the garage, the guys continued ribbing each other, and he realized that what had once been surreal—being part of their lives—might one day become normal.

Headlights lit up the interior of the garage, and everyone turned to see a cop car pulling into the driveway.

Engine idling, the door opened. With an uncomfortable expression, Zach headed toward them, carrying an envelope. "Evening." He nodded, holding the letter out to Hunter.

Scanning it, Hunter let out a slow breath before handing it to Daisy. Ethan came up behind her and read it over her shoulder.

"No." She shoved the letter to Ethan before stalking toward Zach. "You know exactly what he's doing. You can't let him get away with this."

A shock of fear pierced his heart. Cooper snatched the letter out of Ethan's hand.

"This has nothing to do with me," Zach said. "I'm just the officer of the law who's delivering it."

Cooper skimmed it. Stuart had gotten a local judge to issue an injunction shutting down the battle of the bands until an environmental impact assessment could be done. *This is not happening.* "It starts tomorrow," he said to Zach. "You can't shut it down."

"Not shutting the festival down." Zach tipped a chin toward the letter. "Just the competition. Stuart's convinced him it's different from past years when you've had local bands playing. This year, you've got national media attention and a major record label involved, which means all kinds of people flooding into town, bringing security and environmental issues."

Cooper knew from his tone what the man thought of Stuart's bullshit.

"What can we do?" Ethan said.

"Not a damn thing." Zach gave a deep sigh of resignation. "The injunction comes from the honorable Judge Pearson of the Yellowstone County Superior court. And as an officer of the law, I have to enforce it."

"Even if it hurts the town?" Daisy said. "Because this *will* hurt the town. Zach, the media's already here. That means the only thing they'll report is that we tried to pull something off but failed. The investors will think we're incompetent. That means no resort." She shot a quick, desperate look to Ethan. "There's no other hope to revive the economy of this town than this resort. You have two kids going off to college in the next few years. Don't you want them to come back? Raise their families here? That can only happen if our town has a thriving economy. We're about to make that happen."

Zach looked uncomfortable. "I'm sorry, guys. Just doing my job." He turned to go back to his car.

But Cooper stalked after him. "Hang on. You know we're not going to just accept it, so give us some guidance. What can we do to fight this?"

"Fight what? The first act's supposed to take the stage in twenty-four hours." Remi shoved a wheelbarrow, knocking it into the snowmobile. The crash hurt Cooper's ears.

"You'd have to hire an attorney," Zach said. "And file the appropriate paperwork."

"We don't have time." Cooper held the man's gaze. "Come on, man. Work with us."

"There's nothing you can do. You have to argue this in front of the judge."

Cooper's pulse quickened. "You guys know this Pearson guy? How do we get to him?"

"*Get* to him?" Zach said.

"Cooper." Hunter's tone held a warning.

Jesus Christ, he wasn't some fucking thug. "Come on, man. We gave the Gallatin River Authority facts, and they tossed out Stuart's claims. Let's do the same thing with this judge." He was not making that call to Emmie, telling her he'd fucked it all up, and he sure as hell didn't want to see the look in his bandmates' eyes when Kallous joined their tour.

"What about the governor?" Remi asked. "He'll be here tomorrow to judge the event. Can we talk to him?"

"It's not like the guy's our drinking buddy," Ethan said. "I'd rather talk to the judge myself."

Cooper shot a look to the others. "Think. Who do you know that might have access to Pearson? Maybe a lawyer?"

Zach sighed. "You don't talk a judge out of an injunction."

"Stuart talked him into one." Cooper looked to Daisy. "What about Whale's wife? She's a cop. Maybe she's got a lead to the judge."

"And if she does?" Zach asked. "What're you going to do, interrupt his dinner to tell him your side of the story? You piss him off, and he'll hold you in contempt. Look, if there were anything I could do, believe me, I'd do it." He cut a look to Daisy. "Hell, yeah, I want my kids to come home, but Stuart's got us. He wins." Zach headed off to his cruiser.

Bullshit. "Call Whale," Cooper said to Daisy.

As the cruiser backed out, she pulled her phone out of her shorts' pocket.

"What do we do?" Remi said.

"We sure as hell don't cancel anything," Ethan said. "Not until we've run through every possibility."

"Agreed," Hunter said. "We fight it like Cooper said."

"That asshole's not getting away with this," Remi said.

Something niggled at the back of Cooper's brain. "The question is *why* he's doing it."

"Because he wants the attention on him," Remi said.

Cooper shook his head. "His concert's sold out. He's got attention. There's something we're not seeing. What is it about the Battle of the Bands that threatens him?"

"We've already talked about this," Ethan said. "We've got Mickelson Media." But his voice lacked conviction.

Because it didn't make sense. They were missing something.

"Okay, but instead of shutting us down, he could get his own media exposure. Shouts! a big name. They've got one of the biggest manager's in the business. What about this event…" Maybe it wasn't about this event. "Is there any reason he doesn't want you to build the lodge?"

"Of course not," Remi said. "He's the mayor. He ran on a platform of economic recovery. Our success is his."

"Think outside the box," Cooper said. "Stuart's only issue seems to be the venue. He switched it to the Blue Sky Amphitheatre because his bandmates thought it was more upscale."

Hunter perked up. "He spends a lot of time at the Blue Sky Club."

"My mom works there." Cooper pulled his phone out of his back pocket and hit her speed dial. It went straight to voicemail. "Mom, call me as soon as you get this." But he didn't have time to screw around, hoping she'd return his call. "Do you know anything about Stuart Neil Goff? The old Shout! singer? He's trying to shut down the Battle of the Bands, and I need to figure out why before it's too late."

"Good news." Daisy looked up from her phone. "Whale says Judge Pearson's a club member. Which means we might be able to catch him at the Road House."

"On a Thursday night?" Remi sounded skeptical.

"Hang on," Hunter said. "Think about what Zach said. We don't want to get in trouble for harassing a judge."

"I'll take my chances." Cooper looked to the others.

"Abso-fucking-lutely," Remi said. "Who's driving?"

But Daisy had already headed out of the garage, keys in hand. "I am." When she got to the driver's side door, she looked up to see all of them at her car. Her look of determination turned him on. "He's not getting away with this."

The smell of barbecue sauce drifted from the grill, and solar lamps glowed a luminous yellow around the Blackstone's garden. Thumb absently rubbing the moisture on her cold beer, Daisy watched Cooper strum a guitar. Nearby, Hunter plucked the double bass.

She should be singing her heart out. They'd won. Not only that, but they'd taken Stuart out of the equation for good. After hearing them out, Judge Pearson had vowed to press charges against him for filing false claims. He'd only had to skim through her report to realize they'd gone well beyond what was required to use the land safely and responsibly.

Even sweeter, Cooper was jamming with his dad, hanging out with his brothers. It was a beautiful sight.

She should be happy. She *was* happy.

But with every second that passed, the undercurrent of tension ticked up a notch. Because no matter how clear Cooper had been about his intentions, he'd gotten close to her and his family. *It had to change things, for him, right?*

She didn't want to feed and water this sturdy root growing in her heart—because hope sucked. It lifted you up, sent you soaring, and then slammed you right into the mountainside.

And there was nothing she hated more than the suffocating, relentless pain of crushing disappointment.

But…*look at him*. He'd let them in. He'd let *her* in. Wouldn't he want to come back and get to know them better?

The sliding glass door rattled on its runner, and Daisy turned to see Crystal coming out with a huge salad bowl. "Chicken ready?" she called to Nash at the grill.

"Just about."

"Daisy, hon, could you grab the basket of bread on the kitchen counter?" Crystal said.

But Remi was just coming out of the house. "I got it." He swung back around.

"How about I pour the wine?" Daisy reached for the uncorked bottle.

"So, I got a bunch of text messages from you guys," Crystal said. "But why don't you fill in the missing pieces. How'd it all go down with the judge?"

Daisy had a feeling she'd be telling this story for weeks. "Well, we got to the Roadhouse, and the judge wasn't sitting at the bar, so Whale stands up and shouts, 'Anybody got the ear of Judge Pearson?' And, of course, someone did. We lucked out that he was willing to meet with us, but that was definitely because of Whale and the whole bike club brotherhood thing." She reached for a wine glass. "Anyhow, the judge heard us out. I showed him my file with all the work we'd done to meet regulations. He was definitely sympathetic, but it didn't seem like he was going to take any action. And then all of a sudden, Cooper gets up and walks away. I'm thinking, *What the hell are you doing? Don't give up now.*"

Crystal took the basket of rolls from Remi and swiped one before setting it on the table.

"And then a few minutes later," Daisy said. "Cooper comes back with the winning card. He'd called his mom, who works at the Blue Sky Club, and she said that Stuart's a founding board member there. Apparently, they're having some financial troubles—welcome to the hospitality industry—and the Club doesn't want us building a resort so close to theirs. In fact, the only reason the band agreed to a reunion concert at all was to draw people to the Club they all invested in."

"Then why did Stuart say he'd have the concert here?"

"I think he wanted to." He had seemed genuinely sorry to pull the concert from them. "But when the board at Blue Sky heard about it, they realized what it could do for their resort. They were just as worried about their investment as we were about ours."

Crystal set her roll down. "That's shameful. Just shameful. There's no reason we can't have resorts in both towns. It'll liven up the economy of the whole county."

"I know. And they're coming at it the wrong way. Instead of trying to block us, they should be promoting the one thing their resort has that ours doesn't."

"Skiing."

"Exactly. They should be marketing themselves as a ski resort, while we focus on outdoor adventures."

"Hunter says the judge is going throw the book at Stuart."

Daisy smiled. "Yeah, he was pissed at him for abusing the court system."

"Dinner." Nash brought over a huge platter of glistening chicken breasts and legs. "Hey," he called to Cooper and Hunter, who continued to jam.

"Looks like Dad's finally got someone to play with," Ethan said.

Remi dropped into his chair. With one hand he grabbed a roll from the bread basket and the other, he stabbed a chicken breast with a serving fork.

"Wait for everyone to sit down," Crystal said.

"I'm hungry." Remi tore into the roll.

Nash smacked the back of his head. "Can you ever not think about yourself?"

"Hunter? Cooper?" Crystal called. "Let's go."

As usual, Hunter was lost in the music. His whole body moved as he played. Eyes closed, Cooper's fingers moved over the fret, equally lost. It was a beautiful sight.

As if he could feel her gaze on him, he opened his eyes. One side of his mouth curled in a smile and a blush stole across his cheeks.

"*Dad.*"

Hunter looked up sharply at Remi. When he noticed his family seated around the table, he stopped playing. They set their instruments down and joined them.

With Hunter taking the chair beside his wife, the only other available seat was between the twins. Cooper nudged Remi.

"What?" Remi looked around the table, saw the available chair next to him, and dragged it out with a foot. "Sit."

Cooper gave him an uncompromising look.

"What do you want?" Remi seemed genuinely perplexed.

"He wants to sit next to his girlfriend," Ethan said.

"You seriously can't sit apart from her for one meal?"

"That's correct," Cooper said, making Daisy's heart flutter.

Remi made a big deal out of switching seats. "Happy?"

Cooper sat down and reached for Daisy's hand under the table. "Yep."

"So…" Ethan pushed his chair back and stood. Crystal lowered her fork. Nash set his glass down. A strange quiet fell over the table, as the Blackstocks shared meaningful looks with each other. "Before we eat, I just want to say something." Ethan paused with a grave expression. "This is a big weekend for us. You all know how much is riding on it."

At their concerned expressions, Ethan continued. "But it's good. It's all good." He turned his attention to her. "Daisy, none of this would've happened without you. I couldn't ask for a more reliable, intelligent, hard-working—"

"And pretty," Remi said.

Nash smacked him.

"What?" Remi rubbed his arm. "Daisy's beautiful."

Ethan ignored him. He seemed weighted with something, and she wondered what he was getting to. "I was going to say positive. Daisy, you're always an optimist, and you always work your ass off. So, thank you for being our partner."

"My pleasure. I love working with you guys, and I'm excited to watch this place grow."

Ethan blew out a breath. "We had a close call with this whole Stuart thing."

"Guy's a fucktard." Remi stuffed more bread in his mouth.

"Can't believe he tried to sabotage us," Nash said.

"Imagine if he'd gotten away with it," Crystal said.

Daisy squeezed Cooper's hand. "Not with this guy on our side."

"Exactly. And that's what I want to talk about." Ethan glanced at him. "I'm not going to lie, finding out you were…"

The longer he drew out the pause, the thicker the tension grew.

"Dad's bastard." Remi looked over to his dad. "Sorry, but it's true."

"You don't have to be a dick," Nash said.

"I'm not. How else do you want to say it?'

"My son," Hunter said. The simple word was weighted with pride, confidence, and a warning. *Don't ever call him a bastard again.*

"Guys." Ethan's tone shut them down. "My point is that it didn't sit well at first. Mostly because it was a shock, but also because I was wrong about you. Back then and now. And I'm sorry."

"Wait. Rewind. Did Ethan just apologize for something?" Remi asked.

Ethan glared at his brother. "Yeah, and you should, too. You were with me that day. Anyhow, it took a while to wrap our heads around it, but in the meantime, you swept in with your Plan B, got to work, and then handed Stuart his ass. Coop, you saved us."

"You did, man," Nash said.

"Good job, Cooper," Crystal said.

Cooper tipped back his beer bottle and drained it. "You would've gotten there yourselves." He shrugged like it was no big deal.

Daisy didn't know about that. He was the one who'd pushed them to think beyond the obvious. To figure out *why* Stuart was blocking them. He'd pushed it until they'd gotten to the truth.

"You're kind of a slow learner." Ethan grinned at his half-brother. "Here's where you say, 'You're welcome,' remember?"

Cooper's slow-spreading smile lit a fuse in her belly, sending a rush of heat along her limbs. Aside from her, he didn't seem comfortable around anyone in Snowberry. Not his mom, the contractor, the Kneeknockers, and certainly not the Blackstocks. So, it just sent a thrill through her to see him so genuinely happy and at peace.

"Yeah, okay. Sure. I'm a boss." Cooper held up a fist and bumped it against Ethan's.

"Bottom line." Ethan tapped him on the shoulder. "You did it. You're the reason this festival's going to bring in the money we need to build the lodge. Therefore…" He drew in a breath. "You win Eagle's Landing."

Cooper jolted so hard in his seat he knocked into the table. Wine sloshed in glasses, and one of the candlesticks tottered. "No." He shook his head. "Absolutely not."

"Cooper." She said it quietly, but her voice carried in the silence.

He was looking down at his plate, so he couldn't see the shocked expressions around the table. She didn't know who she hurt more for—the Blackstocks or Cooper.

"I can't accept it. It means too much to this family."

"You're part of this family," Crystal said.

Cooper's stricken expression was killing her. She

pressed a hand on his thigh, stroking it soothingly. He stiffened.

"Hey, man." Remi gave him a chin nod. "We had a bet. You won."

"That's ridiculous," Cooper said. "You don't give part of your property to *me*."

"What do you mean, don't give it to you?" Nash said. "It's done." He seemed confused. "It's yours."

"We want you to have it," Hunter said.

Daisy had to look away from the appeal in the older man's eyes.

"Guys," Crystal said quietly. "Give him a moment."

The table went quiet, amplifying the rush of wind through the branches and the creaking trees. His panic clear, she wanted to get him away from the Blackstocks and give him a moment to let it sink in.

With both hands on the table, Cooper cleared his throat. "Thank you. It's a very nice gesture. But I'm going to have to pass."

Oh, this is terrible. Didn't he know this offer—this gift —had nothing to do with winning a bet? The Blackstocks —all of them—had just welcomed him into the family. They fully and completely accepted him as theirs.

For the first time in his life, Cooper had a father who wanted him, brothers, and a stepmom who'd treat him like her own.

How did she convey this to him before he blew it all up?

"I'm on the road more than half the year," he said. "And the rest of the time, I'm working on or recording the next album. In New York."

"The land is yours, son," Hunter said. "When you're ready to build on it, it'll be here."

"Have you seen it?" Remi asked. "That's a big-ass piece of land. You could build a studio." Excitement flared in his eyes, as he turned to his dad. "You could run it."

"I'd like that," Hunter said.

"You could record your albums here," Remi said.

"Wait'll your band comes out here," Nash said. "They're never going to want to leave."

Daisy shot him a look. *Shut up.*

But Nash didn't see. "Think about it. While you guys are working, their families can be out enjoying the mountains, the river. And it's perfect because after being cooped up in the studio all day, you get to come outside to this." He gestured to the mountains. "Who wouldn't want to be out here?"

"Look, honestly, I..." He looked almost wild like he wanted to bolt. "Again, thank you. But it's just not going to work out like that. Our bass player's wife runs a business on her farm on Long Island. Calix's whole family lives there. Emmie and Slater have a kid. They can't just pick up and go wherever they want."

"Don't bands do that all the time? Rent places so they can work on new material?" Nash sounded like he couldn't understand why they were having this conversation.

She was such an idiot. He hadn't changed at all. Sure, he'd gotten more comfortable with them, but he could still get up from this table, walk away, and not look back. He'd have nothing but fond feelings and a pair of her panties.

Cooper didn't do love or deep attachments. He was a free spirit. A rock star. And any attempt to tie him down made him panic.

This should not feel so devastating.

But, God—*God*—it did.

"Wait, are you seriously turning it down?" Remi asked.

"Remi," Crystal said in an admonishing tone.

Her body tensed, waiting for his answer. *Prove me wrong. Prove that you can feel love and make attachments.*

Prove that I'm worth staying here for.

"Again, thank you. But I have to turn it down."

Chapter Seventeen

HE'D NEVER MISLED HER. SO WHY HAD SHE TAKEN OFF like that?

Cooper took the shortcut through the woods, pine needles stabbing his bare arms. Without moonlight in this dense patch of forest, he couldn't see, so he held his hands in front of him, batting away tree limbs and spider's webs.

He couldn't stop replaying it in his head, the way she'd pushed back her chair and excused herself with her usual elegance and grace. But her voice. *Excuse me. I have to get to rehearsal.* It had been thick with emotion.

Did it really matter how clear he'd been? He'd hurt her. The brightest light, the sweetest soul—and he'd messed with her heart.

Emerging from the woods, he stepped into the path of a golf cart whirring by, forcing it to swerve. "Sorry, man."

The guy gave him a conciliatory wave and continued on. Solar lights lit a walkway filled with families and couples out walking or jogging.

He crossed the lawn to her cabin and leaped the steps

to the porch. Digging the keys out of his pocket, he unlocked it and thrust the door open. "Daisy? Daze?"

He knew from the stillness, the emptiness, that she wasn't here.. Her vanilla and honey scent hung in the air like a ghost, and a chill got hold of his spine. He'd prepared himself to lose her on Sunday—not tonight. Not so soon.

Hope toyed with his heart, and he hurried down the hall to the bedroom just in case she was changing her clothes.

She's been here. The tank top she'd thrown on the back of the chair by the window was gone. The jar of lotion she kept on the nightstand? Gone. In the bathroom, he shoved the shower curtain aside. Hope died when he found her shampoo and conditioner missing.

He'd fucked up.

He'd hurt her.

Okay. It wasn't too late. He could make it right.

Cooper threw open the door to the Sugar Bowl, only to find Lia on stage.

Disappointment slammed him.

Where the hell is she? He'd checked the cabin and her mom's apartment. He had no idea where else to look.

Pulling his phone out of his pocket, he scrolled through the most recent messages. Still nothing from her. He shot off another text.

Cooper: I'm at the Sugar Bowl. Where are you?

He reminded himself that this place was her world. *If she's hurting, she'll come here. She'll find her mom.*

He had to talk to her. Let her know…what? That he

hadn't meant what he said? Because he had no business accepting Eagle's Landing. *So how the hell do I make this right?* Leaning against the wall, his shoulder knocked into something. He swung around to catch the framed antique photograph. As he replaced it on the hook, he realized the whole place was covered in family portraits—from the sepia-toned images of the eighteen-hundreds until now. Did Ms. Charbonneau even know half these people? But then, she wouldn't need to know them personally. A shared history bound the people of Snowberry. Their roots meant everything to them.

Cold fear burst open in his chest. He *knew* that, and yet he'd just shit all over the Blackstocks. They'd offered him a thread, a means of weaving himself into the very thing they valued above anything else—family—and he'd rejected it. As if it had meant nothing to him.

He just…he hadn't seen it coming. He'd been so sure they wouldn't want anything to do with him that he hadn't allowed for any other possibility.

It had taken them less than two weeks to accept him as their blood—including Crystal—and he'd given them the finger.

Daisy. Jesus. Of course, she'd bailed on him after witnessing his callousness.

That's not what she saw. Electricity flashed through his body as the full impact of what he'd done slammed him. Because from her perspective, he had a girlfriend that he lived with, made love to with alarming intensity and frequency, a family that had just offered them the keys to their world, and he'd told all of them they meant nothing to him.

Thanks for a few good meals, some excellent fucks.
I'm out of here.

A shock of pain stabbed him. He'd more than hurt her. He'd completely disrespected her.

How do I fix it?

He couldn't take that land when he knew he'd never live here, but could he visit? Spend holidays with them?

What would that mean for the band? The thought of losing his connection to his bandmates bit down hard. It was bad enough that he was the only single guy left—that already separated him. But not spending holidays with them? They'd drift. The connection would fade.

He'd be shut out.

No.

Lia hit a note that snapped his attention to the stage. He'd never have expected that powerful voice on her petite frame. She might not have Daisy's joyful and mischievous stage presence, but she could definitely open for Blue Fire.

Daisy's Mom came out of the kitchen and headed for the bar. *Thank fuck.* He pushed off the wall and hurried over.

Perched on a stool, she ordered a drink and then turned to watch the Kneeknockers.

"Hey, Ms. Charbonneau."

She covered her initial surprise with a tired smile. "Cooper. You can call me Hannah." The bartender handed her the drink, and she thanked him.

"Where's Daisy?"

His abrupt question made her tilt her head and study him a moment. "She's upstairs."

"I tried there. She didn't answer."

Pain whispered across her features. "Maybe that *was* her answer."

Her words blew through him, cold and harsh.

"Just give her some time." She sipped her drink and turned her attention to the stage.

"I don't have time. I hurt her. I need to talk to her."

"I had the impression this was meant to be fun between the two of you?" She barely gave him a moment to answer. "It doesn't seem fun anymore. It might be best to let it go."

"I can't do that."

"Why not? You're leaving in three days, and you're not coming back. Isn't that right?"

"Right. Maybe it was supposed to be fun, but it turned into something more. I…" Jesus, what was he going to say?

"You what? You *love* her?" She set her drink on the bar and slid off the stool. Anger energized her. "Let me tell you something, Cooper, she gets enough of that kind of love from her father. Trust me, he loves the hell out of her when he passes through town." She snatched her drink and strode back into the kitchen.

The roar of an engine forced him to move closer to the guardrail. The truck sped past, spitting out gravel and grit.

And here I am once again, walking 191 alone at night. Except it didn't feel the same. Because tonight he had everything he'd ever wanted as a kid growing up in this town. He had Daisy. He had a family.

A family that offered him a lifetime of Christmas mornings and fighting over the last biscuit and impromptu jams. Which was better than anything he'd ever dreamed of as a kid.

And right then, he got it. *He* hadn't rejected Eagle's Landing. It was the angry, dirty kid still living inside him.

That kid hadn't belonged among those good, clean people, and their gift had paralyzed him. *I don't deserve your prized piece of land.* Because in Snowberry, he was still Ronnie's kid.

The boy who'd slept outside on a pallet of dried pine needles and had awakened when something heavy and determined had shoved him. Who'd rolled onto his back, fear freezing his blood at the sight of those black, beady eyes trained on him.

The kid who'd reached into his backpack and tossed the beef jerky as far as he could.

But the bear had swiped at him anyway, his claws raking across his forearm. Blood had bubbled out of his wound, but he'd had nowhere to go. Because his mom was wasted.

At some point, a man had stumbled out of the house, throwing on a canvas jacket and heading for his truck. He'd only seen the wounded boy because he'd stopped to take a piss in the woods. That man had driven him to Urgent Care, where Cooper had waited hours for his mom to pick him up. He'd heard the nurses talk about him— well, about his mom, really—as if he didn't speak English and couldn't understand words like *loser*, *whore*, and *fucking useless bitch*.

Yeah, *that* kid couldn't understand why the hell people like the Blackstocks would give him their coveted piece of land.

But goddammit, I'm not that kid. And he didn't want that boy inside him anymore. He was safe now, independent—

Cooper stopped walking. *Bullshit.* He didn't feel safe. He hadn't felt safe a single day in his life. When Slater and Derek had chosen him to be in their band, he hadn't felt happy. He'd been scared shitless. Like he'd tricked them into thinking he was a good guitar player. And the truth was that he'd always felt like *they* were the band. He was disposable.

He still thought that. Now that the guys were coupled up, Cooper considered himself an outsider, on the verge of being kicked out.

But he wasn't a fucking outsider. He was a founding member. The lead guitarist. And, more importantly, their *friend*.

He'd watched Derek fall for their minder—and then marry her. He'd been in the waiting room when Emmie had delivered her baby. He was inextricably part of their history.

In a completely different way, he was just as bound to the Blackstocks. He was Hunter's *son*. And—maybe the best gift of all—he was finally with Daisy, the girl of his dreams.

Christ, Daisy didn't see the dirty, angry boy. She saw *him*.

No. Wrong. She did see that boy—she'd had a crush on him—and she still liked him. Admired him for overcoming his childhood and creating this great life.

A life that was a thousand times better for having her in it. He didn't have an answer for their problem—he had to leave; she had to stay. But he did know he'd never felt this way about anyone before. And he never would again.

What the hell was he doing walking away from her?

Cooper pounded on the door. He wasn't leaving until he talked to her. "Daisy. Open up."

The door whisked open, and Daisy stood there looking

fierce in her pajama pants and tank top. "If I haven't made it clear enough, I don't want to talk to you tonight. Just give me some space."

"I don't have time to give you space. Now, let me in so I can tell you what an asshole I am."

Exasperation turned to sharp interest. "I don't need you to tell me. I know." He stepped forward, but she wedged herself between the door and its frame. "But it doesn't matter anymore. The festival starts tomorrow, and that's the only thing I care about."

"Bullshit. We matter. I may not have any answers about us, but I'm not ending it, either. I want you, Daisy. I want to be with you. I want *us*."

"Well, Cooper, there is no us beyond this coming Sunday. You've made that crystal clear. So, since neither one of us can change our situations… Let me rephrase that. Since neither of us *wants* to change our situation, let's end it now. On a good note."

"No."

She shifted into a defiant stance, with a hip jutting out and arms crossed over her chest. "The press will be here in full force starting tomorrow. I'm not going to risk a picture of us going viral. You don't want that for me."

"Of course, I don't."

"Then let it go."

"I can't do that."

"You have to. You have to do it for me. Goodnight." She shut the door.

Cooper stood outside her mom's apartment, the cool night air sinking into his bones.

If he had a solution, if he could give her any kind of commitment, he would shoulder that door open and open his heart to her. But he didn't have one. And, as her mom had said, it wasn't fun for Daisy anymore.

He should go. He even visualized the steps he needed to take down the stairs, across the green, and down the long winding road back to the highway. But his muscles refused to cooperate.

He tipped his forehead against the door, tied to her in a way he didn't understand and didn't know how to handle.

All he knew was he couldn't leave her.

He pulled out his phone and opened his messages. He typed out a text.

Cooper: It won't fade when I go back on the road.

The moment he sent it, the truth rose up and possessed him.

He sent another one.

Cooper: It's never faded. Ten years later, and it only burns brighter.

When the whole truth unfurled, he could smell its fragrance.

Cooper: Pretty sure it never will.

Sliding his phone back into his pocket, Cooper felt stronger than he ever had in his life. He'd leave her alone tonight, give her a chance to work through everything, but he'd be back first thing in the morning with a hot coffee and a warm cinnamon bun.

The moment he turned, the door opened. Daisy stepped out, eyes glistening. She reached for him, pulling him into the house and closing the door.

His mouth was *everywhere*, that hot sucking heat on her skin, his hands gripping, squeezing, kneading her thighs, her ass, her hips.

Drifting in through her childhood window came the distant laughter of people leaving the Sugar Bowl, the crickets in the woods behind the building, and the essence of the mountains: the wildflowers, pine, and dusty earth.

His big hand slid under her body, and he cupped her ass, tightening the fit of their bodies and pressing his cock to her stomach. "Daisy."

The word, uttered with such reverence, made her eyes sting. Of course, she didn't doubt his feelings for her. If she did, she wouldn't have let him in after that last, sweet text.

But she knew what would happen after he left. No matter how intense things felt when they were together, they'd fade when they were apart. Her own father forgot her birthday.

Experience had taught her the reality: long-distance relationships don't work.

His mouth pulled away, and he brushed hair off her forehead. "You with me?"

She nodded, but it was a lie. Half of her was desperate to be with him, to offer him her body and soul. But the other half knew she'd be crushed when he left. When she saw pictures of him partying and surrounded by eager fans, it would kill her.

She had to tell the truth. "I want to be. But I'm scared."

He settled at her side, and she curled around him, wrapping an arm across his chest. She needed his heat, the connection to his body. "I tried to keep it fun. I really did. I let myself fulfill my teenage fantasies, but…"

"It's so much more."

"Yeah." She hated his troubled look because he'd always been honest with her. It wasn't his fault fun had developed into deep, strong feelings. "Honestly, it's been the best two weeks of my life."

"Except the Stuart part."

She hitched up on an elbow. "No, including the Stuart part. Because I got to fight with you. I didn't even realize how much of my life is spent alone."

His eyes widened in surprise.

"No, I know. I'm in this great community of people—the Kneeknockers, the Blackstocks, my mom, my godfathers. And I love them all. I do. But they've got their own lives, their own battles to fight. And, honestly, until you came along, I thought I had everything. But I didn't have this." She tapped his chest. "This connection. This...I don't know what it is." *But it's everything.* "I love being with you. I *like* you. I even love it when we fight."

A naughty smile curved his lips. "There's nothing hotter than Fierce Daisy."

"You know why I like fighting with you? Because of the way you react. I feel like whatever I do, you're still going to be there. You're still going to like me." She caressed his chest, fingers tracing the licks of cobalt blue fire over his heart. "And I'm going to miss it so much when you're gone."

As Daisy and the Kneeknockers finished their set, Cooper stood at the side of the stage. Beyond the packed audience, the Huckleberry Festival was in full swing. Cars jammed the parking lots, and people wandered the South Meadow, sampling food, playing carnival games, and visiting the community service booths.

With the descending purple dusk, lights had flicked on. Strings of them in trees and along the fencing turned the ranch into a magical place, and the people wearing glow-light necklaces and bracelets only accentuated the effect.

Daisy pulled the microphone off its stand. "Thank you all for coming out here tonight!"

The audience went wild, chanting, "More, more, more."

Strutting across the stage in her flared mini-skirt, red cowboy boots, and a black tank top glittering with red rhinestones in the shape of a cowboy hat, she said, "Y'all aren't sick of us yet? We play here all the time."

He smiled at the audience's reaction to her fun, vibrant, and slightly naughty energy.

Tonight was his last night in Snowberry. His last night with her. He tried to tell himself that once he got back on tour, he wouldn't have time to think about her.

But he was full of shit. Because he'd gone way past like or affection. She was in him, part of him, threaded into the very fiber of his soul.

"Seriously, y'all can hear us any old time. How 'bout we shake things up, give you a night you'll never forget? You ever heard of Blue Fire?"

When they answered by whistling, stomping, and shouting, she just dipped her chin and laughed. "Yeah, that's what I thought."

Camera operators from *Entertainment Update* positioned themselves at the side of the stage and in the front row. Flashes lit up the audience.

Just beyond the crowd, a convoy of limos crossed the

wooden bridge, their tires kicking up a cloud of dust. "What's going on?" Cooper asked the sound engineer. A couple of the off-duty cops they'd hired to direct traffic jogged alongside and in front, clearing the way of pedestrian traffic.

"Could be Mickelson."

True. A mogul like that would make a big entrance.

Unless…an alarm set off in his head—*Stuart?* Was that fucker still trying to sabotage them?

No, wait. It couldn't be Stuart. It was Saturday night. He had his own show at Blue Sky.

"You want to hear them play?" Daisy shouted. "I know I do."

He wished she hadn't worded it like that. The audience would be disappointed when only the lead guitarist hit the stage. They'd be expecting Slater, the good-looking, charismatic front man for the band. Or Derek, the badass bass player.

The limos stopped, lined up along the perimeter of the North Meadow.

"Then let's get things started. Ladies and gentlemen, let's give a big old mountain welcome to Blue Fire's lead guitarist and our very own local boy Cooper Hood!"

A stage crew guy handed him his ax, but before he went out there, he motioned the stage manager over. He couldn't afford any fuck-ups. "See those limos?"

The guy nodded.

"Not sure what's going on, but whether it's a VIP or more of Stuart's crap, we need to be on top of it. Get Hunter, Ethan, and all the guys to see what's going on. If this stinks of Stuart in any way, get my attention. We're not going to let the bastard screw this up, you get me?"

"I get you, man."

The guy took off. With one more look at the limos, Cooper made his move onto the stage, toward Daisy who'd crooked a finger, reeling him in like a fish on her line. With his ax in the air, he waved to the crowd and nodded to Daisy.

And just when the drummer started counting out the beat, just when Daisy's boot started to tap along with it, Cooper looked out into the audience.

A huge banner at the back of the meadow strung up between trees read, *We love you, Cooper Hood!* People in the crowd held up posters: *Welcome home, Cooper!* Mrs. Gonzales stood just off to the side, watching him with a proud smile, her hands clasped under her chin.

Mr. Walker sat in a lawn chair, right beside Mr. and Mrs. Tandy, all of them smiling proudly.

And there was his father. Hunter Blackstock. Cooper was too far away to say for sure, but it looked like tears glistened in his eyes.

Fuck. He lowered his head, awash in emotion too big and powerful to name. The muscle in his throat tightened into a hard knot, his palms grew damp, and he closed his eyes to shut it all out.

But a hand touched the small of his back, and he breathed in the one scent in the world that cut through all his fears and insecurities and gave him strength and focus. *Daisy.*

"Ready?" she said.

He nodded, taking one last look at the welcoming audience. He'd had it all wrong. He'd thought this town hadn't given two shits about him, but it turned out they'd tried the best they could in an untenable situation. And now? They were proud of him. They celebrated *him*—not the rock star, but the man who'd become one. It couldn't wipe out his past, but it sure blew out the grittiest parts.

"A one, a two, a one-two-three-four…" Daisy said before her band launched into "Get it, Boy."

With trouble lurking, he had a hard time getting into the rhythm, so he sought the stage manager out in the crowd, watched him talking to Ethan. His half-brother shot a look toward the limos and then took off. *Cool.* Ethan was on it.

Cooper turned his attention to his fingers on the fret and let himself get swept away into the song that had scored a Grammy for Blue Fire earlier in the year.

But the music cut off abruptly, leaving Cooper confused. Daisy grabbed the mic.

"Hang on, hang on. Is it just me, or is something missing?" She turned to her band. "What is it, guys?"

Jason joined her at the mic. "It's a Blue Fire song, but…we're not Blue Fire." He faced the audience. "I think we're going to need the real deal. What do you say? You want the real deal? You want Blue Fire?"

The band started chanting, "Blue Fire, Blue Fire, Blue Fire." The audience joined in.

What the hell were they doing? Misleading the audience was a colossal mistake.

"I know I do," Daisy shouted into the mic. "Who's your favorite band member?"

He should step in. Stop this train wreck before she got the crowd too psyched for something that wasn't going to happen.

Cupping an ear, she shouted, "Slater Vaughn? Is that what I'm hearing?" With a gleam in her eye, she laughed. "Okay, then, how about we get Slater fucking Vaughn up here right now! Ladies and gentlemen, help me give a warm welcome to the Grammy-winning band Blue Fire!"

Shock barreled into him at the sight of his bandmates running out. Ben rushed him so hard Cooper had to put a foot back to catch himself. The drummer hugged him, lifting him off the ground and squeezing him breathless.

"Missed you, man." Ben slapped his back hard enough to sting.

All of them surrounded him. Slater, Derek, Calix, Ben…his fucking brothers. A wall of gratitude and affection crashed over him. It was too much. This whole night…it was too much.

"What the hell are you guys doing here?" He couldn't believe they'd come. He looked to Daisy. *Did you ask them?* Smiling, she shook her head.

"We missed your sorry ass," Ben said.

"I was giving you time with your families."

"You *are* our family, dipshit," Derek said. "And, since you insisted on spending your break away from us, we had to come to you."

"You shouldn't have done that." But then he remembered what Ethan had said, and he drew in a deep breath. "Thank you, man. Means a lot."

Slater held his gaze. "Means a lot to us, too." *You get it?*

Yeah, Cooper thought he really did get it.

"Hey, guys." Daisy gestured to them. "You think you could have your reunion after you play a few songs? These guys want to hear you play."

The audience launched into another chant. *Blue Fire, Blue Fire.* The glow necklaces rocked and bounced in the sea of bodies. And in the middle of all the chaos, all the noise and excitement, his gaze connected with Daisy's. And it hit him hard.

That elusive sense of home he'd been chasing?

He'd only ever felt it with her.

And now that he'd found her, there wasn't a chance he'd give her up.

The moment the show ended, handlers ushered Blue Fire into a tent set up to serve as a green room. VIPs mingled while the press snapped pictures, and journalists waited for their turn to interview Slater and Derek.

Cooper stood among his bandmates, keenly aware of the intense energy flying between them as they caught each other up on the past two weeks. They hadn't been apart this long since they'd first started the band nine years ago. How had he ever thought he might not have a place with them just because he hadn't wanted a family? Their connection had always been this powerful, this real.

"How the hell did you guys pull this off?" Cooper nudged Derek. "I didn't have a clue you were coming."

"Your girl." Ben tipped his head toward Daisy, who was talking to the press about the resort.

"No wonder you 'had' to stay in town for two weeks," Derek said. "And here I was feeling bad that you had to spend time in the 'shithole' where you grew up."

Cooper thought of Snowberry from their perspective...the mountains, the cute, historic town, the winding river...and he burst out laughing. "Yeah. Sucks to be here."

"It was Emmie's idea, though," Ben said. "When you were freaking out about that zoning shit—"

"I didn't freak out."

"He never freaks out." Calix tipped his beer bottle back. "He's too chill."

Cooper gave him a look that said *Exactly*.

"Yeah," Ben said. "So, when you were crying to Em about the big, bad Stuart-man, she figured we could fix everything by playing the event."

"I had it handled, asswipe."

But Slater ignored him. "But we knew you'd never go for it."

"You were hell-bent on 'handling' this on your own," Calix said.

"I didn't want to fuck up your time with your family."

"Why is our break more important than yours?" Derek said. "It's our band, our problem. We solve shit together."

"Don't know why you didn't ask us." Ben sounded almost hurt. "We'd have come out here, no problem."

"He knows that, Einstein," Calix said. "We're here."

"Hell, man, the surprise alone was worth it," Derek said. "Did you see his face? I think he pissed himself."

Without even thinking, Cooper sought out Daisy yet again and found her watching him. She gave him a wistful smile—*how much longer until we can be together?*—and his knees went weak.

Because that was the thing with them—they were always touching. Couldn't keep their hands off each other —even in a crowded room, they needed the brush of their bodies to keep them grounded. He was fucking crazy about her.

Slater blew out a slow breath. "Whoa."

"Fuuuck," Ben said.

"Never thought I'd see the day," Derek said.

"Put a fork in him, man," Calix said. "He's done."

"What're you guys talking about?" Cooper asked.

"No, it's cool," Slater said. "I'm happy for you."

"Happy for what?"

"So, explain this to me," Slater said, changing the subject. "Why the hell are we holding this competition when we have Daisy Charbonneau? Her band's the shit."

"Seriously, man," Derek said. "That girl's got pipes."

"She's a partner in the resort they're building," Cooper said. "She can't leave."

"So, how's it going to work then?" Slater asked.

"The finalists from last night and tonight will play tomorrow and—"

"With *her*," Ben said. "You and Daisy."

"I don't know. She doesn't want a weekend here and there. She deserves better than that."

His bandmates stared at him.

"You're fucking with me, right?" Calix said. "You got a girl like that, and you're walking away?"

"Sometimes you're such a douchewad." Ben shook his head.

"Just to be clear," Derek said. "When we leave tomorrow, you're not going to see her again?"

"Her work's here, and I live in New York. Once we finish the tour, we start the next album, and then we're in the studio." He quit talking because they were all watching him like he was speaking in tongues.

"You're shitting me right now," Ben said.

"What? You don't get it. She can't leave this town. And between touring and working on the next album, I can't come back here for more than a weekend here and there. She doesn't want a Facetime relationship."

Calix fixed his unwavering gaze on him. The dude was intense. Underneath it, though, there was a softness, an understanding. "It's not gonna come around again."

I know that. "Our lives don't sync up."

"Coop, man, seriously," Slater said. "I've known you

a long time, seen you around a thousand different women. I've never seen you look at anyone the way you do her."

"You love her?" The sincerity in Ben's tone hit the target.

Fuck, yes. With everything in me. "I've been here two weeks." *I've known her most of my life.*

"That woman?" Calix elbowed him with the same arm that held his beer bottle. "One in a million."

"You're an asshole if you leave here without puttin' a ring on it," Ben said.

A ring? A bolt of electricity lashed through his body. *Marriage?*

Daisy made her way over to the band. "Hey, guys, I hate to interrupt, but we should probably get you started with the interviews."

"Sure thing." Slater and Derek split off, following the reporters to a corner of the tent set up for interviews.

"So, the Kneekockers, huh," Ben said to Daisy. "Are you Maria McKee's long-lost daughter?"

"I don't think so, but you're not the first to compare us to Lone Justice."

"*You,*" Calix said. "He means you. Your voice, your stage presence. Powerful."

Color rose high in her cheeks, making her even lovelier. "Thank you. That's nice to hear from someone with your talent."

And when she gifted Calix with her glorious smile, the big beast of a man looked like the Queen of England had just knighted him.

Was he really going to give her up tomorrow? Cooper would leave his source of light and heat and happiness and go back to a life that, sure, had some small bits of all that

—bits that glanced off him. But not bits that sank into and nurtured his every cell.

He would never feel for anyone the way he felt about Daisy Charbonneau. And right then, watching her charm his bandmates, he got what they were saying.

He'd never considered marriage, but he knew there was no one else for him. In this lifetime, he had one woman.

Daisy.

Yeah, he got it now. He'd found his woman, and there was no going back. She'd captured him with her smile, with the scent of her perfume on his pillow, with the way her eyes rolled back in her head when he brought her a cinnamon roll and a cup of coffee.

There's no going back.

Once he put a ring on it, he'd get to kiss her anytime he wanted. Every single day for the rest of his life. He could lose count of all the kisses.

I want that.

"Can I talk to you?" he asked her.

All eyes turned on him, making him realize he'd interrupted their conversation.

"Of course." She searched his expression the way she always did, and he loved it. Loved her concern for him. Nobody cared about him the way she did.

How had he thought he could walk away from the one person who got him? Who made him truly happy? After the childhood he'd had, the life he'd built had seemed amazing. Until her. But *this* life, the one he could have with Daisy? Holy fuck, it was beyond anything he'd ever imagined. Snatching her hand, he tugged her away from the group.

"You all right?"

He lifted the tent flap and led her into the woods. Backing her up against a towering pine tree, he cupped her chin, his thumb caressing her graceful neck. The golden light from the tent gilded her beautiful face. "I…"

Her hand closed around his wrist. "What's going on?"

The words took shape in his mind. He could see them, but he didn't know how to get them on his tongue. He'd never said them in his life.

But Daisy needed to hear them. If he had a chance in hell of winning her, he had to tell her what she meant to him. He framed her face in his hands. *Tell her.* "Daisy."

She grasped his wrists with an expression that said, *I'm here.*

"I…" *Say it.* If he wanted a life with her, he had to give her his whole heart. "I love you."

She flinched, her mouth slackening into a soft O.

He took advantage of her surprise and kissed her. Her arms wound around his neck, and she stepped closer. And just like that, the barrier snapped. A tidal wave of love reared back—the powerful tension slowing his blood, pulling on his organs—before it came roaring in, crashing over him, and surging into every fiber of his being. "*I love you.*"

"Cooper." Her voice was rich with affection.

Affection isn't good enough. Push harder. Give her more. "Come with us. Tomorrow. Finish out the tour with us." He saw her confusion and scrambled to make his spontaneous idea work. "We'd have two opening acts. You and whoever wins the final round tomorrow. Come with us, Daisy." He could tell from her features, tight with concern—maybe even anger?—that he hadn't said it right. He'd still withheld. *This isn't how you win the girl.* He had to put his whole self on the line. Crack open his chest and hand her his beating heart. "Come with *me*." *Love me.*

He waited for the happiness that lit her from within to break through her confusion. But it didn't. Instead, the longer she held his gaze, all wide-eyed and shocked, the angrier she seemed to become. "Are you..." She lifted her arms before helplessly dropping them to her sides. "Are you actually asking me to give up my life, my *career*, to go on tour with you? Have you heard *anything* I've said?"

Oh, fuck. All his emotions, so raw, so tender, scuttled back into his heart like crabs in wet sand. Her anger anesthetized his heart. He had to think. Had to pull the moment out of this crazy tailspin and get it back on track. He had to make her understand. "I know how much your career means to you." *I just hoped I meant something, too.* "But you said that once you get the shareholders, all you can do is break ground and pour the foundation. You have to wait until spring to actually build. So, I'm not asking you to walk away from anything. You told me everything's set up. The contractors, the vendors, everyone's waiting for your signal."

Her anger only intensified, and his heart burrowed deeper. He needed to stay present, not hide if he had any chance of convincing her. But before he could find the words, she thumped his chest with both hands.

"Did you think we'd pour the foundation, and then I'd just be filing my nails? I'm a *partner* in this resort. It's a full-time job." Her expression said, *I can't believe this.* "You want me on tour with you."

"Yes. I do."

"And what happens if we don't work out? Am I supposed to just watch you party with your fans?"

Those were the words he'd meant to say. Hope rushed

in, and he reached for her arms. "There *is* no going back. Daisy, what we have, I've never..." *Calm down. Talk to her.* "There's no going back. Not for me."

"You can't really think what we've been doing for two weeks is real. It's been fun because we've been sneaking around."

"Bullshit." *Is that what she really thinks?* "We've been living together. Working together."

"And what happens when the tour ends? Do I go to New York with you? Do I leave my family, my job, my whole life behind?"

"I don't have all the answers. I only know I can't walk away from us. Can you?"

"It's easy for you to stand there and ask me to give up my life because there's nothing on the line for you."

My heart. My heart's on the line. I've never given it to anybody before.

Because it's yours.

"If we don't work out, life goes on for you. But for me? I've given up my job. I've said goodbye to everything I love here. Everything I've worked for."

"But we will work out. This is it—you're it for me."

Perspiration beaded on her forehead. This conversation was *upsetting* her.

"Well, of *course,* you feel that way now—you've got an adrenaline high after a great show. But the minute you're back on the road, I guarantee this, *us*...it'll fade. You're going to forget."

"I am *never* going to forget. Don't you get it? You're in me, Daisy. I think you've always been there. I just didn't think I deserved you before. But now...now I want to be the man who deserves you. And I will. I'll be that man if you let me."

She let out a shaky breath and turned away from him. "I'm handling this about as well as you handled Eagle's Landing." She gave a bitter laugh. "God, how is this happening? I never expected you to…"

"Fall in love with you?" He didn't mean to sound so incredulous, but how could she not have known? Hadn't he shown her again and again with his body, his gestures, the way he hung around her every chance he had?

"I know we have chemistry, but you're so set on living this rock star lifestyle. You're so adamant about never coming back here. I'd talked myself into enjoying what I could have. And now this? You want more."

His bloody, bruised heart couldn't take much more of this. He needed an answer. "More than you want to give?"

Her chin tilted. "Are you going to take Eagle's Landing?"

He recoiled. "What does that have to do with anything?"

"Yes, or no? Are you going to build on your family's land?"

"No." It wouldn't be right to take the parcel that meant so much to them. It should be given to someone who lived in Snowberry permanently. He didn't know if he had it in him to put down roots, but if he did, it wouldn't be in this town.

"What's the point, right?" She pursed her lips, nodding. "You're not coming back." She waited for a response, but he didn't have one. If he said *yes, you're right*, she'd have no reason to be with him. But if he said he might live here one day, he'd be lying.

"Yeah, that's what I thought." With a huff, she turned and walked away.

Chapter Eighteen

SHE SLAMMED THE DOOR SO HARD THE WINDOWS rattled.

"Daisy?" Tying the sash of her pink cotton robe, her mom came out of her bedroom. Face free of make-up, hair damp from a shower, she looked flat-out exhausted, and it broke Daisy's heart.

It also empowered her. It reinforced her decision not to abandon her life for a fling with a rock star. He'd been gone a week, and she'd slept at her mom's place ever since. She'd tried sleeping in their—*her*—bed that first night after he'd left town, but she couldn't do it. Too much anger and frustration. Okay, fine, and too many memories. Because he hadn't just slept with her. He'd nestled with her. An arm snuggled around her waist, his face in her hair at the back of her neck. *Stop it.*

The man lived his life on the road. She lived here, where she was creating hundreds of jobs for her community and making sure everyone's investment turned out well. And within a few years, her mom's schedule would ease. No more of this ridiculous work-only lifestyle.

She breezed into the kitchen. "How about I make us some tea?"

"No." Her mom followed her. "Thank you. I'm about to go to sleep."

Then, she'd make some for herself. Something calming. Like Chamomile. "Me, too. Tea first, though." The top cabinet held a few boxes of herbal teas, but she didn't want lemon or anything zinger. Black cherry?

"Honey, what're you looking for?"

"Chamomile. Maybe lavender."

Her mom opened a drawer and pulled out a box.

"Since when do we put tea in a drawer?"

"Since about two years after you moved out and into your own home. The ones up there"—she pointed to the top cabinet—"are yours from when you'd come home during college. These are mine. It's easier for me to reach."

"Your back's been acting up?"

"Of course, sweetheart. I'm on my feet all day. That's a given."

"I hate that you work so hard." She thrust the kettle under the faucet.

"What else would I be doing with my time?"

"Uh, dating? Living."

"I'm living." Her mom leaned a hip against the counter. "And if I wanted to date someone, I would."

"Working isn't the same as living."

"Seems like you might want to take your own advice." Her mom pried her fingers off the kettle and turned off the faucet. "That's enough, sweetheart. You're just making one mug." She set it on the stove and turned on the flame.

Daisy rooted around the drawer for honey but didn't see any. It had to be here, though. Her mom used honey in her tea. She started pulling out the boxes. Why did one woman need so many types of tea?

"What are you looking for?" Her mom sounded annoyed.

"Honey."

"It's right there." She pointed to the saucer next to the toaster. A tub of golden honey sat on it.

Daisy grabbed it, but the bottom stuck to the dish, making it clatter.

"Dammit, Daisy." Her mom snatched the saucer, rinsed the honey residue off, swiped a dish towel over it, and then set the bottle back on it. "Do you want to tell me what's going on, or do you want to keep stomping around my apartment?"

"I want to stomp. In fact, I'd like to throw things. Can I do that?"

"You sure as hell can." She flicked the dial on the stove, killing the flame. "Let's go."

In her short cotton robe and flip flops, her mom grabbed the keys off the hook by the front door. She led the way down the stairs and into the back of the Sugar Bowl's kitchen. Yanking a drawer open, she grabbed a marker. Then, she opened the printer's paper tray and pulled out a sheet.

Grabbing the tape dispenser, she thrust the paper at Daisy. "Draw his face. Or his name. Whatever you want."

With the image of Cooper fresh in her mind, she said, "Who's face?"

Her mom just gave her a bored look and headed into the walk-in refrigerator.

Fine. Daisy drew a round face with two eyes and a sexpot mouth. But it didn't look like Cooper, so she scribbled long hair.

Her mom came out with two cases of eggs.

"Forty-eight? Really?"

"It's a good start. Let's go." With her hands full, her mom tipped her chin toward the outdoor light. "Turn that on for me."

Daisy flipped the switch, and the narrow alley and woods just beyond lit up.

Her mom strode right into a cluster of trees and set the eggs down on a picnic table the workers used when they took breaks. Plucking the paper out of Daisy's hands, she walked it over to a tree.

Nailed to the trunk was a yellow Bear Crossing sign. Her mom whipped off an egg yolk-splattered sheet of paper and taped Daisy's picture on the sign. "Let the games begin."

"I'm not wasting good eggs on a rotten man."

Her mom came back to the picnic table. "If he was so rotten, you wouldn't be such a mess."

"I'm not a mess. It's over. He's gone. He's having the time of his life. Good for him."

"Yes, I can see how little you care."

"I don't."

"You left your browser window open."

"Whatever." She heard how petulant she sounded, and she kind of liked it. It felt good to pitch a fit, knowing her mom would totally let her. "Trust me, I didn't have to search hard to find pictures of him."

"Looks like he's having a grand time."

Picturing him surrounded by deliriously happy fans cranked her anger.

"Good thing you're too smart to fall for his lines," her mom said. "Because from the looks of it, he's forgotten all about you."

"Mom!" Fueled by a fiery rage, she reached for a cold egg and hurled it at the target.

"Missed it by a mile."

She shot her mom a quelling look. She'd only missed because she was shaking with anger. Grabbing another egg, and then another, she hurled them one after the other. One missed, and the other clipped the edge of the sign. *Screw that.* Like a demon, she grabbed and tossed eggs, working so quickly perspiration dripped into her eyes. In no time, she'd wiped out the first case.

"Better?" her mom asked.

No. She reached for more eggs. "He said he *loved* me." Her voice sounded strangled. Pain and frustration had her throwing them so hard her back leg lifted, and she nearly lost her balance.

"And what did you say to him?"

Regret covered her body in deep bruises, and Daisy fell onto the bench. She hated herself for the one thing she hadn't said. "I yelled at him like he'd just asked me to be the band's whore. And right after that, I yelled at him for being so selfish as to ask me to come on tour with him." Tears burned, and sorrow swamped her. "I'm an evil bitch."

Even if leaving town had been the wrong choice for her, she shouldn't have ended things on such a terrible note. *Oh, God.* He'd told her he'd loved her. That couldn't have been easy for a man who'd never known love. Who'd never been hugged. All the gestures of affection she'd taken for granted, he'd never had. And he'd taken the biggest risk of all. He'd given her his heart.

And she'd spit on it. *I hate myself.*

She just…she hadn't expected it. *At all.*

"Sweetheart?" her mom said quietly. "Do you love him?"

She could almost feel the pop. All that love she'd reined in because she was so afraid of getting hurt sprang free, flooding her. "Yes." *Completely.*

"But you don't trust him."

"You don't build a lasting relationship in two weeks. Look what happened to you and Dad. You gave up everything for what you thought was love. And it didn't work out. You had to raise me on your own."

"Is Cooper anything like your dad?"

She didn't even have to think about it. "No." Her dad was a blast to be around, but the moment things got real, he bailed. If someone needed something from him, he made all kinds of promises, but he never saw them through.

Trying to hold onto her dad was like trying to capture the wind. "He's nothing like Dad."

"Yeah, that's what I thought. And, anyways, our situations are nothing alike. I met your dad when I was eighteen. My parents would only pay for college if I went to a small private school near home. I had to *live* at home. And then I met your dad at a bar on the wrong end of town. And let me tell you, he was more fun than anyone I'd ever met. So, when he asked me to go for a ride, you bet I went." Her mom sat down beside her, reached for her hand, and clasped it between hers. "Honey, I have no regrets. I needed to leave home. I wouldn't have become my own woman if I'd stayed in San Diego. My parents were controlling and protective to the point that I had almost no life experience. If I'd stayed in that town, I'd never have realized my potential." She nodded toward the café. "I'm proud of what I've done. I took a part-time job in a bakery and turned it into a thriving business."

"But you're so tired." Alone was what she really meant. *You're so alone.*

"Honey, what would I be doing with myself if I didn't work?"

"You'd have friends. A boyfriend." She drew in a shaky breath. "Mom, why don't you date Joe? He's crazy about you."

"Ah." Her mom looked off into the woods. "Well. You're an adult now so I can tell you. Your dad wrung me out. Too many years of fighting with him. First, it was trying to get him to love me. To stay with me. Then, it was decades of trying to get him to be a good father. It wasn't until you went off to college that I finally accepted he wasn't willing to give anything. And, I don't know, honey, like I said, it just…wrung me out."

Daisy smiled. "Is Joe anything like Dad?"

Her mom smiled. "No, sweetheart. He's nothing like your dad." She reached for Daisy's hand and gave it a squeeze. "Maybe I'll make him supper tomorrow night. See how it goes."

"He'd love that."

"Yeah. He would."

They sat in silence for a moment, just listening to an owl softly hoot and the low rumble of a private conversation somewhere near the café.

She could admit she wasn't doing such a good job with the Cooper situation on her own. She needed her mom. "What do I do? Cooper's not coming back here. He turned down Eagle's Landing. I mean, he's really not coming back. So, if I go with him, if I give our relationship a chance, then I give up my life here."

"Does it have to be so black and white?"

"I think so." Maybe he didn't even want her anymore. After she'd been so careless with his heart, he might've shut down. Gone back to his old ways.

"I can't tell you what to do. I can only ask you if he's worth giving a chance?"

Daisy couldn't answer because her pulse beat *yes* while her mind screamed, *dear God, no*.

"If you can imagine your life without him, if you think, given some time, you'll fall for someone else, then screw it. Let it go. You had fun for two weeks. But if you think what you had was special, then what the hell are you doing throwing eggs in my backyard in the middle of the night instead of sharing that man's bed right now?"

In the green room after the concert, a roadie came up and clapped him on the back. "Great show, man."

"Thanks." Not in the mood to talk, Cooper tipped back his beer.

"You okay?" The guy looked concerned.

"Sure."

A ruckus broke out around the coffee table, and a woman on ice pick-sharp heels tumbled into him. He caught her around the waist, his beer sloshing out of the bottle. When she righted herself, she said, "Sorry about that." Blonde, slender, with very white teeth, she leaned into him. "Well, if I had to make a fool of myself at least I caught a rock star."

He nodded, waiting for attraction to flare. *Nothing.*

Here's where you flirt back, dumbass. He could at least

fake it, play the role she was looking for. Maybe he'd get into it.

She said something, but it was hard to hear over the roar of conversation and heavy thump of bass. But he understood the question in her eyes and shook his head.

Color rushed into her cheeks, and she nodded before taking off into the crowd.

"Can't believe you let that one go," the roadie said.

"No rush, man." Cooper had his choice of beauties for his evening's entertainment. His bandmates might've gone back to the bus, but the Kneeknockers were eating up the rocker lifestyle. He helped them shut down the party most nights. "Have you seen Lia?"

"No, but I can find her for you." Without waiting for an answer, he took off.

They'd been back on the road for ten days, and Jason's girlfriend hadn't seemed to be enjoying herself much. Mostly, she hung out by herself or had quiet talks with a roadie or the sound engineer. He liked checking in with her, making sure she was okay.

A trio of women approached.

"Hey." The tall blonde thrust her hand out and gave him a firm shake. "I'm Kaitlyn. This is Danni and Taylor. We're DJs at K104 FM."

"Great to meet you."

"You look so lost, standing there all alone."

"Not lost at all." *Totally fucking lost.* "Just waiting for the right invitation."

"You're in luck. We're heading out to a party right now. Want to join us?"

The roadie waved at him from behind the couch, then pointed to Lia, who leaned against the wall, reading the screen of her phone. Was she texting Daisy?

That was a stupid assumption. She was probably reading a book. Or checking her email.

"So," the woman asked. "You in?"

The women were attractive, friendly, and didn't have the groupie-vibe going on, and yet he knew he wouldn't be taking them up on their invitation. He couldn't rouse even a hint of interest. "I'll pass, thanks. Got an early morning."

He'd just gotten his heart handed to him ten days ago. It would take some time to get his mojo back.

"Come on," one of the women said. "It'll be fun."

He didn't have to fuck them or get drunk. He could just go and hang out. Meet some people. What else was he going to do? Go back to the bus and listen to Ben Facetime with his girlfriend?

But the idea of standing around with a bunch of strangers getting drunk or high or whatever just didn't move the needle. At all.

A rush of longing hit him full force. He wanted to be with Daisy.

I miss her.

"Hey, Coop." Lia approached them, giving a brief smile to the DJs. "Can I talk to you?"

"Yeah, sure." He looked to the women. "Give me a second?"

"You got it," the blonde said.

"We'll wait right here," her friend said.

Lia led him to a corner of the room and held up her phone. "Thank you."

"For what?" It took a moment to make sense of what he was seeing. A bank statement. *Ah.* She'd received his donation.

"This is amazing. Thank you so much. I can't wait to

get back home and start putting it to use. I've got so many projects ready to go."

"Happy to do it."

"Yeah, I just want to go home and get started. I wish Daisy—" Her jaw snapped shut and her eyes widened.

"You can say her name." His heart thumped painfully. "It's okay for you to talk about her."

Lia smiled. "She keeps checking in with me. Seeing how I like touring."

"You tell her the truth?"

Lia held his gaze for a moment, then let out a little laugh. "No. I don't want…it's just two and a half more months." She glanced at her boyfriend across the room. "I really want him to have this."

"You think he'll get it out of his system?"

In the center of the room, Jason partied with strangers. He was laughing so hard, his eyes were squeezed closed. Cooper didn't believe for a second that Jason would get anything out of his system. He'd want more.

Cooper just didn't know if he'd get it without Daisy or Lia fronting the band.

"He wants this life more than anything." Lia watched her boyfriend. "If he doesn't take every opportunity to go after it, he'll regret it. He needs to come to his own conclusions about the life he wants to lead. And if he wants a life on the road, I'd rather know now."

"Does it have to be all or nothing?"

She gave him a knowing look. "You tell me."

The strangest sensation came over him, an awareness as cool and clear as a mountain lake. Over and over, he'd told Daisy it was all or nothing. When he'd rejected Eagle's Landing, he'd basically said the same thing to his family. *I'm never going to live here, so I don't need your land.* Remi had suggested building a studio, but Cooper hadn't even considered it. *All or nothing.*

Of course, Daisy wouldn't come on tour with him. He'd only offered her three months.

"I fucked up."

"No, you didn't. She just…"

"I did." But he finally knew how to fix it.

How to win his girl.

A bulldozer emerged through the early morning mist like an alien spaceship invading the ranch. Why Daisy was thinking about spaceships instead of the conversation between Ethan and the project manager, she had no idea. She couldn't seem to concentrate on anything these days.

Since hurling eggs with her mom, she'd started about a dozen text messages to Cooper. But nothing sounded right. If she said she loved him, what would happen next? Would she visit him on tour? Wait for him to finish and then spend Thanksgiving with him—and if so, where?

How did she reconcile loving a man who had no intention of coming back to her hometown? She didn't know what to do with these feelings. Until she had an answer, she didn't see the point in reaching out to him.

The truck rumbled past, bypassing the construction site. *Uh…hello?* Where the hell was it going? It lurched up the dirt road that led to an undeveloped section of the Blackstock Ranch. Daisy grew alarmed when she noticed an eighteen-wheeler with a backhoe loaded on its flatbed falling in behind the bulldozer.

"Guys?" But when she looked over, she realized she

was alone. The guys stood huddled together over a zoning map at the project manager's pickup truck. "*Ethan.*"

He looked up, and she pointed to the rogue trucks. He nodded like everything was all right.

But of course, it wasn't all right. There was nothing up that road. No reason for construction trucks to head up there. *Oh, for goodness' sake.* Daisy jumped into her Camaro and quickly took off after them. Dirt kicked up, bits of gravel pinging the sides of her baby. *Dammit.* She accelerated to reach them before they got too far.

Daisy honked and flashed her brights, but they either ignored her or couldn't hear her over the engines. With the road too narrow to pass, she veered as far left as she could, laying on the horn and frantically waving to get the driver's attention in his rear-view mirror.

Finally, he noticed her and braked. She jumped out of her car and raced over to the guy's window. "Where are you *going*?" She had to shout over the idling engine.

"'Bout two miles up this road."

"There's nothing up there. The only work's down there." She pointed behind her. "At the construction site."

The guy pulled out a clipboard. "I'm supposed to go here." His finger stabbed at a spot on the topography map.

"Let me see." He handed the board through the window, and Daisy followed the red line that led from the entrance of the property up to…her heart lurched painfully. "That's Eagle's Landing."

"Okay…?"

"There's nothing happening there."

"Lady, all I know is it's staked out for clearance, and I'm delivering the equipment."

"That's not possible." She would've known if the Blackstocks had decided to build on that piece of land.

The guy took the clipboard. "We good?"

She backed away. They weren't actually doing anything other than leaving trucks there, so she nodded. "I'll talk to the property owners. Thank you."

The driver motioned to the bulldozer, and they continued on.

This isn't about Cooper, right? He'd been one hundred percent clear on the fact that he wasn't coming back.

I love you. His expression when he'd said those words haunted her. He'd meant them. *I love you.* The words animated her. Invigorated her. Because she loved him, too. And what they had was real. It was deep. And it was strong.

She didn't want to get her hopes up—*oh, dear God, stop being such a wussy.*

Get your damn hopes up. Why not? What's the worst that can happen?

You get disappointed.

Been there done that, still alive to tell the tale.

She got in her Camaro and peeled out, hoping with all her heart that Cooper had decided to build on his land.

"When did he call?" She had to run to keep up with Ethan's long stride. "What did he say exactly?"

"He called a few days ago and apologized for being a dick." Ethan shrugged. "Wants to build a place here."

"Why?"

Ethan turned an exasperated look her way. *Why do you think?*

"If it's about me, why wouldn't he tell me?"

"He's *showing* you, Daze. Means a whole lot more, don't you think?"

She couldn't make out his features through the wall of tears building in her eyes. "Ethan."

"Yeah, Daze?" He stopped walking to brush hair off her damp forehead.

"It would be stupid and frivolous of me to take time off, right? You need me here to build the resort."

"Not building till the spring."

"So, if I took a few weeks off…"

"We could spare you." He shrugged. "Might even be able to stretch it to a month or two."

Tears spilled down her cheeks. Was this happening? Was she really going to do this?

"Go on." Ethan burst out laughing. "Get out of here."

Chapter Nineteen

Blue Fire stood in the wings, ready to take the stage. Cooper shifted restlessly, ready to go.

Except…wait. He didn't see their lead singer. Cooper nudged Ben. "Where the hell's Slater?"

Calix fought back a smile, as Ben gave him a knowing look. What was he missing? He turned to find Slater and Emmie coming out from behind a thick, velvet curtain. Slater tucked in his shirt, while Emmie ran her hands through her long, dark hair.

"Jesus Christ, you two," Cooper said. "We're going on in one minute."

Ben eyed them enviously. "Can't wait till Lee can come on the road with us."

"You even think of doing *that* with my sister," Calix said. "And I'll fuck you up."

As the guys bickered, Emmie gazed up at her husband, smiling at something he said. Cooper hadn't paid much attention to their relationship before, but now it sliced all the way to the bone. He'd been away from Daisy for over two weeks, and he missed her in a way he couldn't have anticipated.

With her, he'd felt whole for the first time in his life. He'd felt completely himself. *I want that back.*

"Need a nap, old man?" Derek said.

"Unlike you, I've got stamina," Slater said. "I'm ready to go. So, let's show California how it's done." He gave his wife a big kiss and then strode to the edge of the stage.

The crowd went wild, as the Kneeknockers finished their set. Lia waved. "Thank you all so much. You guys have been great." She grabbed the mic off its stand. "We're so grateful to Blue Fire for letting us open for them on their tour. They're the absolute best group of musicians we've ever worked with."

A roadie on the other side of the stage shouted, "Encore!"

Okay, that was weird. Why would a *roadie* ask for another song?

"Sorry, what was that? Did I hear someone ask for an encore?" Lia smiled at the guy before turning her attention to the crowd. "Guys, that's Sam. He's one of our favorite roadies. And he wants us to do another song. What do you say? You up for one more tune?"

"What's going on?" Cooper asked. But no one responded.

"So, which one do you want to hear?" Lia set the mic back in its stand.

"'Set Yer Truck on Fire!'"

"Oh." She pretended to be worried. "Gosh…I'm not sure I can do that one justice. I mean, I can sing but not *that* well. There aren't too many people who can hit those notes. Hm." She turned to her band. "What should we do?"

Confused, Cooper turned to find his bandmates watching the scene, riveted. "Seriously, what's going on?" There was only one person who sang the hell out of "Set Yer Truck on Fire," but she was a thousand miles away. Cooper's bandmates were biting back laughter. "What?" Now, he was just pissed.

The roadie took the stage, clapping his hands and chanting "'Set Yer Truck on Fire,'" and within seconds, the whole audience joined him.

"Well, damn, looks like we're gonna have to do that song," Lia said. "Okay, you guys, I need some help. Who can help me out?" Lia pointed at someone in the front row. "How 'bout you? You want to give it a shot?"

Jason and the lead guitarist rushed to the edge of the stage, got on a knee, and reached down to grab someone's hand.

A hand that was attached to a sexy, toned arm. An arm that led to thick, dark hair, all tousled and shiny. And then several people gathered around her, hoisting Daisy fucking Charbonneau onto the stage.

"Ladies and gentleman, I'm happy to present the one and only Daisy Charbonneau."

Holy shit. Voltage struck his central nervous system, and Cooper raced onto the stage, lifted Daisy into his arms, and held her like he'd never let go. Happiness crashed over him. "You're here."

She wrapped her legs around his waist, those red cowboy boots locked over his ass, and cupped his face with both hands. "I love you. I love you so much."

"Fuck, Daisy." He squeezed her tightly. "I thought I was going to have to work a hell of a lot harder than this."

She tucked her face into his neck, her body shaking with laughter.

"Are you coming on tour with me?"

She stroked the hair at the back of his neck. "Well, I was hoping for a little more than that."

"You can have everything. I'll give you everything. I just want to be with you."

"You're building a house." Her eyes shone with tears.

"*We're* building a house, sweetheart. It's for us. It's forever."

All of a sudden, the crowd roared to deafening decibels. Cooper glanced over to see Slater had taken the stage.

"Hey, Coop?" Slater said into the mic. "You and your girl need some alone-time?"

Catcalls from the audience made the band crack up.

"Or do you think you could let the Kneeknockers play their last song so we can get this show started?"

Daisy started to wriggle free, but he couldn't let her go just yet—he'd just gotten her back. So, he held on tight to her perfect ass and gave her one long, deep, kiss that let her know how much it meant to have her with him.

The Kneeknockers started playing "Crazy Little Thing Called Love," and the audience burst into applause.

"Oh, hell, man," Slater said. "Emmie, get out here. I need some lovin' too."

Laughing, Emmie came out onto the stage, and Slater wrapped an arm around her back, dipping her low as he kissed her.

The audience roared its approval, and flashes went off everywhere.

And then the Kneeknockers kicked off "Set Yer Truck on Fire," Daisy took the mic, and Slater, Emmie, and Cooper scampered off the stage.

Surrounded by his bandmates, Cooper watched his

woman belt out the song in her powerful, show-stopping voice.

He had *no idea* how his life had turned out this way. But he'd sure as hell hold onto it with all he had.

Because, with Daisy at his side, he had *everything*.

Chapter Twenty

"Are you nervous?"

And wasn't that just typical of his wife to be worried about *him*? "No, cinnabun. Not a bit." Keeping an eye on the road, Cooper cupped the back of her neck and drew her across the console so he could press his mouth to hers. He gave a little swipe of his tongue, and the love of his life opened for him. The kiss deepened, and Daisy pressed her hand to his chest.

Three years later, and she still responded to him with the same passion and urgency. It turned him the fuck on. He pulled away, placing both hands back on the steering wheel to handle the bend in the road.

"This is exactly what got us into trouble in the first place." She tugged the skirt of her dress, covering those pretty thighs.

Trouble? He smiled. This was the best kind of trouble. Was he scared shitless? Yeah. But in a good way. A really good way. He reached for her hand and entwined their fingers.

"Are you even ready for this? I mean, you've got an

380

international tour coming up. Blue Fire's, like, the biggest band in the world right now. It's a terrible time for *this*." She clutched the little plastic bag.

"It's the perfect time. And you know the band. You know our priorities."

She sighed. "Family first."

"Exactly." It wasn't like Daisy to freak out. "Do *you* not want this?"

But before she could answer, he rounded the bend and got that punch to his system that hit every time he came home. It was almost too perfect to be real. Not the six bedrooms and stone fireplace, not the gourmet kitchen and game room filled with pinball machines, foosball, and air hockey tables.

No, it was the fact that he got to sleep with Daisy Charbonneau every night. He got to pull her laundry out of the dryer and fold her panties and pajama bottoms. He got to bring cinnamon rolls and coffee to her in bed every Sunday morning.

He got Daisy. The girl he'd loved his whole life. It seemed absurd that he'd once thought being a rock star was the best life had to offer. Hell, no. Kissing Daisy any time he wanted? *That* was the best.

On the front lawn, his bandmates played tackle football with their wives and toddlers. Violet, about two weeks away from giving birth to her and Derek's second kid, arched her back.

Daisy watched the pregnant woman with pure fear. Reaching for her hand, he brought it to his mouth and kissed her palm. "Cinnabun."

She turned to him with a look of alarm.

"I'm ready." *I want this.*

Her features relaxed, and she gave him a small smile.

The moment he parked the car, his bandmates stopped playing and shot him chastising looks. They were supposed to be in the studio by ten, but he and Daisy had needed to make a quick trip into town. She couldn't rest until she knew for sure.

He opened the door, holding out his hands in a placating gesture. "I know, I know. Had a little emergency."

The icing on his cake was that his bandmates had loved Snowberry so much, they'd all built second homes —forcing the Blackstocks to move up phase five of the resort development. Now, all five of their families lived close together, sharing a backyard the size of a football field.

The guys kissed their women, crouched to hug their kids, and then met Cooper on the pathway to the studio they'd built at the back of his property.

"We've been waitin' on you, man," Derek said in his growly voice.

"Looks like it's been pure hell." Cooper gestured to the grass stains on the bass guitarist's jeans. He had a smear of something that looked like chocolate on the shoulder of his white T-shirt, where he guessed Derek's eighteen-month-old hellion had wiped his mouth.

"We've got a lot to cover today," Slater said. "And I need to be done in time for dinner with my family."

Daisy led the charge into the studio, and Ben said, "She layin' down vocals today?"

"Nope," she called over her shoulder. "Just need to use the bathroom."

Confusion crossed their features—she could obviously use one of the seven bathrooms in her home, which sat not a dozen yards from the studio—but they let it go.

Once inside, Cooper took Daisy's hand. "Be right with you," he called.

But the guys were busy shaking hands with Hunter and the sound engineers.

"Hurry up, man," Slater called. "No hanky panky in there."

"I would *never*." Cooper gave him a big grin.

"You know we'll be able to hear you," Ben said.

Laughing, Cooper closed the bathroom door. He pulled the box out of the plastic bag and tore it open, handing the stick to his wife. Daisy pulled up her dress and yanked down her white and pink polka dot panties.

Once she finished, she set the stick on top of the box, washed her hands, and turned to look at him. Her eyes were bright and wide with fear. "I want this."

"Yeah?" He knew his wife. She hated getting her hopes up and having them dashed. With his hands on her hips, he drew her closer and gave her a gentle kiss. "I do, too. I want a feisty little girl with her mom's pretty hair and fun-loving spirit."

Tears glistened in her eyes. She looked so damn scared.

"But Cinnabun, we weren't even trying. So, if it doesn't work out this time, imagine what'll happen when we get busy."

He lowered himself down between the toilet and the counter and tugged his wife onto his lap. "I love you, Daisy."

She wrapped her arms around his neck and buried her face in his neck. "I want our baby. And I'm so scared."

"Are you scared? Or excited?"

Her head popped up, and she bit her bottom lip, fighting off a smile. "I'm really, really excited. And if Violet, Emmie, and Mimi can handle raising kids with their full-time jobs and your crazy schedules, then I can, too."

"*We* can. We're in this together. All the way." He kissed her. "Ready to look?"

"It hasn't been three minutes."

"Cooper?" Emmie knocked on the door. "I hate to bother you, but the photographer just showed up."

Daisy got off his lap and opened the door. "I thought we weren't doing pictures until the weekend?"

Emmie peered in, as though casing the joint. "She has an emergency in Hawaii and can only do it today. Right now."

Daisy glanced at him. "How come I don't have Hawaiian emergencies?"

He smiled, but mostly because he caught her subtle grab for the pregnancy stick. She slid it into the back pocket of his jeans.

"When this album's in the can, we'll go DEFCON 1 all over Hawaii's ass."

"Guys, we're already *in* paradise." Emmie led the way out. The studio had cleared, and they found everyone outside.

The photographer had arranged the band against the stark rock wall at the back of Eagle's Landing. Once Cooper joined them, the woman started taking some shots. But then Calix's two-year-old daughter tottered into the frame and plowed her face between his legs. The huge man swept up his little girl, and she buried her face in her daddy's neck.

"Is Mom around?" the photographer asked. "We're not done yet."

"I'm so sorry." Mimi jogged toward them. "I just got a call from the contractor." She gave Calix a thumbs-up.

"Snowberry's first tea house is good-to-go." As she was coaxing her daughter away from Calix, Lilah Dove, Slater's little girl, raced toward him, squealing with joyful abandon, and within seconds all the wives and kids were gathered around, and the photographer was going nuts taking shots from every angle. The lens moved in and out as she got both group and private photos.

Discreetly, Cooper reached into his back pocket and pulled out the wand. Daisy wrapped an arm around his waist, leaning in to see the results.

Two pink lines in the result window. Joy rushed through him so fast and hard he needed to reach for the rock wall. "Holy shit."

His wife wrapped her arms around him. He just held her, neither speaking. He was going to be a dad. Once, he hadn't been able to imagine anything better in life than getting to play guitar for a living. He'd never even considered wanting anything else.

But look at me now. He had the love of his life, his band of brothers, his actual brothers, a damn good father, and now…a kid.

"Is that a pregnancy test?" Mimi asked loudly enough that everyone heard.

The attention of nine grown-ups and four kids turned on them.

Daisy gave him a smile filled with love and pride and hope for a future that was coming up fast. *I love you,* she mouthed.

"Well?" Emmie clasped her hands over her chest.

Cooper gave a nod.

"Oh, my God!" Emmie cried.

"They're pregnant," Mimi shouted. "You guys, they're having a baby."

And just like that, they found themselves in the center of a press of bodies. Slaps on the back, kisses on his cheek, and Daisy's forehead on his chest, as they let all that love rain down on them.

It filled him with an ineffable sense of joy and utter contentment.

The kid who'd started out with so little, now had it all.

Thank you for reading MORE THAN A FEELING! Have you met Slater f**ing Vaughn, the lead singer of Blue Fire? YOU REALLY GOT ME is a slow burn, friends-to-lovers, rock star romance with explosive sexual chemistry, and a soulful rocker who falls for his bandmate's sister. "Slater Vaughn might just be the best book boyfriend I've ever come across." – Obsessed with Romance

Here's the Rock Star Romance series:

YOU REALLY GOT ME
I WANT YOU TO WANT ME
TAKE ME HOME TONIGHT
MORE THAN A FEELING

And check out the world of Calamity Falls, a steamy, small town, contemporary romance series, where each book can be read as a standalone. In this charming town, you'll find alpha male book boyfriends and the kind of strong, supportive women you'll want as your best friends.

KEEP ON LOVING YOU
WE BELONG TOGETHER
THE VERY THOUGHT OF YOU
JUST THE WAY YOU ARE
IT WAS ALWAYS YOU
CAN'T HELP FALLING IN LOVE
COME AWAY WITH ME
WHOLE LOTTA LOVE
YOU'RE STILL THE ONE

Look for YOU'RE STILL THE ONE in June 2021! Grab a FREE copy of ALWAYS ON MY MIND, so you can find out what happened to Pete, Blue Fire's original keyboard player. And come hang out with me on Facebook, Twitter, Instagram, Goodreads, and Pinterest or in my private reader group.

Here's an excerpt from the first book in the Rock Star Romance series—you're going to fall hard for the hot, lead singer and the woman who swore she'd never fall for another rocker!

Keep reading for an excerpt from
YOU REALLY GOT ME by Erika Kelly!

You Really Got me

"OH, BOLLOCKS, *EMMIE*!"

Emmie Valencia's boss hollered so loudly her teeth rattled. And there was a *wall* between them. She pressed the button on her intercom and said, "Be right there." He could be such a baby. Seconds later, the office came alive with excited voices and laughter. Her coworkers hurried down the hall, heading for the foyer.

Frontierland was back from their tour. Which meant . . .

Alex.

Her gut twisted hard. Briefly, she imagined ducking under her desk, maybe dashing to the mail room. But, of course, she wouldn't do that. She could face her ex. No big deal.

In fact, that's exactly what she *should* do. Talk to him as casually as she did the rest of the guys. She hated the way people looked at her whenever he came into the office. Besides, they'd ended it months ago.

One of the interns popped breathlessly into her office. "They're here." Her features flushed, she mouthed, "Flash," and pretended to fan herself. Then, she darted down the hall.

Emmie smiled and shook her head. Even though they worked with bands for a living, everyone got all goofy and fawning when the artists came in.

Except for Emmie, of course. She'd grown up around musicians. She saw beneath the glitter to their tortured, attention- craving, twisted souls. Everyone wanted a piece of them, to be the one to get in, breach the barrier. To win their hearts.

But she knew better. They didn't let anyone in. Not really. They drew people in with their dazzling charisma and then pushed them back when they got too close.

Loving an artist *hurt*.

Obviously, she'd thought Alex would be different. They'd grown up together. Their parents were best friends. *Silly me.* Musicians were musicians. She'd *known* that.

As she pulled papers from the printer, she heard, "Emmie!" in a far more upbeat tone than her boss's. She spun around to find the boys from Frontierland crowding into her office.

Crap, is Alex with them?

She'd keep her cool. Treat him the way she treated the other guys. No big deal. Because *he* was no big deal. Not after what he'd done to her. Lifelong friendship be damned.

"Great job, you guys," she said, as the drummer pulled her to him. They played an outrageous mix of rockabilly, country, and country rock and dressed like badass banditos in leather, vests, and straw cowboy hats. "Have you read the reviews yet?"

"Brenda doesn't make those fuckin' scrapbooks like you do, man." The keyboardist pushed through the others to give her a hug. He smelled of whiskey and patchouli.

"Why couldn't we score Irwin as our A&R guy?" another one asked.

She winced. Her boss wouldn't sign them because she'd been dating their bass player.

As the next guy leaned in for a hug, Emmie made a quick scan of their faces. No Alex. *Good.* But right when the rhythm guitarist belted his arms around her and lifted her off the floor, Emmie caught sight of him.

Her ex, clad in black leather pants and a stretched-out white T-shirt, flirted with the new receptionist across the hallway. Emmie hated that he'd do it right in front of her, of course, but mostly she couldn't believe he thought so little of their relationship that he felt *comfortable* doing it. Like their time together hadn't really counted.

It had to her.

Flash, the lead singer, yanked her out of the other guy's arms and said, "There's my girl." Gorgeous in a rough way, Flash had gotten his nickname because, in the middle of every show, he asked the women in the audience to "Flash me your tits," so he could take a photo on his phone and post it on the band's website. *Classy.* "You gonna marry me yet?"

"I think I'd rather marry your fiancée. She's hot."

Just as his hand skimmed down her back heading for forbidden territory, she jerked her hips and pulled out of his embrace.

"You're no fun, Emmie Valencia."

A sharp pain sliced her heart. Her gaze flicked over his shoulder to the office where Alex and the receptionist shared a quiet laugh. "So I've heard."

"Hey." Tilting his head, he gave her a concerned look. "I'm just playing with you."

"I know." She smiled, hoping to brush away the uncomfortable moment. God, she had to get ahold of herself.

"But if I can't get you to marry me, then can you at least get me one of those bags you got Irwin's kid?"

"You want me to score you the latest Hermès purse?"

"For my fiancée."

Emmie let out an exaggerated sigh. "What did you do this time?" She held her hand up. "Never mind. I don't want to hear. And you don't need me to do it—get yourself on the list. Make a call like I did."

"Oh, come on. We're stuck with Brenda. She doesn't do shit for us. Besides, I don't have your connections. You make shit happen."

"Yes, for Irwin. And I don't *have* connections. I make them when I need to."

"I could make shit happen for you."

Their gazes caught. Behind his incessantly flirtatious vibe lived a shark of a businessman. "You offering me a job, Flash?"

A slow smile ate up his ruggedly handsome features. "Fuck, yeah."

"What kind of job?"

"What kind of job you want?"

Wasn't that just the question? She didn't want just a *job*. She wanted *inside*. Eight years on the periphery of the music industry as Irwin Ledger's personal assistant was enough. She needed to take that next obvious step to A&R coordinator—discovering bands, working with talent—and Flash couldn't help her with that.

Only Irwin could.

"Flash?" his bandmate called. "Leave Em alone and get in here. Bob's waiting."

"We'll finish this convo later." Flash started to go.

"Hey, can you close the door behind you?" She didn't need to watch Alex flirting.

Unfortunately, Flash followed her gaze, got an eyeful of her ex and the receptionist, and then looked back at her with a hint of pity. He pointed a finger at her. "Golden rule, baby. Never get involved with the talent."

She smirked. "So, we're *not* getting married?" So much for her resolve not to make people uncomfortable. "You know what? Leave it open." Her tone said, *what do I care?*

He gave her an appreciative smile before taking off.

"Oh, for fuck's sake," her boss shouted. "Emmie?"

"Coming," she shouted back.

"I can't imagine what's taking you so bloody long. I have a crisis, Emmie. Cri-sis."

She picked up the handset and hit his speed dial. "Crisis as in you scuffed your favorite Bruno Magli chocolate suede loafers, and they don't make them anymore, so you need me to call the designer himself and get a pair custom-made? Or crisis as in the drummer from Wicked Beast fell off the wagon again and can't make the show tonight so I need to get to the hotel and get him sobered up?"

"You mock me. I count on you, and you mock me."

She smiled. "Two seconds." Disconnecting, she grabbed her iPad and spun around to the door . . . only to catch the receptionist pressing her body against Alex.

Oh, hell.

Memories slammed her. Alex's hard chest, the spicy scent of his soap, the creak of his leather. How many times had she held him just like that?

Alex's hand wrapped around the woman's waist, pulling her tight against him. That moment of intimacy, the way Val conformed her body to his, the way her hands cupped the back of his neck, her features soft—it struck Emmie right in her core.

It was so intimate, so sensual. And it hurt. God, it hurt.

Because she wasn't sexy like Val. She just . . . wasn't.

Tucking the iPad to her chest, she leaned back against the wall, out of sight. Why did she let him affect her? It wasn't like she missed him or even wanted him. He'd cheated on her.

The sex is fine. It's just not . . . you're not wild, you know?

You service *me.*

She cringed remembering his words.

A guy wants more than that.

Oh, God. She couldn't bear the memories. She charged out of her office. Just as she turned into the hallway, she saw Alex capture Val's leg, his hand cupping her thigh, as he murmured against her mouth. Expression sultry, Val curled around him.

Emmie had never held him like that. Not with that kind of total abandon.

"Emmie?" Irwin shouted.

"I'm coming." Seeing Val be the woman Alex had wanted *her* to be, the kind of woman who melted around a man, who lost herself in sensation, well, it just made it hard to breathe.

The worst thing was that she'd never felt that kind of passion, that urgency. Not for any guy.

She stood there a moment longer, contemplating barging in and greeting Alex, letting the whole office know she was cool with him. Letting *him* know he didn't affect her anymore.

But then she realized something. She *wasn't* cool with him. She wasn't unaffected at all.

Because he flirted right under her nose with the receptionist, and that was just a lousy thing to do.

Taking a deep breath, Emmie pushed off the wall and strode out into the hallway. She didn't even spare Alex a glance as she hurried into Irwin's office.

She came to a halt when she saw her boss's expression. Lips drawn into a taut line, he held the phone to his ear. When she walked right up to his ultramodern chair, which hung from the ceiling like a hammock, he looked at her with utter relief. Immediately, his features turned slack, and he thrust the phone at her.

Placing it to her ear, she had about two seconds to get up to speed, not having the slightest idea who was on the line.

"He wants me to be there, Daddy. I'm, like, his muse. He said he for sure can't do his best work unless I'm there. Do you want this track to suck?"

"Caroline," Emmie said. "Who're we talking about?"

The girl exhaled roughly. "James. He wants me in the studio with him."

Honestly, Emmie did not have time to deal with this nonsense. "James is a drug addict, Caroline. Your dad had to drop him from the label because he couldn't fulfill his contract. Do you see why your dad wouldn't want you hanging out with James while we're out of the country?"

"So, what, I'm supposed to be all locked up because my dad's out of town? I'm an *adult*."

"Not when your dad's paying your bills, including the lawyer he keeps on retainer for your *indiscretions*."

"Oh, my God—"

"Last weekend the sound engineer got you so drunk you blacked out. Your dad and I spent seven hours racing around the city, out of our minds, trying to find you. You can't blame him if he's not comfortable giving you the run of Manhattan when we're not around."

"You don't even know what you're talking about. Rory didn't *get* me drunk. I thought I was drinking iced tea. I didn't know they were *Long Island* Iced Teas. That's not his fault. We were just hanging out. Besides, it's not like I'm going to be *alone*. You'll be here."

Tipping her head back, she blew out a breath. "Caroline. You know I'm going with your dad. Look, hanging out with James the drug addict is obviously out of the question, but let's come up with a few—"

"No, you're not."

"I'm not what?"

"Going with my dad."

"Of course I'm going with him." She glanced at Irwin, found him examining his laptop, swinging in his chair.

He didn't have a formal office, the kind with the big oak desk facing two guest chairs, a potted plant, and a filing cabinet. Why would he need a desk? No, he had a plush couch, a world-class sound system, a pinball machine, a dartboard, and a Picasso hanging on the wall.

Movement from the corner of her eye had her turning to the door. Alex stood in the threshold, a hint of remorse on his face. Her heart pounded, and her nerves tingled. But before

he could take one step into the office, Irwin flew out of his chair, stalked to the door, and slammed it in her ex's face.

Emmie smiled.

Irwin stalked back to the chair, gripping the metal arm, and set it off rocking again.

"I'm not talking to either of you anymore," Caroline said. "I'm going into the studio with James because I'm his muse and he needs me. And if my dad doesn't like it, then you can just come with us and hang out in the lounge."

"I won't be able to come with you because I *am going to Australia*."

Irwin got up, leaving the leather and chrome chair swinging. He went to the built-in media center that took up one wall and got busy shuffling through his CDs.

"You're not going to Australia. Dad said. God, why are you being such a bitch?"

Emmie closed her eyes, taking a moment before responding. "And so ends my efforts to help you. Here's your dad." With that, she handed the phone back to Irwin. "Hold your ground. She shouldn't be anywhere near James Beckman."

He put the phone back to his ear. "What did you say that made your auntie Emmie hand me back the phone?" His gaze kicked up to Emmie's. "Nothing? Are you sure? She's usually so indulgent with us." His brow furrowed. "A bitch? Ah, well, then. I'm afraid you're on your own on this one, darling. Must go, my love. Kiss, kiss." He hung up on her. "Wretched child, isn't she?"

Emmie smiled, knowing how he adored his only kid. But the smile quickly faded. "So, Australia?"

"Yes, right. Slight change of plans." He ran his hand through his messy, floppy hair. Only the silver streaking through it made him look anything close to his forty-nine years.

"We're not going?"

"That would be a *total* change of plans. Slight means only one of us isn't going."

"Irwin. We leave tomorrow."

"Emmie, darling, I'm sorry, but I can't leave Caroline alone for six weeks. I'm going to need you to stay here."

Okay, wait. Emmie had spent months planning this trip. Two weeks ago, one of the producers had realized his passport had expired. She'd had to wave her wand, cast spells, and rub magic lamps to push his renewal through. She'd planned every detail of their time there, down to finding the coffee shops closest to the recording studios. She'd booked dinner reservations, arranged delivery of industry periodicals to his hotels, and spent months researching and contacting up-and-coming bands.

Oh, and hang on. She'd spent last night *packing* for her boss. Yes, that meant handling his black silk boxers.

Not only that, but this trip meant more than assisting Irwin. She'd gotten him to agree to let her go off and discover some bands of her own. So she could finally get that promotion. But now, the day before departure, he was telling her she couldn't go. Because . . .

"Wait a minute. You want me to *babysit*?"

"Don't be ridiculous. Of course not. You're not changing nappies. You just need to look after her."

"You want me to babysit your daughter." She said it dully, lowering herself onto the plush leather couch. "I'm twenty- five years old, I've worked for you for eight years —" She flashed him a look. "Even as a high school intern I did more for you than your own secretary. And your best use for me is babysitting?"

"You make it sound so trivial. This is my daughter we're talking about. And you're more like a mother to her than her actual mum."

"I'm four years older than her. I'm not like her mother."

"No, you're better than her mum. And something's off with her."

Emmie narrowed her gaze.

"More so than usual. You heard her. She's all screechy." His phone buzzed, and he quickly answered it.

Coward.

She needed to get a handle on this situation. Heading to the window, she glanced out, pressing close to look down at the street twenty-seven floors below. If she focused on the steady stream of pedestrian traffic, the yellow cabs, the exhaust-spewing buses, she could tell herself he really was just looking out for his daughter. But she knew better. It was so much more than that.

Oh, hell, she couldn't hold it back. The unbearable pain of being shut out again rolled in and threatened to *crush* her. God, it hurt.

She wanted in so badly. Why was it so elusive? All these feelings . . . God, it was her childhood all over again. Being shut out of her dad's world for not being creative enough, for not really *getting* him, had made her too sensitive to these slights. Because, truthfully? Artists didn't have a lock on creativity. She had it, too, just in other ways.

The whole reason Irwin valued her as his assistant was for her ability to think outside the box. She'd proven herself at Amoeba Records a hundred times over. So why did he hold her back? Sure, he needed her in this role as his assistant. But she could do so much more.

She knew she was lucky to work for the top A&R guy in the business, at the best record company in the world. She didn't take it for granted, but she also knew it was time for more. If she stayed behind and babysat Caroline, she'd never break out of this role. At some point, she had to take the initiative and actually say no to one of his demands. She had to force him to see her in a more creative role, or she'd never have the chance to explore that side of herself. To unleash it.

Besides—*hello?*—he couldn't function without her, so how could he get through the next six weeks on the other side of the world?

She spun around, pointing a finger at him. "What are you going to do without me?"

He looked alert then. Most of the time he had a dozen *very important ideas* going on in his head all at once, so it was nearly impossible to gain his full attention.

Those sharp blue eyes pierced her, and she knew she had it then.

"Right," he said to the caller. "Emmie will get back to you later." He stowed his phone in the back pocket of his jeans. "I'm taking Bax with me."

Had she been standing on a trap door? Because the floor gave way, and she was in free fall. Baxter Reynolds had started as an intern five years ago. When Irwin hadn't shown any interest in promoting him, he'd attached himself to Bob, one of the other A&R guys.

And *now* Irwin was showing an interest in him? Instead of Emmie?

She didn't know what to say. "Bax?" How was *Bax* better than her?

His phone buzzed, but he ignored it as he came right up to her, close enough that she could smell the Christian Dior cologne she kept stocked for him. He brushed his hand down her arm. "I'm sorry, Em. As much as I need you with me, I can't leave Caroline alone."

"Where's her mother?"

"Well, that's the point, isn't it? I can't count on Claire. But I *can* count on you."

See? When he did that, she caved. Irwin loved his daughter, and who else could he trust to look out for her? His entire family lived in England. Flighty, gorgeous, sexy Claire Murphy flitted around the world on a whim, barely touching down long enough to take care of anything but her most immediate and impulsive needs.

But Emmie needed more. She needed *in*. She couldn't stay his personal assistant forever. So, what should she do? Of course, if Caroline were in any danger, Emmie would have to help. But the girl was twenty-one. And, sorry, but Emmie simply *wasn't* her mother.

She didn't want to let Irwin down, but she was continuing to let herself down if she never took the next step—which meant taking charge of her own career.

She needed the promotion. "I'm not going to babysit Caroline, Irwin. You need me in Australia, and I need to go to Australia to see the bands I've been researching."

He let out a deep sigh. "Truth is, you've set everything up perfectly, as you always do. You've got my every moment organized and arranged to the point that I *don't* need you there."

"But you need Bax?"

"You've given me the list of bands to check out, along with the scheduled times to meet them. So, yes, I need Bax."

"I researched those bands."

"From the privacy of your office. Bax *lives* it, Emmie."

"You're saying I'm not good enough to be promoted?" She felt the sting of it, like alcohol on a blister. *No, no, no.* That was bullcrap. She *was* good enough.

"I'm saying I need you right where you are."

"And I need a career. Not just a job."

His phone buzzed again, and this time he checked the caller ID. "I have to take this."

"No. Please, Irwin. Not until we settle this."

"It *is* settled, Em." He said it gently. "I'm taking Bax." He punched the button on his phone. "Yes?"

"Then I quit."

Irwin's eyes flared. His features burned crimson.

She stood there, letting the words settle around her. The only sound was her own breathing, the only movement the wild and erratic beating of her heart.

Had she actually done it? Quit her coveted job?

"Wait, wait, hang on a moment," he said into the phone.

"I'm sorry, Irwin. I can't keep doing this. You have no intention of promoting me."

And standing on the periphery hurts too much.

He turned back to the phone. "Let me get back to you." Without waiting for a response, he hung up. "You can't quit." He looked utterly lost and baffled. "Why would you quit?"

"I'll find my replacement." She turned to go.

"Good God, Emmie. You cannot leave me."

"You've given me no choice."

"All right, just stop this. Stop it right now. I can't function without you, and you know that. You're threatening me. That's not a good way to get a promotion."

"It's not a threat. I told you I needed a career, and you told me you needed me right where I am. Fetching your Americanos and cajoling your landlord into letting you keep amphibians in your penthouse apartment isn't a career. I can't be your personal assistant the rest of my life. You get that, right? I've loved working for you, but it's supposed to be a stepping stone. You've just shown me it's a cage. I deserve more."

He had a strange expression, like he was listening to an incoming message from an ethereal source. "It's not right for you."

"What isn't?" He'd punched the accelerator on her pulse, making it rev so fast she went light-headed. *This is not happening.* He was *not* shutting her out of this world.

"A&R."

"I . . ." She found it hard to take a full breath. But he was wrong. Of course it was right for her. She pretty much did the job anyway. Maybe not discovering the bands, but . . . oh, God. She needed to breathe. *Deep breaths.* "That's ridiculous. I've been doing it for eight years."

"Em, look, I have to get to the studio. You simply can't quit. I won't allow it. We'll find a way to compromise, right? I want you to be happy."

"I'm not happy babysitting your daughter."

He winced. "Loud and clear."

"I need to know there's a place for me here other than looking through your drawers for a missing cashmere night sock."

Looking pained, he touched her arm, ignoring his buzzing phone. "Let's both think on it. Come up with a solution."

"Am I going to Australia with you tomorrow?"

"No."

She bit down hard on fear. It was scary as hell, but she had to do this.

"Emmie . . ."

She turned and walked out of the office.

About the Author

Award-winning author Erika Kelly writes sexy and emotional small town romance. Married to the love of her life and raising four children, she lives in the southwest, drinks a lot of tea, and is always waiting for her cats to get off her keyboard.

https://www.erikakellybooks.com/

facebook.com/erikakellybooks

twitter.com/ErikaKellyBooks

instagram.com/erikakellyauthor

goodreads.com/Erika_Kelly

pinterest.com/erikakellybooks

amazon.com/Erika-Kelly/e/B00L0MLWUY

bookbub.com/authors/erika-kelly